THE DANGER IN TEMPTING AN EARL

At the Kingsborough Ball

SOPHIE BARNES

AVON

An Imprint of HarperCollinsPublishers

AVON BOOKS
An Imprint of HarperCollins*Publishers*
195 Broadway
New York, New York 10007

Copyright © 2014 by Sophie Barnes
Excerpt from *The Trouble with Being a Duke* copyright © 2013 by Sophie Barnes
Excerpt from *The Scandal in Kissing an Heir* copyright © 2014 by Sophie Barnes
ISBN 978-0-06-224518-2
www.avonromance.com

First Avon Books mass market printing: August 2014

10 9 8 7 6 5 4 3 2 1

"What's happened to you, Lucien . . . ?

"In the course of two days you've not only kissed me but offered to take me to bed as well. I wish you would stop."

"Do you?" With slow deliberation, he reached out and placed his hand upon hers. A jolt of tingling warmth swept through her. "Because if you ask me, you wanted me to kiss you not only at the inn but in the carriage as well, and when I finally did, you welcomed it."

His words were soft and sensual, and no matter how much she longed to tell him it wasn't true, she could not bring herself to lie to him—not about something this important. Instead, she closed her eyes and prayed for him to distance himself from her.

He raised her hand to his lips, kissing the surface before turning it over and scraping his teeth against the back of her wrist. She gasped quite helplessly.

"All you have to do is ask, and the pleasure you seek can be yours."

By Sophie Barnes

Novels

THE DANGER IN TEMPTING AN EARL
THE SCANDAL IN KISSING AN HEIR
THE TROUBLE WITH BEING A DUKE
THE SECRET LIFE OF LADY LUCINDA
THERE'S SOMETHING ABOUT LADY MARY
LADY ALEXANDRA'S EXCELLENT ADVENTURE
HOW MISS RUTHERFORD GOT HER GROOVE BACK

Novellas

MISTLETOE MAGIC
(FROM *Five Golden Rings: A Christmas Collection*)

For my wonderful husband. Thank you for providing me with my very own fairy tale.

Acknowledgments

A book travels through the hands of so many people on its way to publication, and while I may be the one sitting at home, typing away on my keyboard, the efforts made by editors and publicists to make the work shine deserve to be mentioned. I'd like to thank my wonderful editor, Erika Tsang, and her assistant, Chelsey Emmelhainz, for being so incredibly helpful and easy to talk to—working with both of you is an absolute pleasure!

Together with the rest of the Avon team, which includes (but is far from limited to) copyeditor Judy Myers, publicists Caroline Perny, Pam Spengler-Jaffee and Jessie Edwards, and senior director of marketing Shawn Nicholls, they have offered guidance and support whenever they were needed. My sincerest thanks to all of you for being so wonderful!

Another person who must be acknowledged for his talent is artist Jon Paul, who has created the fabulous cover for this book, capturing not only the feel of the story but also the way in which I envisioned the characters looking—you've done such a beautiful job!

I would also like to thank Nancy Mayer for her assistance. Whenever I was faced with a question regarding the Regency era that I couldn't answer on my own, I turned to Nancy for advice. Her help has been invaluable.

My family and friends deserve my thanks as well, especially for reminding me to take a break occasionally, to step away from the computer and just unwind—I would be lost without you.

And to you, dear reader—thank you so much for taking the time to read this story. Your support is, as always, hugely appreciated!

"Though time be fleet and I and thou are half a life asunder, thy loving smile will surely hail the love-gift of a fairy tale."

—LEWIS CARROLL

The Danger
in Tempting an
Earl

Chapter 1

*On the way to the Kingsborough Ball
1817*

"**D**o you think she'll be all right?"

"Who? Sophia?" Lucien asked. "She'll be fine. She's with her nanny, after all." Resting against the squabs of the carriage as they tumbled along the country road, both dressed in their evening finery, he regarded the woman who sat across from him. It seemed as if he'd known her forever—ever since her mother had allowed him to hold her in his arms at her christening. He'd been seven years old then and terrified of dropping her, so he'd stood there stiffly and unsure of himself until his own mother had taken Katherine from him, allowing him to run along and play.

"I'm sure you're right," Katherine said, jolting him out of his reverie. "It's just that it's the first time I'm away from her like this and . . ." She turned her head toward the window and was silent for a moment before quietly saying, "I feel a great responsibility weighing on my shoulders."

Lucien hesitated a moment before responding. Her situation could not have been easy, recently widowed as she was and with a child to raise on her own, but in his opinion she deserved better than Charles Langdon, Viscount of Crossby. Lucien had never cared for the man who'd been married to Katherine for just over a year before meeting an early death. He'd been a cowardly bastard, acquiring an honorable discharge from the army for an illness that Lucien had known to be staged. And then there was his character to consider. Growing up only half an hour's ride from Cresthaven, Lucien had seen Crossby frequently over the years. As young men, they had even attended Eton together. But Lucien had always found Crossby both arrogant and pretentious, flaunting his title wherever he'd gone. And that was without considering his keen determination to best Lucien at everything, even if it had meant cheating. The fact that he'd married Katherine made Lucien wonder if the viscount had ever suspected the depth of Lucien's feelings for her. It was unlikely, he decided, for he'd made every effort to hide them. But if that hadn't prompted the wedding, what had? He was unable to understand Katherine's reason for marrying Crossby.

From what he gathered, their mothers had always been friends, visiting each other regularly for tea, for although their properties didn't border each other the way Katherine's and Lucien's did, the Crossbys still lived relatively close by. Perhaps it was this friendship that had led to a courtship and eventual marriage? Lucien was damned if he knew.

Stretching out his legs, he decided that there was no point in dwelling on the past and allowing his dislike of Katherine's late husband to cloud the evening. This was to be her first social event since becoming a widow, and Lucien was determined to make the evening a smashing success for her. "You have many friends who, I'm sure, will be happy to help you shoulder any burdens you may have," he said. He paused before adding, "Myself included."

Her head, which had been at a slight angle since their departure from Cresthaven Manor, turned now so she could meet his gaze. She leaned forward slightly, bringing his attention to her green eyes, which were large and searching. The corner of her mouth lifted to form a crooked smile. "Truly?"

Lucien knew what was coming, but he refused to look away. He would not be a coward.

"Because if you ask me," Katherine continued, "a true friend does not disappear from one's life for almost two years without word. Had it not been for the kindness of your mother and your grandmamma, I would probably have thought you dead!"

He winced. There was no denying that he had acted poorly toward her. "And I have apologized, have I not?" As if a mere apology would ever repair the breach he'd caused in their friendship. He ought to thank his lucky stars that she was even willing to talk to him, let alone share a carriage. He crossed his arms and sighed. "You know that I've always wanted to travel, so as soon as the war ended and I was relieved of my duties as captain, I decided to take advantage. I hadn't intended to stay away for so long."

"I never received so much as a letter from you," she whispered, her tone bleak. She'd leaned back again, hiding her face from him in the shadowy darkness.

"In all honesty, I thought it would be a waste of time," he said. He heard her scoff. "After all, you were recently married and off on your wedding trip when I returned from Waterloo. Frankly, I didn't think you'd notice whether or not I was back in England."

"You're right, of course. Charles was everything I ever dreamed of in a husband, and I was elated to be his wife. The day he asked me to marry him was the happiest of my life."

Her words made Lucien's stomach curdle. "I know," he said more bluntly than he had intended. "And I've never been happier for you." How he managed to say that with sincerity was beyond him. Perhaps he ought to take up acting as a profession? Hell, he'd been doing it long enough by now to know that he could be convincing.

"Hmm . . . and you didn't think that I would need you as a friend anymore, is that it? That I wouldn't want to welcome you home from the war?" Her tone was not accusatory but filled with curiosity and hurt. When he didn't respond immediately, she reached for his hand, squeezing it gently as her voice whispered through the darkness, "That I wouldn't want to offer you comfort after—"

"Don't!"

The word sliced through the air like a saber. Katherine snatched her hand away and retreated to her corner, her face blurring in the shadows. "Forgive me," she said. Her voice cracked and her cool façade trembled. "I meant no disrespect."

"Perhaps not." He knew he'd wounded her with his rebuke, but it couldn't be helped. "However, I did not seek your company in order to discuss those who are no longer with us—not my father, not Crossby, and certainly not my brother."

Silence settled over them for a while, the churning of wheels and plodding of hooves carrying them onward toward their destination until Katherine finally took a deep breath and said, "Then perhaps I may inquire if you've seen your sister since your return? I know she's missed you terribly during your absence."

"Regrettably, I haven't managed to make time to visit her yet, though I plan to do so soon. I'm happy to hear that the two of you remain in touch, though."

"She has always been a good friend. I have fond memories of us playing together when we were little."

"You certainly kept me on my toes, both of you," Lucien said. He shook his head. "Do you remember when you both got your heads trapped inside the soup terrines that one time? I can't imagine what you were thinking!"

"We were pretending they were bonnets," Katherine said.

Lucien frowned. "Bonnets indeed. I don't understand your reasoning, when I'm sure you both had more bonnets than you knew what to do with at that age."

"Well, it wouldn't have been as much fun with *real* bonnets," she said. "Surely you can see that."

With a sigh, Lucien chose to accept that some things just defied logic.

There was a break in the conversation, a noticeable pause, then Katherine suddenly said, "Lucien, I cannot help but feel as though there's something you're not telling me. As if you're deliberately trying to distract me with amusing conversation about our childhood exploits. But I still have questions that need answering. It makes no sense that you would want to go back to the Continent so soon after returning from the war. Tell me, why did you really leave England again?"

Clenching his jaw, Lucien swallowed with difficulty and tried to block out the roar of blood in his ears. He'd long since erected a wall around his emotions, a wall that he couldn't allow to fail him now when he needed it the most. "Very well . . . I believe my parents felt that since you had decided to tie the knot, I ought to do so as well—especially after what happened to my brother. I had duties, they said, responsibilities to face . . . an heir to produce. Frankly, the last thing I wanted after everything that happened was to find myself leg-shackled to some Society miss when I scarcely felt capable of getting out of bed in the morning. It all led to a rather nasty row, which in turn resulted in my very abrupt departure. To be blunt, I took the cowardly way out and fled."

It was of course a half truth, partly because he'd rather cut off a limb than admit to her what his real reason had been—heartache. Gavin, the brother he'd always admired and looked up to, had longed to go to France and fight against Napoleon, but his position as heir apparent had prevented him from doing so. Ironically, he'd died in his bed instead, consumed by fever. Lucien would never forget the scene that had greeted him after returning from Waterloo; his brother's trembling body glistening with sweat, his parents clutching each other for comfort. It had been devastating.

Sitting at his brother's bedside, Lucien had held Gavin's hand while he'd drifted off to sleep for the last time, his final words being, "You know you love her. Now go and make her yours . . . be happy."

Lucien had sobbed at length thereafter, not only because of his loss but also because his brother would never know that he'd asked him to do the impossible. Unbeknownst to Gavin, Katherine had married Crossby the week before and had departed on her wedding trip before Lucien had returned home. Lucien had never confessed his feelings for her to anyone, but when Gavin had guessed the truth, Lucien hadn't denied it.

A heavy silence descended upon them, one Katherine finally broke by saying, "I'm sorry, Lucien. I had no idea. Your mother never mentioned the argument, although I don't suppose she would have, come to think of it. She's always been very private." A beat passed, and she hesitantly continued with, "Did you and your father ever manage to reconcile before—"

"No," he said, his tone reflecting the anger he felt at himself for acting as rashly as he had, but his heart had been broken and he'd lacked the maturity to accept the responsibilities being thrust upon his shoulders—responsibilities that never should have been his in the first place.

Every time he thought of his father, he was filled with undeniable guilt. He hadn't anticipated his sire's early demise and had always thought he'd return to England soon, share a glass of brandy with him and apologize for acting like a spoilt child. Fate, coupled with his father's weak heart, had prevented him from doing so.

"I'm sorry," Katherine whispered as she reached across the space between them and slowly placed her gloved hand over his once more, in much the same manner as one might approach a frightened child.

It was little comfort, but he appreciated the gesture nonetheless, allowing himself to revel in the sweet agony her closeness offered. If his absence from England had taught him anything at all, it was that no matter how far he ran, he'd never escape the torment of his own emotions. Better, then, to accept them, no matter the consequences. "Thank you," he said, watching her quietly as she withdrew her hand from his, "but it is I who should apologize to you for not returning sooner. Until I arrived home, I'd no idea that you were also in mourning. Mama failed to mention it when she wrote to me about Papa. She implored me to return quickly so I could resume my duties." He held her gaze. "It's been a busy two weeks, though I must admit I am relieved that you accepted my offer of escorting you to the Kingsboroughs' this evening. I had expected you to turn me down."

She chuckled. It was the first sign of amusement she'd shown since his arrival on her doorstep just one hour earlier—their first meeting in four years and with only a brief note sent to her earlier in the day, informing her of his plans to come and collect her. His own estate was close to Cresthaven, so it was only logical that they journey to Kingsborough Hall together, though truth be told, he'd wanted this opportunity for them to talk privately before entering the ballroom. Even so, he was fortunate that she hadn't tossed him out on his ear for his audacity.

"Don't think for a second that I didn't consider it," she said. "However, I must admit that curiosity got the better of me. I decided that it was high time you gave me an explanation. That, and I've never been very good at holding grudges. As neighbors, things might get awkward between us unless we decide to put the past behind us and move on with our lives."

This was promising.

"That said, I do hope you realize that I expect you to earn my forgiveness. I shall have to think of something particularly distasteful . . . like taking me shopping at the modiste's."

Or perhaps not.

He frowned as he imagined himself in a ghastly

little shop filled with fabrics and chattering women. *Egads!*

She must have known what he was thinking, for she offered him a wry little smile and said, "You left, Lucien, without as much as a note to offer me an explanation. I must confess that my feelings were crushed as a result. Surely you didn't believe you could simply waltz back into my life without the slightest repercussion after you so thoughtlessly abandoned me."

Her tone was sweet, as if in jest, but there was an undercurrent of pain behind it that occasionally shone through. Lucien frowned. "You had Crossby," he told her simply. Lord, would this conversation ever end? It felt as if they were going round in circles without resolving anything.

"Nevertheless."

And there it was—the duty he'd had to wait for her to return from her wedding trip and wish her well, to tell her that he was leaving England again and to say good-bye to her properly. Instead, he'd buried his brother long before his time. After the funeral and an admittedly large quantity of brandy to dull his senses, he'd argued with his father. The following day, he'd departed for France, eager to put as much distance between himself, the title he'd never wanted, and the woman who'd unwittingly torn his heart from his chest.

Well, he was back now, and however unprepared Kate might be for his advances, he intended to do whatever he had to do in order to win her. Focusing on his faults wasn't helping, though. It was time for a change of topic. "I must say I'm surprised to discover that your brother-in-law hasn't arrived to claim his inheritance yet."

"Yes . . . I'm not sure what's keeping him, other than a reluctance to take on the responsibility of running his brother's estate. He's very young, after all, and probably believes he has better things to do."

"I can well imagine," Lucien said. He'd met Mr. Lionel Langdon only a handful of times, but it had been enough for him to form a rather negative opinion of the youth—an unruly fellow who'd proven a poor influence on others on more than one occasion. Langdon's older brother had not kept a very tight leash on him, either because he'd felt that Lionel would eventually settle down on his own or because he simply hadn't cared. Lucien didn't know what the reason had been, though he suspected it had been the latter.

"It's just as well, really, since I'm happy to remain at Cresthaven a while longer. Especially since I would otherwise have to share the dowager house with my mother-in-law until other arrangements are made. She and I never did get along very well."

"I can't imagine why," Lucien muttered. In spite of the darkness, he knew that Katherine was scowling at him. He decided to lift her spirits a bit. "But Mr. Langdon, or rather the new Lord Crossby, isn't married as far as I know. I'm sure he'll allow you to remain at the manor."

"Perhaps, though I must confess I'm not entirely sure I wouldn't prefer his mother."

Lucien couldn't help but laugh. "I never thought I'd admit to missing the intrigues of the *ton,* but I find myself looking forward to watching you take on the dowager viscountess and an irresponsible heir with great anticipation. I wonder who will win."

"You're a beast," she said, but there was a lighter tone to her voice than there had been earlier.

"Frankly, my money's on you. You're tougher than you look."

It sounded as if she responded with "You've no idea," but he couldn't be sure, as she quickly followed the remark with, "In any event, my aunt has offered me a position as her companion, so I doubt I'll have to worry about my living arrangements much longer."

Lucien frowned. He'd have to dissuade her from throwing her life away on such an endeavor, but before he had a chance to comment, the carriage came to a swaying stop. A moment later the door was opened by a footman, and Lucien climbed out. He turned to offer Katherine his hand.

The vision she presented was almost otherworldly as her head emerged from the dark interior of the carriage and came aglow with the hazy light from nearby torches lining the driveway. The hood of her cloak was only partially drawn up, affording him a glimpse of her rich, chestnut-colored hair, which was undoubtedly set in one of those complicated coiffures that baffled most gentlemen.

With her hand resting gently upon his arm, Lucien guided Katherine up the front steps of Kingsborough Hall, where two more footmen stood, ready to relieve them of their outdoor garments. Plucking his hat from the top of his head, Lucien handed it to one of them, the action forcing him to remove his attention momentarily from Katherine as he did so. He then unbuttoned his greatcoat and was just about to hand that over as well when he happened to glance in Katherine's direction. He froze.

Dear merciful Lord in heaven!

He remembered her having a lovely figure, but either his memory had done her a great disservice, or she'd matured dramatically over the past four years.

She was turned slightly away from him as she handed her cloak to the other footman, affording Lucien a private moment in which to admire her. The gown she wore had to be of silk, for it was so soft and slippery-looking that he could barely resist the urge to reach out and run his fingers over the fabric. Bright and dazzling, hundreds of beads shimmered upon the bodice. And it was white, of all colors, which was remarkably unusual for a widow. He liked it, though—the allusion to innocence . . . a new beginning.

"Your coat, my lord?" the footman said, reminding Lucien of both time and place.

Handing over the garment, he turned to Katherine. "Are you ready to join the receiving line?" he asked, offering her his arm once more while attempting the blandest expression he could muster.

She accepted with a slight nod, the corner of her mouth rising in a half smile as she placed her hand upon his arm, allowing him to guide her toward the long and ever-progressing line of titled ladies and gentlemen that was making its way toward the ballroom.

Hoping to get back in her good graces, he decided that flattery might be a decent way to begin. Particularly since what he was about to say was utterly true. "May I say that you look absolutely stunning this evening?" Lucien offered as he lowered his head toward Katherine's.

Her smile was hesitant, but if he wasn't mistaken, there was a bit of a glimmer about her eyes. "I see you're just as adept at delivering compliments as always," she said, following her statement with an almost shy "Thank you."

Lucien frowned. "I mean it, Katherine. You know I've always been honest in my praise."

"Yes, but that was when you didn't have an agenda.

Now, however, I believe you're determined to gain my forgiveness by whatever means necessary." Turning her gaze away from his, she looked toward the end of the receiving line. She smiled, but it seemed horribly forced—like an artful façade intended to distract the viewer from what really lurched beneath the surface.

"And what if I am?" he found himself saying, determined to bring her attention back to him so he could study her expression more closely.

She did not disappoint, her face turning sharply toward him as her lips parted with what appeared to be genuine surprise, though only for a moment. For one fraction of a second, his comment had thrown her, but her smile was just as quickly returned to its rightful position, removing all trace of the truth he'd just been made privy to: she was afraid.

Of what, exactly, he couldn't even begin to imagine, but it was a startling moment for Lucien as he stood there gazing back into the depths of the dark green eyes that had haunted him during his travels. The Katherine he had once known had transformed drastically during his absence, and he was beginning to wonder if it might have something to do with Crossby. She'd never seemed very fond of him as a child, always trying to avoid joining her mother whenever she'd gone to Cresthaven on visits. In fact, Katherine had once remarked to Lucien that Crossby chilled her blood—a peculiar observation for an eight-year-old to make, or perhaps very astute. But surely she must have laid these reservations to rest if she'd decided to marry the man. Knowing Katherine, and how romantic she was by nature, Crossby must have charmed her.

None of it made any sense. Katherine had always

been passionate by nature and so full of confidence—traits that seemed lacking in the woman who stood before him now, though she put on a good show for appearance's sake.

He knew better, however.

The girl he'd once known would have offered him a dazzling smile in response to his complimenting her appearance, for she'd been bold and brazen—the outgoing sort with whom there had never been a dull moment. If charades had been suggested, she'd taken the lead, not caring how ridiculous she'd looked in the process, for as she'd said on more than one occasion, "I would rather make a cake of myself and share in everyone's laughter than endure a somber existence."

That exuberance had vanished, though. It was even clear in the way she carried herself. As a debutante, she'd looked regal. Now she just looked as if she'd happily go unnoticed, though she ought to have selected a different gown if that were the case. A widow dressed in white was bound to stand out.

"I like your gown," he said, allowing his fingertips to brush against the edge of her capped sleeve.

"Is it really all right?" She smoothed the fabric with her hands. "The modiste tried to convince me to choose another color—something daring, but I have plenty of such gowns already, and found them all to be inappropriately bold this evening. Given my current situation, I'd hate to appear as though I'm deliberately inviting unsavory attention."

There was little Lucien could say in response, so he decided to just nod and keep quiet.

"You always did have exquisite taste," he eventually said. "A trait I believe you must have inherited from your mother. How is she doing these days, by the way?"

"Very well, thank you," Katherine said as they moved forward in the queue.

"And your father?" Lucien asked.

She hesitated for a moment before saying, "Also in the best of health."

Lucien frowned. "I'm pleased to hear it."

"My lord," she said as they progressed another couple of steps, "I know what you're doing and—"

"And what would that be?" he asked, though there was no question she knew his game, even if he didn't quite know it himself. She knew him better than anyone else and had always had the uncanny ability to pinpoint his motives even when he was unaware that he had any.

She gave him a weak smile. "You're dissembling and trying to distract me with conversation that you hope will put the past behind us and allow us to simply go on as if you never left."

"And is it working?" he asked as he secretly crossed his fingers—not that he was superstitious or anything, but there was no harm in drawing on every bit of luck available to him. Lord knew he needed it.

Katherine sighed and shook her head a little. "You know better than anyone that I've never been able to harbor resentment for any significant amount of time. If you must know, you were forgiven the moment you apologized to me in the carriage." Lucien breathed a sigh of relief. "But that doesn't mean that I don't expect you to make it up to me." Her expression was quite serious.

"By taking you shopping," he said, recalling her words from earlier. He shuddered at the thought of it.

"Later," she said. The corners of her lips edged upward, and a glint of merciless mischief sharpened her eyes. "For now, you may start by offering to dance with Lady Deerford, whom I believe will be present this evening."

Good God!

"Kate," he whispered so no one else would hear, "I'd be thrilled to invite you for a ride, perhaps even a picnic when the weather's a bit warmer. Why, I'll even accompany you to the modiste without complaint if that is what you truly desire, but to make me dance with the marchioness . . . you know as well as I that it will be near impossible for me to extricate myself from her again. Besides, I'd much rather keep your company for the duration of the evening."

She peered back at him from beneath her lashes as if trying to decipher his words, though Lucien doubted she would ever consider their true implication—that what he longed for more than anything in the world was an excuse to be near her as much as possible.

"Gracious, Lucien, you know as well as I that you cannot stay by my side all evening without inviting gossip. Besides, dancing with Lady Deerford would be such a kind gesture on your part." Her eyes narrowed, and she looked at him very suspiciously. "If I were to make a guess, I'd say you're up to something. What is it?"

"Nothing." He could hardly reveal the extent to which he craved her closeness after being away from her for so long.

"Hmm. . . . Well, in any event, I will keep all your suggestions in mind for the future, since they all sound rather tempting. Besides, I doubt I'll be able to fully forgive you after only one dance with Lady Deerford. No, it will take much more effort on your part to restore our friendship to what it once was, if that is indeed what you wish to do." She tilted her head in his direction, and Lucien was finally allowed a glimpse of the woman who'd once been his closest friend and confidante. "For now, however, dancing with the marchioness will suffice."

Not to mention a shopping expedition, a ride, a picnic, and whatever else they'd discussed in less than five minutes. Well, Lucien demurred, at least he'd have ample opportunity to romance the lady now that she'd made herself so readily available to him. He hid a smile and wondered what she would say if she knew what he was contemplating, or that she'd just made his plan so much easier and less likely to seem suspicious. In all likelihood, she'd throttle him, and as much as he enjoyed envisioning such a scenario and where it might lead, he decided not to venture down that avenue for a while yet.

Reaching the Kingsboroughs, Lucien greeted the dowager duchess with a low bow. "Good evening, Your Grace."

Katherine echoed his salutation as he raised the duchess's hand to his lips and placed a kiss upon her gloved hand.

"Lord Roxberry and Lady Crossby, how wonderful it is to see you both," the duchess said once Lucien had straightened himself again. "I do hope that you will enjoy the festivities."

"I'm sure we shall," Katherine said. "Thank you, Your Grace."

"And may I say that you look absolutely ravishing this evening, Lady Crossby," the duke said, presenting Katherine with a slight bow. He turned his gaze on Lucien and smiled with pleasure. "I knew you'd eventually grow weary of traipsing across the Continent alone." He held out his hand, which Lucien readily accepted in a firm shake. "It's good to have you back."

After agreeing to tell the duke all about his travels at the first available opportunity, Lucien donned a black satin domino and escorted Katherine, whose face was now partially concealed behind a black-and-white mask, toward the glittering opulence of the Kingsborough ballroom, where, upon their announcement, all conversation ceased as every head in the room swiveled around to stare in their direction.

Chapter 2

"It appears your return has caused quite the sensation," Katherine said.

Lucien chuckled. "I doubt very much that their stunned silence is my doing, Kate."

"Another compliment?" she asked as his words slipped over her. He was being every bit the gentleman, yet with the realization that all eyes *were* indeed upon her, she suddenly wanted nothing more than to disappear into the nearest wall.

"If you didn't believe me earlier when I told you that you look stunning, you have no choice but to do so now," he whispered.

With her heart fluttering in her chest, Katherine attempted a smile, only to feel as if her face was made of plaster. Gripping Lucien's arm a bit tighter, she steadied herself and took a deep breath. The last thing she wanted was to make a spectacle of herself by collapsing on the floor. No, that wouldn't do at all. Yet there was no stopping her body from trembling as they made their descent toward the ballroom.

"Are you all right?" Lucien quietly asked, his lips close to her ear.

Katherine nodded. "Yes. Perfectly, though I must confess that I am finding it a bit hot in here."

"I can lead you straight through the crowd if you wish and out onto the terrace."

The thought of escape was tempting, but just as she was about to agree, she caught sight of her friend, the Duke of Kingsborough's sister, Louise, who was presently approaching along with her husband, the Earl of Huntley.

"I'm so happy that you were able to join us this evening, Katherine," Louise said. She looked to Lucien. "You too, Roxberry. I'm sure you must have many exciting tales to tell us from your travels."

"Lady Huntley," Lucien said, offering the countess a bow, "a pleasure as always. And I see you've brought me someone with whom to pass the time while you and Lady Crossby share the latest gossip." He grinned toward Huntley.

"I shall be more than happy to save you from having to participate in such inane conversation, Roxberry," Huntley said. His face was serious, but there was a sparkle to his eyes that betrayed him.

"At least our discussions generally arrive at a conclusion," Louise said as she smiled lovingly at her husband. "The same cannot be said of your political ones, where nobody ever agrees with anyone and nothing is ever solved."

"And here I thought you weren't paying attention," Huntley muttered.

Katherine did her best not to laugh at their little exchange, which resulted in a somewhat strangled sound. Lucien glanced her way with a knowing smile, to which she responded with a shrug.

"In case you were unaware," Louise continued, "there is a brain behind these lovely eyes of mine."

She batted her eyelids, while Lucien appeared on the verge of dissolving into a fit of laughter. Katherine didn't feel as if she was faring much better. The Huntleys made a lovely couple, and the banter they so openly enjoyed in the company of others was always a source of great amusement—something Katherine craved. It seemed like an eternity since she'd laughed with complete abandon.

"Heaven forbid I should ever forget it," Huntley said as he reached for his wife's hand and raised it to his lips, placing a kiss upon her knuckles. Their eyes met, and for the briefest of moments, Katherine felt as if she and Lucien had been completely forgotten by the couple. They clearly loved each other, and something inside Katherine twisted.

"Shall we take a turn about the room then?" Louise asked, her question directed at Katherine.

"With pleasure," Katherine said. Stepping away from Lucien and linking her arm with Louise's, she glanced up at him and smiled in an attempt to push aside the awful sensation that gripped her. She'd never been envious of anyone else in her life. Discovering that she was helplessly jealous of her friend was humiliating. "Don't forget to dance with Lady Deerford," she said.

Lucien looked to Huntley. "I don't suppose you'd care to help me flee."

"And risk Lady Crossby's fury?" Huntley asked. He stepped back as if considering the possibility of leaving Lucien to deal with the lady in question on his own. "My good man, when a lady sets her heart on something, whether it be a bonnet or a boon from a gentleman, she will have her way sooner or later, and since that is the case, you would only be a fool for prolonging the issue."

"Is that so?" Lucien asked, eyeing Katherine.

There was something curious about the way in which he was looking at her—something that she was not at all familiar with. It unsettled her, and that in turn made her skin prickle and her stomach quiver in a most uncomfortable way.

"I just adore the comparison you choose to draw between gentlemen and bonnets," Louise said with a laugh directed at her husband as she drew Katherine away, removing them from Lucien's and Huntley's company. "My dear Katherine, you must tell me everything. I had no idea that you were planning to arrive here on Roxberry's arm." This last part was said in a low whisper so no one else would hear.

"Truth be told, I didn't know that he would be accompanying me this evening either. Not until a note arrived from him this afternoon, requesting the honor of offering me escort." Katherine paused, hesitant of how much to share because of what the revelation might reveal about her problematic relationship with Lucien, but she eventually decided that if anyone deserved the truth, it was Louise. She'd become a dear friend during Lucien's absence. "In fact, this is the first time I'm seeing him since his return."

"He didn't call on you before?" Louise asked, sounding properly dismayed.

Katherine shook her head, and they continued on in silence as they passed a few other ladies, nodding politely in greeting as they went. "You know what people will say about this, don't you?" Louise continued when they were once again alone and with no chance of anyone overhearing them. "I mean, I hope that you are prepared, all things considered."

"I can't imagine what you mean," Katherine told her friend. They had reached a small alcove with a bench tucked away inside it, offering a bit of privacy from the rest of the guests. The ladies sat and immediately opened their fans.

"Can't you? Hmm . . . no, I suppose you wouldn't have considered it, since you were away on your wedding trip at the time. But you see, the haste with which Roxberry departed England again following his return from the war has raised a multitude of questions that have since resulted in some very interesting theories," Louise whispered. Hiding behind her fan, she leaned toward Katherine and added, "Theories that are likely to become more fascinating than the questions themselves, given that his first public appearance in what . . . four years or so . . . happens not only after you have been widowed but with you of all people on his arm."

"What exactly are you saying, Louise?" Katherine asked, not liking the implication of her friend's words in the least.

"Surely you must be aware of some of the notions that have flittered through every drawing room these past few years?" When Katherine numbly shook her head, Louise gave her a sympathetic look. "Well, if I may cut straight to the point, there are those who think him irrevocably in love with you. In fact, I daresay that this is the general consensus."

It was as if Katherine's entire world skidded to a screeching halt. Lucien in love with her? Preposterous! Her heart thumped madly in her chest at the very thought of such a crack-brained notion while she gaped back at her friend. "But that's ridiculous," she eventually managed. "Lucien and I have always been close friends. It's only fitting that he would escort me this evening."

Louise shrugged. "What can I say? I suppose there

are always those who would like to turn the simplest thing into a complicated Banbury tale. Although . . ."

The word trailed off into obscurity. With a sigh of resignation, Katherine accepted Louise's bait and asked the question her friend so obviously intended for her to ask. "Although what?"

"Well, if Roxberry *is* indeed in love with you, he couldn't have arrived at a better time, considering that you are just now out of mourning and free to contemplate another gentleman in your life."

"Good heavens, but this is madness!" Katherine would rather eat poison than consider attaching herself to another gentleman, so the idea that this might be the consensus of the entire *ton* was horrifying. "They're wrong, Louise. I've known Roxberry my entire life, and I'm telling you that he has never considered me as anything more than a friend."

Louise nodded. "Perhaps you're right," she said, patting Katherine's arm as if to placate her. "After all, you do know him better than anyone else, so if you are certain in your assessment, then I have no choice but to trust your judgment."

"Thank you," Katherine managed. She felt as if she'd just run a three-legged race.

"However . . . ," her friend added.

Oh dear God, there was more.

"From what I have heard, many believe that he quit England after the war because his heart had been so thoroughly broken by his unrequited love for you that he found it impossible to remain in your presence . . . let alone the same country. They say that this is the true reason why he left." Louise wafted her fan back and forth with increased vigor.

Katherine gritted her teeth and did her best to calm her quaking nerves. "And why exactly am I only hearing of this now, my dear *friend*?"

Louise's hand stilled, and she turned her head to look directly at Katherine. "First of all, it was such common knowledge that I thought you were aware— why, even the society columns made a mention of it for a while. And second of all, I must confess I found it a bit of an awkward subject to broach when you were married to Crossby . . . more so once you were widowed."

Dear God.

"They're wrong," Katherine repeated, desperate now to convince the world that it had made a serious error in judgment. "Lucien left because of the pain his brother's death caused him and because he argued with his father, who was apparently quite determined to see his youngest son married in order to secure the line of succession. Lucien felt trapped, so he fled."

"Or," Louise offered, her eyes appearing unnaturally large all of a sudden, "he did want to marry but could no longer have the woman he desired and decided not to marry at all."

Uncertainty pressed upon her, but Katherine urged it away. No, it wasn't possible. She dismissed the notion with an awkward laugh. "Honestly, Louise! Have you been reading gothic novels again?"

Louise swatted her arm. "I'm being perfectly serious."

Katherine sighed. "Lucien and I were neighbors growing up, and since I didn't move farther away than Cresthaven after I married, we've pretty much remained so, but to make any more out of it than that would be ridiculous. You know that his sister and I are close in age and that we played together as children. Lucien was often there as well, no doubt to ensure that we didn't get into too much trouble. He's like a brother to me."

"Are you sure he feels the same way?"

Following Louise's gaze, Katherine found Lucien and Huntley striding toward them. Huntley's gaze was fixed on Louise in a manner not entirely dissimilar to the way in which Lucien was regarding Katherine. She felt an odd fluttering sensation in the pit of her stomach, but she managed to give herself a mental kick. Surely she was imagining things. Yes, of course she was. Everything Louise had said had addled her brain. Why, the very idea that Lucien's feelings for her ran deeper than friendship was pure nonsense. She straightened her back and rose to her feet alongside Louise, ready to meet the gentlemen. "Of course I am," she quickly whispered, snapping her fan shut in irritation. She was suddenly annoyed that the *ton* would assume otherwise. It was outrageous, really.

"You will be pleased to know that I have just danced a lovely quadrille with Lady Deerford, who, I must add, has recently added a new doll to her collection. When I mentioned you, Lady Crossby, and how much you'd like to give a doll to your daughter, she immediately offered to show you her favorite shops."

Katherine winced. She liked Lady Deerford and was terribly sad for her, especially now that she, like the older woman, was also a mother. It was heartwrenching to imagine the pain of having your child snatched away from you and not knowing what had become of her, as was the case with the Deerfords, whose daughter had been kidnapped twenty years earlier. Still, the thought of shopping for dolls with the lady . . . "I never said that I was looking for a doll for Sophia," she said, frowning at Lucien.

"You didn't?" he asked, looking properly confused. His eyes brightened a second later, and he smiled at her broadly. "Well, then I suppose I must have made a mistake."

Katherine's eyes narrowed. "A mistake that's about to get the better of you, since you have recently offered to take me shopping. We shall accompany Lady Deerford together at the first available opportunity."

To her satisfaction, Lucien's mouth dropped. A snicker brought her attention over to Louise, who was looking terribly amused. "Heavens," she croaked in an attempt to contain her laughter. "For a 'couple' who's not a 'couple,' you're certainly having the most delightful quarrel."

Katherine bit her lip while a slow dread slipped along her limbs. If there was one subject she did not need her friend to broach at the moment, it was the one they had recently been discussing. Thankfully, Lucien appeared to have taken no heed of Louise's blatant remark and surprised Katherine instead by saying, "All talk of the lovely Lady Deerford aside, I was wondering if you would do me the honor of partnering with me for the next set."

Tilting her head, Katherine studied him for a moment. Ordinarily, his question shouldn't have given her pause, except that in all the years she'd known him, he'd never once asked her to dance. Louise must have registered the same thing, for she appeared to be holding her breath while her eyes seemed to say, *I told you so.*

Katherine expelled a shuddering breath. She'd last danced with Charles at the Oakley Ball two years earlier, twirling around beneath the shimmering glow of chandeliers while he'd held her uncomfortably close. She forced away the unpleasant memory and focused on Louise. Her friend was clearly looking for something intriguing to fill her mind and had decided to turn Katherine's and Lucien's longtime friendship into something more. She felt inclined to refuse Lucien's offer to dance on that basis alone. "Thank you," she told him, "but I—"

"Please," he implored as he extended his hand toward her. His deep brown eyes bored into her with such intensity that she could have sworn his gaze touched her soul.

A shiver traced the length of Katherine's spine. Swallowing, she pushed her reservations aside and placed her hand in his. "I'd be delighted to," she said, offering Lucien her best smile.

"It appears we've quite the audience," Huntley said as the four of them took their places for a country dance. He smiled warmly at Katherine.

"Do you suppose they think we might have forgotten how to proceed and that they're expecting us to make a cake of ourselves?" Lucien asked as the music started.

He winked toward Katherine, who was equally aware of all eyes being trained upon them. This was not good. Not in the least. Her stomach roiled, and she feared she might be ill.

"No, my lord. I suspect they are far more interested in discovering why you would ask Lady Crossby to dance when you have never invited her to do so before," Louise said, much to Katherine's horror.

The smile that had appeared on Lucien's face didn't falter as he happily responded with, "How do you know that I have never invited her to dance with me before? Perhaps I did and she declined. After all, it's not as if she just dropped from the sky."

Louise chuckled, and Katherine felt her whole face grow warm. Was it really necessary for the two of them to jest like that at her expense? But before she could come up with a quick-witted remark, the music rose through the air and the first pair of dancers started along the colonnade.

Pushing all feelings of discomfort aside with the hope of enjoying the dance, Katherine looked across at her partner. He hadn't changed overly much since she'd last seen him four years earlier. His hair was still the same dark color it had been then, his eyes almost black beneath two distinguished eyebrows.

Katherine's gaze settled on his nose. It seemed a bit more crooked than she remembered, forcing her to wonder if he might have had an altercation with someone during which it had been broken.

Louise stirred at Katherine's side as she stepped forward to meet her husband. They turned about, a vague flurry of movement in the corner of Katherine's eye as her gaze wandered down to Lucien's mouth. It was a nice mouth, she decided, and she was immediately struck by the realization that this was the first time in all the years she'd known him that she'd actually spared it any thought at all. In fact, if someone had asked her yesterday if she could describe his features, she'd probably have gotten it all wrong.

She frowned. Was it possible to know someone your whole life and only have a faint notion of what they actually looked like? She reprimanded herself for even considering such a possibility and more so for paying such close attention to what he looked like now. Once again, Louise's words were having a most annoying effect. Yet in spite of her best efforts, Katherine found it impossible to ignore the observation that her mind had been struggling to resist since Lucien had arrived at Cresthaven earlier that evening—that he was far more handsome in reality than he'd been in her remembrance of him. In fact, there was something hard and masculine about him that she'd overlooked in the past, perhaps because of how well she'd known him. Or perhaps the war had taken its toll on him and he'd changed. It was difficult to tell.

An elbow nudged her waist, and she was shocked to discover that she'd missed her cue. With a muttered apology, she accepted the hand that Lucien offered and allowed him to turn her about. "You appeared to be deep in thought just now," he said as they stepped closer to each other with both hands clasped together. "I hope nothing's troubling you."

"Oh, not at all," she said, hoping to dismiss the notion and hating how strangled her voice was sounding. Surely he would know she was lying, because really, what could be more troubling than discovering that she'd seen the man she was presently dancing with thousands of times before without really seeing him at all? She eyed him discreetly as they passed along the colonnade of dancers, noting how broad his shoulders appeared beneath the snug fit of his jacket.

"Is something amiss with my attire?" he asked without so much as turning his head in her direction.

Her eyes immediately jerked away. She looked straight ahead. "No," she said. "Of course not."

"Then why do you continue to study me as if I'm some rare artifact that the Hunterian might consider putting on display?"

She swallowed and took a breath. "It's an age since I've seen you last, and the carriage was too dark for me to notice if you've changed much during your absence."

"And have I?" he asked as they turned about once more.

"Actually . . . no, I don't believe you have. In fact,

you're exactly how I remember you, though I think perhaps your nose is a bit more . . . notable than before."

They moved apart, taking up positions across from each other. Katherine looked toward the other dancers, determined not to meet Lucien's gaze, which would allow him the chance to discover her lie. She still wasn't sure of what her revelation meant or how to address it, but she suddenly knew one thing with startling clarity—Lucien was a fine-looking man indeed, and there would be a multitude of young ladies eager to make him theirs now that he was not only back but also unmarried and in possession of a desirable title. She snuck a glance at him again and berated herself for not noticing before how handsome he looked.

Good Lord, what was happening to her?

She'd known the man her entire life, and not once before had she considered his appearance. She wasn't quite sure if she ought to chastise herself for her negligence or applaud herself for not being shallow. The issue was most confusing, more so with Louise insisting that the *ton* would assume there might be more between them than mere friendship.

It was her turn to dance with Huntley while Louise partnered with Lucien, crisscrossing between each other before being handed back to their rightful partners. "I broke it in a fight about a year ago," Lucien said as they linked arms and spun about.

"I thought you might have," Katherine said. They returned to their places in the colonnade and waited while other couples danced along it. And then it was their turn again. They stepped toward each other and she put her hand upon his arm so he could guide her along while the other dancers watched.

"By the way," she said, ignoring the shyness that

plagued her, "I have to compliment you on your dancing. You haven't stepped on my toes once. What a pity it is that we haven't partnered before—I quite enjoy it." She looked up at him with a hesitant smile just as he turned his head to meet her gaze. The corner of his mouth tilted and a dimple formed. Katherine blinked. If this was how he looked at other women, it was a wonder he hadn't yet married. Surely every unmarried lady must have had him on her mind at least once.

"As do I," he told her smoothly.

There was a mischievous playfulness to the way he spoke that completely caught Katherine off guard, making it difficult for her to discern if he'd moved onto a different topic without her and had just referred to something else entirely. Not knowing how to respond, she kept quiet and focused on the dance, afraid that if she spoke, she'd sound like a girl straight out of the schoolroom. Her irritation grew. She didn't like this effect he was having on her—how uncomfortable he was making her feel, when she'd always been accustomed to an easy camaraderie between them. Perhaps his lengthy absence was to blame and they required more time in which to become properly reacquainted.

Having completed their progress, they resumed their places in the colonnade while the music faded. He bowed and she curtsied. When he offered her his arm and asked if she would care for some refreshment, she accepted, then proceeded to ponder the awkwardness between them while she sipped her champagne.

There was no doubt that she was a very different woman than the one he'd left behind, and since that was the case, he might be a very different man than the one she'd last seen. Four years could have a dramatic effect on a person, depending on their experiences during that time, and he had not only been to war but had lost his brother as well. It would have been ridiculous for either one of them to expect the other to have remained unchanged.

Accepting a dance with a gentleman who'd just offered, Katherine excused herself to Lucien and returned to the dance floor with her new partner. She hoped that she and Lucien could find a means by which to rebuild the closeness they'd once shared, though she expected that doing so would take time and effort on both their parts. One thing was for certain—she could never allow him to know what she'd been through in his absence. Telling him would only give rise to unnecessary arguments filled with anger and pain—emotions she had no desire to stir up again.

Chapter 3

Lucien watched from the sidelines while Katherine danced a quadrille. He was painfully aware of the age-old possessiveness that gripped him, especially when she was in the company of another man. He took a lengthy sip of his champagne. It had been both wonderful and torturous to dance with her, the mere touch of her hand heating him deep within, even though she wore gloves. Keeping his true feelings for her at bay had not been an easy task. Indeed, it had been not only frustrating but also harder than ever before—a true effort in discipline. Or perhaps he'd just forgotten with time how easily she affected him. Perhaps it had always been this difficult. He was damned if he knew.

Katherine laughed in response to something her partner said, and Lucien took another sip of his drink, fighting the urge to storm out onto the dance floor and claim her as his own. He had to be patient with her and progress slowly if he was to open her mind to the idea of sharing her future with him, for he knew all too well that she had never viewed him as anything more than a dear friend and brother-figure—the boy who'd taught her how to skip stones across the lake and whistle with a blade of grass. Lucien winced. He had fond memories of those days gone by, but he'd also never given Katherine a reason to consider him romantically, perhaps because he'd thought she deserved better. As a second son, he had not been able to offer her the title that she, as the daughter of a baronet, ought to have. This feeling had only been amplified when he'd overheard their mothers talking one day over tea. They'd been discussing the coming Season when Dame Bethany had distinctly said, "It would be such a feather in Katherine's cap if she could land a peer."

"I must confess that I've always liked the idea of her marrying one of my boys," his own mother had said with careful deliberation.

"Oh! Do you really suppose Lord Leveen might consider making her his viscountess? After all, she's quite a bit younger than him."

"Actually, I was thinking of his brother, Lucien. He's always seemed very fond of her, so I'm sure he'd treat her well."

"Er . . . yes, of course. I suppose that might be an option as well." *In the event that all else fails,* Lucien had imagined her thinking. "Didn't he just buy a commission in the army, though? I have to tell you, Lady Roxberry, that as much as I like Lucien, he cannot offer her nearly as much security as a man of Lord Crossby's stature, for instance, can."

Lucien hadn't stayed to hear the remainder of what had been said, but he recalled with sharp clarity how inadequate he'd felt. Even now, years later, he felt his heart squeeze in his chest. Things were different now, however. He'd witnessed the horrors of war and suffered the loss of his brother. Nothing could have opened his eyes more to the fleeting fragility of life. No, he would not waste another moment wondering about "what if's." Instead, he would do everything in his power to win Katherine, but in order for him to do so, she would have to develop an awareness of him . . . to realize that he was not some nonsexual being but a man capable of fulfilling her every desire.

Christ. It would not be easy, and if he failed, he would in all likelihood lose the most important friendship he'd ever had. The risk was great, to be sure, and in the event that it all went pear-shaped, he would no longer be able to flee the country as he had before—not with the responsibility of earl resting upon his shoulders. But his brother's dying words still echoed through his mind. *Make her yours.* Lucien tightened his hold on his glass. No matter the heartache he'd suffered, he'd been offered a second chance, and he was determined more than ever before to risk everything if there was but a speck of hope that Katherine might one day return his affections.

Gritting his teeth, he watched as Katherine's dance partner leaned a bit closer to her—too close—and whispered something in her ear. She blushed and looked away.

Damnation!

"It's good to see you again," a deep voice spoke.

Lucien blinked. He'd been so lost in thought that he hadn't noticed anyone coming up beside him. He turned his head to find Lord Winston, the Duke of Kingsborough's brother, at his left shoulder. "You too," he said as he shook Winston's hand. He'd always liked both him and his brother, even though Winston was quite a bit younger than Lucien.

Winston plucked a champagne glass from the tray of a passing footman. He took a quick sip before saying, "I'd like to offer my condolences. Not only for your father but for your brother as well. They were good men, both of them, and they shall be dearly missed."

Lucien nodded. He knew that Winston and his siblings had recently suffered a similar blow when their father had taken ill and died a little over a year earlier. Lucien's mother had written to Lucien, informing him of the news in the same straightforward manner with which she addressed all the events that ought to be known by a future heir to an earldom. He returned the sentiment to Winston, and they stood for a moment in companionable silence until Winston broke it by saying, "You must have seen some marvelous places while you were away."

Lucien nodded. "I can't deny enjoying the opportunity to travel the Continent after the war. The countries differ dramatically from north to south and east to west in both culture and climate."

"I've been thinking of taking Lady Winston and the twins to see Paris and Rome."

"Ah, yes . . . I attended the premiere of Rossini's opera, *The Barber of Seville*, in Rome back in February. It was indeed a spectacular affair."

"I'll have to invite you for dinner one day so you can tell us more about it—advise us on the best places to visit, where to stay and where to dine."

Lucien chuckled. "I'd be happy to." Looking toward Katherine, who was still twirling around on the dance floor, he wondered if he'd ever have the opportunity to share these places with her.

"It would be a lovely way for Lady Winston and me to celebrate our next anniversary." Lord Winston paused for a moment before saying, "Speaking of which, I suppose you're planning to get yourself settled soon. Will you be attending the marriage mart this coming Season?"

"I must confess that the notion nauseates me," Lucien said.

Lord Winston nodded. "I daresay my brother shares your sentiment, though I suppose he will have to suffer it eventually if he is to do his duty—as will you."

Lucien snorted. "Not if I can help it."

His friend eyed him suspiciously for a moment. "Don't tell me you already have someone in mind. Some foreign beauty hidden away at Roxberry Hall, perhaps?"

Lucien smiled. "Nothing quite that exotic, I fear."

"Hmm . . . if you ask me, I always imagined you'd marry Lady Crossby—before she married the viscount, that is."

Lucien raised an eyebrow. "Oh? And why is that? Don't tell me you're planning to expand your business by publishing a newspaper and that you're secretly looking for a good story."

Lord Winston laughed. "No. I'm quite content with what I already have—no thoughts of expansion—but I've always been of the opinion that you and Lady Crossby would make a very good match."

Lucien snorted again. "We are merely friends."

"And yet I couldn't help but notice that you danced with her this evening . . . for the very first time."

"Are you always this astute?"

"Actually, it was my wife who pointed it out to me," Lord Winston confessed.

Lucien grinned. "Well, you may tell her ladyship that I thought it only proper to ask Lady Crossby to dance, since this is her first public appearance in so long. I merely meant to offer my support."

"How very good of you."

"And," Lucien added, "you may remind your wife that I also danced with Lady Deerford this evening, and I can assure you that I have no designs on her."

"I should hope not," Winston choked out.

Lucien took another sip of his drink, adding, "And I have every intention of dancing with a few more ladies this evening. Perhaps I'll even ask your wife, or do you suppose she'll wonder if I'm trying to seduce her as well?"

"I daresay I—"

"Ah! There you are, my dear," a warm voice crooned. "I've been looking everywhere for you since my arrival, but there are so many people and too many blasted feathers about, blocking my view."

Turning to his right, Lucien bowed toward the lady who had just spoken. "Grandmamma," he said. "It is absolutely delightful to see you again."

"Oh tosh! You make it sound as if it's been an age since we saw each other last, when it's only been a few hours." The old woman flicked her wrist and peered at Winston, who'd also greeted her with a bow. "My lord, I simply must compliment you on this evening's celebration. The floral arrangements are absolutely breathtaking."

"Thank you, Lady Roxberry, but this is entirely my mother's doing."

"Nevertheless, I am thoroughly impressed. This is not the first Kingsborough Ball I've attended, you know, but I daresay it promises to be the most memorable one."

"If for no other reason than the pumpkin carriage Mama acquisitioned for the occasion," Winston murmured, then quickly changed the subject by saying, "I see you have no refreshment, my lady. May I have the honor of fetching you a glass of champagne?"

Lady Roxberry's eyes narrowed ever so slightly. "Surely one of the footmen can save you the effort."

Leaning toward Lucien's grandmother, Winston lowered his voice to a conspiratorial whisper. "I fear that whatever they bring will not be to your liking."

This was met with a loud guffaw from her ladyship, and try as he might, Lucien found it impossible to stop himself from laughing as well, for what only few people knew was that Lady Roxberry favored brandy over anything else and that she oftentimes drank the stuff watered down and from a champagne flute so she might appear more sophisticated and ladylike to others.

"In that case, I give you my sincerest thanks, Lord Winston," Lady Roxberry said. "I shall look forward to your speedy return."

"I assume Mama is here somewhere as well," Lucien said as soon as Winston left, "and that you did not leave her at home."

"Unfortunately I had no choice, my dear—she claimed a megrim, and I could hardly accuse her of being dishonest. After all, it might very well be true . . . this time."

"I doubt it," Lucien muttered with mixed feelings of annoyance and concern. If only his mother could get herself out of the rut she was in. He was certain that socializing would help, but how could it when she was determined to barricade herself in her bedroom?

"Well, at least I managed to get here, though I did arrive a little later than I'd planned. I daresay you chose to take the best carriage when you set out." Lucien's grandmother heaved a great big sigh and looked around the room. "Now, where is Lady Crossby? I haven't seen the dear girl since Crossby's funeral. It would be nice to talk to her under more agreeable circumstances."

"You'll find her just over there," Lucien said with a nod toward the dance floor.

"Have you danced with her yet?" Lady Roxberry asked.

"Yes," he said.

Lady Roxberry nodded. "Good." She didn't elaborate, leaving Lucien with the uneasy feeling that he hadn't quite understood her meaning. He hadn't a chance to contemplate it much, since she spun toward him with startling speed, pinned him with an even stare and said, "You're quite a handsome devil, you know, just like your father was and your grandpapa before him."

Lucien blinked, taken aback by the force of her tone. "Thank you for that compliment, biased as it is," he murmured. He leaned toward her and smiled. "You're quite lovely as well."

Her cheeks dimpled. "Oh tosh! You needn't flatter an old bird like me, Roxberry. I'm well aware that I resemble a prune." She looked toward the dance floor, and her lips immediately thinned. "I must say I don't approve of the gentleman Lady Crossby is currently dancing with. You ought to step in and save her, Roxberry. Why, look at her, she's positively scarlet! Whatever can that man have said to her?"

Lucien had no desire to contemplate it.

"Oh dear," Lady Roxberry said, sounding perfectly distressed. "She looks so terribly unhappy, don't you see?"

Lucien did, and it made him want to grab Katherine's dance partner by the scruff of his neck and give him a good shake. No doubt the man had just propositioned her.

Thankfully, the dance soon drew to a close. An idea began to form inside Lucien's head. He looked at Katherine as she curtsied to her partner. The man offered her his arm and began leading her away from the dance floor and toward the refreshment table. Lucien forced himself to remain where he was and quietly asked his grandmother, "Who do you suppose will be the most sought-after lady this coming Season?"

The old woman eyed him suspiciously. "I believe the Earl of Rockly's youngest is showing great promise. She had her debut last year but declined the attention of all the gentlemen vying for her hand. She is not only considered an incredible beauty—a diamond of the first water, as they say—but she is also reported to be delightfully charming."

Lucien craned his neck and looked around the room. He spotted Daniel Neville in one corner and made a mental note to greet him later. "I don't suppose you know if she's here this evening? Lord Rockly's daughter, that is?"

Lady Roxberry's smile faded. "If you're thinking of focusing your attention on her, I daresay you're wasting your time and efforts."

Lucien nodded. "All the same, I do believe I'll give it a go. What is her name, by the way? I don't believe I recall it, though if I'm not entirely wrong, she's one of five. Is that correct?"

"Spot on," Lady Roxberry said, craning her neck as she looked about. "Her name is Lady Julie, and I do believe she's just over there with her mother and her sister, Lady Serena. Lady Julie is the one wearing a light pink gown and a silver mask with matching pink feathers on one side."

Setting his eyes on Lady Julie, Lucien wasn't surprised by what his grandmother had told him, for she was the typical slim-figured, blonde-haired woman that most gentlemen found appealing. Her youth, however, was not something that Lucien cared for in the slightest. Nevertheless, he would speak to her in the hope of striking a bargain. "Perhaps you would be so good as to introduce me?"

For a moment, Lady Roxberry looked as though she might dig in her heels. Instead, she gave a curt nod, placed her hand upon the arm Lucien offered her and allowed him to escort her across the room. A moment later, they were greeting the Rocklys and making small talk.

"I must say I'm very pleased to find you in attendance this evening, Lord Roxberry," Lady Rockly said. "It shows a certain . . . enthusiasm on your part to take your new role as earl seriously."

"Oh indeed, I take it most seriously," Lucien said. He knew exactly where this conversation was heading and hoped to prevent the countess from making a more specific comment. "But for the present I am simply hoping to enjoy the next set with Lady Julie if she is available and would care to dance."

Lady Julie responded with a pleasant smile, but it was the look in her eyes that surprised Lucien, for it conveyed a bland disinterest that he would have found insulting had he been pursuing her in earnest.

"How kind of you to ask," she said as she linked her arm with his and allowed him to steer her toward the dance floor.

"You need not concern yourself with how to be rid of me," Lucien muttered as he took Lady Julie by the hand at the start of a cotillion. "I have no interest in courting you."

Relief washed over her features, and she finally offered him a proper smile. "I hope you will forgive me, my lord. I mean no offense, but I invariably find myself exhausted by the end of these events, having danced until my feet begin to blister. I just wish I wasn't quite so sought after."

Lucien sympathized with her. The marriage mart could be terribly exasperating. "Your mother just wants to make a brilliant match for you, that is all."

"And therein lies the problem, I think." Lady Julie sighed. "She wants me married off to a peer, but I . . ." She snapped her mouth shut and looked away.

"You have developed a tendre for an untitled gentleman? Is that it?"

Her eyes grew large with worry. "I cannot believe that I allowed you to discover as much when I haven't even confided in my sisters. No one knows—not even him. Please, my lord, you mustn't—"

"Not to worry," he assured her in a low murmur as they wove their way between the other couples. "I promise you that nobody will discover your secret. However . . ." Tilting his head a little closer to hers, he whispered in her ear.

A sharp intake of breath conveyed her surprise, and for a long moment Lucien wasn't sure of how she would reply. Eventually she gave a little nod. "As long as you promise you'll be a gentleman."

He smiled down at her. "You have my word on it."

Katherine had in all likelihood never been more confused than when she'd watched Lucien leave the ballroom with Lord Rockly's daughter on his arm following their dance together. Surely Lady Julie was too young for a man of Lucien's age and experience—

not that he was old or anything, or that she had any clue as to how much experience he had exactly, but it was a fair guess that it surpassed that of Lady Julie. Katherine felt the heat rise in her cheeks at the unbidden contemplation that had entered her mind. This was Lucien, for heaven's sake. It was completely unseemly of her to be wondering about his prowess in regard to any woman.

She sighed deeply and tried to concentrate on what the two gentlemen in her company were saying, except she was finding their conversation terribly mundane—something to do with sheep breeding and agriculture. With a little bit of luck, Louise would hopefully notice her dilemma and come to her rescue, but it was an entirely different woman who eventually materialized at her side. "Lady Roxberry! What a pleasure it is to see you again. It's been far too long." She turned toward the two gentlemen, whose names she couldn't even remember. "If you'll please excuse me, I believe I'll take a turn about the room with her ladyship."

"Yes, of course," one of the gentlemen said, "though I do hope to speak to you again later. There is a rather . . . delicate matter I wish to discuss."

Silence reigned while she stared back at him, wondering what exactly he might be referring to. He shifted a little, looking mildly uncomfortable, and then it struck her that he wanted to ask her what five other gentlemen had already asked—if she would consider becoming his mistress.

Good heavens!

Managing a polite nod and a "Yes, of course I'll give the matter some serious thought" that didn't sound too appalled, she took her leave and walked away alongside Lady Roxberry.

"I imagine that it must be a bit like making your debut all over again, with all the attention you've been getting," the old woman said with a glimmer to her eyes.

"It is worse," Katherine confessed. "There are certain things a gentleman would never dare say to an innocent, but give him a widow and he'll happily whisper his every desire in her ear. I find it deplorable, really, and rather embarrassing."

Lady Roxberry laughed. "And yet I do believe it's been a while since any gentleman has offered *me* such a proposition. I can't imagine why, for I don't feel a day over twenty, even though my looking glass keeps insisting I'm old."

Katherine smiled at her fondly. She'd always loved Lucien's grandmother and her frank disregard for other people's opinions. If there was a lady in England who could cut straight to the heart of a matter before tea had even been served, then it was she, the bold and daring Lady Roxberry.

"My dear," the dowager countess was now saying. "Have you considered remarrying?"

A shiver ran down Katherine's spine at the very idea of allowing another man the right to lay his hands on her. "No," she said. "I don't believe another marriage is in my future. My focus will be on Sophia. There will probably be a few changes once my late husband's brother arrives to claim his inheritance, though. My mother's sister, as you probably know, is the Countess of Marlowe, and she has recently contacted me, inquiring if I would consider becoming her companion."

"I don't believe she has any children, does she?" Lady Roxberry asked.

"She does not, which makes the offer all the more

appealing, for she has promised to offer Sophia whatever opportunities her own children might have had."

"Hmm . . . I suppose that does sound tempting, though I'm not sure how you would manage to include a lover in that scenario. However, if you chose to become someone's mistress . . . ," Lady Roxberry said in a manner that belied her scandalous suggestion.

"I could never," Katherine gasped. She knew the lady was forward, but to say such a thing in public was beyond shocking. Glancing warily about to ensure that nobody had heard, she said, "I don't think it wise for us to continue this discussion here."

Of course, this was Lady Roxberry she was talking to, so she ought to have known that the subject would not be so easily terminated, and indeed it wasn't. "Don't be a prude, Katherine. You're a widow with a child, not an inexperienced debutante. Surely you don't imagine yourself alone for the rest of your days without a man to tend to your needs."

Good God!

"I assure you that I shall be quite all right on my own," Katherine said.

Lady Roxberry turned her head and looked at her with those knowing eyes of hers. "You say so now, my dear, but you are young, and you deserve to be loved again."

Katherine began to shake her head, but she caught herself just in time. "Perhaps," she said, hoping to placate the lady and put an end to the uncomfortable conversation.

"But you are probably right to wait and take your time deciding what you really want for yourself. In the meantime, I am hoping to get my grandson settled, though I'm having a difficult time ascertaining what he wants. The two of you have always been close friends, of course, but that's neither here nor there, considering the keen interest he's showing in Lord Rockly's daughter, Lady Julie, this evening."

Katherine stilled. "I'm sure the two of them have only just met."

"Oh, indeed they have, but only because Roxberry specifically asked me to introduce him to her. Of course I couldn't say no, though I can't help thinking that she's not the right match for him."

Something fierce and protective began to unravel inside Katherine, and she simply couldn't stop herself from saying, "I'm sure he will come to that realization on his own. After all, he is hardly a fool. I trust him to make the right decision when it comes to choosing a bride." She could scarcely believe that rushing into marriage with a woman he didn't really know was something Lucien would be able to accept in the long run.

Lady Roxberry waved her jewel-encrusted fingers nonchalantly. "My dear, Lucien is the heir to an earldom, and as such, he will do his duty come what may. Now, he and Lady Julie may have little in common, it's true, but since he specifically asked me to point out this year's most desirable catch, I do think he's paying attention to pedigree. There's no denying that Lady Julie is of good breeding, not to mention beautiful and a delightful conversationalist to boot. I have no doubt that she'll become a magnificent woman with time."

"It seems so superficial of him though—completely out of character," Katherine said. "Forgive me, my lady, but I find it difficult to believe that he would consider marrying a woman whom he barely knows." She found it nearly impossible to keep an edge of bitterness from her voice. What on earth was wrong with her?

Lady Roxberry gently patted Katherine's arm. "Unfortunately, my dear, how well he knows the lady is of little significance when compared with her ability to produce the heir he needs."

Katherine halted her progress and turned toward the dowager. It was a hard truth to face—the aristocratic obligation to procreate no matter the cost. Making a brilliant match was always of greater importance than whether or not the parties involved were capable of getting along with each other. It was absurd!

Katherine sighed. All she wanted to do was go home and crawl into bed. This conversation had made her feel dismal. "It just seems rather rushed," she confessed, "and so unlike Lucien, who's always given a great deal of thought to even the most trivial of things."

"Well, war can have a life-altering effect on a man. With everything he's lost, I do believe the only thing on Lucien's mind right now is building a future so he can leave the past behind him."

"Yes, of course," Katherine said as her eyes darted toward the terrace doors. She wasn't ignorant of the effect war could have on any person. Lucien had changed, and she was suddenly alarmingly aware of just how much. The innocent playfulness of his features had been worn away and replaced by hard lines—a silent account of all the horrors he'd seen—and there was something harsher about the way he spoke. Yes, when circumstance required it he could shove it all aside and pretend that he was still the same carefree person, but one would be a fool to ignore the pain and anger that surely gripped his soul.

But for him to throw himself away on a woman he'd only just met, just because he believed she'd make a suitable countess . . . It wasn't jealousy that washed over her. No, that would be ridiculous. She was just concerned for him and the choice she feared he might make. An urgent need to see him, to speak with him and advise him, assailed her. "If you'll please excuse me," she managed to say to Lady Roxberry, "I don't feel quite myself. I believe I'm in need of some fresh air."

"I have some smelling salts if you think that might help," the dowager offered.

"Thank you, but I believe I'll be fine once I get out into the garden."

"Then I will accompany you," Lady Roxberry said. "It's the least I can do."

Appreciating the old lady's proposal, Katherine gave her a grateful smile and said, "How kind of you to offer."

Chapter 4

"**H**ave you loved her for a very long time?" Lady Julie asked with marked curiosity while she and Lucien posed for the sketch artist inside the pumpkin carriage that was sitting on the lawn.

"Longer than I'm willing to admit," Lucien replied.

"In that case, I wish you every bit of success. Love matches are rare among our set. I'd like nothing better than to have played a part in making one happen."

"You are very kind to say so, my lady. I will wish the same for you, though I must warn you that the gentleman whose attention you seek may be in need of reformation first."

Lady Julie gave a small chuckle. "I may be young, my lord, but I am not naïve. Mr. Goodard is a notorious rake, and I am well aware of that. However, I have every confidence that he will come up to scratch if the right woman comes along to spark his interest."

"And I suppose you have every intention of being that woman?"

"Well, that goes without saying, does it not?"

Lucien couldn't help but smile. If there was one

thing his current companion didn't lack, it was confidence and determination. "You sound very sure of yourself, Lady Julie."

She turned her head just enough to look him in the eye. "That is because I believe that a task is best accomplished if you know that you are capable of doing it." She returned to her pose and added, "If you believe you are going to fail, then you've already given up before you've even begun, in which case there's very little point in trying at all."

Lucien blinked. It was as if a very old and wise woman resided within Lady Julie's youthful body. "Mr. Goodard has no idea how lucky he is that you have set your cap for him, though I daresay he'll find out soon enough."

They finished their sitting in silence and accepted the sketch from the artist as they alighted from the carriage. "I must say that's rather good," Lady Julie said as they stood side by side, studying the image. In a low whisper she continued with, "Don't look, but it appears as if your heart's desire is on her way over here right now, and looking not the least bit pleased, I might add." She then looked up at him in a most adoring way as she raised her voice and said quite sweetly, "He's captured your likeness so well, my lord, though if I am to be truly honest, you're far more handsome in person than the drawing suggests."

Lucien had to struggle not to laugh—especially since he was close enough to Lady Julie to see the hint of mischief in her smile. There was no doubt in his mind that she would take Mr. Goodard by storm, and the more he thought about it, the more he looked forward to watching that inevitable romance unfold.

"I was hoping to find you here," Katherine said as she approached with his grandmother at her side.

Lady Julie had been right about Katherine not looking pleased. In fact, she looked veritably annoyed—a state of being that would require further investigation in order for him to determine the cause. He could only hope that Lady Julie was to blame.

"Oh?" Lucien asked.

Katherine's eyes met his briefly before gravitating toward Lady Julie. "I'm afraid I've yet to make your acquaintance," she said. Her smile appeared a touch too forced. "I am Lady Crossby, a longtime friend of Lord Roxberry's. I do hope you'll forgive my intrusion."

"Of course," Lady Julie said. "Indeed, I'm happy that you chose to join us."

Katherine's smile broadened. "How kind you are, but I must confess that I was hoping to steal his lordship away from you for a spell." She returned her gaze to Lucien. "Considering how long it's been since we've seen each other, I thought it would be nice for us to have a little talk—the way we used to."

Lucien's heart made a leap. That last bit sounded very competitive and territorial, yet he couldn't be sure. He looked to his grandmother for guidance, but she was of no use whatsoever in revealing Katherine's motive for seeking him out, though she did leap into the middle of the conversation by saying, "And while you do, I shall take the opportunity to discuss something very important with Lady Julie."

Lucien frowned. He couldn't for the life of him imagine what that something might be and found himself wondering if he'd missed something. Unsure of how to react to the situation, he decided not to ask any questions and merely play along instead. "I would enjoy that a great deal, Lady Crossby," he said, "as long as Lady Julie doesn't mind me walking off with another woman."

"I must admit that I was hoping for a quiet stroll with you myself," Lady Julie said. "However, I am also terribly curious about what Lady Roxberry has to say."

"Well, if you will please come with me, I shall tell you," Lucien's grandmother replied as she took Lady Julie by the arm and steered her away.

Lucien frowned as he watched them leave. He felt as if he was somehow missing the plot. Well, at least now he finally had Katherine all to himself, outside, away from the crowd, and in a dark garden lit only by the occasional torches that lined the paths. He offered her his arm. "Will you walk with me?"

"I hope you're not too disappointed in your change of company," Katherine said as he guided her toward the far end of the garden. "I apologize if I was rude in demanding your attention—I meant no insult to you or to Lady Julie—but you see . . . well, the thing of it is that I couldn't help but notice how taken you seem to be with her, and I . . . err . . . well, she is rather young."

Lucien glanced over at Katherine. Her profile was shadowed, and it was impossible for him to tell if she was voicing her concern because she genuinely feared he might be acting too rashly and making a mistake, or because of some deep-rooted jealousy that had begun to bloom inside her. So he merely shrugged and said, "Perhaps, though I must admit that I find her absolutely enchanting. She's not the least bit empty-headed, but incredibly witty and smart. Frankly, I think she would make a fine wife for any gentleman seeking to marry."

"And is that what you want, Lucien? To marry?"

Only if I can marry you.

"It is certainly something that I have begun to

consider." She didn't respond to that, so he said, "I'm an earl now, Kate. Sooner or later I will need an heir. I see no reason in prolonging my search for a bride when I have a duty to do so eventually."

"No, I suppose not," she said, her voice holding a hint of uncertainty. "But since you've only just returned and this is the first time I'm seeing you in so long, I suppose I imagined that we would be able to spend some time together the way we used to."

"I see no reason why we can't still do that," he said.

She laughed, but it was the sort of laughter that betrayed her calm composure. "You know as well as I that a courtship will take up a great deal of your time." She fell silent. He sensed that she was struggling with whether or not to say something more, so he said nothing and merely waited for her to continue, which she eventually did. "I would like the opportunity to spend some time with you before you settle down and start a family—a chance for us to become reacquainted, to talk about the last four years we've been missing from each other's lives and for you to share with me your experiences from the war. I think it's important that you—"

"If you think that I am going to tell you or anyone else about something that I don't even wish to think about, then you are wrong," he clipped as the muscles in his arms tightened.

"Forgive me," she said in a rush of trembling words. "I just thought . . ." She shook her head. "I'm sorry."

Lucien frowned. Where was the Katherine who'd once used a slingshot to knock down apples from the highest branches of an apple tree, who'd urged his father to eat less pudding and his mother to favor blue rather than yellow when selecting her gowns? She seemed so skittish and unsure of herself now by comparison—so unlike the Katherine he'd left behind when he'd gone to join the army. "Is that it?" he asked her, hoping for a glimpse of the spirited woman he'd fallen in love with. "No quick response or set down to put me in my place?"

She eyed him cautiously, took a deep breath and finally said, "Very well. I realize you've had some unpleasant experiences since we last saw each other, but that doesn't give you the right to be curt with me or to dismiss what I am saying. If you've no desire to discuss what happened, you may tell me so in a polite manner, but know this, Lucien Marvaine—I am your friend, and I only have your very best intentions at heart."

Having come to an abrupt halt, Lucien stared down at the vision before him. This was the Katherine he loved and adored—a woman who was willing to fight any battle for those she cared about, even when it meant telling them what they least wanted to hear. What struck him by surprise was how stunned she looked—as if she couldn't believe the words that had just popped out of her mouth and regretted saying them.

Something wasn't right with her, and Lucien had every intention of getting to the bottom of it. For now, though, he would have to be content with settling the issue she'd initially broached in regard to the courtship she believed he would soon embark on. "Would you like me to postpone finding a wife in favor of spending time with you instead?" he asked. Maintaining a calm demeanor was becoming a very trying effort indeed. Especially when every nerve in his body was on full alert and his heart was racing away at a frantic pace.

"I know it may sound selfish," she told him hesitantly, "but when we spoke earlier this evening, I was under the impression that you wanted the same. So yes, if you could wait a while to seek a wife, I'd love nothing better than for us to talk, catch up on lost time, perhaps even go riding together the way we used to—mad races across the countryside."

The corner of his mouth tilted. "You are aware that I always let you win, right?"

Her chin rose a little, the gesture angling her face as she said, "I've no such notion. As far as I am concerned, I outrode you every time."

This brought a helpless bark of laughter from him. "Very well, then," he said, his voice still ringing with mirth. "You have convinced me, if for no other reason than to allow me the opportunity of proving myself a far superior equestrian than you."

"Do you remember when you took Patricia and me fishing that one time?" she asked, changing the subject.

"At the lake on the edge of my property? How could I forget, when you refused to listen to reason and lost your balance as a result? You were a sight to behold, with your wet hair falling into your eyes as you sputtered and splashed about as if you were drowning." He couldn't help but smile at the memory. "If I'm not mistaken, the water was only knee deep."

"Not my proudest moment, I must admit, but I was grateful that you didn't make fun of me at the time. Instead, you behaved very gentlemanly as you scooped me out of the water and dried me off."

Lucien felt his stomach tighten. Everything had changed between them that day—for him, at least. Holding her slight body in his arms as her wet muslin gown had clung to her every curve, he'd become startlingly aware of his own masculinity and of the woman she'd been turning into. She'd been sixteen years of age and he'd been three and twenty.

He recalled how much he'd regretted his sister's presence that day—was still embarrassed by it. But Patricia had denied him the opportunity of stealing a kiss. Later, when he'd had the time to contemplate the situation more clearly, he'd been glad to have been denied the chance to press his advances. It would only have complicated his friendship with Katherine, especially since she'd been destined for something greater than marrying a second son whose future had lain with the army. Since then, he'd withdrawn from her, kept his feelings in check, and breathed a sigh of relief when the army had called him away to fight against Napoleon. He'd needed distance.

"I will call on you tomorrow," he told her now. "If that is agreeable with you. We can spend the afternoon together, riding or fishing—whichever you prefer."

"Why not do both?" she said as they turned down a walkway that would bring them back toward Kingsborough Hall. "I'll ask Cook to prepare a picnic for us to enjoy, providing the weather isn't too cold."

It was late April, but the last few days had shown a marked rise in temperature, particularly during the afternoons, which had been filled with sunshine and cloudless skies.

Drawing her closer, Lucien lowered his head to whisper in her ear, "Just dress appropriately, Kate, and I'll bring a blanket."

There was nothing suggestive about what he said, yet Katherine felt a slight tremor wash over her in response to his words and his closeness. She'd nearly been reduced to a bundle of nerves when she'd asked him to postpone a courtship. The last thing she wanted was for him to think she had a romantic interest in him, which, of course, would be absurd, even though she couldn't dismiss that she'd found herself in a constant state of confusion the entire evening. Her reaction to Lady Julie had made no sense at all, nor had the persistent possessiveness she'd suddenly felt toward Lucien when he'd mentioned the prospect of marriage.

She glanced up at him with a modicum of discretion, aware more than ever before of the strength that resided in the arm she was holding. He really was an incredible specimen, if such a term could even be used to describe a man. Charles had been handsome—beautifully so—but his body had been slimmer. Lucien, on the other hand . . . a fleeting image of what his chest might look like in a state of complete undress gave rise to thoughts of toned flesh and broad shoulders. She shook the image away, bewildered by her reaction. Never before had she considered him in that way, yet she'd done so repeatedly in the space of only a few hours.

"You seem very preoccupied all of a sudden." The sound of his voice breaking the silence startled her. "Anything you'd like to share with me?"

Not in a million years!

"I was just thinking about Sophia," she lied, hoping he'd believe her. The orange glow from a torch flickered against the side of his face, illuminating it enough for her to see his frown. "I believe I would like to return home soon so I can check on her."

"Let us at least stay for the fireworks display. We can leave immediately after if you like."

Katherine nodded her consent, for she had been looking forward to seeing the sky light up with bright bursts of color. It would be a shame to miss it.

"Will I have a chance to meet Sophia tomorrow?" Lucien suddenly asked.

The question surprised Katherine, for Lucien was the first man to voice even the slightest interest in her daughter; why, even Katherine's female friends had made it clear that an infant had no place in polite company. They preferred to enjoy their tea undisturbed while the children were left with their nannies. "If you like," she said. "I'm sure she'd be happy to make your acquaintance."

"Truly?"

"She's only six months old—she's not very judgmental."

Lucien laughed. "I must confess that I've missed your wit while I've been away."

"Oh? Are they all very dull on the other side of the Channel?"

"No, I can't say that they are. In fact, most were very forthcoming, though I suppose my rank did help. But I should have liked to have shared with someone some of the things I saw and experienced during my travels. It would have been nice to be able to talk about them."

"I see no reason why you can't still do so—I'd love to hear about your adventures." She meant it, for while he'd told her that he'd missed her wit, she had missed so much more, she realized—she'd missed the companionship he'd always offered her, a companionship she'd never shared with anyone else, least of all with her husband.

Even now Katherine's throat tightened at the memory of what her wedding night had been like.

"Are you all right?" she heard Lucien ask.

Her breath caught. "Yes," she managed.

"You seemed so distant all of a sudden," he said as

they approached the stairs leading back up to the terrace. "I hope I've not distressed you in any way, for if I have, then I can assure you that—"

"You have not," she said, forcing a smile. "I'm just tired, that's all. I find that being a mother, as wonderful as it is, can also be quite exhausting."

"But you have her nanny to assist you. Surely you must be able to get a decent amount of rest." He sounded genuinely concerned.

"One would think so, but I find myself awoken now by the slightest sound. It is as if my body is on constant alert, and each time that happens, I rise to check on her."

"She sleeps close to you, then?" He did not try to mask his surprise.

"In an adjoining chamber," she said, annoyed that he would dare to judge her on something like this. He had no right.

"I hope you do not think I disapprove, Kate. On the contrary, your devotion to your daughter is nothing short of admirable. Why, there are so many people who care not one whit for their children, abandoning them to their nannies and governesses at every available opportunity. I'm glad to see that you're taking an interest."

It was not what she had expected him to say, and the surprise caught her off guard—so much so that she failed to watch her step, the tip of her slipper catching the hem of her gown and tripping her. For one faltering second, she felt the loss of control as her balance wavered. They were halfway up the stairs, so a plunge would hardly be painless, but just as she feared she would surely topple backward, a strong arm reached around her waist and held her steady.

Katherine's breath caught with relief as she tilted

her head back and looked up at Lucien. "Thank you," she said. His dark brown eyes stared back at her with an intensity she found most unsettling. It was then that she realized how close he was holding her and how rapidly her heart was beating against her chest. She took a breath, aware that she might be responding to him in a most inappropriate way, but then she caught herself and pushed the notion aside.

Silly girl.

Of course her pulse would be racing after what had just happened. To think that it had anything to do with Lucien would be ridiculous. Clearly Louise had muddled her head with all her talk of Lucien returning with the intention of courting her. And yet, when he distanced himself from her, she felt bereft. It had felt good to be held by someone, no matter how brief it had been.

"Let's get you inside," he said as they continued up the stairs, their arms linked so he could assist her. "I believe a refreshment will do you good."

Chapter 5

"Lady Huntley and Lady Winston," Lucien said as they approached the two women who were standing close to the terrace doors. "Would you care for some lemonade? I'm about to fetch some for Lady Crossby and thought you might enjoy a glass yourselves."

"How very kind you are, Lord Roxberry," Lady Winston said, her voice soft as she spoke. "We'd appreciate that very much, wouldn't we, Lady Huntley?"

"Oh, indeed we would."

"Very good, then—I'll be right back." Leaving Katherine with Louise and Lady Winston, Lucien walked off, moving confidently through the crowd until he disappeared from Katherine's sight.

"How was your stroll in the garden?" Louise asked.

Her question sent an uncomfortable rush of heat up Katherine's arms and across her chest. "Quite lovely," she admitted, immediately irritated by the gleam in Louise's eyes. She decided to quash whatever notion her friend had of her and Lucien developing a relationship that went beyond the bounds of friendship. "Before arriving here, I was unsure if our relationship would ever return to what it once was, but during our walk it almost felt as if he never went away at all—as if things were just the way they used to be between us. Once he marries, this will probably change to some degree, since his wife will require more of his attention, but that is how it should be, don't you think?"

"He's spoken to you about his intention to marry?" Louise asked with marked curiosity.

"He made it clear that since he must eventually do his duty, he might as well get on with it, or something to that effect," Katherine said. Why on earth was her heart beating so fast?

"And has he told you whom he intends to court?" Lady Winston asked.

"It appears he may be considering Lady Julie," Katherine replied, albeit a little reluctantly.

"Well, I cannot accuse him of not having good taste," Louise said. "Lady Julie will make a fine countess, to be sure."

The comment gripped at Katherine's insides, filling her mind with images of Lucien saying his vows to Lady Julie. To her dismay, she did not feel the least bit happy at the thought of it. "If you will please excuse me," she said, "I will just pay a quick visit to the ladies' retiring room."

"I hope you're not unwell," Lady Winston said.

"No, not at all," Katherine told her, attempting a calm tone to her voice even though her stomach was turning itself inside out and she feared she might be ill. "Indeed, I feel wonderful! It's so good to be out among friends again." And then she turned and hurried away, hoping that neither woman remarked on the way in which her words had faltered.

Reaching the other side of the ballroom, she was

just about to turn down the hallway that would take her to the ladies' retiring room when she spotted Lucien, his head bowed toward Lady Julie as he spoke to her. There was an intimacy between them that irritated Katherine beyond reason, and in spite of herself, she felt her whole body grow stiff as she watched the pair. Fearing they might see her, she made up her mind to continue on her way, when a low voice stopped her. "They make a fine match, don't you think?"

Vexed by the question, Katherine spun around to find Mr. Goodard, the Duke of Kingsborough's friend, standing close to her, his deep blue eyes trained on the same couple she'd been watching moments earlier. While she had met Mr. Goodard once or twice before, she had never spoken overly much with the man, and it annoyed her now that he'd noticed where her attention had just been riveted. "I'm sure they do," she said, her words a little terser than she would have liked.

"I must confess that I'm a little surprised by Roxberry's eagerness—I wouldn't have thought Lady Julie his type."

"No? And why is that? He's been gone from here for quite some time, Mr. Goodard. Who knows what his tastes are like these days?"

Tearing his gaze away from Lucien and Lady Julie, Mr. Goodard fixed his eyes on Katherine and frowned. "You seem . . . piqued, my lady. Do you not approve of the choice your friend has made for himself?"

A nervous laugh escaped her. "Rest assured, sir, he has not made a choice yet. For heaven's sake, the two of them have only just met."

"Hmm . . . perhaps that is true. However, love

matches sometimes take little more than a minute to be formed."

A love match?

Why, it was preposterous to think that Lucien had been so easily struck by Cupid's arrow. She looked toward him again just as he laughed in response to something Lady Julie said, his hand reaching out to rest for a moment on her arm. Something awful rose inside Katherine at that moment—something she did not like or understand in the least—and it took every ounce of restraint she possessed to quell it.

Feeling miserable, she bid Mr. Goodard a good evening and continued on her way, ignoring the hush that filled the room behind her and the dim sound of the duke's voice as he started to speak to his guests. All she could think of at that moment was that she had to get away.

Pushing open the door to the retiring room, she was thankful to find the space empty, allowing her some peace. She was sick of having to discuss Lucien's intention to court either her or Lady Julie. Both notions aggravated her, and not for entirely dissimilar reasons. After all, Lucien had only just returned. Why couldn't she and he just enjoy each other's company in peace and quiet without everyone eager to draw unwarranted conclusions? Why had everyone decided that just because he spoke to Lady Julie, the two of them would likely be wed? It wasn't likely at all, Katherine decided, no matter what his grandmother might think of the matter. Lucien would never attach himself permanently to a woman he'd only just met. Unless of course Mr. Goodard was right. What if it was love at first sight?

No. It cannot be.

Louise's words from earlier filled her mind. *"There*

are many who believe that his heart had been so thoroughly broken by his unrequited love for you that he found it impossible to remain in your presence . . . let alone the same country." It couldn't possibly be true, could it? Katherine shook her head. Of course it wasn't true. Louise was wrong. She had to be, but even if she wasn't, what did it really matter? Katherine had sworn that she would never remarry, and she would not want Lucien to think that she might if that was what he hoped for. No, it would be better, then, if she encouraged him to pursue Lady Julie, even though the thought of doing so did not sit well with her at all.

Lady Julie is perfectly lovely, Katherine told herself as she made her way back to the ballroom. Everyone said so, did they not? And besides, she ought to trust Lucien's ability to determine whether or not a woman would make him a suitable wife. However, when she returned to the ballroom and found the two of them dancing and smiling happily at each other, she didn't enjoy the emotion that flared up inside her. Dear God, she wasn't jealous, was she? The answer came in a flash, unnerving her even further. But how on earth could that be? She made an attempt to focus on what she was feeling as she watched the pair move about the dance floor.

This was what she'd always dreamed of when she'd contemplated her future, and as awful as it was, she couldn't stop herself from wishing that it was she and not Lady Julie who was being gazed upon right now with adoration. Furthermore, she felt as if she'd just gotten her friend back, only to have him snatched away from her again without any warning.

Swallowing the pain that threatened to return in full force, Katherine averted her gaze from Lucien and Lady Julie and headed for the terrace, only to find her path blocked by a tall, dark-haired gentleman with whom she was well enough acquainted to know that she had no desire for his company. "If you'll excuse me, Lord Starkly, I'm in no mood to hear whatever proposition you wish to make at the moment."

The man, however, was as rude as always, and rather than allow her to pass, he took her firmly by the elbow and steered her forward. Well, at least they were heading outside, which had been her goal in the first place, but she would have so much rather accomplished it on her own. "What do you want?" she asked once he'd led her over to a low bench and she'd seated herself.

"I sense you're not very eager for my company," he said. His voice was gruff.

"You sound surprised."

He didn't answer immediately but expelled a deep breath instead and lowered himself slowly onto the bench beside her. "I must admit that I was hoping you'd be here this evening. When I saw you last, at Crossby's funeral, you looked so pale and weary that I couldn't help but worry about you."

"I'm better now, so you needn't concern yourself," she said, looking away.

"And yet I find myself doing precisely that." He paused before saying, "I know you're unlikely to trust what I say, given my reputation, but I wanted to offer my services, in case there's anything you need."

She drew back. "Are you propositioning me, my lord?"

"No." His words were firm. "You deserve better than to be insulted in such a manner. Katherine, I—"

"You are being entirely too familiar, my lord. I

don't believe I have ever given you permission to address me so liberally." If only he would leave. She hated how scornful she sounded and how angry she felt, but seeing him had reminded her of things she'd rather forget, and it was rapidly ruining her evening.

"Forgive me, my lady," Starkly said. "It was not my intention to upset you, just to let you know that should you need anything—anything at all—I'm more than happy to assist."

He rose then, bowed toward her and wished her a pleasant evening before walking back inside. Katherine stared after him, fighting back the tears that burned in her eyes.

Rising, she headed for the stairs leading down to the lawn below.

"There's a waltz starting, Kate," a deep familiar voice spoke. "I was hoping you'd agree to dance it with me."

A flutter stirred her stomach as she turned to face Lucien. Determined not to allow anything to cloud the mood when she was in his presence, lest he become suspicious, she tamped down the nerves that had lingered from her conversation with Starkly. "What about Lady Julie? Wouldn't you rather take her for a walk in the garden so you can become better acquainted?"

"I must admit that I did intend to suggest it, but her sisters asked her to take a turn with them, so I'm afraid she's otherwise engaged at the moment."

"How disappointing that must be for you," Katherine said, attempting a lighthearted tone even though his confession made her feel like the rejected toy that only gets played with while the favorite one is being cleaned or mended.

He laughed and shook his head with amusement.

"Not at all. Indeed, I'm thankful for a chance to spend a bit more time with you."

"Oh?" Her spirits began to rise a little.

"If you must know, I couldn't help but notice that you were talking to Lord Starkly. I thought I'd better ensure that he didn't say anything untoward. The man doesn't have the best reputation."

Linking her arm with Lucien's, Katherine allowed him to lead her back toward the ballroom. "If you're inquiring as to whether or not he made any inappropriate suggestions, then the answer is no, he did not."

"I'm relieved to hear it."

"Others have, however, but I have turned them all down. The last thing I need right now is a scandal."

They entered the ballroom, where the shimmering glow of light from the chandeliers overhead bounced off each and every piece of jewelry present so they sparkled like stars. Smiling down at her as he led her onto the dance floor, Lucien said, "I take it you hope to remarry?"

His arm came about her waist as they took up their positions for the waltz. "No," she said. "I merely hope to raise my daughter without tarnishing her name."

The music started and Lucien took the lead, his hand pressed firmly against her back as he guided her forward. "A husband would permit you to do so," he said. "Especially if you make the right match for yourself. A husband will grant you security, Kate, not to mention friendship and . . . so much more."

"Good heavens," Katherine gasped. Heat rose to her cheeks, and she couldn't help but look away. "You're as bad as your grandmother!"

Lucien grinned. "She made a similar suggestion, did she?"

Katherine was not about to repeat what Lady Roxberry had said to her about a woman having "needs," so she just nodded and said, "She did."

"Well, if war has taught me anything, it is how fleeting life can be and how much more we might accomplish in the time we have if we'd only be more candid and less fearful of what others might think."

Returning her gaze to him, Katherine noticed that all traces of humor had vanished from his face, and as she stared back up at his soulful expression, she felt her heart ache for him and all that he had been through. "There is such a thing as propriety to consider, Lucien. One cannot always utter the first thought that comes to mind."

"One ought to be able to do so among family and close friends," he countered.

Uncertainty threatened, and Katherine felt herself frown. "I've always imagined that you and I were very straightforward with each other. Are you telling me that hasn't always been the case?"

Pulling her a little closer, he whispered in her ear, "You were an innocent when last we met, while I was a man with some experience. It goes without saying that there were certain subjects we could not discuss."

Oh dear God, she was going to burst into flames right there on the dance floor. "We ought not even discuss such things now," she muttered. How she was capable of speech in the midst of such discussion was beyond her.

"Oh, Kate," he told her cheerily as he spun her about. "I only have your best interests at heart, and while you may be opposed to the thought of remarrying right now, I have every intention of getting you to change your mind. Indeed, I plan on seeing you properly settled now that I've returned, and I shall do so by helping you find a husband."

"A wha-a-a-t?" Surely he was joking.

"You may not think you need one, but I know you, Kate—you're a romantic at heart, always have been since you were a little girl. Don't think I haven't forgotten how fascinated you were by the story of Odysseus and Penelope. It wouldn't do for you to live out the remainder of your days without a man at your side, or in your bed, if you prefer." He winked.

Katherine gasped, but before she could think of an appropriate response, Lucien said, "I know I ruined things by staying away as long as I did without sending word to you, but I still think that our history offers us a closeness that ought to allow me to be direct with you without you getting overly appalled, especially since you know how deeply I care for you."

"I'm very pleased to have you back," she told him. "Even though you're being terribly bold with the advice you're giving."

There was something wolfish about him as he pressed her closer still. "I am simply all too aware of the pleasure that can be had between a man and a woman, and I would hate to see you miss out."

If she spoke now, she knew she would stammer like an imbecilic fool, so she held silent while the spicy scent of him washed over her, caressing her senses and drawing out an awareness of him that she'd never sensed before. It was making her feel rather dizzy.

"So," he went on in a very businesslike manner (clearly without sensing her lack of composure, which was probably for the best), "I shall start looking for a suitable gentleman for you—someone handsome enough and smart enough to hold your interest."

"I really wish you wouldn't," she said, finding her voice. "As I've said, all I want right now is to forget all this talk of courtship so you and I can make up for lost time. What I truly desire is a friend, not a husband or a lover, for that matter."

"Very well," he acquiesced, "but if you happen to change your mind, I do hope you'll let me know so I can find you someone of whom I approve."

Katherine felt her whole body tense up. The way he said it made her wonder if perhaps he'd disapproved of Charles and might know the truth about her marriage, but she could see no trace of such knowledge in his features. She breathed a sigh of relief. "Yes," she said. "If I ever decide to take a husband or"—she hesitated as she struggled with being as forward as he had been—"a lover . . ." Lucien looked annoyingly amused as she repeated that word. ". . . then you shall be the first to know."

Bowing his head toward her ear, he quietly whispered, "I certainly hope so."

The maelstrom of emotion that flooded through her was enough to leave her not only breathless but also imagining the most wicked things possible—not with a faceless stranger she'd yet to encounter, but with Lucien, of all people. Good Lord, whatever was she going to do?

Chapter 6

"**I** believe it's time for the fireworks," Lucien said when the waltz ended and they stepped away from the dance floor. "Let's go outside so we can find a good place from which to view them before it gets too crowded."

Katherine accepted his arm with only the briefest hesitation. There was a most delightful blush to her cheeks, but her eyes held a wariness about them that made Lucien wonder if perhaps he'd been too bold toward her when he'd spoken of lovers, passion and secret desires.

It was time for him to pull back a little, so rather than pursue the issue, he said instead, "We can have our portraits drawn in the pumpkin carriage once the fireworks are over."

"What a splendid idea. I should like that very much," she said as they passed through the throng of people gathering on the terrace and started down the steps toward the lawn where they'd spotted the duke and his mother, the duchess.

"Oh look, I see that Mr. Goodard is there as well, along with the Winstons and the Huntleys."

"But who is that lady with the blonde hair standing next to the duke?" Katherine asked. "I don't believe I've ever seen her before."

Spotting the lady in question, Lucien had to admit that he didn't know either. "I'm sure we'll find out soon enough," he said as they stepped down onto the gravelly path at the foot of the stairs. Crossing it, they headed for the lawn.

"Even with her mask there can be no denying her beauty," Katherine murmured.

There was something so utterly sad about the way she said it—a sense of melancholy that reminded Lucien of her reaction earlier in the evening when he'd complimented her on her looks. Once again, he wondered if it might be possible for her not to realize how beautiful she truly was. Intent on setting her to right, he halted their progress and turned her toward him. "Indeed there cannot," he said. Her entire posture seemed to wither before his eyes, and he knew then beyond any shadow of a doubt that Katherine's confidence in herself had been drastically shaken during his absence. There would be a better opportunity to discuss the reason for this later, however, so he merely looked her squarely in the eye as he continued with what was the absolute truth. "And yet she pales in comparison to you."

"Lucien, I . . ."

"You are beautiful, Kate," he told her firmly. "I always thought you knew that."

Katherine's lips parted ever so slightly as if she meant to say something, but instead of words came a rush of air. Her eyes glistened, and she looked more vulnerable than she'd done at the age of six when she'd sprained her ankle after falling from her horse. Her bottom lip had quivered then, Lucien recalled, but she hadn't shed a tear, and he knew that she wouldn't do so now either, no matter how difficult this conversation might be for her. He decided to cheer her up a bit by saying, "Besides, most gentlemen prefer brunettes anyway."

It took a moment, but then she smiled. "That's not what I've heard."

"Well, whatever you've heard is all wrong. Blondes can be had by the dozen in England, whereas brunettes and redheads . . . well, don't even get me started on those."

To his delight, she finally laughed and slapped him playfully on the arm. "You're absolutely incorrigible."

"My lady, I never said that I wasn't." Winking at her, he resumed walking, only too well aware of how desperately he longed to haul her against him so he could kiss away the pain from behind her lovely green eyes. If this was Crossby's doing, Lucien had a good mind to march into hell and drag the man out by his hair so he could challenge him. But, for the meantime, he somehow managed to keep his rising anger at bay and said, "By the way, I do believe Mr. Goodard might be perfect for you."

The look of horror on Katherine's face was absolutely charming. Lucien smiled to himself, for he had known that Katherine would balk at the idea.

"You cannot be serious," she said.

"He's a very amicable gentleman once you get to know him."

"Well, in that case, I suggest you pair him off with Lady Julie instead—she's also very amicable." The sweet smile she gave him was not to be ignored, for it was laced not only with irony but also with . . . dare he hope . . . a touch of exasperation?

"I suppose I could, but where would that leave me?"

She eyed him assessingly. "Since you're so eager for us to speak our minds, I may as well tell you that it will never work. She's entirely wrong for you."

"Is that so?"

"Quite."

"Well, if not her, then who? Who would you suggest I marry?"

"Well, I . . . ," she started, but her words trailed off into thin air.

"Yes?"

"As your friend, I would recommend that you take a moment to consider your options, since marriage is, after all, for life. You wouldn't want to leap too hastily into something you cannot get out of again." Her words, as wise as they were, were tight and concise, as if she'd shut herself off emotionally as she'd said them. "Besides, you did promise to postpone a courtship in favor of spending more time with me."

Lucien nodded. "You're right, although considering my situation, I won't be able to do so indefinitely. If anything were to happen to me, the Roxberry title would go to my second cousin, George."

Katherine scrunched her nose. "The ginger-haired fellow who thinks himself superior to everyone and once threw your cat down the stairs?"

"Precisely."

"Well, we can't allow that to happen."

"So you see my dilemma? The sooner I marry and produce an heir, the sooner I'll stop Mama and Grandmamma from throwing themselves into the Thames—which is precisely what they'll do if George inherits."

"Right. Well, in that case, there's really nothing for it, I suppose. You *must* get yourself married." She looked at him conspiratorially. "Let's contemplate it this coming week, shall we?"

"When I take you fishing?"

She laughed—a sound he'd dearly missed. "Or after our race, which I have every intention of winning."

A bright burst of color exploded in the air. Looking ahead, Katherine nodded politely at her host, the Duke of Kingsborough, who had turned toward them with a smile just as the next firework rose in the sky. It was accompanied by a loud bang coming directly from Katherine's right, and as she turned her head instinctively toward it, she saw to her horror that a woman whom she did not recognize was hanging limply in the arms of Mr. Neville, heir to the Marquess of Wolvington.

Dear God in heaven, she's been shot!

Chapter 7

It was like a scene taken from a nightmare. Fireworks continued to explode against the night sky while the crowd watching from the terrace cheered and clapped, oblivious to what had transpired on the lawn below. Katherine spun toward Lucien, but he was already leaving her side and rushing to help. "Stay back," he said as she made to follow.

"I can't just stand here and do nothing," she muttered, distressed by the fear in Neville's eyes.

"Get her on the ground," the duke said as he removed his jacket for the victim to lie on. He shoved a wad of fabric toward Neville, who was now kneeling at the lady's side, alongside Lucien, Lord Winston and Mr. Goodard. "Put this on her wound, add some pressure and try to stop the bleeding. Winston, I'm leaving you in charge here while I try to find out what the devil happened." The duke then shot to his feet and took off at a run, heading toward the terrace.

Katherine gasped as the woman's sleeve was pulled back to reveal an ugly, blood-smeared wound. Seeing how quickly it was seeping through the compress, Katherine started grabbing at her skirt with trembling fingers, but a hand stopped her. "Don't ruin your gown," the Duchess of Kingsborough told her. "There are plenty more cravats and handkerchiefs for us to use should we need them."

"We should probably get her inside," Lord Winston said. His voice was gruff. "The wound will need cleaning, and I'm sure she'll be more comfortable too."

"I couldn't agree more," the duchess said, her mouth set in a firm line of determination. "And since we've no way of knowing how serious the lady's injury is, I suggest we hurry."

Following the duchess's orders, Neville scooped the woman up into his arms and strode quickly toward the stairs leading up to the terrace, while everyone, with the exception of Lucien and Katherine, followed behind.

Katherine's throat worked convulsively as Lucien came toward her. "Are you all right?" he asked.

She ignored his question. "Shouldn't you be going with them so you can help?"

"I fear I'll only get in the way," he said. "Her wound needs to be cleaned, and that won't require more than two, possibly three, people at most. Besides, I'm sure the duke will have sent for a physician to tend to his guest."

"She just . . . she looked so awfully pale. And her face . . ." Katherine met Lucien's gaze and immediately recognized the truth that glowed in his eyes. "That was Lady Rebecca, wasn't it?"

Lucien nodded. "Yes, I daresay it was."

Katherine nodded as if in a daze. She felt weak and out of breath. Never in her life had she witnessed such an awful occurrence.

"Come," Lucien said as he placed his arm around her shoulders. "You've had a shock. I think it best if I take you home so you can rest."

Katherine blinked, realizing that he was absolutely right. Never before had she known such a desperate longing to be with her daughter, for seeing a woman almost killed before her very eyes was a stark reminder of how fragile life could be. "Yes," she said, allowing him to guide her forward, "I would appreciate that a great deal."

"**A**ny news on the mill in Ancoats, Mr. Simmons?" Katherine asked her secretary the following morning as she leafed through the pile of papers that were spread out before her on the desk. She still had trouble deciphering some of the legal jargon, but with Mr. Simmons's help, it was getting easier.

"I was just about to mention it to you, my lady, since I just received a letter from the owner this morning, assuring me that your terms have been met."

"And are you inclined to believe him?"

"It would be foolish of him to lie when we can easily check the validity of it. Then again, he may have underestimated your dedication and think you unlikely of calling on him again anytime soon."

Katherine pondered this a moment. "You're probably right. Would you mind riding up there to ensure that what he says is true?" she asked, recalling how filthy the factory had been when she'd first visited it. It was clear that Charles hadn't cared about the work conditions at the mill while he'd been alive, but Katherine felt differently about it. As an investor, she had a responsibility toward the people who were helping her build and sustain her fortune. "I would come with you, but it would be difficult bringing Sophia along, and I'd rather not leave her."

"You needn't explain," Mr. Simmons told her

kindly. "You're a wonderful mother to her, my lady. The rest of the staff is in agreement."

It meant a lot to Katherine that he said so, for she'd been nothing but a bundle of nerves in recent years, always feeling as if she'd been walking on glass. Being allowed the opportunity to succeed at something was gradually restoring some of her shattered confidence. "I'll start making the necessary arrangements, then," Mr. Simmons said. "Perhaps you even have some new ideas that you wish for me to discuss while I'm up there—ways in which to increase profitability?"

"Oh . . . I don't know. Allow me to think on it," Katherine told him. "Thank you for looking out for my investments for me. Your help and advice have been invaluable to me since my husband's death."

"Think nothing of it, my lady, for it is my job to do so." He looked as if he wanted to say more, but he hesitated.

"What is it?" Katherine asked.

"I hope you won't mind my saying so, but I must admit that I was surprised when you initially told me of your decision to continue with your husband's work. It's unusual for a lady to show such interest in these things . . . men's things, if you'll forgive me. I confess that I imagined you'd simply leave it all to me, and . . . well, I'm embarrassed to say that I didn't think you capable. But I am impressed with the decisions you've made so far. The companies you've chosen to invest in have since given high returns. Indeed, your income has almost doubled over the course of the last year, and it's all thanks to you."

Katherine couldn't help but blush. It pleased her that Mr. Simmons had noticed how well her hard work had paid off. She'd spent weeks secluded in the study after Charles's death, going over his documents and trying to get to grips with all the ledgers—the vast records of Cresthaven's income and expenses.

It had been a daunting job, but it had also been a very rewarding one, for she was now aware of the specifics regarding each company her late husband had invested in and could discuss them properly with Mr. Simmons, allowing her the chance to be involved.

After sinking a portion of her own money into a couple of companies, she found it particularly fitting that she should be a part of the process. "You are very kind to say so," she told the secretary, "even though I still have a lot to learn."

A knock at the door brought Katherine's attention to Carter, the butler, who had just arrived. "Lord Roxberry is here to see you, my lady—I have shown him into the parlor."

Katherine's heart did a funny skip. After returning home last night, she'd spent a great deal of time contemplating the peculiar effect Lucien had had on her at the ball. Removed from the fairy-tale splendor of it all, her mind had cleared, and she'd decided that the way in which her nerves had quaked and her heart had pounded in his presence had been nothing more than the product of a magical setting, a few insinuating words from her friend and perhaps a bit too much champagne.

Today was a new day, however, and she had a job to do. If Lucien insisted on getting himself married, then she was going to make certain that he attached himself to the right woman. It was possible that Lady Julie would turn out to be the perfect candidate, for although she'd implied otherwise, Katherine hadn't dismissed the idea, considering how smitten Lucien had seemed to be with the lady. But since this was her dearest friend's future at stake, Katherine wanted to be absolutely sure that he was making the right decision. Therefore, being the practical sort, Katherine had made a list of all the ladies she thought suitable (and with whom she could see herself enjoying tea or shopping for fabrics, which of course was an essential factor).

"Thank you, Carter," she told her butler as she gathered up her papers and put them in a neat pile. "Perhaps you could ask if he'd like a cup of tea. I'll just be a moment."

"Yes, my lady."

"Oh, and Carter?" The butler halted and turned back toward his mistress. "Please inform Cook that his lordship has arrived and that she should start to prepare the picnic basket."

With a nod, Carter strode off. Katherine rose, as did Mr. Simmons. "We'll talk again later," she said as she went to the door. "We've yet to decide if we're going to sell the stock in that coal mine in Durhamshire."

Heading toward the parlor, she stopped briefly in front of the mirror that hung in the foyer and took a quick peek at her reflection. Noting that she looked a little pale, she pinched her cheeks but then admonished herself for her silliness. This was Lucien she was meeting—a close friend whom she'd met on countless occasions before and who was hardly going to care one way or another about her coloring. The thought stilled her as she gazed back into the eyes of her reflection, unnerved to discover how much Lucien's perception of her suddenly mattered. She sighed. Lord, she was being ridiculous! And yet . . . a faint voice whispered to her that things had been different between them last night and that she had not been as indifferent to him as she would have liked herself to believe. Pushing a lock of hair back into place, Katherine quickly dismissed the notion. Now was not the time to be having fanciful ideas, especially when the gentleman in question was presently waiting to see her.

But when she stepped into the parlor with a smile on her face, ready to greet him, her mouth went instantly dry and her stomach almost felt as if it was turning itself inside out—a feeling that was not in the least bit comfortable but apparently hard to avoid as she took in Lucien's appearance.

Gone was his black evening attire and his neatly groomed hair. Instead, he wore a dark blue jacket with beige, snug-fitting breeches and black Hessian boots. His hair was slightly mussed, with a few stray tendrils brushing against his forehead. Good heavens, he looked like a prime figure of a man as he stood there casually gazing out of one of the windows. Perhaps she ought to have taken greater care in selecting her gown that morning, because right then, without the slightest bit of warning, her conviction that Lucien did not affect her in any way fell apart in its entirety. There could be no denying that without as much as looking at her, he'd taken her breath away. The realization flustered her, but she had no time to consider the implication of it, since he turned his head just then, spotted her and immediately came toward her.

"Good morning," he said, bowing from a respectable distance.

Disappointment swept over Katherine. No kiss upon her hand? *Idiot*, she chided herself as she returned his greeting. It was midmorning, the magic of the previous evening had departed the instant

Lady Rebecca had been shot, and considering how well acquainted she and Lucien were with each other, it would be absurd for him to go around kissing her hand at every available opportunity. Still, she couldn't help but be a little put out by him not doing so, especially since she presently felt as if he'd reached inside her chest and touched her heart.

He of course felt no such thing toward *her,* or he would have at least suggested that they marry each other now that he was in the market for a wife. Not that it mattered, of course, since *she* had no intention of acquiring another husband.

Oh bother!

"Have you received any word from the duke regarding last night's incident?" she asked, both out of concern for Lady Rebecca and because she was desperate to concentrate on something other than Lucien—impossible as that was when he was standing before her looking so rugged.

"Nothing yet, I'm afraid." He tilted his head. "You mustn't worry, though. Considering her wound, she ought to be fine as long as she gets proper treatment—I'm sure of it."

"That is a relief to know." Silence fell between them. The clock ticked away on the mantelpiece. Katherine's fingertips toyed with her skirt. "Have you seen many such wounds before? During the war, I mean."

"I've seen my fair share. More than I care to remember, I'll admit."

A shadow fell across his brow, and Katherine chided herself for posing the question. In all likelihood, she'd just reminded him of his brother. "I'm sorry," she said.

Drawing a deep breath, he pushed the air out slowly.

"I brought my curricle along. Since you mentioned having a picnic, I thought we could drive over to the lake and go fishing—save the race for another day?"

"Are you trying to postpone losing to me?" Katherine teased, eager for a bit of easy banter and hoping that it would relax her agitated nerves.

"Not in the least. I was merely trying to protect you from the truth—that I have always allowed you to win." He flashed a cheeky smile.

"First of all, I don't believe a word of it, and second of all, if you were a true gentleman, you would not be so ready to tell me of your superior riding skills. Instead, you would have allowed me to remain ignorant, providing of course that what you say is true— which it is not."

He laughed, a low rumble that sent frissons scurrying across her skin. "I daresay I'll never understand the workings of a woman's mind, not even yours. I imagine it's quite a muddle in there."

Crossing her arms, she tilted her chin in defiance. "And yet we do excel at keeping all our thoughts in order."

He leaned toward her and frowned, as if attempting to look inside her head. "Tell me, for I've always wondered, is there a specific part of your brain that you devote to gossip?"

Keeping a straight face was becoming exceedingly difficult, but at least the humor was distracting her from other things, like the curve of his mouth as he smiled and the same spicy scent she'd smelled on him as they'd waltzed. Her stomach began to tighten, so she redoubled her efforts to concentrate on the conversation. "Of course," she said. "How else am I to recall which lady caused a scandal by falling into the arms of a scoundrel?"

"How indeed?"

His eyes darkened for a moment, and as much as Katherine wished to look away, she could not. It was almost as if he was somehow testing her.

"There is also a special compartment allotted to gowns, bonnets and"—she waved her hand—"shoes."

Lucien's lips began to pucker, then he suddenly burst out laughing. Katherine smiled. This was what she'd missed—this easy camaraderie between them. She watched as he wiped his hand across his eyes and straightened himself. When he'd gone to join the army, she'd been nineteen years of age and had inappropriately flung her arms around him in a tight embrace when she'd told him good-bye. She longed to do so again now, for it would be bliss to be held by him. Fearful of the reaction he'd stirred in her since yesterday, however, and recalling how startled he'd been by her forwardness four years ago, she decided that doing so would likely be a very bad idea.

Instead, she smiled at him politely and gestured toward the door. "If you'd still like to meet Sophia before we leave, I can take you through to her right now."

Sitting next to Katherine, Lucien whipped the reins, pushing his horses into a canter, their hooves thudding against the graveled driveway. Eyes straight ahead, he did his best to quell his pounding heart.

Follow your plan and you shall have her. Do not rush this.

When she'd entered the parlor and he'd turned to look at her, it had taken every ounce of restraint not to stride across the floor and pull her against him.

Gone was the silk and lace she'd worn to the ball, replaced instead by a modest morning gown that ought to have dampened his desire. Instead, it had only made him more eager to rip away the plain muslin with which she was garbed in hopes of revealing that extra bit of skin she'd displayed last night.

A wave of heat crashed over him. No, this pursuit of his would require finesse, for although she was responding to him in a most delightful way, he also sensed a great deal of resistance. She'd said she'd never again marry and that she had no plans of ever taking a lover—that she was content to remain alone. And yet, whenever he touched her, it was almost as if a flame sparked to life in her eyes. Oh, the lady might insist she had no needs, but Lucien knew better, and in time, he had every intention of showing her how skillful he could be at fulfilling them.

An ache settled in his loins and he found himself clenching his jaw, his fingers gripping the reins as he urged the horses onward. "Your daughter is absolutely charming," he said, settling on a topic that he knew would appeal to her and that he hoped would distract him from his wayward thoughts. "She looks a lot like you."

Katherine chuckled. "I think it's too early to say so, but thank you." Even though his eyes remained on the road, Lucien could sense that Katherine was looking at him. "You know," she finally said, "I always suspected that you would be good with children, but I must admit that you are better than I ever imagined. Seeing you hold her as you did, tickling her belly and making her chortle, was very touching indeed. I daresay you'll make an excellent uncle for her."

The compliment warmed his insides, even though he hoped his position as uncle would be a fleeting one and that he would soon become the babe's papa through marriage. He felt the edge of his mouth curve upward. Today would mark their first day of courtship, even if he was the only one who knew it. It was all part of the plan he'd forged to heighten her awareness of him as a man—a man in need of not just a wife, but a lover as well—and little by little he meant for his every touch and whispered word to melt her insides until she could no longer recall a time when she did not want him.

Ah, if only it worked, for the alternative was not a pleasant one.

Arriving at a cluster of trees, Lucien parked the curricle, jumped down onto the springy grass below and secured the horses. He then helped Katherine alight, his hands resting firmly upon her waist as he lifted her down. Her cheeks appeared rosier now than they had earlier, he noted, and rather than release her immediately as he ought, he held her in place with one hand while the other rose to her cheek, his fingertips brushing gently across it. "Just a bit of dust," he said. "There . . . all gone."

Stepping away from her, he handed her the fishing poles, then grabbed the picnic basket and a blanket and gestured for her to lead the way along the path that would take them through the trees and down to the lake. He was not the least bit oblivious to the dazed expression on her face. His efforts, it would seem, were already having a remarkable effect. He tried not to smile too much.

"Do you prefer a spot in the sun or in the shade?" he asked once they reached the edge of the water. The weather was beautiful—bright and sunny, with a clear blue sky. It was warmer than it usually was this time of year.

"I think the shade might be too chilly, don't you? I would personally welcome the sun's heat. If we lay the blanket out over there," she said as she pointed to a flat, grassy spot next to the lakebed, "we'll even be able to anchor our fishing poles using those rocks."

Agreeing with her reasoning, Lucien spread out the blanket, placed the picnic basket at one end of it and asked Katherine to take a seat, which she promptly did, folding her legs neatly beneath her as she carefully placed the fishing poles to one side.

"Have you been fishing since the last time we came here together?" Lucien asked. He was trying to envision what her life had been like in his absence.

"When I made a cake of myself by falling into the water? Your sister has never allowed me to forget it, you know."

He hadn't wanted to mention the incident again, as he'd hoped to avoid embarrassing her, but when he met her gaze, he couldn't help but notice how bright her eyes were. Her lips twitched and she laughed. He smiled in return. "I trust you'll avoid stepping out onto a slippery rock today."

"You can count on it, and in answer to your question, no, I have not."

"Well, it's all very simple, if you recall." He removed a small jar from his pocket and took off the lid. "Just pick a worm and place it on the hook."

With a stiff nod, Katherine quickly removed her gloves, just as he'd known she would, and reached inside the jar to retrieve her prize. It was one of the things he'd always loved about her—how grounded she was, the sort of woman who never fussed over getting her hands dirty. She could be prim and proper when necessary, but in her element, which had always been outdoors, she never worried about spoiling her clothes or whether a spider might be crawling up her arm. Indeed, she was more likely to take a closer look at said spider and remark on its beauty.

Picking a worm for himself, Lucien slipped it onto his hook and looked at Katherine. She appeared to be struggling with hers. "Do you need some help with that?" he asked, his eyes riveted upon her fingers.

"If only it would stop wriggling so much, it would make the task so much easier."

Lucien suppressed a bark of laughter. "Yes, because that is precisely what any other creature would do—wait limply to be impaled."

She looked at him with a frown. "Are you trying to put me off?" She appeared to make another attempt, but once again the worm maneuvered itself away from the hook.

Deciding to take advantage of the situation, Lucien leaned over and placed his hand on Katherine's. "Like this," he said as he adjusted her hold on the worm. Putting his arm around her shoulders, he then showed her how to hold the hook properly in place while he helped her bait it. He didn't linger once the job was done but removed himself immediately from her person and rose to his feet, taking his fishing pole with him. "Now all you have to do is toss the line in the water. I can help you with that as well if you wish."

"Err . . . no thank you . . . I mean, I'd like to attempt it on my own."

She moved hesitantly, he noticed, and with less determination than when she'd selected the worm. In fact, she looked adorably unsettled, for which Lucien had to applaud himself. If he wasn't mistaken, his closeness and touch had had the desired effect. Casting his own line into the water, he watched as Katherine did the same. Unlike her previous attempt eight years earlier, she remained on solid ground this time and did not slip or fall as her line flew neatly out over the water, the hook landing with a satisfying plop. "Ha!" she shouted, her eyes bright and her smile unwavering as she turned toward Lucien. "I did it!"

"So you did," he grinned. She was mesmerizing in her victory, her face glowing with more happiness than he'd seen in her yet since his return, as if some heavy burden weighing her down had been momentarily dismissed. He eyed her quietly as she secured her fishing pole between the rocks and returned to the blanket.

Following her, he could not help but notice the gentle sway of her hips as she walked or the grace with which she took her seat. The memory of her wet gown hugging her every curve flashed before him so powerfully that he forgot himself, emitting a groan at the sudden discomfort it wrought.

"Are you all right?" she asked, all wide-eyed concern.

Taking a deep breath, Lucien sank down onto the blanket and crossed his legs. "Yes. Quite. Shall we see what your cook has prepared?"

With a nod, Katherine reached for the picnic basket and flung open the lid, revealing a bountiful feast of mincemeat pie, smoked herring, some cheese and a bottle of wine. To their unfettered delight, there were crêpes with strawberry jam for dessert.

"Are you still an avid gardener?" Lucien asked as he bit into a slice of pie.

"Yes," she said. "I love watching my plants flourish, which I suppose explains why spring is my favorite time of year."

"Your daffodils do look lovely lining the driveway—don't think I didn't notice."

Katherine beamed at him. "They do brighten things up, don't they?" She gave him no chance to respond before saying, "I allocated part of the back garden to herbs and vegetables last year. Can you believe that Cresthaven did not have a vegetable garden? You must come and see it during the summer, for I have every confidence that the tomatoes I have recently planted will be among the juiciest in the county."

"I do not doubt it for a second," Lucien remarked, though he could well enough imagine other juicy things he'd like to sink his teeth into, like Katherine's plump lower lip, for example.

"And what about you?" Katherine asked. "Was all as you expected it to be at Roxberry Hall when you returned? You must forgive me, but I quite forgot to ask last night. How terribly thoughtless of me."

Lucien grinned. She was prattling on as if she was nervous. Her hand reached for her glass, and, raising it to her lips, she took a hasty sip of her wine. "Not at all," he said. "In fact, everything was mostly as it was when I left, though I do believe my absence and my father's death have forced Mama and Grandmamma to see more of each other than either of them would have wished."

"I always thought they got along rather well, or at least that's how it appeared."

Arching an eyebrow, Lucien selected a piece of cheese. "Their opinions differ greatly on most issues, as does their method of conveying them." He took a bite of his cheese.

"I suppose your grandmother does have a tendency to be more forward than your mother, whom I've always considered quite reserved."

"Precisely."

There was a pause, then Katherine quietly said, "I

believe they agree on at least one thing, though, and that is that you must marry."

Meeting her gaze, Lucien felt his pulse quicken. "True," he said.

She looked away and reached for one of the pancakes. "And . . . as promised, I have considered some . . . possible candidates."

Lucien felt his eyes narrow. Was it just him, or was she deliberately trying to busy herself with something—anything at all—that would not require her to look at him as she spoke? How very interesting. "And?" he asked, feeling suddenly cheeky, "is Lady Julie on your list?"

Katherine's eyes flew toward his, her lips parting ever so slightly while her chest began to rise and fall in a flurry. "Yes," she told him pertly as she smoothed the skirt of her gown. "You seemed quite taken with her, so I thought you'd be pleased to have her included."

"Oh, I am," Lucien murmured, for it could not be more obvious than if Katherine had actually told him so herself that she did not care to contemplate his marrying Lady Julie. "I'm very pleased indeed."

"But she is not the only one on the list, of course. I've also included the Earl of Mayhaven's eldest, Lady Theodora, the Earl of Thisdale's daughter, Lady Annette, and the Duke of Sylverton's daughter, Lady Charlotte."

"Fine ladies, I'm sure," Lucien murmured. He studied her for a moment before saying, "How exactly did you end up married to Crossby? I never had the impression that you were particularly fond of him."

Her posture grew rigid. "I admit that I always found him a bit self-obsessed when we were younger, but then he went to war and . . . when he returned he was entirely different. He was attentive and kind." She plucked at her gown. "The first time he called, he brought me wildflowers, which I considered surprisingly sweet, as I would have expected a man like him to bring roses."

Lucien clenched his fists, recalling how Crossby had once declared that any woman could be had with a bouquet of roses. Lucien had challenged the statement by saying that he knew of at least one who'd rather have wildflowers, and Katherine's name had been mentioned in that context. "My understanding is that you married him rather quickly," he said.

Katherine nodded. "Our courtship was quick, but such is often the case these days. I didn't have my sights on anyone else and neither did he, so when our parents discovered how well we were getting along with each other, they encouraged us to marry."

"I'm sure your parents were especially pleased by the match you made."

"I believe so. They always hoped I would marry a lord, so when Crossby's intentions became clear, they urged me to accept, so I did." She took a breath and relaxed her shoulders. "But what about you? I'm sure you must have seen some wonderful places during your travels."

Lucien took a sip of his wine. "Crossing the Alps was a spectacular experience." He shook his head at the memory of it. "The beauty there is so enormous that it surrounds you, draws you in and leaves you utterly breathless. Italy was remarkable too, the Roman architecture unlike anything you've ever seen in England."

Katherine leaned forward. "Did you see the Colosseum?"

"I did," Lucien said.

"Oh, it must have been a magnificent sight," she sighed. "I'd love to visit it myself."

"Perhaps you will," Lucien said, deciding to add Rome to the list of potential destinations for their wedding trip.

"I'm not so sure," Katherine said. "My intention is to become a companion to a lady who's never set her feet outside of England and who I doubt has any intention of ever doing so."

"So much more reason for you to marry an adventurer," Lucien suggested. "You know, I can see you as the wife of a privateer, sailing the high seas and such."

Katherine rolled her eyes, but her words, "We'll see," were promising. She raised a rolled-up pancake to her lips and took a tentative bite.

Averting his gaze, Lucien looked at the lake and considered jumping into it. If there was ever a time when a cold swim would be more than welcome, it was now. Frustrated, he rose to his feet and went to check on the fishing poles. He'd ventured down a dangerous path, he realized, one from which he dared not veer, even as it challenged his tightly reined sense of control.

With his back turned toward Katherine, he took a deep breath and expelled it, deliberately pushing the tension out of his body. He needed to relax, to calm the blood that pumped so furiously through his veins each time she spoke, fluttered her eyelashes or puckered her lips. Christ, how he longed to throw himself on top of her, to declare himself her humble servant, to love her . . . pleasure her . . . fulfill her every desire, as he'd wanted to do so often over the past years that the mere mention of her name set his insides aflame. He loved her, yes, but by God if he didn't also lust after her like a youth who'd yet to know a woman's touch.

On a heavy sigh, he looked over his shoulder at the spot where she was sitting, delicately licking some jam from her fingers after finishing her pancake. Feeling his restraint grow taut, Lucien returned his attention to the lake and to the fishing lines that pierced the surface. One of them squirmed, rippling the water.

"It appears you've caught a fish," Lucien said as he picked up Katherine's pole and started to reel in the line. A small ide emerged, wriggling from side to side. Crouching down, Lucien carefully held the tiny fish in his hand and began prying the hook out of it.

"Poor thing," Katherine murmured.

Her words drifted over Lucien, startling him with her closeness. He hadn't realized she'd gotten up and come toward him; he'd thought she'd still been seated at a comfortable distance from his aching heart. It was all too much, the force with which she drew him. He felt a muscle twitch in his cheek in response to the strained expression he forced into place as he desperately sought to keep his feelings for her at bay. And yet her voice beckoned with its sweetness, allowing him no choice but to turn his head and look up at the woman who stood beside him. His gaze traveled the length of her legs, past the spot where he knew her thighs to be, to her belly and the rounded softness of her breasts. Abruptly, he rose, almost knocking her sideways in his haste to regain some of his crumbling composure.

Being the gentleman that he was, his arm reached out instinctively to steady her. "Forgive me," he said. "That was terribly clumsy of me."

Her eyes, which had been focused on the fish, met his for the briefest of moments before traveling down to the spot where his fingers still rested against her elbow. He withdrew his hand, apologized again and began to busy himself with freeing the fish—anything that would calm his racing heart in the wake of what he'd just seen in the depths of those haunting green eyes: confusion twined with fear. But beneath those emotions he'd glimpsed something else—something he'd been dreaming of for years: raw, unfettered desire.

The fish squirmed between his fingers as he unhooked it, offering barely a splash as Lucien tossed it back in the lake. Drawing a deep, fortifying breath, he stood for a moment just staring at the water, allowing himself the luxury of reveling in his progress. It was much too soon for him to act on his feelings for Katherine, but there was no harm in congratulating himself on his efforts, for it was clear to him now that she was no longer indifferent to him . . . that something in her regard had shifted.

"Shall we pack up and head back?" he asked. "I feel a chill coming, and I'd hate for you to catch a cold." Tilting his head, he looked at her as she stood there beside him.

She frowned, then nodded. "Yes. I suppose we ought to." Her words, slightly breathless, reflected her bewilderment.

Lucien smiled as he went to retrieve the picnic basket. Things were most assuredly progressing as he had hoped, and as long as he persisted with the right amount of patience, he had every confidence that Katherine would soon be his.

"May I call on you again tomorrow?" he asked her later as they drove up the driveway toward Cresthaven. "We could have that race we discussed and finally settle the matter of who is the fastest."

"Then I suggest you choose your horse carefully," she said with a smile, "and consider the stakes."

"Oh, believe me, Kate, I've been considering the stakes for a very long time," he murmured.

She looked at him, all wide-eyed and with that same bewildered fear she'd made him privy to at the lake. "What are you saying?" she asked.

"That I know you well enough by now to realize that you'll never allow me a moment of peace if I happen to lose—not when I've told you you've no chance of winning."

"Oh," she said as they pulled up to the front steps.

Jumping down, Lucien rounded the carriage and helped Katherine alight. Was it just his imagination, or did she actually gasp when he seized her about the waist? Determined not to give himself away yet, he released her as soon as she was on the ground and offered her a gallant bow, while a footman fetched the picnic basket and fishing poles. "It was a pleasure seeing you again," he said.

"Likewise," she said.

There was a pause that felt like a hesitation, as if she intended to say something more, but when she didn't, Lucien wished her a pleasant afternoon, climbed back up onto the seat and whipped the horses into motion. It had been a productive day for him in terms of steering his relationship with Katherine in a new direction, though there could be no denying that he would have to use restraint where she was concerned. She wasn't ready for his advances yet, and if he rushed, he'd only succeed in scaring her off. This he felt like a certainty deep within his bones.

Something had happened to her in the time they'd

spent apart, something that she was attempting to hide, though her smiles failed to mask the fear and pain within her. Whatever it was, Lucien meant to uncover it, because however much he wanted to make Katherine his, he wished to see her happy so much more.

Chapter 8

"**M**r. Goodard! What a surprise," Katherine said, setting her book on the table as she rose to greet her unexpected guest the following afternoon. She'd been expecting Lucien, who was supposed to arrive at any moment, and had decided to wait for him in the parlor, where the light was particularly good at that time of day.

"Lady Crossby," he said. "I hope you'll forgive the intrusion, but I couldn't stay away after our conversation the other evening. You seemed distressed by what I said, and I haven't felt comfortable about it since. I hope you'll accept my apologies."

"Of course I will, though I daresay there's nothing for you to apologize for. If I appeared distressed in any way, it was only the result of my own folly." She studied him a moment. He was a striking man—tall and handsome, with honey-colored hair and deep blue eyes. "Since you did come all this way, though, I do hope you'll stay for tea. Lord Roxberry will be joining us as well."

For a spell, it looked as though Mr. Goodard might decline, but then he nodded, slapped his gloves against his thigh and strode further inside the room. For a man who'd appeared in complete control of himself on the few occasions she'd seen him, Katherine couldn't help but notice that he seemed mildly uncomfortable. "Please have a seat," she offered, gesturing to a chair clad in gray and lilac damask silk.

Sweeping aside his coattails, he accepted her offer, although his posture remained remarkably stiff. "May I ask for your advice, Lady Crossby?" he abruptly asked, surprising her twice in the space of five minutes.

"Certainly, Mr. Goodard." How curious! They'd only recently become acquainted with each other through Louise and Huntley, so she found it odd for him to seek her opinion on anything.

A maid entered with a tray holding a teapot, cups and a plate full of triangle-shaped sandwiches. As soon as she had once again departed, Katherine reached for the teapot and poured them each a steaming cup. "Milk and sugar?" she asked.

"Just sugar. One spoonful if you please."

She handed him his cup, and he accepted it with a polite "Thank you."

Picking up her own cup, Katherine sat back against the sofa and waited for Mr. Goodard to enlighten her. He was biding his time, it seemed, which only made her all the more curious about the subject.

"Lady Crossby," he eventually began, then paused. For several seconds he just sat there, peering at her in a most discomforting way. "Considering your friendship with Roxberry, I thought you might know . . ." He took a breath and eventually blurted, "Are you by any chance privy to his plans for the future?"

"Sir?"

"What I mean to ask is whether or not you're aware of any interest he might have for a certain lady."

"May I ask which lady you're referring to?" Katherine asked. "I would hate to draw my own conclusion in case it is wrong."

He set his cup on the table and picked up a sandwich instead. "It's Lady Julie."

Katherine stilled as she considered this. She really wasn't well enough acquainted with Mr. Goodard to be having this sort of conversation, but she also wasn't opposed to the idea of him courting Lady Julie. Lord Rockly's daughter was all wrong for Lucien, so if another gentleman could take her off his hands, that would be splendid. It would also allow Katherine a bit more time to consider a better match for her friend, since she wasn't convinced that the other ladies she'd chosen were perfect either. "Am I to understand that you are making your inquiry because you have developed a tendre for the lady yourself?"

It was a bold question, considering their brief acquaintance, but Mr. Goodard didn't scoff at it or walk away. He held his ground, and in doing so, he heightened Katherine's opinion of him. "I cannot lie to you, my lady. She has me completely smitten—however demeaning that might be for any gentleman to admit." He chuckled, perhaps to hide his embarrassment.

"And you wish to know what Roxberry's intentions toward her are?"

Mr. Goodard inclined his head. "I merely wish to know if I would be wasting my time in pursuing her."

"Surely that is for Lady Julie to decide."

He chuckled. "Quite so, though I must admit it would ease my mind greatly if I didn't have to compete with a man like Roxberry."

Katherine frowned. "I hope you're not criticizing him, for if you are—"

"Rest assured, my lady, I was doing quite the opposite. What I mean is that I do believe he's sent many a female hearts aflutter on numerous occasions, handsome, charming and . . . titled that he his."

"I'm sure you have your own merits, even if you do lack the title. Indeed, if I were to choose, I would choose character above title any day."

Mr. Goodard's expression grew somber. "You speak as though from experience," he said.

Her heart skipped a little in her chest. She forced herself to smile. "It's just my opinion. But, regarding your question, I fear it would be wildly inappropriate of me to speak of my friend's confidences to anyone. Good heavens, whatever must you think of me to imagine that I would?"

"Rest assured, my lady. I hold you in the highest regard." He sat back against his seat. "But we both saw how cozy they looked with each other at the ball, whispering together and dancing not one but two sets. If you ask me, it's quite apparent that Roxberry has set his sights on Lady Julie. So much so that I daresay you won't be violating his trust by discussing it."

"It's a matter of principle," she said, "and if Roxberry's regard for Lady Julie is indeed as apparent as you say it is, then I don't see the need for you to question me about it."

"You are right, of course. Please forgive me." He took a sip of his tea. "But I do believe I was correct in surmising that you disapprove of his choice, for indeed you did not look the least bit happy when you saw them having that little tête-à-tête at the ball."

"Good grief," Katherine gasped. "You really are every bit the scoundrel."

He inclined his head and smiled broadly. "So they say."

"I ought to ask you to leave."

"And yet you're too polite to do so." He set his cup on its matching saucer. "Not to worry, though—I'll see to my own departure, though I would like to offer you a bit of advice before I go. If you will permit?"

She wasn't sure if she ought to allow such forwardness from a renowned rake, but curiosity got the better of her and she nodded.

"Be honest with him, Lady Crossby. If you think Lady Julie is wrong for him, you should tell him so, as his friend. He values your opinion."

Katherine couldn't help but doubt Mr. Goodard's sincerity. "Why do I get the feeling that you're only trying to win Lady Julie for yourself?"

"Well, of course I am," he said, surprising her with his candor, "but that doesn't mean I cannot look out for everyone else's best interests at the same time."

Katherine felt the urge to roll her eyes, but she refrained. "The only person's interests you're looking out for, sir, are your own."

"Tell me I'm wrong," he pressed. "Tell me that you're happy on Roxberry's behalf."

"I . . ." Oh, what was the use? It was as if this scoundrel knew of the turmoil she was suffering through—the doubt and confusion.

Understanding flickered behind his eyes. "You cannot, can you, my lady? Indeed, if I am not mistaken, you think he would be better off with someone else entirely . . . someone like . . ."

No. Surely he wouldn't.

" . . . you, perhaps," he finished.

Katherine's mouth dropped. She stared back at Mr. Goodard. Eventually she shook her head. "No. No, that's not what I was thinking at all."

"Forgive me, Lady Crossby. It was impertinent of me to suggest it, but it does seem logical."

"I don't believe it's anything of the sort." She was lying to herself and to Mr. Goodard in the process. The worst of it was that the glint in his eyes made it clear that he was aware of it. Folding her hands in her lap, she straightened her back and looked straight back at him. "Very well. I must confess that I have considered it . . . fleetingly, of course . . . since the Kingsborough Ball." Why on earth was she confiding in this man she barely knew when she'd scarcely admitted it to herself? "But considering all the gossip that was circulating about us that evening, I hardly think it surprising. Do you?"

He shrugged. "Perhaps not. Then again, I wouldn't be the least bit surprised if the two of you were to marry. In fact, what astounds me is the possibility that Roxberry would have an interest in any other woman at all."

"You flatter me, sir, but I don't believe his interest lies with me."

"And if it did? Would you marry him if he offered?"

Katherine's gaze drifted toward the window. It was sunny outside, with a slight chill—perfect weather for working in the garden or going for a ride. "I don't believe I'd care to remarry," she whispered. She returned her gaze to Mr. Goodard, who was watching her a little too closely for comfort.

"Well, so much for my plan," he said. "I was beginning to think it would work out rather nicely if you could steal Roxberry away from Lady Julie so I could have her all to myself!"

Katherine wasn't sure if she ought to have been amused or outraged by such a statement, but then

Mr. Goodard laughed, and she felt herself relax. "You are a rogue, aren't you? Now that I think of it, I'm not so sure I like the idea of a match between you and Lady Julie. If memory serves, you did quite a few deplorable things in your youth."

"Hasn't every man?"

He had her there. Even Lucien had probably gotten up to a bit of mischief back in the day, though she would have been too young at the time to have been aware of it. A knock sounded, and Carter appeared in the doorway. "Lord Roxberry has arrived," he announced. "And he is accompanied by Lady Julie. Shall I show them in?"

The smile that had captured Katherine's lips at the mention of Lucien remained plastered to her face as she numbly nodded in response. Daft. That was what she was. She suddenly realized how much she'd been looking forward to seeing him again and how annoyed she now was at the prospect of having to share his attention.

"Are you unwell?" Mr. Goodard asked.

"No," she managed, even though she felt faint. "I'm quite all right, really." Feeling restless, she rose just enough to reach for the flowers on the table, intending to busy herself with rearranging them, but her agitated state caused her to forget herself and she moved too hastily, knocking her knee against the table. The vase tilted and Katherine instinctively pitched forward, determined to catch it before it fell over completely and made a mess, but another hand shot out and grabbed it.

Katherine gasped. She knew she'd lost her footing in the midst of all this and that she would soon be landing on the table, most likely at the exact moment when Lucien and Lady Julie would enter. What could possibly be more embarrassing? She had the answer to that question soon enough when her downward progress was halted by Mr. Goodard. He pulled her back so swiftly that she went tumbling right into him. His arm came around her shoulders to hold her steady, and in his hand he held the troublesome vase.

"Thank you," Katherine managed. She was just about to step back when a movement caught her attention out of the corner of her eye. Looking toward it, she felt her face grow hot at the sight she beheld— Lucien and Lady Julie staring back at her with wide-eyed astonishment.

Of all the things Lucien had expected to encounter upon his arrival at Cresthaven that day, this was most assuredly not one of them. Standing there in the doorway to Katherine's parlor, he couldn't help feeling like the biggest fool that had ever lived as his eyes settled on Katherine and Mr. Goodard, of all people. The man was a known rake, and the way in which he was holding her . . . it looked like an exceedingly passionate embrace. "Forgive us," Lucien said, recalling that he'd brought Lady Julie along in the hope of stirring some feelings of jealousy in Katherine. By God, he'd ridden all the way to Kingsborough Hall to fetch the lady, fully aware that he'd promised Katherine he'd refrain from an immediate courtship so the two of them could spend some time together. It was pathetic, really, yet here she was looking disturbingly intimate with Mr. Goodard. "It appears we're intruding on a private moment."

"Not at all," Mr. Goodard replied as he disengaged himself from Katherine and bowed toward Lady Julie.

"Lady Crossby and I were merely discussing a conversation we had the other evening. I feared I might have upset her, so I came to offer my apologies."

"I see." Lucien noticed the vase in Mr. Goodard's hand. "The flowers are lovely, by the way."

With a broad smile and gleaming eyes, Mr. Goodard turned to look at Katherine, who still appeared mildly dazed. "Yes, I thought it a pity that they should go to waste."

Lucien was finding it difficult to breathe. Hadn't Katherine just told him that she had no intention of marrying or of becoming anyone's mistress? She couldn't have changed her mind, could she? "Forgive me, Mr. Goodard," he found himself saying, "but as Lady Crossby's friend, I must insist on knowing what your intentions are." He felt Lady Julie's hand upon his arm in a gesture of comfort. What a blow this had to be to her as well.

"My intentions?" Mr. Goodard looked confused.

"They had best be honorable, or I will personally call you out."

Katherine's eyes widened. "You will do no such thing. Mr. Goodard has done nothing wrong."

"Then please explain why he was being so familiar with you just now," Lucien said. Noting the look of alarm in Katherine's eyes and the tightening of Mr. Goodard's jaw, Lucien realized his mistake. In his frustration, he'd embarrassed Katherine horribly in front of everyone.

Mr. Goodard stepped toward him, undoubtedly intent on admonishing him for his thoughtlessness.

With tremendous effort, Lucien reined in his annoyance, determined to salvage the situation before he and Mr. Goodard came to blows. "My apologies," he said, perhaps a bit too hastily. "I meant no disrespect. I am just surprised, that is all, but since Mr.

Goodard *is* here and Lady Julie was good enough to join me, there are now four to our party. What say you if we go for a ride together? I know we discussed a race, but perhaps we could visit the old ruins for a game of hide-and-seek instead?"

Katherine looked skeptical, and Lucien knew that she had not yet forgiven his public insistence that she explain the nature of her relationship with Mr. Goodard. Thankfully, Lady Julie's youthful spirit applauded the idea of a game of hide-and-seek. "Oh yes!" She clapped her hands together while her eyes implored them all to agree. "It's been so long since I've played."

"Then we mustn't disappoint you," Katherine said, eyeing Lucien with some degree of reservation. "It's lovely weather for a ride, so I suggest we leave behind the carriage."

"Would it be all right if my maid remained here in the meantime?" Lady Julie asked. "I mean, I brought Sarah along to chaperone, but if Lady Crossby is there, then I think I'd rather give my maid a little time off—she'd love to see your garden, my lady."

Katherine smiled, and Lucien caught his breath. "I think that would be acceptable, Lady Julie. Is she very fond of gardens, then?"

"Oh yes, and yours is one of the most famous ones. In fact, she could barely keep her enthusiasm at bay as we approached, isn't that so, Lord Roxberry?"

"Her interest was very much apparent," he said, his eyes fixed on the only object of his own interest—Katherine.

"**Y**ou surprise me," Lucien told Katherine as they rode along the dirt road that would take them a couple of miles away from Cresthaven and to the ruins of an old medieval castle. Lady Julie was not an expert horsewoman and had fallen behind. Lucien knew he probably ought to have remained at her side, but when Mr. Goodard had seemed more than willing to oblige, Lucien had taken the opportunity to ride ahead alongside Katherine, leaving Lady Julie to enjoy the company of the man she loved. Well, one of them deserved to be happy on this wretched day.

"How so?" Katherine asked.

"I think you know perfectly well," he muttered. Finding her like that with Mr. Goodard had made him glum and raw with jealousy. He hated the feeling.

"I can only assume that you are referring to the unfortunate situation you found me in with Mr. Goodard upon your arrival."

"Indeed I am." He angled his head so he could look at her and was immediately taken aback by the sight, for she held her chin high, jaw firmly clenched while her eyes drove into the horizon. Swallowing any reservations he had about continuing with this issue, he said, "I only want what's best for you, so unless Mr. Goodard is proposing marriage, I beg you to reconsider your actions."

She didn't respond right away, but he could see that her throat was working, as if she was struggling with finding the right words. "I told you just the other night that I have no intention of remarrying. Do you really suppose that I would change my mind so quickly?"

"Then it is as I feared," Lucien muttered, his heart slamming against his chest as he tried to digest what she had told him. "He has propositioned you and you have . . . please don't tell me that you have accepted."

"Do you know," she said, her voice disturbingly

quiet, "that of all people, I never thought that you would have questioned my judgment."

"Then give me a reason not to," he blurted.

"I shouldn't have to." She looked at him then, her hair falling in soft tresses around her face. "Considering all that you know of me, you should be able to trust that I will do the right thing. Instead, you have presumed the very worst, not only of me but of Mr. Goodard as well."

"How so?"

"It's silly, really, but just as you were arriving, I lost my balance while trying to straighten the tulips. Mr. Goodard caught not only the vase but me as well, which I daresay was fortuitous, or you might have found me lying on the floor instead."

It sounded like a perfectly reasonable explanation, but Lucien didn't entirely believe it. In his opinion, it seemed far more likely that Mr. Goodard had tried to use the vase to his advantage—as an excuse to play the knight to her damsel in distress. Katherine, on the other hand, had been gazing up at him all dreamy-eyed. Lucien's stomach twisted. All he could think of was pulling her off her horse and shaking her until her teeth clanged together. She was completely wrong for Mr. Goodard. She should be with *him*, Lucien Marvaine, Earl of Roxberry—the man who'd loved her since she'd slipped and fallen into the lake at the tender age of sixteen.

Christ, what a mess!

Untangling it would be harder than combing out the knots in Katherine's hair when she was eight years old and had gotten jam in it. How she'd managed it, Lucien wasn't aware, but she'd been too afraid to go to her maid for help, since she would only have informed Katherine's mother. Instead, the little sprite had thrust a comb into Lucien's hand and begged him to do the job for her. Which of course he had, although the chore had taken the better part of an hour.

Fleetingly, Lucien wondered if Mr. Goodard would have been so obliging. He forced the thought away. If Katherine planned to dismiss her embrace with Mr. Goodard as something meaningless, then he had no choice but to give her the benefit of the doubt. Not unless he wanted to lose her friendship forever, which was precisely what he feared might happen if he failed to assure her of his faith in her.

"**T**his is splendid," Lady Julie announced as she and Mr. Goodard rode into what had once been the bailey of a solid stone fortress. The walls had long since begun to crumble, leaving a jagged silhouette against the background of the sky.

From far above, the twitter of birds reached their ears. Looking up, Katherine spotted a nest. It was sitting on a ledge that had probably once been part of a window. It was years since she'd last been out here, and she couldn't help but note the extra bits of moss and weed that squeezed between the cracks in the stone.

Dismounting, Katherine led her horse over to a tree that had sprung through the ground in a corner, then she secured the reins to a low branch. "Shall I go first?" she asked, looking over her shoulder at the others. "I don't mind doing the searching." It would give her an opportunity to reacquaint herself with the ruin at a more leisurely pace than if she had to run and hide.

"I think we ought to draw straws," Mr. Goodard said as he dismounted. "What do you think, Roxberry?"

"It sounds fair enough to me," Lucien said. Already on the ground, he went to help Lady Julie down, his hands lingering about her waist just a second longer than required.

Katherine watched the display with an aching heart. She looked at Mr. Goodard, who looked just as depressed as she felt. It was no good. Lucien was clearly smitten and Lady Julie equally so, evident in the way her gaze never veered from Lucien's.

Picking up a pair of twigs, Katherine snapped them in half so three of the pieces were of equal length while one was half an inch longer. Her hands were trembling and her heart was beating somewhere closer to her belly than to her chest. Damn her for listening to all the stupid gossip. There was no merit to it, yet it had made her think of Lucien in a new light. Tragically, he clearly didn't feel the same way about her, or he wouldn't have been treating Lady Julie as if he'd already begun courting her.

She felt a hand upon her arm and looked up to find Mr. Goodard staring down at her. "I know it isn't easy to watch, but you must be strong, my lady."

"Perhaps it's for the best," she whispered. "I'm not sure I can give him what he wants anyway."

"Discussing strategy?" Lucien asked as he approached with Lady Julie on his arm. His eyes met Katherine's and she instinctively took a step back. There was something fierce in his gaze that quickened her pulse. She didn't understand it, but it made her wary.

"Just preparing the straws, or, in this case, twigs," she said, her voice a little weaker than she would have liked. Holding them in her fisted hand, she extended them so they could each pick a twig.

"Oh!" Lady Julie squealed with excitement. "Looks like I'll be hiding."

"Me too," Mr. Goodard said.

"And I'll be seeking for the lot of you," Lucien said as he drew the longest one. "I'll stay here and count to fifty."

Determined not to lose a second of precious time, Katherine hurried through an archway toward the gaping doorway of the keep. All was still within, the air cooler between the confines of the large walls than it had been outside in the sun. Looking up, Katherine saw nothing but clear sky dotted by the occasional cloud. At the far end stood the remains of a staircase that would lead her up inside one of the towers. When Katherine reached it, she started upward, her feet a little unsteady on the steps, which sloped and sagged with age.

"Mind if I join you?"

Spinning around with such speed that she nearly lost her balance, Katherine scowled at Mr. Goodard. "What are you doing here?" she whispered.

He shrugged. "You seemed to know where you were going, so I decided that you probably know of a good spot in which to hide."

"But you can't possibly hide *with* me. You must find a place of your own," she insisted as uneasiness claimed her. If Lucien was prepared to turn Mr. Goodard's steadying hand in the parlor into an amorous embrace, there was no telling what he would think if he found her hiding with Mr. Goodard. Having always valued Lucien's high regard for her, Katherine hated the thought of disappointing him.

Mr. Goodard frowned. "I don't think I've enough time for that now, and besides, the rules say nothing about not being allowed to hide in the same location as someone else."

"We ought not be alone together," she said. "It isn't appropriate."

"It's just a game, Lady Crossby, and since you already know that my intentions lie elsewhere, I daresay you've little to worry about. Besides, you're a widow now and entitled to a little fun. No?"

Katherine hesitated. She looked toward the doorway of the keep through which Lucien would probably be arriving any minute, and then at Mr. Goodard, who was looking mildly impatient. Taking a deep breath, Katherine made her decision and continued up a few more steps until she knew she was hidden from view. She then seated herself on the chilly stone. Mr. Goodard immediately plopped down next to her. "You ought to have followed Lady Julie instead," Katherine muttered.

"I doubt she would be swayed by amorous advances in a ruin," he said. "She is a debutante after all, and—"

"Oh no! I should have stayed with her," Katherine said, feeling suddenly remarkably guilty about her own determination to get away. She hadn't spared Lady Julie a thought.

"So much more reason for you to be thankful that I am here with you and not with her."

"But what about Roxberry? If he is hoping to—"

"Calm yourself, my lady. Roxberry is a gentleman. He would never do anything untoward."

Katherine knew he was right, yet she couldn't stop her treacherous mind from imagining Lucien and Lady Julie in a lover's embrace while she sat on these cold steps with Mr. Goodard at her side. It was not the least bit heartwarming.

As soon as Lucien finished counting to fifty, he set out with the express purpose of finding Katherine as quickly as possible. Seeing her in private discussion with Mr. Goodard had swiftly stirred his ire once more, and he was convinced more than ever that Mr. Goodard was determined to make Katherine his, even if she was unsuspecting of his intentions. Lucien's pace quickened. He couldn't lose her to that man.

Fists clenched, Lucien strode through the archway, where he knew one, possibly two, people had gone— he'd heard their fading footsteps. It didn't surprise him. The keep had always fascinated Katherine, so he'd suspected from the very beginning that she would choose to hide somewhere in there.

Entering it, he paused to listen, the flutter of wings catching his ears as a bird darted back and forth. Continuing his progress, he strode to one of the towers and looked up, but found nothing. Perhaps he should climb the stairs? He decided against wasting time on that, for he knew that Katherine would not have forgotten the warning he'd issued when he'd first taken her and Patricia here all those years ago. The building was in decay and had to be treated with respect unless one planned on getting hurt.

Again he paused to listen, and he became aware of the quiet falling of pebbles, as if part of the structure had just been disturbed. It had come from the opposite tower, and Lucien now hastened toward it, his strides long and determined. As he came closer, however, he heard voices and immediately softened his footfalls.

"Who knew that we would one day be more than mere acquaintances?"

Lucien froze as he recognized Mr. Goodard's voice.

"Not I, though I daresay Roxberry must have thought we'd get along splendidly."

"And why is that?"

There was a slight pause before Katherine said, "The other night at the ball, he suggested I set my cap for you." Lucien gritted his teeth as he was once again reminded of his own idiocy. What the hell had he been thinking?

"Did he really?" Mr. Goodard asked. "But surely he must know that you don't intend to remarry."

Lucien breathed a sigh of relief. If Mr. Goodard was aware of this, then surely he'd stop pursuing her. He reminded himself of the man's reputation and muttered an oath.

"Yes, of course he does, but he seems quite determined to see me properly settled again regardless, perhaps because he's contemplating the matter himself." She sighed, and Lucien took a quiet step closer. "He's only just returned, yet I feel as though I'm already losing him again. Once he marries, I'll see less of him, of this I'm certain."

A smile tugged at Lucien's lips. Katherine cared about him and she wasn't planning to marry Mr. Goodard. Perhaps there was hope yet.

"Not to worry," Mr. Goodard said. "You have me now, and I have every intention of seeing to your happiness."

Whatever elation Lucien had just felt plummeted at those words. So there *was* something between them! They might not be contemplating marriage, but they sure as hell weren't planning an innocent evening at the theater either—not when they were hurrying off to hide together like this. Hot anger rushed through his veins. What a fool Katherine must think him that she would imagine he'd believe that ridiculous story of how she'd ended up in Mr. Goodard's arms. And to think that he'd actually told her Mr. Goodard was amicable! Why, the man was no better than Crossby!

Placing one booted foot on the bottom step, Lucien dipped his head through the opening of the stairwell and looked up. There, seated right next to each other on the narrow step, were Katherine and Mr. Goodard. Lucien's hands clenched at his sides. "It appears you've been found," he grumbled. Stepping back, he turned on his heel and walked away.

Disappointment flared through him, both at himself and at Katherine. She'd denied any wish of becoming a mistress when he'd discussed that possibility with her, yet she seemed quite prepared to do so now. Why? Clearly his little tableau with Lady Julie had been a wasted effort. Katherine still viewed him as a brother figure—either that, or she simply didn't find him the least bit attractive, which was not a very flattering notion in the least.

A pitter-patter of footsteps sounded behind him, then he felt her hand tugging at his arm. "Are you all right?" she asked. "You seem to be in a rotten mood all of a sudden."

Pulling his arm free of Katherine's fingers, Lucien continued on his way. She fell into step beside him. "I don't understand you," he said. "When you last spoke of your future, you told me clearly that you have no intention to marry again or that you would ever wish to become a man's mistress. I cannot believe you would change your mind so quickly on a matter of such great importance."

"Lucien, you're completely mistaken in the assumption that you're making." Her voice was thin but sharp.

Halting, he turned to look at her, his longing for

her an acute pain that hugged his soul. Mr. Goodard
stood a few paces further away, and as Lucien held
his gaze, a potent surge of envy fanned through him.
It was raw and it was basic. Lucien closed his eyes,
willing it away for fear that he might intentionally
harm a man who wasn't standing across from him on
a battlefield. Except this was a battlefield of course,
and there was a very real war being waged over
Katherine. "So you say, yet I continue to find the two
of you together like this. If you were a debutante, I
would have to insist the two of you marry. But you
don't want that, do you?" Expelling a deep breath, he
said, "You'll invite scandal if you associate with him
in any other capacity than as his wife."

A cry for help drifted toward them, preventing
Katherine from responding. Lucien raced outside,
followed swiftly by Mr. Goodard. They rounded
the corner together and peered over a low wall, immediately spotting Lady Julie, who was lying on
the ground a little way off, her legs twisted beneath
her. "Please see to Lady Crossby's comfort," Mr.
Goodard said, his voice tight as he clambered over
the wall. "I'll tend to Lady Julie."

Lucien hesitated. How remarkably odd of Mr.
Goodard to be more concerned with Lady Julie all of
a sudden than with Katherine. Knowing that he was
supposed to be courting Lady Julie, if only in pretense, Lucien started to protest, then stopped himself. This was what Lady Julie would want—for Mr.
Goodard to run to her rescue. And besides, Lucien
had no issue at all with seeing to Katherine in the
meantime, in spite of their argument.

Turning around, he started back toward the keep
and found her hurrying toward him. "Is Lady Julie
all right?" she asked, her eyes wide with alarm.

"I believe she'll be fine."

Katherine made as if to move past him, but he stayed her with his hand. "I ought to go to her," she said. "Lady Julie is an innocent, and as you say, Mr. Goodard is a renowned rake. Her parents would be very displeased with me if I failed in my duty as chaperone."

He didn't unhand her, but he moved a little closer until they were standing side by side, with Katherine facing one way and him the other. His hand held her arm, and from beneath the snug wool of her jacket, he could feel her tremble—a restless urge to get away from him, perhaps? Or something else? "And here I was, hoping for a moment to be alone with you," he murmured in reply.

"And why is that?" Her voice hitched ever so slightly, her breath escaping her lungs in a shudder.

He tightened his hold on her, met her gaze and turned around so he could lead her back toward the others. She was right—they could not leave Lady Julie completely alone with Mr. Goodard. "Because I cannot help but be concerned for you."

"You needn't be," she said, her hair catching in the breeze while her eyes scanned the landscape— grassy hills blanketed by patches of heather beyond the castle walls.

"How can you say that when you are entertaining the notion of becoming Mr. Goodard's mistress?"

"I don't believe I ever told you that I was. On the contrary, I think I was very clear with you when I said I have no intention of doing anything of the sort," she said as they rounded the corner, bringing Lady Julie back into view. She was standing up now, supported by Mr. Goodard. Katherine gave Lucien a firm look. "*You* are the one who insists on dismissing what I am telling you in favor of drawing your own conclusions."

"Can you blame me? I just found you alone with the man for the second time today, so either fate is having a very good laugh at your expense, or you're not being completely honest with me."

Katherine sighed. She sounded weary, and the pain in her eyes made Lucien wonder if he was indeed wrong to doubt her. "Time will tell, I suppose." She shook her head. "But what difference does any of it make, when you have planned to marry Lady Julie?"

The words were so quiet that he scarcely heard them—as if she'd been talking to herself and hadn't intended for him to hear. But he had, and her words cut straight through him. "I haven't *planned* to do anything of the sort," he told her roughly.

"Is Lady Julie aware of that?" Katherine asked, her voice tight as she stared back at him with defiance. "I can't imagine what life has been like for you these past few years, but I never considered you the sort of man who'd toy with a lady's emotions." Yanking her arm away, she went to join Lady Julie and Mr. Goodard, leaving Lucien with much to consider. Had she been speaking of Lady Julie or of herself just now? he wondered. Following her at a respectable distance, he pondered their heated exchange until the edge of his mouth slowly curved upward. He was beginning to suspect it might be the latter.

The ride back to Cresthaven was a tedious one, not so much because of the pace they were keeping due to Lady Julie's sprained ankle, but because Katherine suddenly wanted to be completely alone. She'd never been the sort of woman who feigned disinterest in order to win a gentleman's attention or pretended her preferences lay elsewhere so he would redouble his efforts at winning her. Those were the sorts of games played by sophisticated Society misses, which she'd never considered herself to be.

No, she'd grown up in the country, the daughter of a baronet, and while she'd been to London on more than one occasion, she'd always been relieved to find herself returned to the fields and meadows that surrounded her home. She liked simplicity. Getting embroiled in lies and deception did not sit well with her, especially when it involved Lucien, with whom she'd always been blatantly honest.

At present, however, honesty was proving extremely difficult. How was she to tell him of all the conflicting emotions tumbling through her, when she barely understood them herself? She was confused, and as a result, she was desperately unhappy, so it was a relief when they finally arrived back at Cresthaven and Lady Julie announced her desire for immediate departure. "I'm sorry, Lady Crossby, I've had a lovely time visiting you this afternoon, but I'd like to get back to Kingsborough Hall so I can have a rest."

"Would you like me to escort you?" Lucien asked.

"There's no need for you to trouble yourself, Roxberry," Mr. Goodard said, "considering it's on the way to my own home. I'll be happy to escort Lady Julie."

Lucien hesitated, as if he wasn't quite sure how to respond. Eventually he nodded, stepped toward Lady Julie and bowed over her hand. "I'll call on you soon, my lady," he told her as he helped her up into her carriage.

She smiled down at him and said, "I'll look forward to it with great anticipation."

And then the carriage rolled away with Mr. Goodard riding alongside it. Katherine watched it move down the graveled driveway until it turned a corner and disappeared from sight. "I want to apologize to you for earlier," she said without looking at Lucien, who stood silently at her side. "I never meant to imply that your feelings toward Lady Julie are disingenuous. It's none of my affair whom you choose to marry, and truthfully, she is very likeable, if perhaps a bit young. I'm sure she and I will get along very well if you do decide to make her your wife."

"It is I who should apologize to you, Kate. It wasn't my intention to return here only to chastise you—especially not after everything you've been through."

She winced. "I daresay it can't compare with everything *you've* been through, Lucien." She turned toward him then. "I've never lied to you, you know, and everything I told you today is true. I've no intention of forming an attachment of any sort with Mr. Goodard. That you would even suspect such a thing . . ." She fought for composure.

"Once again, I apologize, but it was difficult for me to think anything else, given the man's reputation and your recent state of widowhood." He moved as if to take her hand in his, but instead he just stuck his own hand in his pocket.

"I know," she said, "but whatever choice I make, I want it to be *my* choice. You just have to trust in my ability to do what is right for myself and for Sophia." She smiled at how sheepish he suddenly looked. "That aside, Mr. Goodard did flatter me with his attention today, but contrary to what you might think, he remained quite courteous and made no attempt to press his advances." She paused to consider that for a second. Curious, that; not once had he given the impression of being a libertine. "Is it so terribly wrong of me to appreciate the regard of a handsome gentleman?" she asked, continuing her line of thought. "I am a woman, after all, and while I might choose celibacy, I still want to know that I can catch a man's interest, even at the ripe age of four and twenty."

Lucien laughed. "How heartless of you to speak of age, Kate, when I am seven years your senior."

"But you're a man. It's entirely different."

He sobered. "Well, if you ask me, you'll still be beautiful fifty years from now."

She couldn't help but smile. "What about sixty years from now?"

He appeared to ponder that quite seriously and eventually said, "Hmm . . . I'm not convinced your looks will last for quite that long."

She slapped him playfully on the shoulder. "You're a beast!"

"I am only trying to be honest," he said, sounding affronted. "I thought you'd appreciate that."

"Well then, Lucien, since you're being so honest, why don't you tell me what you're really hoping to accomplish by chasing after Lady Julie, since you say you're not intending to marry her."

Taking Katherine by the arm, he led her back inside the house and toward the parlor. "I believe I said I hadn't made a decision yet either way."

"But you cannot continue to act as if you're courting her unless marriage is your goal. It isn't honest, and frankly, I fear for her feelings," Katherine insisted. She couldn't believe that Lucien would be so heartless as to give a lady false expectations.

"I wouldn't worry too much about that, my dear." They arrived in the parlor and he guided her toward the sofa, where she took a seat while he remained standing. "For you see, it has come to my attention that Lady Julie might be happier with someone else."

"Oh, Lucien," Katherine gasped, inadvertently reaching for his hand and squeezing it with her own. "I'm so sorry. She seemed so taken with you."

He grimaced, then raised her hand to his lips and kissed her knuckles. She shuddered. "Perhaps we should use that as a reminder that things aren't always as they appear," he said as his breath brushed over her, filling her with warmth. He straightened. "I will bid you a good day now, Kate, for I must return home. Will you allow me to visit you again tomorrow?"

"I will look forward to it," she said as he straightened himself and took his leave.

Chapter 9

Awakened that night by a muffled sound coming from Sophia's room, Katherine threw back her covers and started to rise, intent on checking on her daughter. Most likely, her feet had gotten tangled in her blanket again, as was often the case these days, for she was turning into quite the restless sleeper. But an out-of-place rustling gave Katherine pause, and her increased heart rate warned her to beware. Reaching for the drawer of her nightstand, she swiftly snatched up the pistol her father had given her after Charles's death when she'd mentioned how secluded she'd felt in the massive house. "Who would stop a potential intruder?" she'd asked.

"One of your footmen, most likely," her father had said.

The words hadn't appeased her. Things had changed now that she had a child to protect.

"Take this, then," her father had said as he'd handed her the pistol. "It will ease your concerns, having this by your bedside."

Holding the weapon steady, Katherine now approached the room where her daughter slept. Fearful of what she might find, she prayed that it was merely her imagination playing havoc with her senses.

It was not. As she held her breath and peered through the darkness, she saw a slim figure dressed in breeches and a tight-fitting jacket silhouetted against the window, his posture slightly hunched as he stood over Sophia's crib. A chill flew down Katherine's spine, but she steeled herself, wary of acting rashly and putting Sophia at risk. For now, at least, it appeared as if the stranger was merely watching her sleep, though Katherine dared not contemplate his reason for breaking into Sophia's room in the middle of the night. Nevertheless, Katherine decided to wait and gauge his intent, hoping that he would eventually distance himself enough from the crib to provide a clear shot, should that be necessary.

It felt as if an eternity passed, though it was probably no more than a minute before the stranger turned and started in Katherine's direction. Backing up, Katherine returned with silent footfalls to her room, raised her pistol and aimed it at the doorway. She waited until the man came into view, then said, "I suggest you make your intentions known before I put a hole in you."

There was a beat of silence as the stranger froze, no doubt contemplating his next move. Katherine stared back at him, her concentration pinned on his hands. One of them was slightly concealed from her line of vision, so it was impossible for her to tell if he carried a weapon.

"I don't suppose we can just pretend this never happened?" the stranger asked.

Katherine took a sharp breath. She'd been so certain that it was a young man, from what little she'd been able to discern of the clothing, but the voice belonged to a woman—a noblewoman, judging from her aristocratic tone. Clenching her jaw, Katherine tightened her hold on the pistol and shook her head. "No," she said.

The woman tilted her head. "Well, in that case, I suppose I shall have to take what I came for."

Katherine had no chance to ask what that might be as the woman dropped to the floor, rolled over and vanished to the opposite side of the bed. The next sound Katherine heard was the soft click of a pistol being cocked. They were equally armed, but the other woman had one advantage—she knew exactly where Katherine was standing.

Lowering herself quietly to the floor, Katherine edged her way around to the foot of the bed, then paused to listen. All was silent. With her heart pounding in her chest, Katherine looked across at her dressing table, her eyes concentrating on the mirror that was sitting on top of it. It was difficult to see anything of significance, given how dark the room was, but she kept her eyes on it anyway as she continued to listen for the slightest sound, attempting all the while to keep her breathing low and even. A moment passed, then a sudden flicker of movement caught her eye. Katherine focused on the spot on the mirror where she'd seen it and immediately noticed it again, ever so slight but enough to reveal the woman's location.

Sitting quietly, with her pulse rapidly thumping in her throat, Katherine was still trying to figure out how to subdue the intruder and divest her of her weapon when she heard the woman move. Looking at the mirror, Katherine could no longer see her, and this unsettled her. She didn't enjoy the idea of being caught by surprise.

Carefully raising her head, Katherine peered over the edge of the bed and squinted through the darkness. It only took her a second to spot the dark outline of the woman who was now standing in the far corner of the room. Raising her pistol as silently as she could manage so she could support it against the bed, Katherine prepared to fire a wounding shot.

To her surprise, the woman was swiftly across the floor, making Katherine's aim exceedingly difficult. But then the woman paused, as if something had caught her attention. It took Katherine no more than a second to realize that she had seen her reflection in the same mirror.

Acting on instinct, Katherine flung herself against the floor just as the woman pulled the trigger and fired at her, stirring the air with a thunderous roar. A wail arose from the adjoining room as Sophia awoke, but Katherine paid her daughter no mind this time. Instead, she leapt to her feet, raised her own pistol with lightning speed, aimed and fired, evoking an anguished yell from the woman, who immediately dropped to the floor.

Not sparing her another thought, Katherine raced from the room, locking the door firmly behind her. Grabbing Sophia from her crib, Katherine hugged her tightly against her chest. She was just about to ring for Carter when the door to Sophia's chamber burst open and the man in question materialized before her with Mrs. Burke, the housekeeper, and a footman named Thomas in tow. "Forgive the intrusion, my lady," he said, looking rather sleepy-eyed, "but I could have sworn I heard a shot."

"So you did," Katherine said, her voice sounding awfully shaky. Thankfully, Sophia's cries had lessened to a mere whimper as she snuggled her head against her mother's neck. It wouldn't take long before she was sleeping peacefully again. "A woman broke in. She fired at me, but her aim was off, so she missed, upon which I shot her. She's in there." Katherine nodded toward her bedroom. "I locked the door so she wouldn't be able to escape, though I'm not even sure that she's still alive."

"Dear me," Mrs. Burke said, looking ashen. "Thankfully you and Lady Sophia are unharmed, but what on earth are we to do about the woman you shot?"

"We're going to have to open the door and take a look at her," Carter said. "Thomas and I will see to it." He handed the oil lamp he'd brought with him to Mrs. Burke, who turned up the light before setting the lamp on a small table.

Staying back, her whole body trembling, Katherine watched as Carter and Thomas unlocked her bedroom door and peered inside the room. "We'll need another lamp, Mrs. Burke, but it appears as if the intruder is lying motionless on the floor."

Katherine shivered. Surely she hadn't killed the woman? She waited while Mrs. Burke lit another lamp and handed it to Carter, then Katherine stepped hesitantly forward in order to get a better look. "Good heavens!"

Raising his head, Carter looked up at Katherine from beneath a pair of bushy eyebrows. "Do you know her, by any chance?"

"I . . . yes, I believe so, though not very well. Is she dead?" Her voice sounded faint to her own ears.

"No, she's alive and will be on her feet in no time," Carter said. He turned the woman's head to the side and peered down at the back of it. "Your shot only clipped the side of her chest, my lady. Looks like she knocked herself unconscious when she fell to the floor—most likely on the nightstand, I'd imagine. In any case, she has a nasty gash right here on her head, so she'll probably wake up to a horrible headache."

"What should we do with her?" Thomas asked, looking at Katherine.

Katherine looked at each of her servants in turn and realized that they were all waiting for her to advise them on how to proceed. Her heart was still beating ridiculously fast, and she was still clutching Sophia in her arms, most likely taking as much comfort in the embrace as her daughter was. "Well, I . . . I suppose we ought to alert the authorities." Thomas yawned, as did Carter. "However, since it is the middle of the night and she hasn't been mortally wounded, perhaps we ought to wait with that until morning. What do you think, Carter? Does that sound reasonable?"

"A splendid idea, my lady," Carter said.

"Well, in that case I think we should probably put her in a locked room for now so she can't get into any more trouble."

"And which room would you suggest?" Carter asked.

Katherine looked at him. "I don't know . . . somewhere she cannot escape from, I suppose, and without any items that she might be able to use to her advantage."

"We could always tie her up," Thomas said.

"Good heavens," Mrs. Burke said. "We're not that barbaric, surely."

"Indeed we're not," Katherine said, "yet we mustn't forget that she came armed into our home in the dead of night and didn't hesitate to fire her pistol at me. We would be fools to trust her, so as much as I dislike the thought of restraining anyone, I believe that Thomas has the right of it. We will bind her wrists and ankles and place her in the cellar . . . perhaps in the butler's pantry, if you will allow it, Carter?"

Carter nodded. "I was thinking of it myself, my lady. The room can be secured, and with the china locked away in the plate closet, there isn't much of anything for her to use as a possible weapon—especially not if she's been tied up."

"It's settled, then," Katherine said. Going back into her daughter's room, she walked across to the crib and carefully returned Sophia to the comfort of her mattress. "I trust there must be some rope in the stables that you can use?"

"I'll fetch some right away," Thomas said, heading for the door.

"In the meantime," Carter said, rising from his position next to the unconscious woman and walking across to where one of the pistols was lying, "I suggest we reload this thing in case we need it."

"Must we really?" Mrs. Burke asked, looking not the least bit comforted about the prospect of being in the vicinity of a loaded pistol.

"As her ladyship has pointed out to us, this woman, whoever she may be, poses a threat. I intend to get some answers out of her, and I do believe she'll be more cooperative if I happen to be pointing this at her." Carter swiped the pistol off the floor and glanced at it briefly before looking at Katherine. "I'll need powder and shot, if you please."

Half an hour later, the intruder had been tied and gagged and carried down to the butler's pantry, where Carter and Thomas had placed her on a small cot that they'd brought in from the storage room. "Thomas has agreed to guard her for the next two hours, at which point I will relieve him until you rise, my lady," Carter reported to Katherine before adding, "may I suggest a glass of brandy to calm your nerves and help you rest?"

Katherine nodded. "Yes, thank you, Carter. I believe that would be most helpful."

"Will that be all, my lady?" Mrs. Burke asked once Carter had provided Katherine with the promised drink.

"Yes, thank you for being so helpful. I'll see you both in the morning."

"Well, just ring if you need anything, my lady," Mrs. Burke added as she and Carter exited the room, leaving Katherine alone with Sophia. Katherine doubted she'd get any more rest that night, for she was still quite shaken by the events that had taken place. Yet the brandy must have done the trick, for it wasn't long after she'd climbed back into bed that she drifted off to sleep.

"Lord Roxberry to see you, my lady," Carter announced the following morning just as Katherine was finishing her breakfast. She'd been planning to go and check on her prisoner, intent on hearing her story before they called the constable, but that would clearly have to wait.

"You may show him into the parlor," she replied. "I'll be with him shortly."

Katherine stifled a groan as she took a sip of her tea. When Lucien had suggested he call on her again today, she'd looked forward to it, but so much had happened since then that she'd actually managed to forget he was coming. Her body heated and tingled.

She'd been distraught after their recent outings, unable to understand why her stomach fluttered or her heart pounded in response to his slightest touch. Her troubled thoughts on the matter had not lessened as she'd lain in bed the previous evenings, wondering what it might be like if he felt the same way . . . what his lips might feel like pressed against her own.

She chastised herself for contemplating such a possibility even as her body began to ache with need. Dear God, she hadn't felt such longing in years, and to feel it now for Lucien was making her most uncomfortable, particularly since, too fearful of what she risked losing, she would never be able to act on it. Besides, he'd probably never see her as anything more than the girl he'd given piggyback rides to when she'd been little. She clenched her jaw. How on earth had this happened? Perhaps his grandmother was right and she *should* take a lover.

No, she hadn't the courage to undress in front of any man. Not anymore.

Taking one last sip of her tea, she considered her current dilemma—getting rid of Lucien so she could deal with the fact that she was holding a lady hostage in her cellar. Deciding that there was nothing for it but to get on with the matter at hand, she got up from the table and headed for the parlor.

"Good morning, Kate," Lucien said the moment she entered. "Ready for a dash across the English countryside? The weather's perfect for that race we've been discussing, and since neither Mr. Goodard nor Lady Julie appear to be joining us, I thought you might be up to it."

"About that . . . I fear something unexpected has happened."

"Oh? Nothing serious I hope." With a frown, he

stepped toward her and peered at her face. "Now that I think of it, you do look rather pale. Are you ill?"

"No, I'm actually perfectly fine," she said, willing him to drop the subject and be on his way, but that was of course too much to ask of Lucien.

"And I'm the king of Russia," he said.

"Russia doesn't have a king," Katherine told him carefully. "They have an emperor."

"Precisely! Now, are you going to tell me what's really going on, or am I going to have to lure it out of you? I have special techniques specifically designed for such a thing, and I'm really quite eager to employ them."

Katherine sighed, and Lucien's frown deepened when his joke failed to elicit the slightest bit of laughter from her. "Good God," he said. "Something's really troubling you. Just tell me what it is and I'll do whatever I can to help." When she hesitated, he placed his hand on her arm and looked into her eyes. "I mean it, Kate."

She hadn't planned to share last night's incident with him—or with anyone else, for that matter—until she knew more about the break-in and the reason behind it. From the looks of it, one of the windows had been unlatched. But Katherine had to admit that there was something very comforting about having Lucien there with her, so she found herself nodding and saying, "Very well. If you were serious about those techniques of yours, then by all means, follow me."

Whatever Lucien thought Katherine might show him, he was not prepared to find a woman tied and gagged in her cellar—least of all the Countess of Trapleigh.

Holy bloody hell!

He looked at Katherine, who was standing very still at his side. "I'm guessing there's a good explanation for this?" he said.

She nodded, then related the details of what had happened, while Lucien did his best to maintain a calm demeanor. "My butler has made the occasional effort to get her to talk, but his attempts have been unsuccessful so far. Each time he removed the gag, she started screaming. Eventually he thought it best to keep it in place so she wouldn't distress the other servants."

Lucien turned his attention to Lady Trapleigh. The shapely figure he recalled from when he'd last seen her had been concealed beneath layers of men's clothing. What surprised him, was how young she still looked. What a pity she hadn't been sensible enough to avoid attaching herself to scandal. She might have remarried then, but now . . . well, there wasn't a gentleman in all of England who'd marry a woman who had done what she just had.

A thought struck Lucien, and he stepped toward Lady Trapleigh. "Do you mind if I remove her gag?" he asked Katherine, though he did not look in her direction, his entire focus riveted upon the woman who'd attempted to kill the love of his life.

"Of course not," Katherine said. She shifted her feet. "I know this isn't quite de rigueur, but given her position, I thought she deserved the opportunity to offer an explanation before I called the constable."

Flexing his fingers, Lucien pulled up a chair, then tugged away the length of fabric that had been bound around Lady Trapleigh's head. He took his seat in front of her.

"Lord Roxberry," Lady Trapleigh purred. "What a pleasant surprise."

Lucien didn't think there was anything pleasant about it in the least—especially not when Katherine said, "You are acquainted with each other, then?"

"Intimately," Lady Trapleigh said, batting her eyelashes as she smiled at Katherine.

Lucien winced. As much as he longed to deny that Lady Trapleigh had ever tended to his needs, he could not. The fact was that he was no better than any of the other countless lovers she'd had—a man so desperate with desire that he'd imagined it might be quenched if he'd only lose himself in any woman other than the one he really longed for. He'd been wrong, and now Katherine was here to bear witness to his weakness.

Casting aside his embarrassment, he chose not to look at the woman he loved, narrowing his gaze on Lady Trapleigh instead. "What in God's name are you playing at?" he growled.

"You think that you will be able to convince me to say more than Lady Crossby's butler was capable of?" Lady Trapleigh asked, the edge of her lips curling with defiance. She snorted and tossed her head to one side. "As if you have anything of greater value than what I've already been offered."

Lucien stared back at her. "As far as I know, you've never committed a crime before." He narrowed his eyes. "Someone gave you an incentive. But to do what, exactly?"

Lady Trapleigh gave a little shrug—a gesture of such indifference that Lucien had to stop himself from placing his hands about her neck.

"I had a pistol, my lord. Surely you can draw your own conclusion."

From behind him, Lucien heard Katherine gasp.

He'd known she'd probably suspected the same, but suspicion was one thing—*knowing* was something else entirely. "You have very little with which to commend yourself, my lady, yet in spite of it all, I've never thought you cold enough to commit murder."

"Hmpf!"

"Was it also you at the ball? The shot that struck Lady Rebecca?"

Finally, a hint of emotion—regret—appeared in Lady Trapleigh's eyes. "That was a mistake," she whispered. "One I meant to rectify last night."

So, the widow wasn't completely devoid of a conscience. She was sorry to have struck down Lady Rebecca. "Tell me," Lucien said. "Who asked you to do this?"

"I cannot tell you that."

"Why not?" he asked. "You are not some simpering debutante, Lady Trapleigh, but a woman of experience—a strong woman. What could anyone possibly do to make you kill an innocent woman?"

There was a beat, during which the tension in the room grew palpable. Lady Trapleigh stared back at him with burning intensity. "My son," she finally confessed. "He'll have him killed if I don't meet his demands."

Lucien blinked. Of all the damnable things he'd thought Lady Trapleigh might say, this was the most unexpected. It wasn't possible though. Everyone knew that the widow had no children. "You're lying," he said.

She shook her head. "No, I'm not."

The words were the first she'd spoken that actually rang true. "If you need proof," Lady Trapleigh continued, "you need only look at the miniature inside my jacket pocket. I never go anywhere without it."

Reaching forward, Lucien dipped his hand into her pocket until he felt something soft against his fingers. Scooping it out, he discovered a small parcel of linen, held together by a silk ribbon. Lucien placed it in the palm of his hand and unwrapped it, revealing an oval piece of enamel-sealed ivory with Lady Trapleigh's likeness painted upon it. In her arms, she held an infant. Lucien stared at it for a moment, then expelled a deep breath. "You need to tell me what you know," he said. "And in return, I promise that I will do everything in my power to return your son to you."

"Don't you understand?" Her composure finally snapped, and her eyes welled with tears. "I was given one week in which to see it through, and that was three days ago. If news of Lady Crossby's death doesn't reach London by Thursday, Tobias will die."

"Well, he's as good as dead unless you start talking," Lucien clipped, "because I'll never let you harm as much as a hair on Lady Crossby's head. That leaves you with only one chance at saving your son—by trusting in my ability to help you and telling me everything you know about the man who's behind this."

Rising, Lucien walked over to Katherine, who was standing in the doorway precisely where he'd left her. He turned toward Lady Trapleigh. "We'll give you a moment in which to make your decision."

Something shrewd swirled behind the widow's eyes. She smiled slowly. "I believe you know what it's like to feel as though your heart is not your own, Lord Roxberry."

Every muscle in Lucien's body tightened. He glared back at the countess, willing her to keep quiet. The last thing he needed right now was for her to offer

Katherine any reason to suspect his true feelings for her, since doing so would likely ruin everything. Katherine was vulnerable, so although she might be warming to the idea of taking their relationship to a new level, she wasn't ready to make the leap just yet. For now, Lucien would have to continue on his path of seduction with subtlety, or he would likely frighten her away. "You know nothing of me," he muttered.

"Oh, but I do," she purred as her gaze swept over him. Leaning back in her seat, she chuckled briefly before turning serious once again. "That aside, I have no reason to trust you—no assurance that you'll help me save my son."

"I am a gentleman, Lady Trapleigh. My word is my honor."

She nodded. "Just be aware that if I choose to help you and you decide to throw me over, Lady Crossby will be as good as dead. The man blackmailing me is not to be trifled with. He will only send others in my stead, and Lady Crossby will have no choice but to live the rest of her life looking over her shoulder in anticipation of another attack—an attack which, I assure you, will come, sooner or later."

Lucien didn't reply this time but stepped out into the hallway with Katherine. He closed the door to the pantry behind him. "She's right," he said as soon as it was just the two of them. "If she was hired by someone to kill you, that person will only send another assassin as soon as he discovers that Lady Trapleigh has failed. Additionally, her son's life has just become our responsibility. We must discover the person behind this in order to save you both."

Katherine nodded. "Yes, of course." Averting her gaze, she swallowed hard. The evidence of last night's ordeal was prevalent in her features.

"Can you think of any reason why anyone would wish to harm you?" he asked.

Her eyes snapped toward his. "No," she said with a slight shake of her head.

Her eyes began to glisten, but she held back the tears that threatened to fall. God, how he hated seeing her like this. Unable to help himself, he reached out and pulled her toward him, his arms coming around her in a tight embrace. "I promise you, Kate, that we will find whoever's behind this," he whispered against the top of her head as his lips brushed her soft chestnut curls.

"Thank you," she murmured.

Her words, spoken against his chest, heated his skin, and all he could think of in that instant was how good she felt in his arms and how desperately he longed to kiss her. Now was not the right time, however, for she was overset and only seeking comfort. No, when he eventually kissed Katherine, he wanted her to want it because of *him*, not because it might offer a moment's escape from her troubles. So when she leaned back a little and gazed up at him with a look of keen expectancy, he reined in the temptation to lower his lips against hers and took a step back, placing a decent amount of distance between them. "I believe we're in agreement, then," he said. "I shall go and inquire if she is willing to accept my offer."

"**W**ell?" Lucien asked as he returned to the pantry.

Eyeing him with a great deal of wariness as he seated himself in the chair opposite her, Lady Trapleigh did not look the least bit eager to assist. She clenched her jaw. Lucien waited. Her choices were limited, and he knew that she'd been weighing them while he'd spoken to Katherine.

"If I refuse to help, you won't find the man you seek and Lady Crossby will remain in danger. My son, however, will be as good as dead, for I will have failed to do what was asked of me." Drawing her lips into a thin line, she nodded. "I will tell you what I know, but you must swear to me that you will hurry to London immediately in case word gets back that my attempt on Lady Crossby's life was unsuccessful." Her eyes filled with emotion and she whispered, "Tobias is only two years old—you must save him."

"Then tell me the name of the man who is threatening your son so that I may hunt him down and make him pay for his crimes."

The edge of Lady Trapleigh's lips rose slowly to form a crooked smile. "The man you seek is called Donovan. He runs a large crime organization in the City that's mostly involved in art forgeries, fixing races for a few desperate members of the *ton* and assuming their debt whenever it suits his own interest."

Lucien nodded. "I've heard of the man," he said, recalling an acquaintance of his who'd fallen on hard times once. The poor fellow had sought Donovan's help, but the burden of being indebted to Donovan had been too great, and the man had eventually taken his own life.

"Lord Bath recently lost one of his country homes to Donovan when he couldn't pay back his loan," Lady Trapleigh continued. "I'm sure his lordship regrets not selling the place to pay off his gambling debts sooner, when he had the chance to do so, but then again, desperate men are often rash and stupid."

"I agree with you there, but that doesn't explain

why this Donovan fellow would want to harm Lady Crossby."

Lady Trapleigh's eyes shifted to a spot behind Lucien. "Have you no idea why I was asked to come here?"

"None at all," Katherine said.

Lady Trapleigh frowned, as if she found that very hard to believe. "It's because of your business dealings, Lady Crossby. They are a threat to Donovan, and nobody crosses a man like him without paying the price."

"What on earth are you talking about?" Katherine asked with a trembling voice.

"I don't know the specifics," the countess confessed, "only that he considers you an obstacle and that he hopes to eliminate you as soon as possible."

"Can you tell us where to find him?" Lucien asked. He felt a keen urge to pummel the man, if not worse.

"It is my understanding that he likes to frequent a gaming hell on Piccadilly—a place called Riley's."

"And his appearance? If you can give me a description, he'll be easier to locate."

"Alas, I cannot help you there," Lady Trapleigh said, "for I have never so much as laid eyes on the man—at least not as far as I am aware. The two instances when Donovan sought me out, I was unable to see his face. The man is fond of hiding in the shadows."

Lucien clenched his fists, his nails digging into the palms of his hands as cold, unabated fury surged through him. "Then how the bloody hell do you suppose I find him? How can you even be sure that he'll be at Riley's? Christ almighty, woman! I thought you'd be able to help when in truth you've given me nothing but a supposition to go on."

"It is better than nothing. Besides, you have the

name of the man you're seeking now, which is more than you had before." She leaned forward a little and tilted her head. "I haven't slept my way through the majority of noblemen in England without becoming privy to a bit of information here and there, and I'm telling you that Donovan can be found at Riley's. I have no doubt on the matter."

"Then that is where we'll begin," Katherine said.

"We?" Lucien asked, turning toward her. "If you think you'll be joining me on this mad journey, then you're—"

"What?" she asked, eyes flashing as she stepped toward him. "I've no intention of waiting here for your return when my life is the one being threatened. You must be cracked in the head!"

"You won't be able to show your face in public. Nobody can know you're there in case word gets back to Donovan that you've survived," Lucien said, hoping to dissuade her.

"I'm sure we can find a way to accomplish that," Katherine replied, stubbornly crossing her arms.

Lucien groaned. "What about Sophia?"

Silence reigned for what seemed an eternity before Katherine finally said, "In light of what has happened and what might yet happen if Donovan sends another assassin after me, I do believe she would be safest if she's not in my company."

It made sense, of course, as much as Lucien hated it. The whole ordeal had put a bitter taste in his mouth. "I will send my valet to inquire about the validity of this first," he muttered, his eyes settling once more on Lady Trapleigh. "If what you say is indeed true, then Lady Crossby and I will journey to London in search of Donovan while you remain here, out of sight. In fact, you will stay in this pantry until you receive word of Donovan's arrest."

"Lord Roxberry, I—"

"Enough!" He leaned closer to the widow until the tip of his nose almost touched hers. "If one of Donovan's men sees you strolling about the grounds or lounging in the parlor, they'll know something's off. In fact, I daresay it would be best if you remained behind lock and key."

"You mean to hold me prisoner?" Lady Trapleigh asked.

"After everything you've done, I wouldn't trust you not to stab either one of us in the back at the first available opportunity," Lucien said, "so unless you prefer to speak with the constable, I most certainly do intend to keep you under restraint."

Lady Trapleigh nodded, but the look she gave Lucien suggested that she hoped for fire and brimstone to fall on his head.

"Excellent," he said, quite eager to leave Lady Trapleigh's presence so he could be rid of her altogether. Turning his back on her, he followed Katherine out into the hallway and closed the door behind him, locking it for good measure. He shut his eyes for a brief second, took a deep breath and expelled it, then looked to Katherine, who was staring back at him with grave concern. "What a distressing start to the day," she said.

He nodded. "In the event that we do end up going to London, where will you send Sophia?" he asked. "She can't remain here."

"I know, but don't worry. I have a plan—one that I will share with you in private, should anyone happen to overhear." She was being cautious, Lucien realized, most likely in the event that Donovan's men did show up and threaten her staff. There was no telling what a man or woman might confess if the situation was dire enough. It was wise of Katherine to consider this.

Without warning, she reached for his hand, sending a pulse of heat up his arm as her fingers curled around his. Her eyes met his and he found that he was suddenly struggling to breathe. There was something about the way she was looking at him . . . something urgent that made him grow weak. "Thank you," she said, her voice so soft it was but a breath of air.

Doing his best to tamp down the rush of desire that swirled up inside him, he raised her hand to his lips and placed a tender kiss upon her knuckles, lingering for just a second longer than what was appropriate.

"Lucien?"

His name, spoken with wonder, stirred his blood like nothing else. God, how he longed to press his lips against hers, to strip her of her gown so he could pay tribute to the beauty beneath, and to offer her his love in the most elemental way possible. Heat surged up his legs and straight to his groin, where it proceeded to tease and torture until he hardened.

"I have to inform my valet so he can be on his way," he told her hastily as he released her hand. Time was of the essence if they were to save Tobias. Besides, Lucien needed distance, distraction and something to cool his ardor if he wasn't to make a complete fool of himself. With a curt nod, he took his leave, pleased by how bereft she looked as they parted ways, her lips slightly parted and her eyes filled with curiosity.

Chapter 10

As soon as Lucien left, Katherine hurried upstairs to the nursery, almost sagging with relief at the sight of Sophia lying on a cushion on the floor, arms waving about as she tried to grab the crystal that her nanny, Mathilda, was dangling over her head. "My lady," Mathilda said when she spotted Katherine. She made as if to get up off the floor, but Katherine stopped her with a staying hand.

"May I join you?" Katherine asked.

Mathilda nodded with enthusiasm. "Of course! I'm sure her ladyship would be delighted to play with her mama."

Katherine chuckled as she settled down on the floor beside her daughter and offered her one of her fingers. The little imp latched onto it quickly enough, chortling in response to her success while offering Katherine a necessary distraction. Her nerves were still on edge after Lady Trapleigh's interview, as she continued to fear for her own safety, as well as for Sophia's. It would be impossible for her mind to find peace until Donovan was stopped.

Picking up Sophia, she walked across to the

window and looked out, singing softly as she did so. She couldn't see it from where she was standing, but she knew that Roxberry Hall sat solidly beyond the farthest hill, just right off the forest that bordered both properties. "Do you have a small bell, by any chance?" she asked Mathilda as she turned away from the window.

"Yes, my lady. Sophia finds it very amusing to listen to."

"In that case, please fetch it and we will offer her some entertainment."

The sound of footsteps caught Katherine's attention a while later. Turning her head, she found Carter standing in the doorway. "Lord Roxberry has returned," he said. "I've taken the liberty of showing him into the parlor."

"Thank you," Katherine told him, unable to believe how quickly her time with Sophia had flown. "I'll be down in just a moment."

The calm she'd felt while playing with her daughter ebbed away at the thought of Lucien. They had a serious concern to deal with—a threat that had to be removed—in addition to the fact that she'd almost been killed. That ought to have been enough to keep her growing feelings for Lucien at a distance, but for some reason she could not explain, it wasn't. Least of all when he was under her roof and would soon be in her presence. Dear God, she'd felt it the night of the ball when he'd held her in his arms, then during the days since, both at the lake and at the ruin. Today it had been overpowering—a growing desire for him to want her the way she'd begun wanting him.

Never before had she considered him in such a way, yet now . . . good heavens if he hadn't returned to her life more handsomely rugged than ever. He'd filled out in his absence, and there was now an edge of resolve to his masculinity that appealed to her feminine side—so much so that she found herself in a constant state of want whenever he was near. She knew she ought not think such things and that she especially ought not feel them toward Lucien. Why, he'd known her his whole life. Whatever would he think of her if he discovered that she longed for him to kiss her with abandon?

She dared not imagine, fearing that he too would look at her with disapproval . . . that he would reject her just as easily as Charles had done. She never would have thought that anything could hurt her more than the way in which her husband had spurned her, but she realized now that this was untrue. If Lucien discovered her unexpected yearning for him and failed to reciprocate, she knew she'd never survive the heartache that was bound to follow.

Nothing about him suggested that he had developed a tendre for her. If anything, he'd seemed a bit standoffish—more serious than he'd been four years ago, but that was to be expected, all things considered. Additionally, he'd been showing a keen interest in Lady Julie, even if their brief acquaintance had proven fruitless.

The point was that he'd made his choice in a potential wife known. What did it matter if Lady Julie's interests lay elsewhere, when it was she, not Katherine, who'd captured Lucien's attention? Katherine shook her head. No, Lucien Marvaine had given her no reason at all to believe he considered her anything more than a dear friend. Except perhaps one . . . the way in which he'd paused most inappropriately with his lips upon her hand. Yes, it had been brief and subtle, but it had happened nonetheless, and she in turn had felt like a girl thrust into the midst of a turbulent storm, her knees more wobbly than ever.

Katherine sighed as she made her way down the stairs. She'd sworn she'd never again allow a man to hurt her, that she simply wouldn't allow any man to get close enough. The problem was that Lucien had already been close and her reaction to him had snuck up on her with such stealth that she'd been caught completely off guard.

Confused, Katherine paused when she reached the bottom of the stairs. Clearly she was overthinking the whole situation and driving herself mad in the process.

Heavens, what a muddle!

And yet . . . if there was any chance at all that he might reciprocate her feelings, then she was prepared to dive in headfirst and grasp with both hands whatever he had to offer, no matter how much it terrified her to do so. Because if there was one thing Katherine longed for above all else, it was to be loved, and she was willing to face her greatest fear if there was but the slightest chance she might achieve that.

Heart pounding in her chest, she crossed the floor to the parlor door. Rejection—the humiliation of it and the pain it had wrought—still clung to her like a wet cloak, impossible to shake off. If Lucien would only give her some indication, something more than a lingering kiss on her hand to suggest that he wanted more from her than friendship. She slowed her pace as stark realization dawned. If Lucien had even the slightest interest in her, he would not have offered Lady Julie his attention instead. Once the matter with Lady Trapleigh was settled and Katherine no longer required his help, Lucien would probably find another eligible young lady to pursue. Her stomach churned as the unwelcome thought of him sharing his future with another woman ran through her mind. Sharp awareness stabbed at her heart. It would be unbearable for her to watch.

Shaking off her misgivings, Katherine reached for the handle, aware now of what she had to do. She had to reach for the moon and the stars or risk drowning in despair; she had to ignore the anxiety that shackled her; she had to do everything in her power to discover if Lucien might want her too. Propriety and fear be damned, she was going to cast herself into the abyss that yawned before her and do the unthinkable—she would seduce the Earl of Roxberry.

"Kate," Lucien said, rising the moment she made her appearance. "Mr. Dawson has already set out. He ought to be back by this time tomorrow with the necessary information. In the meantime, I will remain here, with you."

Although the idea of keeping Lucien close was tempting, Katherine couldn't help but rebel. "You cannot possibly," she said. "Whatever will people say if it becomes known that you spent the night here?"

"I suppose they'll assume that you and I have become lovers," he said somewhat blandly.

"And scandal will rain down upon both Sophia and me as a result."

"It is only for one night, Kate, and to be blunt, I would rather take such a risk than allow another as-sassin the opportunity of attacking you."

"After last night's incident, I'm sure I can depend on the footmen to see to my safety."

"Perhaps," he acquiesced, "but I'd rather see to the matter myself. Allow me to keep watch in front of your bedchamber with one of the footmen."

Katherine hesitated. "Servants talk, Lucien. Even the ones that I trust can be tempted to gossip." She paused, unsure of what to do. Was safety of greater importance than her reputation? Absolutely—especially when Sophia was to be considered. "I will ask my lady's maid to sleep in my room with me, then. If anyone says a word afterward, she will vouch for both of us."

A smile dimpled Lucien's cheeks. "It's settled then. In the meantime, you ought to prepare your valise in case we do travel to London tomorrow, and once that is done, I believe we ought to enjoy each other's company for the remainder of the day." A spark lit in the depths of his dark brown eyes. "Indeed, I cannot tell you how pleased I am to share your company for such an extensive period, my only regret being the circumstances."

Katherine's legs felt wobbly. "I couldn't agree more," she said. A heavy pause hung between them until she found herself saying, "I suppose I ought to go and pack then?"

He took a step toward her. "Yes, you should."

"Right." She then turned sharply about and exited the room, her nerves completely frayed and her stomach all jittery. Blast it all, how was she supposed to seduce the man when she could barely think straight whenever he was near? Not to mention that she had never even considered attempting something so bold before. In all likelihood, she would achieve nothing more than making a fool of herself in the process.

"Shall we take our tea in the library?" Katherine asked after lunch. "I've recently acquired the fifth edition of the *Encyclopædia Britannica* and would love to show it to you."

"A wonderful idea," Lucien said. "I have the fourth edition myself, you know."

"Do you? Then I doubt you'll be very impressed, as there's very little difference between them."

"All the same," he murmured as he followed her down the hallway, "I'm sure we'll enjoy looking at some of the articles." Frankly, he didn't care what he was doing to pass the time, just as long as they were doing it together.

"There's a really good one about botany," Katherine was saying.

Lucien smiled to himself. "I was rather thinking of the one about chemistry."

A puzzled expression caressed her features as she swiftly glanced at him over her shoulder. When she didn't respond, Lucien decided to hold silent as well.

"Shall I pour us each a cup of tea?" Katherine asked as soon as they arrived in the library, where the tea tray was already waiting on a table between two armchairs.

"Certainly," Lucien replied. "I'd love to have some."

Seating herself, Katherine tended to the tea while Lucien took the other chair, his eyes riveted upon the graceful curve of her wrist as she poured. His chest tightened as he imagined them spending many more such moments together.

"Now, stay right there," she said as soon as she was done, "and I'll be right back."

Agreeing to do as she bid, Lucien leaned back against his chair, picked up his teacup and took a sip while he watched Katherine walk toward a stepping stool on wheels. Bending over, she then began to nudge the piece of furniture forward, along the length of the room. Lucien almost choked on his tea, his pulse quickening at the sight of her delectable derriere sticking up in the air, even if it was covered by layers of fabric. She came to a stop, having no doubt arrived at the part of the bookcase where the book she sought was housed. Lucien expelled a deep breath. He reached for a strawberry tart and was just about to take a bite when Katherine raised her skirts ever so slightly and stepped up onto the stool.

Lucien's mouth went instantly dry, for the figure she portrayed as she reached up toward one of the shelves, the fabric of her skirt still clutched between the fingers of her other hand so that her ankles came into view, was not one he could tear his eyes away from. By God, did she have any idea of what she was doing to him? Of the torment she was causing? No, of course not.

"I've got it," she told him triumphantly as she stepped down onto the ground with a leather-bound volume clasped against her chest. She smiled, and he knew that he was under her spell, held captive and incapable of escape. "Since you are the guest, I thought I'd bring you the volume you suggested—the one on chemistry."

With a cough, Lucien set his tart aside. "How thoughtful of you."

She grinned. "Don't think I don't have a secret agenda."

"Oh?"

"I'm really just trying to placate you so you won't complain once we get to the article on botany."

"I see," he drawled. "So what you're saying is that you wish to indulge my wishes before indulging your own?"

She looked at him with hesitation. "Quite," she eventually said.

"As grateful as I am for such consideration, Kate, I would never put myself before you in any regard."

"I know that," she said. "Please know that I will be eternally grateful to you for everything you're doing in order to help with this awful situation. It means a lot to me, having you here for support." Flipping open the book, she handed it to him, her fingers brushing his as she did so.

Lucien's heart shuddered. Had the gesture been intentional? He hoped it had been, but there was nothing in her expression or bearing to indicate that this was the case. He blinked, shook his head and bent over the text before him. How the devil would he ever survive the long night ahead? Standing outside her bedchamber door within feet of her bed was going to be hell.

Seated in the parlor the following afternoon, Katherine busied herself with some embroidery while Lucien helped his driver ready the carriage. After returning from London an hour earlier, Lucien's valet had informed them that word of Lady Crossby's business proficiency had recently spread due to questions being asked by some men of dubious repute. Worst of all, however, was Mr. Dawson's account of an accident that had occurred on Regent Street the previous evening when a fabric shop, La Belle Anglaise, had caught fire. Thankfully nobody had been harmed, but most of the shop's contents had been ruined. What Lucien and Mr. Dawson hadn't known until Katherine had mentioned it, however, was that she had sunk a great deal of her own money into that business in her desire to help the proprietress—a woman Katherine had known since childhood, as she had once been Katherine's governess.

"Miss Pinket?" Lucien had asked.

"She's Mrs. Brown now," Katherine had told him. "I feel terrible for her. Especially if this is indeed Donovan's doing, for then I am entirely to blame for her loss. Heavens, but she must be devastated, poor woman. I'll have to find a way to help her through this."

Lucien had smiled reassuringly. "I'm sure the insurance will cover most of it."

"Yes, you're probably right," Katherine had said, happy now that she'd made that a prerequisite for her investment.

After discussing the matter a bit more, Lucien had finally declared that they should depart for London without further delay. It appeared that Lady Trapleigh's story rang true and that Donovan was indeed stirring up trouble. With both Katherine and Lady Trapleigh's son at stake, Lucien didn't dare hesitate a moment more. He was determined to find Donovan himself and put an end to the man's deviousness.

Straightening her back, Katherine was just getting started on another daisy when Lucien appeared in the doorway. Heavens, he was handsome with his hair all mussed and his cravat in slight disarray.

"The carriage is ready," he announced, eyeing the door, which remained ajar. "Do you still wish to come along, or do you think it best for me to go alone? I only ask because now is the time to say so if you have reconsidered. We depart in ten minutes."

"Do you prefer to travel alone?"

"This has nothing to do with my preferences, Kate. I'm only concerned for what is best for you and for Sophia."

Warmth enveloped her heart and her worries

eased. "Then I shall join you as planned." She gestured for him to take a seat opposite her own, which he did. Leaning toward him, she lowered her voice to a whisper. "I'm sending Sophia to Bath with her nanny. My parents are there at present, though everyone believes them to be in Scotland. You see, I wasn't completely honest with you when you asked about my father's health. He hasn't been feeling himself lately, and the doctor believes that taking the waters will help."

"I'm so sorry, I—"

"Mama insists he will be fine, and I believe her. He simply worries a lot about everything—always has—and I daresay his concerns have given rise to a slight depression." Unwilling to discuss the reason behind her father's concerns, Katherine quickly continued. "The point is that nobody is likely to look for Sophia there. She ought to be perfectly safe, or at least more so than she would be with us as we chase after this Donovan fellow."

Lucien frowned. "Kate," he began, "I must confess that I was taken aback when Lady Trapleigh mentioned Donovan's reason for targeting you. It never occurred to me that you would be so successful at doing business—to the point where you would actually be considered a threat to anyone. Forgive me for asking, but how on earth did this come about?"

"After Charles passed away," Katherine said, "I continued to support his investments and gradually began making a few of my own during the last year, with the help of Mr. Simmons, my secretary." She then told him of her struggle to understand the ins and outs of the finance world, how to determine risk, and of Mr. Simmons's unwavering patience with her.

When she finished, Lucien just stared at her,

dumbfounded. "And are all of these investments of yours doing well?"

"Remarkably so. The income is enough to sustain Cresthaven, the staff that it employs and whatever necessities I might have."

"I'm not sure what to say," he admitted, for it was the truth—she had quite literally struck him dumb.

"You're surprised?"

"Well . . . yes, I suppose I am. I'm also terribly impressed, if you must know." She looked pleased by his praise, so he added, "To think of everything you've been through—losing your husband and having to raise a daughter immediately after, all while taking charge of Crossby's affairs. I daresay it's rather remarkable!"

She was blushing now and looking adorably bashful. "It eased my mind, I think—having something with which to busy myself when I was not with Sophia. The garden doesn't offer much diversion during the winter."

Lucien nodded. He understood all too well the need for distraction that followed on the heels of loss. "I don't mean to rush you," he said, changing the subject, "but considering our time limit, I suggest we make haste and head to London immediately. Are you ready?"

"Yes," she said, setting her embroidery aside and rising. He rose as well. "I just need to fetch my pelisse."

"And Sophia?"

"She and her nanny are ready to take one of my carriages, but nobody, not even the driver, is aware of where they are going yet. They'll be informed as soon as they're ready to set out—which they will do before us."

She looked up at him then, hope brimming in her

eyes, as if she longed for him to save her. Her life and trust had been placed in his hands, and he felt both honored and humbled as, seizing the moment, he pulled her against him, enfolding her in his embrace. "It will be all right, Kate," he muttered, hoping to soothe away her concerns. God help him, but even her touch, separated as it was from his skin by layers of clothing, still scorched his soul.

Swallowing hard, he set her away and took a step back. "I'll wait for you here while you gather your things."

"Should I bring a chess set along for the ride?" she asked as she tilted her head, eyes sparkling with mischief while a smile spread its way across her lips.

Struggling to keep his eyes off those lips, Lucien met her gaze. "Only if you promise that you won't mind me winning."

Her breath hitched ever so slightly and then she blushed, but before he had a chance to examine her response any further, she swatted him playfully on the arm, which of course threw him completely over the edge. "As if that's likely to happen." Her eyes twinkled with merriment and . . . dare he hope . . . a secret promise? Sweeping past him, she headed for the door. "I will return momentarily, and then we will be off."

Seated across from Katherine as the carriage tumbled toward London, Lucien quietly watched while she unwrapped a velvet-clad parcel and revealed the chess set she'd spoken of earlier. With her attention fixed on setting up the pieces while the carriage jostled and bounced about, Lucien was granted the luxury of allowing his eyes to roam over her body—a body he'd recently held in his arms. His blood stirred at the memory of it, and he found himself cursing the pelisse she now wore for denying him a proper glimpse of her breasts. Thoughts of what they would look like, feel like, in the palms of his hands were swift to follow. With a muttered oath, he crossed his legs and peered out the window at the passing countryside. Was it possible for a man to go blind from unfulfilled lust? he wondered.

"Black or white?" she asked, requesting his attention.

Abandoning the view, he gave it to her without hesitation, his lips tilting as he took in the chess set that presently sat haphazardly balanced upon her lap. "A lady ought to be afforded the opportunity of making the first move," he told her smoothly. "I'll choose black."

She did not look at him, though he sensed she wanted to, for her head had jerked a little when he'd spoken, yet her eyes had remained on the board and the pieces upon it as if her full concentration had been required to keep them steady. Biting her lip, she selected a pawn and moved it forward.

"When was the last time you played?" He moved his knight.

She shrugged. "I don't recall." She was being evasive.

Lucien raised an eyebrow. "Why don't you try?"

Tension built between them, so thick and heavy that Lucien half expected to hear a clap of thunder within the confined space of the carriage. Heart hammering in his chest, he watched as she plucked the bishop from the board and set him on a diagonal path. The game they played was not a simple one but dangerously demanding. Driven by a base desire to claim her as his own, Lucien pushed for honesty, testing her defenses and denying her the comfort that avoidance offered.

"If you must know, I haven't enjoyed a game in some time. Not since the last time you and I played together."

Moving his other knight, he asked the only question that seemed important at that moment. "Why?"

"Does it really matter?" Her voice was barely a whisper as she spoke. "After all, it is only a game."

Something about the way she spoke made him want to toss the blasted chess set aside so he could ravage her right there upon the seat of the carriage.

If he didn't know any better, he'd think she was toying with him . . . speaking in double entendres intended to heat his blood. Surely not. Katherine would never be so bold, but then he recalled the subtle display of her ankles yesterday in the library, the unintentional view he'd been given of her derriere, the accidental brush of her fingers against his, and the thought that she might be threatened to push him over the edge.

Hell, standing on guard in front of her bedchamber had certainly tested his restraint. On more than one occasion he'd considered bursting through the door and climbing into bed with her, no matter her maid or footman. *Christ!* He had to find a way to regain control. After all, he was meant to be seducing *her,* not the other way around.

With a good measure of wariness, he eyed her as she twirled her fingers around the bishop. The motion mesmerized him. She licked her lips. For the millionth time that day, Lucien fought for control. "So, tell me more about your investments," he said as she abandoned the bishop and moved another pawn instead.

"Ordinarily, I wouldn't discuss the particulars with anyone," she said, her hands steadying the chessboard as the carriage hit a hole in the road.

"And ordinarily I'd tell you that you're wise not to, but in this case, I think you must. Donovan is after you because of your business dealings, Kate. Making me privy to the specifics might help us figure out why. Besides, you know you can trust me, don't you?"

For the first time since they'd started playing, Katherine removed her eyes from the chess set and looked directly at Lucien. Her gaze was studious, assessing and pensive. Lucien forced himself to remain still, even though he felt like shifting beneath her scrutiny. Slowly, she nodded. "Yes, I do," she said. She dropped her gaze to her lap. "Your turn."

Without thinking, Lucien moved his knight straight into the path of her bishop.

"You're not concentrating," she chided as she claimed the piece.

No, he wasn't, but how could he when his body was raging to touch her? "So will you tell me about all of your holdings willingly, or will you force me to squeeze the information out of you?" He was clasping onto a very thin thread, he realized, but if she'd only talk to him about her business, perhaps he could force his torrid thoughts away from the sweep of her neck as she bowed her head and from the oh so tempting wisps of hair that curled against her cheeks.

She chuckled with unabashed amusement. "I'd like to see you try."

Her words, soft as music, spilled over him, teasing and luring until he felt his resolve waver. God have mercy on his soul, he wasn't going to make it. He clenched his fists, nails digging into his flesh. Did she have any idea of what she was doing to him? Of course not. She would never be so cruel. "Very well," he said. "If I win this game, you will owe me three favors, one of which will consist of full disclosure in regard to your investments."

"You do realize that I'm merely having a bit of fun, don't you? That I intend to tell you eventually? I'm not a fool, Lucien. I realize that it's in my own best interest to do so."

"Nevertheless, I would like to have some guarantee."

"Very well then." She watched as he moved a pawn. "What will the other favors consist of?"

"That, my dear, will be a surprise."

She scrunched her nose. "I'm not so sure I like the sound of that."

"Afraid of the unknown?" Leaning forward, he hesitated briefly before saying, "You've never been a coward."

Her chest rose and fell with rapid breaths. "Things change."

Indeed they did. He could sense her apprehension, her fear of having no choice but to do as he asked, but Lucien wanted answers, and he would not allow her to back away now. "Perhaps," he allowed, "but you're still not a coward, or you would have gone with Sophia to Bath while I went chasing after the villain."

"Maybe," she agreed.

"So will you rise to the challenge?"

She claimed his bishop, raised her gaze from the board and smiled broadly. "By all means."

There could be no denying the importance of the game, for she felt it in every move she made. She'd never lost a game against Lucien and had always considered herself a superior player. But as the game progressed, she began to realize that he might have been serious when he'd suggested that he would win instead of her. Indeed, she was losing, and she was losing fast, which only served to prove how important winning had to be for Lucien. He wanted those favors, and the anticipation of discovering what the last two would consist of stretched her nerves.

"Checkmate." The word hung in the air as Katherine stared down at her cornered king.

"Well played," she said in reply. Raising her gaze, she met Lucien's. Her mouth went dry. Gone was the tepid look of affection he'd always bestowed upon her. The emotion that shone in his eyes was powerful . . . heated . . . more raw than what she'd ever dared dream of evoking in a man. Her pulse quickened. She wanted him, and yet she didn't. Heaven above, she didn't know her own mind!

The carriage jolted, scattering the chess pieces even as she made a grasp for them. It was to no avail. All she had left was an empty board, which was presently being plied from her fingers by Lucien. Katherine swallowed. If only she could still her pounding heart. To think that she'd entertained the idea of seducing him! How naïve of her to think herself sophisticated enough for such a challenge when instinct now told her to retreat. "I believe you wanted answers," she said, grasping for something sensible with which to steady herself. A serious conversation would do.

"First things first," he murmured. His hand settled upon her knee and she almost leapt away from him. Except of course there was nowhere to leap to. Besides, she'd longed for this these past few days . . . had no doubt instigated this moment with her suggestive comments. But it was happening too fast. She wasn't ready. Would she ever be? Probably not, because she was terrified.

"Katherine," he pleaded. "Please look at me."

She did and was instantly rendered breathless by the level of fear staring back at her. It mirrored her own, yet it was tightly wound with fierce determination. Everything was about to change between them. She could feel it in her veins and she was helpless to stop it.

"I no longer have the patience for pretense or for keeping my feelings for you at bay when my greatest wish of all is for you to be mine." Taking her hand in his, he brushed her wrist with his thumb until tiny sparks of heat danced across her skin. "If there is any chance at all that you will welcome my advances, please give me a sign. I cannot bear the thought of not knowing, when the mere sight of you, your very presence, stirs me like nothing else ever will."

"I . . ." The word was almost a croak. She tried to speak again, not knowing what she would say, but words failed to come.

Lucien's hand, still touching hers, toyed with the edge of her kidskin glove. Katherine watched, enthralled as he gently peeled it away so he could caress her bare flesh. Heat washed over her, dizzying her senses. Their eyes met, and Katherine could not look away as Lucien raised her hand to his lips and, with the utmost reverence, kissed her pulse.

Pure pleasure flooded her insides, curling and building until it rendered her breathless. "Forgive me," Lucien said, "but I cannot seem to stop myself. I need to know what it's like to kiss you."

The words barely registered before he was on the seat beside her, pulling her toward him and lowering his mouth over hers. Their lips met, and as they did, every wicked thought he'd stirred in her these past few days collided, crashed over her, and made her desperate for more. Her hands reached for his shoulders, curling into the fabric of his jacket as his tongue traced her lower lip. Katherine's insides melted with desire as it pooled between her thighs. Her lips parted, inviting him in, and he was instantly there, his tongue exploring with deliberate strokes while he pushed her back against the squabs of the seat, her breasts flattening against his chest.

A groan filled the air. His or hers? She wasn't sure. All she knew was that his kiss would not be enough to satisfy the need that roared to life inside her, filling her breasts until they ached for his touch.

"You've no idea how long I've wanted this," she heard him whisper as he kissed his way along the edge of her jaw while desperate fingers worked at the ribbon holding her bonnet in place. The silk fastenings slipped apart and the bonnet tumbled away.

Katherine didn't spare it a thought but leaned her head back instead, offering Lucien the curve of her neck. "Tell me," she begged.

Licking and nibbling, he coaxed from her a sigh. "Years, Kate." One hand settled on her thigh while the other found the curve of her breast. "Years of sleepless nights wondering what it might be like to touch you like this . . ." He gave her a gentle squeeze and she arched her back in response. "Imagining the feel of your body against mine, my name upon your lips as I give you pleasure . . ." She whimpered, entirely too helpless to resist reaching for more. His scandalous words had brought her to a point of unrestrained wantonness from which there could be no return. She wanted the pleasure of which he spoke—

wanted it more desperately than she'd ever wanted anything else in her life. "You've no idea how many times I've thought of peeling away your gown so I could kiss the skin beneath."

Katherine gasped. His words, undoubtedly meant to seduce, served instead as a stark reminder of her imperfections. For a heartbeat, she'd allowed herself to forget, but now, as he spoke of undressing her and of bearing witness to her ugliness, she was assaulted by a flood of unpleasant memories that sent her crashing back to reality.

Placing her palm against Lucien's chest, she gave him a slight push. "I'm sorry, but I . . ." Her voice was breathless. "This is happening too fast."

Lucien stilled, then pulled back. She knew he was looking at her, even though she dared not look at him, instead keeping her attention fixed on one of the chess pieces as it rolled from side to side on the floor. Silence descended, and he removed himself to the opposite bench. There was a beat, and then he asked the one question she dared not answer. "What are you so afraid of?"

Katherine shrugged one shoulder. Her gaze rose warily to meet his. "Nothing," she said, "but I have told you that I have no intention of remarrying or of becoming someone's mistress, so really, where will all this lead?"

"To the altar, I had hoped."

"I just told you that—"

"Yes, you did." His voice was terse, his face set in grim lines. "Kate, you know that I must marry. Are you telling me that you would rather I choose another woman for my wife?"

"I was under the impression that you had already considered doing so. After all, Lady Julie—"

"Is in love with Mr. Goodard, as I'm sure you already know," he said. "She means nothing to me. More to the point, she never did."

"But at the ball and the other day when she and Mr. Goodard came to Cresthaven . . . your intentions toward her were so clear."

He shook his head. "My only intention was to find out whether or not you cared."

Katherine gasped as it all became startlingly real. "You used Lady Julie to try and make me jealous?"

"No. She and I had an agreement." He paused before saying, "You know, Mr. Goodard's keen interest in Lady Julie when she hurt her ankle, coupled with your reaction to my recent embraces, have enlightened me greatly."

"You're being unbearably arrogant right now," she said as annoyance fanned through her. "If there was one thing I always thought I could count on from you, Lucien, it was honesty. Why would you deliberately trick me like that? Have you so little regard for my feelings that you would give no second thought to playing games with me?"

"On the contrary, I feel very deeply for you, which was why I had to know if there was any chance you might feel the same toward me."

"Well, I don't." The lie, born from the pain of his deception, quivered upon her lips.

"I don't believe you," he said, leaning toward her, "not when you responded the way you did to my kiss. Can you honestly tell me it wouldn't bother you if I were to press such advances on another lady?"

Katherine opened her mouth to speak, to tell him she wouldn't care in the least, but jealousy soared and words failed her. Lucien smiled with smug satisfaction. "I thought so," he said, settling back against the squabs. "Something is holding you back, stopping you from grasping on to what you want, and I have every intention of discovering what that something is, not only because I want to convince you to marry me, Kate, but because I genuinely care about you. I hate to see you suffer."

"So much has happened while you've been away." She longed to explore the possibilities of this attraction between them, but fear held her back even as she tried to fight it.

The glint in Lucien's eyes softened. "Kate," he told her gently as he placed his hand over hers, "we've come too far for you to back out now, and just so you know, I have every intention of slaying whatever dragons you're hiding. After all, I still have one favor to ask of you, and I intend to use it wisely."

Oh no.

"Lucien . . ." She eyed him warily.

"Don't worry. I won't make good on it until I'm sure you're ready. I'm not a beast, Kate—I want you to be willing."

Heaven help her if he wasn't speaking of taking her to his bed. To her complete and utter dismay, her body did not revolt at the idea. On the contrary, she felt heated from the inside out, perhaps even a little excited, if she was to be completely honest. A loud pitter-patter on the roof brought her amorous thoughts to a halt. It had started to rain, and from the sound of it, they'd hit a torrential downpour.

Opening the window a notch, Lucien called to the driver, "We'll stop at the next posting inn for the night." Once the window had been closed back up, he looked at Katherine. "No sense in being reckless."

"Quite right," she muttered.

"With this weather, it will be nightfall before we

reach London, and that's if we don't get stuck in the mud on the way there. I for one would like to avoid having to get out and push the carriage."

"I didn't argue," Katherine said.

"No, but you looked as if you disapproved."

Crossing her arms, she stared back at him. It was impossible to stop from smiling when he was scowling at her as if she'd just denied him his favorite treat. Recalling his advances, she acknowledged that indeed, she probably had. Her cheeks heated with the realization. "I do not disapprove of being cautious," she told him, "but in light of what has recently transpired within this carriage I must admit I think it remarkably coincidental that we should find ourselves trapped together at an inn during a rainstorm. Sounds like something out of a novel, if you ask me."

His eyebrows drew together. "Are you suggesting that I have some control over the weather? That this is all part of my secret plan to seduce you?"

She laughed, hoping to make light of his suggestion. "I wouldn't dare."

"Wouldn't you?" A smile touched his lips. "As far as I recall, you've always been more daring than most ladies ought to be, balancing on fallen-down tree trunks and leaping over rivers." Leaning forward, he raised his finger to her lips and gently swept it across the sensitive flesh. "The rain *is* a coincidence, as you say. Still, I am glad for it, for I can think of no better way to spend the evening than by continuing to convince you to submit to your wishes."

"My wishes?" she croaked. "You have no—"

"You betray yourself, Kate, for your eyes, the blush upon your skin, the occasional hitch in your breath all speak of a longing that you are determined to deny. Don't worry though." His eyes were bright with excitement. "I have every intention of kissing you again before the night is over."

The carriage rolled to a stop and Lucien stepped out, his hands reaching for her so he could help her alight. Her thoughts hadn't moved past his last statement, but somehow she managed to rise from her seat and reach out, ready to accept his hand. He caught her by the waist instead and swung her into his arms, the rain heavy upon them as he strode through puddles in order to reach the front door. Pushing it open, he set her down carefully and followed her inside, leaving the coachman to see to the horses and their luggage.

"Thank you," Katherine said. She'd still managed to get wet, even though he'd carried her, but at least her slippers had avoided the mud.

"You're very welcome," he said, not looking at her. His attention, it seemed, was on the man coming toward them. "Good evening, sir. Are you the innkeeper?"

"I am," the man said with a curt nod. He was an old and weather-beaten sort, who walked slightly hunched over and with a bit of a limp. "I trust you'll be needing a room for the night?"

"Indeed. It's coming down heavily out there. Thought it best not to risk the horses or the carriage."

"Quite right," the innkeeper said as he grabbed a key from a hook on the wall. "If you'll please follow me."

"Forgive me," Katherine said, halting both men on their way toward the stairs, "but is it possible for us to have two rooms? We're not married, you see."

"Oh, I say! Indeed it is. You must forgive me. When I saw you come in together, I just assumed that you were," the innkeeper said, returning for another key.

Shaking his head, Lucien grabbed Katherine by

the elbow and leaned toward her, his lips brushing the edge of her ear. "You just *had* to ruin things, didn't you?"

Turning her head, Katherine saw that his features were completely relaxed, his eyes dancing with amusement, while his grin was one of boyish mischievousness. She smiled in return. "But of course," she said. "A joint room would be far too easy, and besides, everyone knows that most men enjoy a good challenge."

"Is that an invitation?" he asked, his murmur so soft that nobody else was likely to hear, his tone so enticing she could practically feel it caressing her skin.

Swatting his arm to make light of it all, she chuckled, "By all means, you're willing to try." Heavens! Why on earth would she say that? She'd baited him—quite brazenly at that—and without being the least bit certain of how far she was willing to go. But for some inexplicable reason, the words had been a natural response to his—familiar and so very similar to the way in which they always sparred with each other. Except this time, there would be consequences, and she wasn't the least bit sure if she was prepared to face them.

Apprehension still gnawed, yet there could be no denying the feelings he stirred inside her. Never in her life had she felt so at ease and flustered in a man's presence. It was most unsettling. And then of course there was the kiss. She'd pushed him away, fearing what it might have led to, but by God if she hadn't enjoyed every marvelous second of it for as long as it had lasted. He'd promised to kiss her again—this very evening—and the thought brought a flutter to her belly. Perhaps if all they could do was kiss, then that would not be such a bad thing.

Reaching the top of the landing, the innkeeper showed them each to their rooms with the promise that a bath would be brought up for each of them before dinner.

"I'll see you later then," Lucien said once the innkeeper was gone. Katherine stood in the doorway to her room, looking back at him, her eyes helplessly seeking his mouth. "Shall we say seven o'clock in the dining room?"

She blinked, then nodded, feeling quite out of sorts and perfectly stupid. If only he wouldn't have dangled the promise of another kiss before her. "That sounds fine." With a nod, he started inside his room, his door almost closing when a thought struck her. "What about our luggage? We'll need dry clothes after the bath."

"I'm sure my coachman will have someone send it up." He'd popped his head back out into the hallway. "Don't worry, Kate—you'll be warm and dry in no time."

Oh, she wasn't worried about that. Not really. What she *was* worried about was her own sanity and how she'd prevent herself from being reduced to a complete imbecile. How on earth had this happened to her?

Removing her sodden bonnet, she placed it on a table, water pooling beneath it as it dripped. Her pelisse came off next, below which her gown was remarkably dry, save for the hem. Even so, she felt chilled to the bone, most likely from the damp. It would be good to enjoy the warmth of a bath.

Crossing to the window, she stared out at the pouring rain as she waited for the servants to arrive with her tub and water. It looked like the wind had picked up, tugging as it was on treetops and hedges.

Lucien had certainly made the right decision stopping here. She glanced toward the far wall, her heartbeat picking up at the thought of him there, just beyond her vision. He'd been wetter than her, or so he had seemed, and she couldn't resist wondering what he was doing. Was he standing by the window too? And if he was, what was he wearing? Surely he'd taken off his greatcoat by now. But what of his jacket . . . his waistcoat . . . his shirt . . . ?

A knock sounded and Katherine's heart leapt. Heavens! What inappropriate thoughts she was having lately. "Come in!"

Four maids appeared, two carrying a tub while the others brought pails of steaming water. Behind them followed a young boy of roughly fifteen years, with tousled hair. Setting Katherine's valise just inside the door, he bowed awkwardly and took his leave. It took no more than five minutes for her bath to be ready, and as soon as she was alone again, she wasted no time in removing the rest of her clothing and slipping into the welcoming heat of the water. Leaning back, she reached for the soap and proceeded to wash herself, then she closed her eyes and allowed herself a moment to simply enjoy being soothed.

A thud sounded, and her eyes snapped open. She stared at the wall, certain that it had come from the other side of it—Lucien's side. Whatever was he doing? She strained to hear more. Voices could now be heard, accompanied by what sounded like a rush of water. Settling back, Katherine smiled. His bath was being readied. There were footsteps, a few more voices, and then the distinct closing of a door—his door. Silence reigned for what seemed an eternity, and Katherine realized that she was holding her breath. What had the world come to that she should find herself so anxious to know his every movement? It wasn't reasonable in the least.

There was another thud, this time dimmer than the first. It was followed swiftly by yet another. If Katherine was to make a guess, she'd say he'd just thrown two heavy objects across the room. Books came to mind first, for the sound was not dissimilar to what she imagined a leather-bound novel would produce. No, that made no sense. He was preparing for his bath, after all, which meant he'd likely removed his boots and tossed them aside.

Sucking in a breath, she carefully listened anew. Curled around the edge of the tub, her fingers held on tight, as if she feared she might slip beneath the surface and drown if she dared to let go. Try as she might, she heard nothing else and swiftly admonished herself for prying. What business was it of hers if Lucien was getting undressed and climbing naked into a tub of steaming hot water? She groaned, wondering briefly if her soul was beyond saving. This should *not* have been happening!

Rising, she reached for a towel, swiftly patted herself dry and stepped out onto the hardwood planking, her feet leaving wet prints behind her as she moved about. This was all his fault, she decided. *Annoying man!* In the space of four days he'd managed to turn her insides to goo. With no more than a glance in her direction she was ready to throw herself at him, to crawl all over him and make a complete cake of herself in the process, no doubt. It had never been like this between them, yet he'd confessed a desire to kiss her for years. Blast him, but he'd made it impossible for her to think straight with his sudden advances bowling her over with surprise. She was not prepared for it, yet she wanted him to hold her again as he'd done back at Cresthaven . . . to kiss her with abandon as he'd done in the carriage. Lord, it had felt so incredibly good.

Again she cursed, this time more fiercely as she tore open her bag and snatched up a clean gown, even more annoyed when she found herself wondering if Lucien would approve. Damn, he'd made a mess of it all, and she had every intention of telling him so over dinner. And then she'd tell him that this had gone far enough—that they couldn't possibly go on like this unless he wished for her to drive herself mad. Yes, his advances had to stop . . . but not until he followed through on that promise of his to kiss her. Again.

Her heartbeat quickened, and she allowed her head to fall into her hands. Oh, what was the use of resisting when she wanted to do anything but? Looking over her shoulder, her eyes scanned the back of her thigh, sobering her and strengthening her resolve. She had a very good reason to resist temptation, she reminded herself. And if she was to avoid further heartache, then she'd be wise not to forget it.

Climbing out of his bath, Lucien dried himself off and strode across the room, comfortable with his own nudity and not in the least bit troubled by the arousal that showed. The warm water had done little to cool his desire for Katherine. She'd heated his blood with that sharp-witted tongue of hers, the hint of amusement forever on her lips and the occasional shy glance from beneath her thick black lashes.

When she'd asked about her clothing, he'd been half tempted to tell her not to trouble herself on that score—that he'd just as happily see her dressed in nothing at all—but he'd stopped himself, deciding that saying as much would be taking his advances a step too far. He was a gentleman, after all—surely he could muster a bit more flair.

Still, the thought of her naked curves stretched out in a tub of hot water no more than ten yards away at most had only served to increase the lust he'd felt for her in the carriage. By God, he'd actually kissed her! He wasn't sure if he ought to regret it, considering how promptly she'd pushed him away, but what he'd told her was true—she'd responded to him, and her doing so had heightened his longing for her like nothing else possibly could have. She wanted him, even if she was too confused, uncertain or scared to admit it. And she *was* scared—he'd seen it in her eyes.

Donning a crisp white shirt, a fresh pair of breeches and a dry pair of socks, Lucien pulled on the boots he'd tossed across the floor earlier, slipped into a cream-colored waistcoat and put on his navy blue jacket before stepping out into the hallway, where he almost collided with Katherine. "I beg your pardon," he said, liking the low timbre of his own voice. It sounded both masculine and confident. Confidence was good, even though he secretly felt like a young lad about to ask a girl to dance for the very first time.

"Lucien, I . . ."

She was breathless, and he decided that this could only be a good thing. "Was your bath to your liking?" he asked.

To his surprise, her cheeks flushed a delightful shade of pink. She swallowed, looked away and eventually said, "Very much so." She bit her lip for a moment before saying, "And err . . . how was your bath? Also agreeable, I hope?"

"Oh, indeed it was." He stared at her until she

brought her eyes back to his, then he held them for a beat and smiled, offering her his arm as he did so. "Shall we?"

She appeared momentarily flustered, but then she straightened herself, squared her shoulders and gave him a curt nod. "Certainly. In fact, I've been thinking of the best way in which to discourage you."

"Discourage me from what?" he asked, loving the way in which she ground her teeth and rolled her eyes. She was charming even when she was vexed. Well, he'd clearly put her out of sorts, for which he silently commended himself most highly.

"You know from what, you scoundrel," she muttered as they approached the stairs. She smiled, dazzling him with her beauty. "But fear not, for I do believe that I can be just as cunning as you. I've decided to have onions for supper."

Lucien barked with laughter. "Well, you really are determined to put me off, aren't you, Kate?"

"Not especially, but you know how competitive I've always been."

"Then perhaps I ought to kiss you now, before you have your meal." Grabbing her wrist, he spun her sideways until she was backed up against the wall of the corridor with his hands braced on either side of her. He leaned in, inhaling the sweetness of her scent, and her breath quivered—he both heard and felt it. "Temptress," he murmured in her ear.

"I . . . I don't know what you mean."

"Oh, but I believe you do, Kate. Indeed, you've been subtle in your suggestiveness, but don't think I haven't noticed that flirtatious look in your eyes, the occasional touch when no touch was needed or that slight display of your ankles yesterday."

"What exactly are you saying?"

He leaned back. "I think you know. Granted, it took a while before I was sure, but I daresay it's quite clear that you're hoping to seduce me, though I've yet to determine if this is a deliberate effort on your part or merely a reaction to my irresistible charm."

Her eyes were wider than he'd ever seen them before. "Why . . . you . . . ugh!" Giving him a push, she moved past him and started down the stairs.

He hurried after her. "Truth be told, I have to say I rather like the idea."

"Whatever is happening between us," she said, "whatever might *yet* happen . . . kisses are one thing. What concerns me is what they may lead to."

So she was worried about the lovemaking, even as her body practically begged for it? Hopefully he would soon be able to ease her concerns on that score. They arrived in the foyer, and he offered her his arm.

"Kate," he said as he led her through to the dining room and across to a corner where a table had been prepared for two. "There is so much pleasure to be had if you'll only allow me to show you."

"I won't be your mistress," she told him bluntly.

"I wasn't suggesting you would," he whispered as he pulled out a chair for her. She seated herself, and he lowered his lips to her ear. "Marriage, on the other hand . . . any chance you've changed your position on that?"

She looked at him then, her eyes narrowing ever so slightly while her fingers toyed with the napkin that lay beside her knife. "Lucien . . . ," she began, "are you—"

"Would ye care for some wine?" a waitress asked, materializing at the side of the table.

Katherine bit her lip and Lucien clenched his jaw.

Of all the damnable moments to be interrupted. He wanted to know what Katherine was going to say, blast it all! "Certainly," Lucien replied.

"I'll bring a decanter, then. As for your meal, we've roast chicken with potatoes and herbs or mutton stew with some bread on the side."

"I'll have the chicken," Katherine said, and Lucien seconded that choice.

As soon as the waitress was gone, he leaned forward and crossed his arms on the table. "You were saying?"

Katherine scrunched her mouth, as if she regretted what she'd been about to ask him. She probably hoped that the waitress's arrival would have made him forget that she hadn't finished her sentence. He wouldn't allow her to withdraw her question, though, and continued gazing at her until she eventually pushed out a deep breath. "I was merely wondering if . . . if you're attempting to court me."

"Whatever gave you that idea? Surely not my mention of marriage?" His lips quivered, but he couldn't laugh. Not now.

"Please don't mock me," she said, the vulnerability in her voice going straight to his heart. "I couldn't bear it—not from you."

The pain he'd caught in her eyes earlier had returned, filling Lucien with a keen desire to wrap his arms around her and hold her close. He wanted to protect her, to keep her safe from harm and from whatever fears haunted her. "Forgive me, but I thought I'd made my intentions clear."

The hint of a smile played about her lips. "Oh, in a manner of speaking you have, very much so."

"I don't follow."

"You've admitted to flirting with Lady Julie in

order to draw my attention, leaving me with no choice but to wonder what else you might have said or done with that specific purpose in mind." Her cheeks turned crimson and she lowered her voice to a whisper. "You've also kissed me and promise to do so again, but that is not courtship, Lucien, not even if marriage is your final goal. There is nothing romantic about it—just bull-headed stubbornness on your part, especially when I've told you repeatedly that I won't remarry."

"You haven't said so today," he said, attempting to make her smile. She did not, and he knew there was no getting around the issue this time. He had to confront her. "Tell me why," he said.

"I beg your pardon?"

"You say you do not wish to remarry, but you haven't once offered me a good reason, so tell me now—why won't you even consider it?" His words were curter than he'd intended, but he was becoming increasingly annoyed by her dismissal when it was clear that she was fighting both of their desires, not to mention that he'd risked his heart by kissing her earlier and she was not being the least bit gentle with it.

The waitress returned with their wine, poured them each a glass and sauntered off after announcing that their food was on its way.

Katherine's breath was coming fast, Lucien noticed. The conversation was distressing her. "It isn't something I wish to discuss," she finally said.

"Not even with me?" Reaching out, he placed his hand over hers. "You used to trust me."

Katherine looked down at the hand that touched her own. How much larger it was. She didn't pull away. Had no desire to. Instead, she felt comforted. Lucien cared for her, and she realized then with startling clarity that he would never hurt her the way Charles had done. "I still do," she whispered, "and one day, I will confide in you, just not today. Please, let us enjoy each other's company the way we used to."

"I don't think anything will ever be as it used to between us, Kate." His eyes searched hers. "I've kept my feelings at bay for so long. Now that they're finally out in the open, I cannot possibly deny them."

"I just wish you wouldn't be quite so pushy," she said, annoyed with herself for sounding so churlish and with him for making her so. She took a deep breath. If he could be brave, then so could she. "I'm not enjoying this uneasiness between us. I feel uncomfortable, confused and completely out of control."

"I think that's a good thing," he said, his mouth curving slightly.

She snorted. "Do you really?"

"It can only mean that you're affected by my incredibly masculine presence."

He waggled his eyebrows, and Katherine almost choked on her wine as she laughed in response. "Oh yes, I'm sure that must be it."

"Are you still wondering about that kiss I promised you?" He studied her, and as he did, she felt herself grow warm. "Judging from your delightful hue, I can see that you are. Well, the day is almost over, so it won't be long now."

"You see! That's exactly what I mean!" Lucien stared at her blankly. Clearly he didn't understand her frustration. "You return unexpectedly, dance with me unexpectedly, kiss me unexpectedly and then promise to do so again, all in the space of four days. The relationship we've had with each other for the past twenty-four years has been turned completely on its head. I don't know where I stand with you anymore or what I am to think. It's very distressing."

The waitress returned and placed a plate before each of them. "Would ye care for anything else, my lord? My lady?"

"Not right now," Lucien said, waving her off. "Thank you."

Stabbing her chicken, Katherine began cutting it into tiny pieces, conscious that Lucien was watching her with raised eyebrows.

"You just don't want to consider that you actually like me . . . in that way," he said as he sliced a piece of his own chicken and stuck it in his mouth. "The sooner you accept that you do, the easier this will be for you."

Katherine glared at him. He was the very personification of male arrogance at the moment. "I ought to call the waitress back," she muttered. "I forgot to order that onion."

Lucien watched her quietly while she ate. "You respond to me, Kate," he finally murmured. "You cannot deny it."

Her heart was pounding furiously in her chest. They were in public, for heaven's sake. Their subject of conversation was outrageously inappropriate, yet it was one of the things she'd always valued about their friendship—their mutual openness with each other. She shook her head, too embarrassed to meet his eyes but determined to be honest. "No, I cannot."

He didn't say anything further, but he did make a sound that sounded more like a deep growl than anything else. Katherine swallowed and focused on her food. She'd confessed the effect he had on her, and she knew that there would be no stopping him now. He would kiss her again soon, and as she hastily finished her meal, she couldn't help but look forward to it with great anticipation in spite of her fears. The only thing she had to do now was prevent them both from getting carried away.

Upon finishing their meal, Lucien pushed back his chair and went to Katherine. He offered her his arm, which she accepted. The tension between them was tighter than it had ever been before. She'd admitted that she was not unaffected by him. He'd known this already, of course, but having her confirm it had been a boost to his ego—the encouragement he'd needed to continue his pursuit. But she'd made a valid point. If he was trying to court her, then he was doing so in a very primal manner and without the least bit of romance.

With her hand tucked away in the crook of his elbow, he guided her out of the dining room and toward the stairs. He wanted her—desperately so— but now was not the time for that. She was wary and fearful, and he would be wise to restrain himself or run the risk of losing her trust. Leading her to her bedroom door, he stood aside and allowed her to enter. He made no attempt to follow. "If you wish to invite me in," he said, "I will kiss you, but I promise that I won't attempt to do anything else. It's your choice."

Her breath shuddered a little as she looked up at him with big round eyes, the green in them bright and filled with longing. Stepping back, she opened the door a little wider. "You've had me rattled all day with the anticipation of it, wondering when and where you'd make good on your word. I do believe I must accept—for the sake of my nerves."

Grinning, Lucien offered her a bow, followed her

into the room and closed the door behind him. He leaned against it as he studied her. She hadn't moved away, and if he reached out his hand, he would be able to grab her by the wrist. Instead, he straightened himself and moved toward her, his eyes on hers, and then on her mouth. Her lips were a deep rose, full and ripe for kissing. His gaze slid lower, to the swell of her breasts, the skin there glowing in the light of an oil lamp that sat on the dresser. Her breath was coming hard, her hands clenched stiffly at her sides. She was nervous—even frightened perhaps. What she probably didn't realize was that so was he.

Raising his hand, he laid his palm against the curve of her cheek. She shivered a little and he stepped closer still, his arms embracing her as he sighed deeply with contentment. Her arms came hesitantly about his waist. By God, it felt good to be held by her. He wanted more—indeed, he longed to tear her gown from her body so he could admire her figure. It would have to wait however. For now, he simply tilted her head with his hand, his thumb brushing her velvety-soft skin as he did so. She closed her eyes and he leaned closer, carefully lowering his lips over hers. So plush.

He placed one hand on her waist and pulled her against him, her breasts flattening against his chest as she sucked in a breath. She steadied herself and tightened her hold on him, her hands splaying across his back in the most sensational way imaginable. He was hot and he was hard, but the last thing he wanted was to frighten her. So he nibbled her lip hesitantly and ran the tip of his tongue across the edge of it. Sighing with pleasure, she gradually parted for him.

Against his chest he could feel the furious beat of her heart as he swept inside her mouth, his tongue meeting hers, coaxing it to follow his lead. She did, her skill increasing with every stroke until she was every bit the passionate woman he'd always suspected her to be, her fingers clutching at the fabric of his jacket as if she hoped to somehow pull him closer. He knew how she felt—this desire to be as one—for he felt it too. She wasn't ready, though, and he'd promised himself not to rush into anything that either of them might regret in the morning.

With pained reluctance, he reached for her hands and plied them away from him, then took a retreating step backward. Her cheeks were flushed, her lips swollen and her eyes dazed. "I will bid you good night now," he said, backing away toward the door. The quicker he left, the less likely he'd be to change his mind and do something stupid. "Sleep well."

"Th-thank you. You too." She touched the tips of her fingers to her lips, her eyes not leaving him for a second. It was almost as if she'd just made a confounding conclusion.

Whatever it might be, Lucien hoped it was in his favor. He opened the door, bowed toward her and made his escape, closing the door firmly behind him as he did so. For a moment he just stood there in the dark corridor, his feet rooted to the floorboards. That kiss had been magnificent—indeed, it had been so much more. It had been a silent exchange of emotion, and his heart soared, for he knew the secret of her heart now. She wanted him just as much as he wanted her. He stared at her door for a moment and seriously considered storming back inside and tossing her on the bed.

With a groan, he spun on his heels and crossed to his own room.

Chapter 11

"Where are we going?" Katherine asked as they rolled into London the following day and the carriage continued past Crossby House.

"To Patricia's," Lucien said. Katherine had always gotten on well with his sister, most probably because they were close in age. "You'll be safe there while I pay a visit to Riley's."

"You don't think she'll mind?" Katherine asked him skeptically. "Your sister is expecting her third child, Lucien. I imagine the last thing she needs right now is to entertain an unexpected guest."

"I'm sure she'll appreciate the company, not to mention that I'm rather looking forward to seeing her again after all this time. Besides, I'll return soon enough, and then we can continue on our way."

"Whereto, if you don't mind me asking."

"Why, to Roxberry House, of course," he said, as if it had been no less proper than taking her for a stroll in the park.

Katherine stared at him. "You cannot be serious!"

It was difficult not to laugh as understanding flashed across her face, stirring a blush in her cheeks.

Oh, fear might urge her to push him away, but Lucien now knew that everything he'd ever dreamed of could be his, provided he went about obtaining it in the right way. His gaze fell to the lips he'd so recently kissed. God, she'd felt good in his arms—better than he could ever have imagined, and so willing . . . so responsive and bold.

He pondered the way in which she'd retreated from him in the carriage the day before. One moment she'd been lost in passion; the next, it was as if a wall of ice had slid into place. What had prompted such a sharp reaction? His words? *"You've no idea how many times I've thought of peeling away your gown so I could kiss the skin beneath."* Lucien frowned as he focused on what had happened. She'd grown rigid—distant—her eyes brimming with pain that courted terror, like a rabbit caught in a trap with dogs approaching. He hadn't mentioned undressing her since, and she'd been more willing when he'd kissed her the second time—lost in the moment.

"On the contrary," he said, "I've never been more serious about anything else in my life."

"But it's preposterous, Lucien." Her eyes darted about. "Don't you see how scandalous it would be? Why, there are many who are already of the opinion that . . . that . . ."

"That what?" he asked smoothly. He could see her struggling with the words as if she wanted to speak them but couldn't quite get herself to do so.

Averting her gaze, she said, "That we are lovers."

"Ah, but we are not, are we, Kate?"

Her eyes shot toward his. "Certainly not!" Her blush deepened. "However, if I cross the threshold of your home unchaperoned and it becomes known that

I spent the night, there's no telling what the gossips will say. I don't want scandal to tarnish my name or Sophia's, Lucien. Please try to understand."

He studied her closely, noting how severely her worries marred her features. Come what may, he had to do everything in his power to protect her. "Your life is in danger, Kate. For that reason alone I've no intention of letting you out of my sight. You will stay at my home, and since you're a widow, whatever scandal may erupt will be minimal. Besides, I do not plan on you arriving through the front door for all the world to see. You will enter the house at the back entrance, dressed in maid's clothing, and with a hood pulled over your head. Provided my servants keep quiet, which I daresay they will if they wish to receive the bonus I intend to give them upon your departure, nobody will be the wiser."

"Good Lord," Katherine murmured. "You've really given this a lot of thought, haven't you?"

"Let's just say that I am not taking the matter lightly."

With her eyes resting solemnly upon him, Lucien registered the moment when resignation overcame her. "Very well, but only if you promise me that you will make no attempt to kiss me while I am there."

Lucien grinned. "My dear, I could never do that. Especially not when I'm hoping to do a whole lot more!"

The carriage came to a halt outside his sister's town house and Lucien stepped out, politely assisting a very flustered-looking Katherine so she could do the same. He'd taken a leap, aware of what he'd been risking, but he'd had no choice in the matter. It wasn't possible for him to go on with his life without at least trying to win the hand of the woman he loved, and he'd grown weary of being cautious when instinct was telling him to be bold.

He sighed as they walked up the front steps in awkward silence. Perhaps he should have told her what was in his heart—perhaps then she'd know he'd never judge or accuse her, no matter what might have happened to put her in the state of despair she was in. He rapped on the door with the knocker.

"Welcome, my lord," the butler said as the door swung open. "What a pleasure it is to see you again."

"Thank you, Travis. It's good to be back. Is my sister at home?"

"She is indeed, my lord." Once they'd divested themselves of their outdoor garments, the butler said, "If you'll please follow me, I'll show you through to the parlor and let her know that you are here."

It took no more than five minutes before Patricia entered the room, her arms enfolding Lucien in a tight, if not somewhat difficult, embrace, given her condition. She smiled broadly. "I've missed you terribly, you know," she said, "but I'm so glad to see that you've brought Katherine along with you. She and I have so much to discuss."

"We do?" Katherine asked, looking mildly surprised.

"Certainly," Patricia said. "It's been far too long since we last spoke, and now that Lucien has returned, I daresay we've a good topic to start on. Some tea?"

Lucien chuckled as they all took a seat, his sister already pouring from the teapot that one of her maids had brought in. Katherine's composure was most assuredly being tested today. She looked as if she'd happily dive under the Persian carpet in order to escape. "Thank you," she said instead.

"As a matter of fact, I was hoping that you might be able to entertain Katherine for a couple of hours while I run an errand," Lucien said. "I know it's a bit late in the day, but there's an issue I wish to resolve with the utmost haste."

"Oh dear," Patricia said. "That sounds terribly serious. Any chance you're willing to tell me what's going on?"

Lucien told her while she held silent, her eyes flickering with emotion as he spoke.

"Right," she said as soon as he was finished. She looked at Katherine. "My brother's correct, you know. The first place these people will look for you is in your own home. I'd suggest you stay here if it weren't for the children. I'm sorry, but I cannot risk putting them in danger."

"No, of course not," Katherine said. "I would never even have thought to ask it of you."

Patricia smiled. "However, if you do as Lucien suggests, then there's really no reason why anyone should discover your whereabouts, not to mention that I have every confidence that he will guard you with his life. Really, Katherine, you couldn't be in safer hands."

With a mere nod, Katherine raised her cup to her lips and took a sip of her tea. Was there a trace of embarrassment to her composure? Concealing his chuckle with a muted cough, Lucien sent a silent word of thanks to his sister and decided he'd best be on his way if he was to achieve anything before nightfall. Rising, he bid the ladies a good afternoon, offering each of them a polite bow.

"If you'd like Gray to accompany you, he's over at White's," Patricia said, her smile warm as she spoke of her husband. Lucien nodded his thanks and assured his sister once again that he would soon be back. As soon as the door closed behind him, Patricia turned to Katherine wide-eyed. "Heavens! What on earth has transpired between the two of you?"

"I don't know what you mean," Katherine hedged, hoping to avoid the subject she knew Patricia was eager to broach.

"Is that so? Then perhaps you'd care to explain why you currently share the same hue as those roses over there and why you scarcely dared look at him the entire time he was here."

Blast Patricia for being so astute. Well then, no point in beating about the bush so to speak, no matter how loathe Katherine was to be candid. Bracing herself, she said, "He kissed me yesterday—once in the carriage, and once at the inn at which we were forced to stay on behalf of the weather."

Clapping her hands together with obvious delight, Patricia squealed. "Finally! Have you any idea how long I've been hoping for this?"

Katherine shook her head, dumbfounded by Patricia's joy.

"Years, Katherine. Why, the two of you are obviously perfect for each other."

"We are?"

"Of course! But then Lucien went to war, you married Lord Crossby, and well . . . I doubted it would ever work out. I'm so pleased to know that it finally has."

Katherine frowned. "Actually, it hasn't really."

"What do you mean?"

Patricia's face fell, leaving Katherine with the unexpected urge to tell her that she and Lucien were practically on the way to the altar. She couldn't be dishonest, though, and found herself saying, "Well, I'm not so sure it's what I want." She sighed. "No, that's not entirely true. Since seeing Lucien a few days ago for the first time in four years, I've started to think of him in a new light. It's very peculiar and rather uncomfortable really. In fact, as reluctant as I am to admit it, I began hoping that he would kiss me—strange as that was— but then he did, and now . . . oh, I no longer know my own mind."

"You're clearly conflicted," Patricia mused. "Is it because you're afraid that if you don't suit—though I'm positive you will—things will be awkward between you? That you can no longer be friends?"

"That's part of it, I suppose."

"And the other part?"

Meeting Patricia's gaze, Katherine took a shuddering breath. She'd never told anyone of the pain that splintered her heart, yet sitting there in Patricia's parlor with a cup of tea, she felt an overwhelming urge to confide the truth to her old friend. "If you must know, I'm afraid he'll find me wanting, and I daresay I would not be able to bear it."

There was a brief silence, then the rustle of fabric as Patricia rose from her seat and came to sit next to Katherine on the sofa. She took Katherine's hand in her own and said, ever so gently and with the utmost kindness, "My dear, it's no secret that Lucien is exceedingly fond of you. He always has been, even though I'm not so sure he realizes how aware everyone in his family is of his feelings." She chuckled, gave Katherine's hand a gentle squeeze and said, "What reason would you possibly have to believe that he would think you anything less than perfect?"

Katherine felt her lower lip begin to wobble as her eyes began to burn. She would *not* make a spectacle of herself by crying, yet it was becoming awfully hard to stop the tears that threatened as her throat began to ache. "Crossby didn't approve of me," she whispered.

"But he was so eager to marry you . . . he seemed so smitten."

"Everything changed on our wedding night," Katherine confessed as she wiped away a tear with the back of her hand. "*He* changed. However attentive he'd been before, he grew suddenly cold toward me, and when we . . ." She drew a ragged breath. "He told me I repelled him, that . . . that looking at me made him feel ill. Of course the drinking didn't help, and neither did the opium. In fact, he was generally in a foul mood, and for whatever reason, he seemed to enjoy taking it out on me."

"I'm so sorry," Patricia whispered as she drew Katherine into her arms, "so very sorry indeed. I had no idea."

"I did my best to hide it," Katherine said, accepting the handkerchief that Patricia offered, "though I'm not sure I would have been able to continue doing so forever."

Shaking her head, Patricia rose and walked across to the sideboard, where she proceeded to pour a brandy. "I can't even imagine what it must have been like for you," she said as she handed the tumbler to Katherine. "You should drink this—it will help soothe you."

Katherine gave her a feeble smile. "Thank you."

Resuming her seat, Patricia waited while Katherine took a sip of her drink. Then Patricia said, "It's not my place to tell Lucien what you've just confided, but I do think that *you* ought to. You know what you want in your heart, but as long as you allow your past to fuel your fears, you'll never be truly happy."

"What if—"

"You can build your whole life on 'what if's' and grow old with regret in the process. You have a chance to make things work between you, Katherine," Patricia said as she smiled with devilish cheekiness. "More so now that you'll be sleeping scandalously close to each other."

"Patricia!"

Lucien's sister chuckled. "Don't tell me you're not secretly looking forward to living beneath the same roof as him."

The room felt overwhelmingly warm all of a sudden. "I must admit that I find it both terrifying and thrilling."

Patricia nodded knowingly. "Consider this— Lucien kissed you because he has every intention of marrying you. If there's one thing I know about my brother, it's that he would never jeopardize his relationship with you for anything less."

"**D**id you find Donovan?" Katherine asked Lucien as they headed over to Roxberry House later that day. After saying good-bye to Patricia and thanking her for her hospitality, Lucien had led Katherine out through the back of the house and helped her into a waiting hackney.

"Not yet," he told her grimly. "I inquired after him at Riley's—said I needed help with a debt. The consensus among the employees and the patrons was unanimous however. Nobody knew of a man by that name."

"And do you believe them?" Katherine asked.

"I confess I'm not sure what to believe anymore,

but I did tell them that I intend to return tomorrow in case someone would like to convey a message to him. If Lady Trapleigh has been honest with us, Donovan ought to thrill at the opportunity of getting another aristocrat under his thumb."

When they arrived at Roxberry House, Katherine gave Lucien a determined look before pulling the hood of her cloak over her head. "I'll see you inside," she said as she alighted from the carriage. She then stepped brusquely forward and gave the wooden door leading into the mews a loud rap. A moment passed before one of the grooms appeared. "Yes?" he inquired.

"I'm the new housemaid," she said.

With a curt nod, he opened the door just enough to grant her entry, then slipped the bolt back into place the moment she was through. Hooves clattered along the cobbles on the opposite side as the hackney continued on its way. It would make its way through a few more streets before returning to the front door, where Lucien would enter, unaccompanied.

"You must be the lady we were told to expect," an elderly woman said as Katherine stepped inside the lobby and pulled the door shut behind her. "I'm Mrs. Ellis, the housekeeper."

"Pleased to meet you," Katherine said, smiling politely.

"Oh, I can assure you that the pleasure is entirely mine. Now, if you will please follow me, my lady, I'll take you upstairs to the parlor. According to the missive I received from his lordship, I do believe he'll be arriving at any moment and will wish to see you." Leading the way down a long corridor while Katherine followed, Mrs. Ellis spoke over her shoulder. "There are also a few details that must be addressed, as I'm sure you are aware. Mr. Parker, the butler, will be joining us, since he has a few concerns of his own that he'd like to bring to his lordship's attention."

Katherine could only imagine. Lucien might have been the master of the house, but that didn't mean the staff would have been pleased with the idea of an unmarried lady moving in. Her suspicion was quickly confirmed when Parker met her in the foyer. He nodded stiffly but didn't smile—not that butlers were particularly prone to smiling, but still. . . . He looked positively acerbic. "The curtains have been drawn in the parlor, Mrs. Ellis. You may show her ladyship in," he said.

No other words were exchanged as Katherine quietly followed the housekeeper into an elegant room set in beige and burgundy tones. She'd been here before, accompanied by her parents years ago, when Lucien's father had still been alive. It was not very different from what it had looked like back then, with Gauss's *Disquisitiones Arithmeticae* still visible on the bookstand.

Crossing the floor to a chair upholstered in a beautiful striped silk, Katherine took a seat while Mrs. Ellis remained standing by the door. The clock ticked away on the mantelpiece. Reaching for the teapot that sat on a tray before her, Katherine poured herself a cup, not because she particularly felt like having tea but because she longed for something to busy herself with until Lucien arrived.

The sound of a door opening and closing, followed by voices in the hallway beyond, had her straightening. She set down her cup just as Lucien strolled into the room looking every bit the charming gentleman and with the hint of a smile about his lips. Katherine sighed with relief, thankful that he was finally there to help her through the awkward business of dealing with his servants.

"You look as lovely as ever," he said with a wink in Katherine's direction—a gesture that made her insides squirm. "Lady Crossby will be staying here at Roxberry House as our guest," he continued, addressing Mrs. Ellis and Parker. "She is to be treated in the manner her station requires, and if she gives you an order, you are to follow it without complaint." Parker was looking increasingly green about the gills, but he said nothing. "Furthermore, nobody outside this house is allowed to know of her presence. There will be a twenty-pound bonus for each member of staff capable of keeping her visit here a secret, but, should anyone happen to let it slip that Lady Crossby is here, they will be sacked without notice or reference. Is that understood?"

"Yes, my lord," Mrs. Ellis and Parker spoke in unison.

Lucien studied his employees in turn and with a good deal of gravity before leaning back on his heels and saying, "Very well, then. Do you have any questions?"

"If I may," Mrs. Ellis began, "I was wondering which bedchamber I should direct her ladyship to."

"You may put her in the one adjoining my own," Lucien said without preamble.

Katherine squeezed her eyes shut. She'd never been quite so humiliated before in her life. Though she would not argue in front of the servants, she had every intention of berating Lucien for his thoughtlessness. She opened her eyes, surprised by the bland expressions on the butler's and housekeeper's faces. If they objected to the idea of an unmarried woman sleeping in the bedroom that would one day belong to their master's wife, it did not show.

"And regarding her ladyship's clothing?" Mrs. Ellis asked. "Will she continue to dress like a servant, or do you have something more appropriate in mind?"

"At present, the less attention we draw to her presence here, the better. Just so you understand the severity of the situation, you ought to know that Lady Crossby's life is at risk. Two attempts have already been made, and I'll be damned if there's to be a third. For now, I have hired a new housemaid. That is all anyone outside this house needs to know."

"You have our full support in the matter, my lord," Parker said. "We'll do everything in our power to keep her ladyship safe from harm, isn't that so, Mrs. Ellis?"

"Absolutely," Mrs. Ellis concurred.

"And in the event that I am not at home, Lady Crossby will remain upstairs and out of sight," Lucien said as he looked at Katherine. "Agreed?"

Deciding that arguing would serve no purpose, Katherine nodded. No matter how much she dreaded being confined to her bedroom, she knew that Lucien was only trying to protect her.

"If that is all, I should like to go and talk to the rest of the staff," the butler said as he turned to Mrs. Ellis. "Shall I ask Edith to go upstairs and ready her ladyship's room?"

"That would be most helpful, Mr. Parker. Thank you," Mrs. Ellis replied.

The servants exited the parlor, and Lucien approached Katherine, claiming the seat next to her. "I do believe I've ruffled their feathers," he said, meeting her gaze.

"What did you expect? That they would nod their

heads demurely as if you're not courting vast amounts of scandal by bringing me here? Speaking of which, was it really necessary of you to insist I sleep in the room adjoining your own? Surely there must be other rooms available."

"Of course there are." His voice was completely serious. "There are three reasons why I want you to stay in that room, Kate. First, it faces away from the street, which makes it more difficult for someone to discover that I have a secret houseguest. Second, if a potential assassin were to make it all the way upstairs, which is of course unlikely, then I'll be close at hand."

"And the third reason?" Katherine asked when Lucien failed to continue.

His eyes swept over her, brightening as a smile captured his lips. "I do believe you can figure that out on your own."

"Good heavens!" She sounded breathless—like a ninny fresh out of the schoolroom. Swallowing her embarrassment, she squared her shoulders and stared right back at him. Whatever game he was playing at, she wasn't having much fun with it. "Is this an elaborate scheme of yours, Lucien? Why, if I didn't know any better, I'd think you concocted the whole thing so you could lure me into your bed—'Hurry, Kate, you'd best get under the covers so I can protect you.'" She rolled her eyes while Lucien barked with laughter. "Honestly, do you think me a fool? Whatever thoughts of seduction you have, I suggest you keep them to yourself, and if you do make any attempt at climbing into my bed, I'll scream—make no mistake about it."

Stifling his laughter, Lucien nodded. "Very well. Although . . ."

"Yes?" she asked hesitantly.

"In case you change your mind, I'll have no qualms about making you scream."

Flames burst to life within her. "What's happened to you, Lucien? You were never so forward, yet in the course of two days you've not only kissed me but offered to take me to bed as well. It's most unsettling, and frankly, I wish you would stop."

"Do you?" The words were but a murmur, yet they hummed through her, stirring her awareness. She nodded, for she'd lost the ability to speak. With slow deliberation, he reached out and placed his hand upon hers. A jolt of tingling warmth swept through her. "Because if you ask me, you wanted me to kiss you not only at the inn but in the carriage as well, and when I finally did, you welcomed it." His words were soft and sensual, and no matter how much she longed to tell him it wasn't true, she could not bring herself to lie to him—not about something this important. Instead, she closed her eyes and prayed for him to distance himself from her. He raised her hand to his lips, kissing the surface before turning it over and scraping his teeth against the back of her wrist. She gasped quite helplessly as heat rushed between her thighs and her breasts began to swell against the tight muslin of her bodice. "All you have to do is ask, and the pleasure you seek can be yours."

"I don't . . . ," she rasped, tugging her hand away from his.

Leaning back, he rose to his feet with a chuckle. "Oh, but I think you do. Now come along and I'll show you to your room."

Chapter 12

Stepping out into the street the following morning, Lucien cursed his forwardness. What the bloody hell had he been thinking last night, talking to Katherine as if she'd been a common doxy? Certainly, she was a widow, but she was also a lady—one who, if her constant blushes and moments of shyness were anything to go on, was also quite inexperienced when it came to being romanced. How the devil such a thing was possible, Lucien couldn't fathom, yet he'd sensed that while he'd most assuredly affected her with his candor, he'd also succeeded in frightening her. Good heavens, but she'd barely stepped inside her bedroom before bidding him a hasty good night and shutting the door in his face.

Lucien grinned at the memory, for she'd apparently forgotten about the connecting door between their rooms and had practically leapt one foot in the air when he'd popped his head through and told her to sleep well.

"To White's, if you please," he told his driver as he climbed up into his landau. It was eleven o'clock and he was admittedly fleeing his own home, determined to be gone before Katherine emerged from the confines of her bedroom. Clearly, she was just as embarrassed as he after last night's exchange.

Settling back against the squabs, he stared out at the passing buildings. He had to get his head on straight and focus on the business regarding Donovan instead of chasing Katherine around like a lovesick pup. Christ, he was making a bumbling fool of himself and scaring her off in the process.

"Roxberry! What a pleasant surprise," the Earl of Laughton said, greeting Lucien upon his arrival. "It has been an age. My sincerest condolences on the loss of your brother and your father. They were good men, both of them."

"Thank you, Laughton. I appreciate you saying so. As you know, it takes a while to adjust," Lucien said, referring to the loss of the earl's own father many years ago.

"Indeed it does," Laughton replied.

They shared a moment of silence before Laughton broke it by saying, "Care to share a drink? I'm actually sitting just over there with Barrymore and Carlyle. You're welcome to join us if you'll only allow me to fetch the betting book. I was on my way to get it just now when you arrived."

Deciding that a brandy in good company was precisely what he needed, Lucien waited for his friend to return with the book in question, then accompanied him over to where the others were sitting. "So, what will you be betting on today?" he asked the three men as soon as the necessary pleasantries were out of the way.

"Funny you should ask," Barrymore said as he leafed through the pages. He set the book on the table and pushed it toward Lucien. "Take a look for yourself, old chap."

Glancing down, Lucien read the words on the page before him and frowned. "You can't be serious," he eventually said, looking up.

Barrymore shrugged. "Since you were seen waltzing with each other at the Kingsboroughs', you and Lady Crossby have been on everyone's lips. I can't tell you how many people hurried back to Town from that ball, determined to place their bets before it was too late. Some were sure you'd already proposed to her in secret."

"But that's preposterous!"

"Are you sure about that?" Carlyle asked him seriously, "because I'm planning to bet a thousand pounds on you and Lady Crossby tying the knot before the end of the Season."

"You have to admit, it does seem rather odd that you would appear so publically with her the moment she's out of mourning," Laughton added. "Are you telling us that there's nothing more than friendship between the two of you?"

"That's precisely what I'm telling you," Lucien said. At least that was all he was going to say on the matter at present.

"Perhaps so, but if it's all the same to you, I'm going to trust my instinct on this, and my instinct says otherwise," Carlyle said as he tossed back his drink. Leaning forward, he dipped the quill that Laughton had placed on the table into the accompanying inkwell and scribbled his name in the book. He then got up and said, "It was good seeing you all again. Especially you, Roxberry—it's been far too long. Regrettably, I have an appointment that I must keep, so I really must be off."

"Is it business or pleasure that's depriving us of your company?" Barrymore asked.

"Well, there's a striking young heiress who's willing to part with a Rembrandt, so it may prove a bit of both if all goes smoothly," Carlyle said as he thrust his hands into his pockets and leaned back on his heels with a broad smile.

Barrymore grinned. "I don't suppose you'd let me join you?"

"Not a chance," Carlyle told him. "But if you're still interested in the other lady we were discussing earlier, then I can tell you that she usually goes for a stroll in the park with her beagle around this hour."

"In that case, I must be off as well," Barrymore said, taking his leave along with Carlyle.

Lucien watched them go. "Care for a game of cards?" he asked Laughton.

"Certainly. But if I win, you'll have to tell me what's really going on between you and Lady Crossby. I could use the advantage."

"I'm afraid I'll only disappoint you then, for what I said before is true. She and I have no plans of marrying."

"Hmpf! More's the pity, if you ask me," Laughton said, reaching for a deck of cards and starting to shuffle. "I've always thought the two of you would be perfectly suited for each other."

Lucien winced. If only Katherine agreed. Somehow, he'd have to change her mind. "I don't suppose you've ever heard of a man by the name of Donovan?" he asked, deciding to change the topic of conversation. He needed to concentrate on why he'd really come here—to get answers.

Laughton shook his head. "Doesn't sound familiar. Why do you ask?"

"A friend of mine's in a bit of trouble," he lied, offering the story he'd fabricated on the way over. "After falling into debt, he went to Donovan for help, but apparently the man's unsatisfied with how fast my friend is able to pay him back—started issuing threats and so on. Anyway, I thought I'd try to locate the blighter myself—get the matter settled so my friend can relax." Lucien trumped one of Laughton's cards. "I wish he would have come to me first, but I believe he was too proud."

"Pride can certainly lead to a man's downfall," Laughton said. He frowned. "Surely your friend must know where to find him though?"

"Apparently, Donovan tends to find *him*, not the other way around, though he did mention seeing him at Riley's once or twice. I went over there yesterday to try and locate him, but everyone was very tight-lipped."

Laughton shook his head. "Sorry, I can't help you with that, I'm afraid. No reputable gentleman would ever set foot in a place like Riley's, no matter what." He gave Lucien a meaningful look.

They finished their game and Laughton took his leave with the excuse that his mother expected him to put in an appearance at her soiree later. "Best of luck with finding this Donovan fellow," he said to Lucien as they parted ways. "I hope your friend gets out of this mess quickly and trust that you will advise him to avoid such people in the future."

"Will do," Lucien said, rising to shake his friend's hand. He cursed himself as soon as he was once again alone. The lie had yielded no result, and he was no better off than he'd been when he'd arrived. Instead, he'd wasted two hours on meaningless small talk.

"**I** think you and I ought to have a little chat," a voice murmured just behind Lucien's left shoulder.

Spinning around, Lucien almost came nose to nose with a familiar face. "Starkly! What the devil?"

The corner of Starkly's mouth edged upward. "It's good to see you too, Roxberry. Now, if you will please follow me." With no other word, the earl walked off, leaving Lucien with little choice but to do as he'd asked.

"**I**s Lord Roxberry at home?" Katherine asked Mrs. Ellis when she finally managed to pull herself together and venture downstairs. After her conversation with Lucien last night, Katherine had lain awake for hours on end, contemplating Lucien's every word. As a result, she'd slept in and had (in the hope of avoiding Lucien for a little while yet) asked to have her breakfast delivered to her room. She'd taken her time with the meal, since she'd asked for the newspaper to be sent up along with it, and she savored the distraction that considering new investment opportunities offered.

"I'm afraid you just missed him, my lady. He's gone out," Mrs. Ellis informed her.

Katherine breathed a sigh of relief, thanked the housekeeper and made her way back upstairs, determined to follow Lucien's advice that she remain out of sight when he was not at home. Stepping onto the landing, she glanced right, toward the bedchamber where she'd spent her entire morning. The thought of returning there held little appeal, so she decided to go left instead, toward a spacious salon, perfect for entertaining informal visitors like close friends and family.

Venturing inside, she considered again the words

Lucien had spoken to her the previous evening. *"All you have to do is ask, and the pleasure you seek can be yours."* At the inn, he'd accused her of trying to seduce him, and he'd been right. Well, somewhat at least. Her main goal had been to uncover his intentions. Now that she knew what they were, she could scarcely form a coherent thought whenever he was near. But was this yearning he'd stirred within her so blatantly obvious? Was she really that transparent?

Trailing her fingers along the edge of a Hepplewhite cabinet, she let out a sigh. Of course she was, or Lucien would never have said such a thing—nor would he have risked the security of their friendship by kissing her in the carriage or continued in his pursuit of her at the inn. It was as if he could read her mind, but if that were the case, did he also know the depth of her fears?

Crossing to a piano that stood in one corner, Katherine seated herself on the bench and opened the cover. Should she even be afraid? This was Lucien, after all. She'd known him her whole life and trusted him more than she'd ever trusted anyone else. Her fingers skimmed across the keys, evoking a soft and languid melody. Her fears were likely unfounded when it came to Lucien. He would never want to hurt her, not deliberately at least. But what would happen if she took that leap, discarded her inhibitions and concerns and allowed him the right to undress her? There was always the risk that he wouldn't like what he saw, that he'd reject her just as Charles had done.

Her finger hit a wrong note. She blinked, steadied herself on a deep breath and resumed her playing. Lucien would certainly be more tactful about it but she would know that he found her wanting, and the pain that would bring—to be looked upon with distaste by someone so dear to her heart—would crush her.

"Lady Gray was just here, inquiring about you, my lady," Parker announced from the doorway.

Stopping in mid-tune, Katherine turned to face him.

"But since his lordship is not at home, I thought it too suspicious to invite her in," the butler added. "However, she did ask me to give you this."

Rising, Katherine went to retrieve the book that Parker was holding. "Thank you," she said. With a nod, the butler took his leave, and Katherine lowered her gaze to the book—*Emma*, by Jane Austen. She opened it and discovered a note:

> *Dear Katherine, I know how difficult it must be for you to be confined in this way, but it is necessary, though I shall miss your company today. The book is a gift, one I consider appropriate under the circumstances. I hope you will find it amusing and that you haven't yet read it. Until we meet again, your friend, Patricia.*

Katherine couldn't help but smile at the kindness as she walked across to an armchair, book in hand. She was determined to get started on it right away so she could discover what Patricia had meant by finding it appropriate.

Recalling the last conversation they'd had, Katherine couldn't help but wonder if the book might have something to do with her relationship with Lucien. Most likely, considering that Miss Austen's books were all terribly romantic. Katherine shook her head. Patricia knew of her reservations, yet she'd championed her brother, urging Katherine to offer him the same degree of honesty, insisting Lucien wouldn't hurt her.

But what if he did so unintentionally? Was that a risk Katherine was willing to take? Bowing her head, she stared down at *Emma,* now resting in her lap.

Lucien had known her since the day she was born. He'd watched her grow—had been her closest friend for so long. Didn't she owe him the truth?

Katherine frowned. Lucien had returned, and he'd done so with a clear purpose. Surely it couldn't have been easy for him to confess his true feelings for her, to risk their friendship in pursuit of something more. He'd taken a leap, no doubt fearing rejection, yet he'd been willing to suffer it if there was but a chance. And what had she done? She'd led him on, only to pull away, frightened of what he would think of her and doing to him exactly what she was so afraid he might do to her. She took a breath, her jumbled thoughts aligning until everything became clear. She loved him, and if Lucien was brave enough to take the leap, then she must be so as well, because the very last thing she wanted to do was break his heart.

"Are you seriously telling me that Lady Trapleigh was the one who fired the shot at the ball?" Starkly asked as he handed a brandy to Lucien.

"You sound surprised," Lucien said, accepting the drink.

Starkly's face was inscrutable. "I must confess that I am rather. I hadn't thought her capable of committing murder."

"Nor had I, but then again, she does have incentive." Lucien studied the earl for a moment, took a sip of his brandy and said, "Do I detect a degree of concern on your part?"

"Things aren't always what they seem, you know," Starkly said. "I think you ought to have a seat." He indicated a leather armchair. Lucien claimed it somewhat hesitantly, upon which Starkly sat down on a similar one, facing him. "I'm not sure if it's wise of me to tell you this, but considering your own involvement, I do believe you ought to know the truth. A lot has happened during your absence, and while I can't be sure of what Lady Crossby has shared with you, I do feel a strong obligation toward her."

"What do you mean?" Lucien asked, not liking the sound of that in the least, considering the earl's disreputable reputation.

"Crossby was my friend. Generally I would meet him in Town, but there was one time when I rode out to Cresthaven in regard to an issue that required my assistance. Unfortunately, he'd already had a glass of brandy too many by the time I arrived."

Lucien stiffened. "What are you trying to say, Starkly?"

The earl stared into his glass for a long moment. "I thought they were happy. At least it appeared that way on the few occasions I saw them together in public, but after returning from war, Crossby was often in his cups, and that was not all. He took a liking to opium as well."

"Good God!"

"Precisely." Starkly served Lucien an even stare. "Look, I tried to talk to him about it—convince him that he was heading down a dangerous path. Then, on the day I visited, I actually witnessed the effect his addiction was having not only on himself but on his wife as well."

"And you said nothing, I suppose?" Lucien glared at Starkly.

"You are wrong about that, Roxberry. Crossby may have been my friend, and as such, I attempted to help him, but I was not about to allow him the right to degrade Lady Crossby in my presence."

A cold shiver ran down Lucien's spine at the thought of what Katherine might have suffered. "What did you do?"

"It isn't looked kindly upon when a man interferes with another man's domestic affairs, but there is such a thing as right and wrong, and since my conscience wouldn't allow me to turn a blind eye, I threatened to call him out unless he mended his ways."

Lucien stared at him, stunned that a man he'd never liked and had always thought the worst of had acted so completely differently from what he would have expected. "Does Lady Crossby know about this?" he asked.

Starkly shook his head. "I believe she resents me for bearing witness to her humiliation, and for being the friend of a man I'm sure she must have despised."

"But surely he must have heeded your warning, or the two of you would have dueled."

"All I know is that he never gave me a reason to make good on my threat. Whenever he and Lady Crossby were seen together, they appeared no different than any other married couple, but there is no telling how they fared behind closed doors."

Lucien's jaw tightened. No wonder she had no interest in remarrying. Her experience with Crossby had put her off, and not without reason. Anger rose to his head in a crushing ball of heat. He had an urgent desire to hit something, or someone, for the distress that Katherine had been submitted to.

"I'd like to help her now if you'll allow it," Starkly was saying. "I find it curious that Lady Trapleigh is involved when . . . did she tell you why she did it?"

"She says a man named Donovan has taken her son and that he'll kill him if she doesn't kill Lady Crossby first. Funny thing is, I never would have guessed she had a child."

Starkly nodded. "She had him two years ago when she claimed to have gone to Scotland. He's being raised at an estate in the Lake District."

"You seem to know a lot about it," Lucien said, frowning. "Don't tell me the boy is yours."

"No, it's nothing like that." Starkly fell quiet for a moment. He took a sip of his brandy, looked Lucien squarely in the eye and said, "I've heard of this Donovan fellow before, but I've yet to come across him myself."

"Lady Trapleigh says he frequents Riley's. Whether she's right about that or not, I don't know, for when I went over there last night, nobody admitted to knowing a man by that name."

"In other words, either Lady Trapleigh is mistaken, or she's being dishonest."

"Or the people I asked were trying to protect their own skins."

"That's certainly another possibility." Starkly paused, took a sip of his drink and set the glass on the table. "You say you left Lady Trapleigh locked up in the butler's pantry at Cresthaven?"

"That's correct," Lucien confirmed.

"Is there any chance that she might escape? She's never been the trustworthy sort—always sneaking off to entertain one paramour or another even while she was married."

"I asked Lady Crossby's butler to send word if

anything strange or unusual were to happen, though I do believe he would do so anyway—he seems reliable enough."

"A wise decision nevertheless," Starkly said. "On a different note, I trust you're keeping Lady Crossby safe and . . . out of sight?"

"I'm not a fool," Lucien said.

"Of course not. I didn't mean to imply that you are." Leaning forward in his seat, Starkly gazed at Lucien. "She's a lovely woman who deserves to be happy . . . promise me you will protect her. Whoever we're up against is either extremely clever or unbelievably callous—perhaps both."

"I will protect her with my life if it comes to that," Lucien said, a little stunned by how much Katherine's well-being meant to this man and perhaps even a little affronted that Starkly would presume that he might fail in his duty toward Katherine.

Starkly nodded as he leaned back in his chair, the leather squeaking in response to his movement. "I'm quite familiar with Riley's by the way, in case you'd like me to accompany you on another visit to the establishment."

Lucien considered his offer. There was something appealing about not having to go back there again on his own, even if it did mean sharing Starkly's company for an extended period of time. Besides, if he did happen to find the man he sought, it would probably be best if he wasn't alone. "Thank you," he said. "I was actually planning to go back there this evening. You're welcome to join me."

Starkly smiled. "I think it best if I do. Considering what Donovan has done, he'll be lucky to escape you with his life—should you happen to find the man, that is. I'd hate to see you hanged when things between you and Lady Crossby are finally beginning to shape up."

Lucien snorted. "I wouldn't waste your money betting on that just yet, but if we can at least put her mind at ease by finding the man who's after her, then I'll be happy enough."

Chapter 13

Roused from her sleep by the sound of a door closing, Katherine sat up, her gaze going immediately to the book still clutched in her hands. After supper, she'd returned to the upstairs salon and dozed off on the sofa while reading *Emma*. She looked at the clock on the mantelpiece. It was almost midnight. Stretching a little to alleviate her aching muscles, she prepared to rise and make her way to bed, when the door swung open.

"Forgive me," Lucien said, his large frame blocking out the hallway beyond, "I didn't mean to startle you, but when I saw the light beneath the door I thought it best to check if one of the oil lamps had been forgotten."

"Quite right," she said, still feeling sleepy.

He nodded, paused and held up a small parcel. "I brought you this," he said, placing the item on a table next to where he stood. "It's not much, but considering your love of gardening, I thought you might appreciate a botany book. It was on display in a shop window and . . . well, it made me think of you."

Katherine could practically feel her heart expanding as she straightened herself. "Thank you, Lucien. I'm sure I'll enjoy reading it very much." She prepared to rise so she could go and examine the gift, but something about Lucien's bearing stopped her. He seemed so distant.

"Well, I believe I'll wish you a good night then," he said, turning to go.

"Lucien!" His name had the desired effect, halting him in his tracks. He turned back toward her, one brow raised in question. "Did you discover anything while you were out?" she asked.

He nodded slightly, a lock of dark hair falling against his brow bone. "It appears my bait worked," he said, sounding weary. "When I returned to Riley's this evening, I received a message from Donovan. I'm to meet him four days from now to discuss my financial difficulties."

Katherine's eyes widened. "I don't like the sound of that, Lucien. It's much too dangerous."

"What would you have me do, then?"

She regarded him steadily. "You could take some Bow Street Runners with you."

Stepping further into the room, Lucien sighed. "You know as well as I do that Donovan will probably slip through our fingers if he suspects that my request for help is disingenuous. You mustn't worry, though. I've spoken to Lord Starkly—"

"Please don't tell me you've had anything to do with that man. He's not to be trusted!"

Lucien just stood there, looking back at her with the most peculiar expression, until he eventually said, "Starkly is not as bad as you think. He's actually quite determined to help you."

Katherine scoffed at the notion. "I doubt that very

much." This whole thing was growing more absurd by the second.

"And why is that?" Lucien asked, looking remarkably interested all of a sudden.

Unpleasant memories flooded her mind, and she became lost in them.

"Katherine?" a deep voice prodded.

Blinking, Katherine looked at Lucien. "Forgive me," she said. "I believe I was woolgathering there for a moment." She shook her head. "Starkly doesn't have the best reputation. Surely you know that, Lucien. He's always looking for a new mistress, not caring one way or another about what happens to his previous one once he tosses her out. There's nothing honorable about him."

"Well, in this case, he's on our side. You needn't worry about him."

Was Lucien seriously telling her to trust Lord Starkly? If there was one person she'd rather have nothing to do with ever again, it was him. "What reason do I have to believe he won't double-cross us?"

"Because I'm telling you he won't." Lucien crossed his arms, his gaze dark with shadows cast across his brow.

Katherine swallowed hesitantly. "Is everything all right between us, Lucien? You seem irritable."

He sighed, then shook his head. "Honestly, Kate, I'm exhausted. This whole business—worrying about your welfare and feeling as if I'm making no headway whatsoever—has put me out. The last thing I want to do right now is risk further rejection from you by pressing my advances, nor do I wish to pretend that I've no desire to kiss you whenever you are near. In short, I'd rather avoid you altogether for a while so I can focus on solving the puzzle that Lady Trapleigh has presented us with."

Drawing on every bit of courage she possessed, Katherine rose to her feet and went toward him. He didn't move but watched her warily as she approached. "I haven't been fair to you," she said, while doing her best to ignore the increasing pressure in her stomach. "You leapt off a cliff without knowing how far the fall would be or whether the landing would be hard or gentle. I ran like a scared little rabbit, too afraid to follow you over the edge."

"What are you saying?" His voice was gruff and he looked tense, but he did not flinch, his eyes steady upon her.

"There's a lot I've neglected to tell you. My confidence, not only in others but in myself, has been severely shaken during your absence. I . . ." She took a deep breath. This was it, the moment of truth. "I fear you won't want me once . . . once . . ." Oh God, she couldn't say it. Not to him at least; no matter how much she wanted to share her pain with him, she just couldn't seem to bring herself to cross that line.

"Once what?" he pressed.

Closing her eyes, she became acutely aware of her heart hammering furiously against her chest. She was nervous and she was afraid. *Calm yourself,* she chided. This was Lucien. He would never hurt her. Not willingly at least, a faint voice taunted. Biting down on her lower lip, she took courage. Without allowing herself the chance to argue the point, she blurted, "Once you see me in a state of undress." There. She'd said it, however mortifying her confession might be.

There was a beat. The clock on the mantel ticked away loudly. Katherine cringed, wishing she could take back the words she'd just spoken. She felt like a fool standing there, her eyes squeezed shut while heat rushed to her cheeks. But then she felt Lucien's arms creep about her waist, the hard planes of his chest as he pressed her against him, holding her as if he feared he might lose her. The scent of him— rich sandalwood clinging to the wool of his jacket— wafted over her, comforting her with its familiarity.

She'd no idea how long they stood there. It seemed like forever, and when he finally made to pull away, she was reluctant to let him go, needing him now more than she'd ever needed anyone before in her life. Leaving her by the door, he crossed the floor to a table where an oil lamp glowed. Picking it up, he returned to Katherine and held his hand toward her, saying only one word. "Come."

Skeptical of his intentions, she placed her hand in his with great hesitation and allowed him to lead her through the hallway and across the landing to her bedroom. Opening the door for her, he told her to step inside. Her skin prickled sharply when she realized he had followed. She'd known he would, yet the fact that he had was sending her mind reeling. A click sounded—the lock to her bedroom door sliding shut.

"What are you doing?" The words tumbled from her mouth on a surge of panic.

"I think you know, Kate," he told her, setting the oil lamp on her dresser. "There have been too many lies between us. It's time for honesty now and for you to be loved the way in which you deserve."

"But—"

"No more buts," he told her gently as he came toward her. Reaching up, he traced his fingers along her cheek, brushing away a stray strand of hair in the process. "I've waited much too long for this."

He leaned forward, Katherine's eyes fluttered shut and she felt the soft brush of lips against hers. This kiss was different from the previous ones. It wasn't rushed or calculated, but careful . . . assessing. With trembling fingers, Katherine reached for him, pulling him closer until she felt herself pressed up against him, her heartbeat keeping pace with his. It dawned on her then: however calm and collected he seemed, he was anything but, and the realization humbled her.

Lucien knew he would have to tread lightly so as not to frighten her off again. She was skittish, and with good reason. Whatever had happened, she didn't think herself worthy of a man's affection, fearing she might repel him instead. The very idea that this was what troubled her not only angered him but also made him aware of just how slowly he would have to take this. He nibbled her lower lip to gauge her willingness, and the response was incredible—a sigh wrought from deep within her chest; a flutter of air that teased and tempted.

He drew her closer, his arms sliding firmly down her back as he kissed the corner of her mouth. A slow succession of kisses followed, each placed lovingly along her cheek, at her temple, and finally upon her brow. He needed her—desperately so—but he would revere her first, show her that she had no cause for alarm where he was concerned.

Stepping back, he took her hand in his and led her toward the full-length mirror that stood in one corner of the room. He placed her before it and stepped behind her, hands on her shoulders as he kissed his way along the sweep of her neck. "Look at yourself, Kate," he murmured. "Look at how stunning you are." Their eyes met in the mirror, unwavering while he unpinned her hair so the thick mass of curls could tumble down her back. Sweeping it aside, Lucien went to work on the buttons of her gown, remembering to place a tender kiss against the back of her neck between each one.

"I cannot tell you how long I've dreamed of this moment," he whispered against her ear when all that remained was slipping the gown from her shoulders.

"And I fear your dreams may not live up to reality," she said. Her voice was soft, her eyes still bravely fixed upon him in the mirror, but there was a note of sad regret to her words that tore at his heart.

"We'll just have to see about that." And before she had a chance to protest, he released his hold on her gown, allowing it to drop to the floor. He felt her flinch. "Don't ever be embarrassed to let me see you, Kate. My desire for you is complete—I want you with every fiber of my being, every piece of my soul."

She smiled ever so slightly—somewhat shyly. "You haven't even seen that much more of me yet, Lucien, for I am still quite concealed by my undergarments."

"Then I suggest we do something to change that." Pulling at the laces of her stays, he soon discarded the item, allowing her chemise to fall in soft folds about her body, the translucent fabric hinting at the delectable figure she kept hidden beneath. "No fears," he murmured as he slipped his fingers beneath the fabric and trailed them up along the backs of her thighs.

A gasp escaped her when he reached her bottom, and then another when he scraped the sides of her breasts. Pulling the fabric over her head, he flung it aside to reveal Katherine in all her glory—more beautiful than he'd ever imagined. Christ, he wanted her, to bury himself deep inside her, to claim her as his own. It was primal, this feeling that swept through him, hardening him to the point of despair.

"Well?" she asked, daring him to give his verdict.

"You're incredible," he said. "More beautiful than any other woman I've ever laid eyes upon."

"You needn't lie to me, Lucien." Bitterness traced her words.

Lucien tensed. "I wouldn't dream of it." Something fierce inside him broke free. "Don't you dare tarnish this moment between us with self-doubt, Kate. I've always been honest with you, so if I tell you that you're beautiful, then it's because I mean it."

"But what about the marks . . . the blemishes." Her voice was but a sad little whisper as she stood there trembling, whether from cold or from humiliation Lucien dared not consider. He blinked. "What marks and blemishes?"

"Don't you see them? There's a red one on my thigh and three brown ones on my back?"

Lucien looked closer. He spotted the red one immediately due to its size—roughly that of a grown man's hand. The brown ones were more discreet. "They're just birthmarks, Kate. Surely you don't imagine they'd have any influence on my feelings for you or the fact that I crave you more than I do air? Has this been the root of all your concerns?"

She nodded, and through the dim light of the glowing oil lamp, he saw that her eyes glistened with tears. Dear God, what the devil had happened to cause this level of upset in her? He didn't need to voice the question out loud, for he suspected that he already knew the answer. Crossby.

"Listen to me, Kate," he told her firmly as he turned her toward him, tilting her chin up with his fingers so he could look her in the eye. "You'll always be everything I've ever wanted in a woman, and my desire for you will never diminish." Lowering his mouth over hers, he kissed her then with unabashed hunger, his tongue pressing against the seam of her lips until they parted, granting him entry. A groan escaped in response to his sudden advance, but her arms came about his neck and she clung to him, her body pressed against his own as he ravished her mouth, tasting that warm moist heat of her until he feared he might expire from sheer lust.

They came apart on a shared gasp. "I think you know enough to realize I'm telling the truth when I say I desire you," Lucien said, his hands stroking down her back until he reached her bottom and pressed her against him. "Do you feel it?"

"Heavens," Katherine breathed.

"Turn around," he said. "Face the mirror and allow me to worship you."

"But my stockings and shoes—"

"Make it so much more exciting, don't you think?" Standing behind her, he trailed his fingers over her shoulder, across her chest, down over her belly and along her hip. "I like you like this . . . still partly dressed yet with all the necessary areas available to my touch. Your breasts . . ." He heard her suck in a breath as he reached up and filled his hands with her plump flesh, delighting in the way she relaxed against him, her lips parting on a slight murmur as he pinched her pebbling nipples.

"Does that feel good?" he asked.

Good? It felt incredible. Indeed, Katherine had never in her life believed it could feel quite like this. Why, he'd barely touched her at all, yet her body was already responding, humming with expectant vigor. "Yes," she sighed as she leaned into his warmth.

Angling his head against her, he gently bit the side of her neck. A burst of quivers shot through her, almost buckling her knees. "Oh God," was all she could manage to say.

Lucien, wicked man that he was, merely chuckled against her flesh. "If only we'd done this sooner," he said, meeting her gaze in the mirror as he slid one hand over her belly, producing a tremor. "Have you any idea of the torturous nights I've spent fantasizing about you?"

Speechless, Katherine could do nothing but shake her head while her heart hammered furiously in her chest.

"I've thought of touching you in the most intimate way possible . . . of sliding my hand between your thighs and stroking you right there, where you ache the most. Tell me, Kate, are you aching there now?"

His scandalous words swept through her, expanding her need until it pooled in the exact place he'd just mentioned. Indeed, she found herself aching for his touch. Unable to lie, yet incapable of speech, she nodded once more. He rewarded her with a kiss against the side of her neck. "Would you like me to relieve the ache for you?" His fingers played lightly across her skin. "To love you the way you deserve to be loved?"

His question shot straight to her heart. Of course he'd phrased it in such a way that she couldn't be sure exactly how he meant it—if it could be construed as a declaration of sorts. She dared not ask, fearing that whatever his feelings toward her were, they would not match her own. "Yes," she whispered, and then more forcefully, "please, Lucien. I need you."

"Good, because I need you too, Kate, more than you can possibly imagine." He grazed his lips against her bare shoulder as he nudged her legs farther apart with his hands, opening her up . . . preparing her for his touch.

The image that met her gaze in the mirror was indeed a scandalous one, for she stood now in a wide stance, still clad in her stockings and slippers, with Lucien's large frame looming behind her. His left hand covered one breast while his right rested upon her hip. "You look so inviting," he murmured, tugging gently at her nipple while his right hand stroked down her thigh. "A man would have to be mad not to want you."

His eyes held hers, and it was as if the veil concealing the truth for so long was finally lifted, allowing Katherine to see the beauty of which he spoke. What did it really matter if she had a few birthmarks when Lucien looked at her the way he did? The marks had never concerned her until Charles had mocked her for them, filling her with doubt and a crippling sense of worthlessness, but it was also clear to her now that Charles had never cared for her. With Lucien, however, it was different—he made her feel desirable.

"Show me," she whispered, empowered by the hunger consuming his eyes.

He chuckled lightly, teasing her skin with the warmth of his breath.

And then those skillful fingers of his swept between her legs with feather softness—a caress so gentle it was scarcely there at all, yet it tortured Katherine's sensitive flesh, evoking a moan of pleasure from deep within her chest. Heavens, it felt good—better than she'd ever thought possible. She tilted her hips, seeking more. "Again," she pleaded, not caring how desperate she sounded or how embarrassed she'd likely be by this newfound wanton behavior of hers when she woke the following morning. All she could think of right now was the present and how desperately she wanted Lucien's fingers to continue their ministration, for she sensed now that there could be more between a man and a woman than she'd ever thought possible.

Mercifully, he stroked her again, with added pressure. Still, it wasn't enough, not when complete unrest had taken over her body and embers curled inside her, threatening to tear her limb from limb. She needed something, though she knew not what, but instinct told her that Lucien was the only person capable of sating this overpowering need that stirred within her.

Eyes locked with his, she watched as he parted her folds, the indecency the image offered sending wave upon wave of pleasure soaring through her. Good Lord, but she had to be the most wanton woman on the face of the earth. And then she felt one of his fingers slip inside her, filling her the way she longed to be filled. "Yes," she sighed as he moved in and out. His other hand released her breast and came down to stroke some magical part that sent sparks flying.

"You're just like I imagined," Lucien murmured. "Better even. So responsive . . . so welcoming . . . so ready. Come for me, Kate. Reach for your pleasure. Let yourself go."

His words, coupled with his touch and the erotic image they portrayed in the mirror, buzzed along her every nerve, building the pressure within her until, on an unexpected pulse of energy, a thousand tingles burst through her. "Oh God!"

"That's it," Lucien murmured, his lips tenderly kissing her shoulder as he wrought every last bit of pleasure from her until she felt well and truly drained. He held her quietly for a brief time after, before turning her in his arms and lowering his mouth over hers, his kiss fierce with passion.

Katherine clung to his broad shoulders, reveling in the thrust of his tongue, the primal demand and possession it signified. "Lucien," she gasped when his mouth left hers to kiss its way along her jawline. She needed to tell him how momentous the moment between them had been—sensed that it was of the utmost importance that she did so. So she placed her hands firmly against his chest, gave him a little nudge and took courage. "I cannot offer you my innocence," she said, embarrassed by the subject but knowing that she had to put the feeling aside and tell him the truth.

He shook his head. "I know that, Kate." He moved to kiss her again, but she wouldn't let him.

"What I *can* tell you is that no other man has ever made me feel the way you just did. I mean, I've never . . ." God, this was difficult. She sighed, closed her eyes and whispered, "I didn't realize it could be so incredible."

Strong arms came about her waist, holding her close. "Thank you, Kate. You've given me a beautiful gift—one that I will always cherish."

His breath was raspy, and she suddenly became aware of the hardness that pressed against her. He needed her just as much as she needed him, and she wanted suddenly, quite desperately, to do for him what he had just done for her. She'd never undressed a man before and felt a little uncertain about doing so now, but then she reminded herself that Lucien could be trusted and that he would not ridicule her for anything. She knew that now, and the thought that she'd recently feared he might felt remarkably silly.

Reaching up, she went to work on his cravat, an intricate knot that was really quite annoying when haste was of the essence. Cursing the piece of linen, she evoked a laugh from Lucien, who was watching her with merriment dancing in his eyes. "Should I help?" he asked.

"No need," she said, determined to finish the task on her own. With a slight tug, she managed to loosen the fabric, and it eventually gave way. She smiled, pleased with her achievement.

Lucien stared down at her. He could scarcely believe that this was really happening, that his foremost wish had finally come true. Katherine was his after all these years. It was miraculous. Joy flowed through him, filling him until he felt his heart might burst. Unable to keep away from her, he reached out and placed his hand upon her waist while she went to work on the buttons of his shirt. He needed the closeness, the contact, the evidence that she was really standing naked there before him in spite of her insecurities.

She'd placed all her trust in him this evening, and the notion humbled him beyond measure. He realized just how difficult it must have been for her to undress in his presence, with the fear of rejection so forceful in her mind. But the marks that had coiled themselves around her and held her prisoner were of no consequence to him. He loved her for the woman she was, for her kindness, her sense of humor, her devotion to those she cared about and for her intellect. Physically, she would always be the most beautiful woman of his acquaintance. Nobody else would ever compare.

His groin tightened with the need to claim her, to love her as much as he possibly could. Christ . . . to watch her face as she found her release once more, this time with him inside her, almost had him shoving her aside so he could make haste with his clothes. Her confession earlier . . . knowing that he was her first meaningful lover had spoken to his male ego and filled him with pride.

His shirt finally slipped from his shoulders, and, shrugging his arms out of it, he let it fall to the floor. "Allow me to remove my boots," he said, stepping back so he could give one of his Hessians a hard tug. Tossing it aside, he quickly removed the other as well, along with his socks. He stood before her now, in nothing but his breeches and not the least bit embarrassed about the proof of his desire, evident as it was beneath the snug fit of the fabric. Her fingers came toward him hesitantly, the touch of them as light as fairy dust as they skimmed along the edge of his waistband.

Lucien sucked in a breath and raised his hand to one of Katherine's breasts, delighting in its fullness. He'd be damned if he would be the only one getting tortured, and he delighted in the sigh of pleasure that escaped her when he found her nipple and squeezed. "The faster you get me out of these breeches, the faster we'll both be able to find what we seek," he murmured.

"I . . ." A blush rose across her chest and traveled to her cheeks. She paused and held completely still.

Lucien studied her closely. The fingertips that rested at his waistline were trembling ever so slightly, and there was something apprehensive about her—a nervousness to complete the task she'd set for herself. It dawned on him then, so forcefully it was almost as if he'd been punched in the chest: not only was this the first time she'd experienced the pleasure of lovemaking but it was also her first time undressing a man . . . touching him like this. "Take your time," he soothed, reigning in his urges, "there's no rush. However, I want you to know that I crave your touch. I long for you to be bold, Kate, and I promise that you'll get nothing but gratitude in return."

She nodded, still hesitant, it appeared. Lucien held his breath, waiting for her to proceed and wondering if she would. The last thing he wanted was for her to back away, so he drew on every ounce of patience he possessed, immensely relieved when she finally began unbuttoning the fall. Happily, her fingers began moving with increased confidence and speed until he sprang free, brushing against her hand. With a startled gasp, Katherine pulled away, but Lucien caught her lightly by the wrist, halting her retreat. "Relax," he whispered. "It's just me, the same person you've known your whole life. I'll never judge you for anything. You're safe with me."

"I know that, Lucien, truly I do. It's just—"

"I love you." There. He'd said it. With three little words he'd torn away whatever barriers remained between them, hoping that their powerful meaning would be enough to save Katherine from the burden of her past.

She gazed back at him with wonder pooling in the depths of her eyes. Lucien's heart knocked against his chest as he stood there, completely vulnerable in every conceivable way, with his manhood thrusting toward her and having just offered her his heart. Would she reciprocate? Did she even feel as strongly for him as he did for her? Fear reared its ugly head, and he opened his mouth to speak—to offer her a way out of the awkward moment he'd just created. But then she spoke, cutting him off, and the words that slipped from her lips were like a concerto rising through the silence. "Oh, Lucien, I love you too. So very much my heart aches with it."

His own heart soared with elation and he brought her hand back to the waistline of his breeches. "Then don't hold back. Know me the way you know yourself—let the last barriers between us fall away. Explore me just as I've explored you, because truth be told, I'm really quite desperate for you to do so."

A smile captured her lips and a small chuckle escaped her. She took a deep breath, and then, gloriously, she tugged his breeches down over his hips, freeing him completely. Stepping out of them, he raised her hand to his lips and placed a kiss against the back of her wrist before lowering it to his aching manhood. "Don't be shy," he murmured when he felt her flinch. "There's nothing wrong with what we're doing."

Tentatively and with his guidance, she curled her fingers around the hard length of him. The pleasure of her touch upon him was intense, and when he showed her how to move her hand smoothly back and forth, it was all he could do not to stop his eyes from rolling back in his head from the sheer ecstasy the movement wrought. He ran his hand over her hip, squeezing the flesh of her left buttock before continuing down behind her. She groaned with pleasure when he found her center once more, his fingers fueling her lust and increasing her wetness until she was more than ready for him.

Unfurling her hand, he scooped her up in his arms and carried her to the bed, where he placed her gently against the pillows before climbing up between her thighs. He kneeled there, gazing down at her while his hands roamed up over her legs, over her hips, across her belly and onward to her full breasts. She sighed when he cupped them, arching against his touch as he kneaded that tender flesh. "Tell me you want me," he said, desperate to hear her invitation spoken aloud.

"I need you, Lucien." She tilted her hips toward

him, leaving no doubt as to where exactly she needed him most.

This was it. The moment he'd dreamed of for so long was finally upon him, and the responsibility that came with it washed over him. He had to make this good for her.

Placing himself at her entrance, he eased himself inside. "You'll tell me if there's something you don't like?" His voice was tight with anxiety and the strain of holding back.

"Yes," she murmured, rocking toward him, inviting him closer.

Pushing himself forward, Lucien reveled in the feel of having her around him—the welcoming warmth and the tightness. "Bloody hell," he gasped, fearing for his control. It felt like a very thin thread was about to snap at any moment.

"Is everything all right?" Katherine asked, wide-eyed with concern.

He nodded, took a breath to steady himself. "It's just . . . I've spent years imagining this and now . . . it feels so damn good, Kate. I don't want to frighten you, but I don't think I can hold back any longer."

"Then don't," she whispered, reaching up and dragging him down for a kiss. "Claim me, Lucien. Make me yours."

Primal instinct took control of his body at those words, and restraint fled. Pulling back, he drove back inside her, the movement forcing a groan from his throat. He did it again, and again with increasing speed, watching as Katherine's eyes glazed over, her breath coming in short pants as she moved in time with his thrusts, her skin flushed and her breasts rocking back and forth with the motion. Tremors started to rise up his legs, and he knew he had to lower the pace if he was to take Katherine with him. But it was beyond his control, and he was powerless to stop it.

But then, just when he felt his climax rising, her muscles quickened, contracted, and his name was flung from her lips as she shuddered around him. Lucien followed in her wake, the rush of energy bursting through him, carrying him forward in an upward spiral until he knew without a doubt that he'd just found heaven. On a sigh of sated satisfaction, he drifted back to earth and to the soft comfort of the bed, where Katherine waited. He placed a tender kiss upon her lips before settling down beside her and hugging her body against his own. Curling to match his shape, Katherine nestled her head against his shoulder and sighed with contentment.

"Are you happy?" Lucien asked, simply to hear her voice.

"Unbelievably so," she murmured. "Are you?"

"I can't remember when I was more so," he said. Allowing his hand to trail along her waist and over the curve of her hip, he placed it on top of the red mark and added, "Indeed, I feel extraordinarily blessed to have won the attention of the loveliest woman in England."

Turning her head, she gazed at him, and he saw in her eyes such gratitude that had he been standing, it would have brought him to his knees. "I love you," she whispered. "I'm sorry it took so long for me to realize that you wouldn't care about the marks."

Lucien hugged her closer, still desperate to prove that he would never judge her like that. "It's quite all right," he said, brushing his lips against her cheek. "You've been hurt and had good reason to be wary." He hesitated, cautious about what he wanted to say next. Their relationship had progressed with startling speed and without agreeing on how to proceed after. She'd said before that she'd no intention of marrying again. What if that was still true? He couldn't stand the thought of her rejection—not now, after everything they'd shared. She loved him though, had told him so just now. Surely that meant she wanted to be more than his lover. Didn't it? Swallowing all apprehension, he decided to ask the question that would clarify where they stood with each other. "Kate, you will marry me, won't you?"

She didn't respond, and Lucien realized she'd fallen asleep. Expelling a deep breath, he closed his eyes, knowing that the matter would have to wait. Hopefully he'd find the courage to ask her again later, and he silently prayed that when he did, she'd answer him "yes."

Chapter 14

Stirring a spoonful of honey into her tea, Katherine sighed with exasperation and stared across at Lucien, who was happily reading his morning paper. Three days she'd been trapped inside his house, not even able to look out the window at the passersby and with nobody save Lucien for company. Not that she didn't enjoy his company, of course, but he'd seemed very reserved lately, considering how forward he'd been before—almost as if he'd accomplished his goal, and now that he'd bedded her, his appetite for her was sated.

It bothered her, not only because she was more than eager for him to make love to her again but because she was beginning to doubt his intentions. He'd spoken of marriage with great enthusiasm before, but he hadn't mentioned it since, though he did occasionally approach her as if he meant to say something of great importance. To her increasing frustration, he never did and would invariably end up saying something banal about the weather instead. Then he'd frown at her the way most men frowned when studying something that puzzled them, and eventually he'd give her a kiss upon her hand or her cheek.

In short, the blazing heat of a few days earlier had cooled dramatically.

Katherine sighed again. It was only made worse by the tedium of her situation. She needed something with which to distract herself from the threat that loomed and from her worries about Lucien. Her greatest fear, of course, was that he hadn't found her pleasing after all—that the birthmarks had repulsed him and that he was too kind to say anything about it because he didn't wish to hurt her feelings. Logic told her this wasn't the case, considering how eager he'd been during their coupling, yet she couldn't help but worry.

She stared at him as he turned a page of his paper. Whatever was going on inside that thick skull of his, he wasn't doing a very good job of easing her concerns. "I'd like to host a dinner party," she found herself saying, her voice curt and irritable.

"You know that's impossible," he said, lowering the paper so he could look at her, his eyes filled with sympathy. It was the last thing she wanted him to feel toward her.

"Why?" she protested. "We could have your sister and Gray over."

"That wouldn't be much of a party," Lucien murmured.

She felt like flinging her teacup at him. "Even so," she said, tempering her tone, since she knew that screaming her head off was unlikely to work in her favor, "it could be fun. We could play whist after supper, perhaps even charades."

He studied her for a moment. "You know how concerned I am for your safety, Kate, particularly following the missive we just received from your secretary."

The letter worried Katherine as well. Apparently there had been another fire—this time at the mill in Ancoats. It couldn't be a coincidence that her investments were being targeted in such quick succession. After breakfast, she would send letters to the other enterprises, warning them to beware.

"Until we find the culprit behind the threats against you," Lucien continued, "I'd rather be overly cautious than risk . . ." He winced. "I just want us to be careful. That is all."

"And we are being. I wouldn't be leaving the house—they would come here. I don't see why anyone should be the wiser, when you know as well as I that they can be trusted."

"Of course I do."

"Then please invite them over. You cannot possibly imagine how difficult it is for me to just sit here day in and day out. You at least have the excuse of going to your club—a freedom which you've been taking great advantage of lately. I don't think it's the least bit fair."

"I've been trying to gather information about Donovan."

"Yes, I am aware. However, if things don't change soon, I am likely to go mad." Rising, she crossed the floor to the door. "You've been warned."

"Very well. You may host a dinner."

She turned around slowly, as if she feared that any sudden movement might change his mind. "Are you certain?"

"I understand how difficult the situation must be for you. You've been shot at, had your home broken into, been separated from your daughter and removed from your familiar surroundings to be locked away in a house that isn't your own and with nothing to entertain you, except for me of course, whenever I am here, which I haven't been often—admittedly. In my opinion, it's a wonder you're not mad already."

Smiling, she walked back toward him. He set his paper aside and stood, his hand seeking hers. She accepted it. "We'll be careful," she promised, aware that his greatest concern was for her safety. She loved that he cared, but too much caring could also be stifling.

He nodded, his lips pressed together even as he made an effort to smile. He was worried, yet he was bowing to her wishes. He truly was a wonderful man. If only he'd kiss her now with all the passion he'd shown for her before. She remained where she was, so close to him that it would scarcely take any effort at all for him to pull her into his arms.

"Kate . . ." His voice was hoarse, and for a moment it looked as if her prayers would be answered. Commanded by the sound of her name upon his lips, she met his gaze, but where there had once been heat, there was now doubt and trepidation.

"It's all right," she said, pulling away from him and taking a step back, the loss of his touch stirring an ache in her chest. "You needn't explain. I understand."

He frowned. "Do you?"

"Oh yes." Heaven above, she was going to die right there on the dining room floor. Her heart was breaking, and she feared she might soon cry before him if she didn't hurry things along and get herself out of there quickly. "However, if it's not too much trouble, it would please me greatly if we could at least remain friends."

"Remain friends?"

"I see you disagree." She nodded, willing back the

tears that threatened to fall. "Well, I suppose that's what I get for wanting the moon, the stars and sun. I'll leave you to your paper."

Turning about on her heel, she started forward, only to be halted by his hand upon her arm. "Kate," he said, his voice thick with emotion. "I don't—"

"Where is she?" The sound of a female voice echoing through the hallway came toward them, followed swiftly by the rapid clicking of heels upon the floor.

"My lady!" Mr. Parker's voice.

"I insist on seeing my friend or if not her, then Lord Roxberry. Surely he must be able to—" Louise appeared in the doorway, her eyes widening as she spotted Katherine. Mr. Parker came up behind her with hastily spoken apologies. "My dear!" The tension left Louise's voice as she enveloped Katherine in her arms.

Lucien dismissed the anxious butler with a request that more tea be brought in.

"Heaven above, I can't tell you how relieved I am to find you, and in good health too, from the looks of it." Stepping back, Louise smoothed the front of her skirts and looked at Lucien. "My lord, I hope you will forgive my dramatic intrusion, but I was so terribly worried. I went to Cresthaven to call on Katherine, you see, but was informed that she had departed for London after being attacked in her home the previous evening."

"That was very informative of her staff," Lucien said stiffly.

Louise smiled. "You'd be surprised how easily some tongues can be loosened, especially since the servants know how fond I am of Katherine. I left for London the next day and went directly to Crossby House, but when the staff there told me they hadn't seen their mistress in months, I grew very alarmed indeed. The next logical place to inquire was here."

"And I'm very happy you did," Katherine told her. "Is Huntley in town with you?"

"Oh yes—he refused to let me travel alone. Mind you, we shan't stay long. I promised Mama that I would only be gone for a couple of days. With Kingsborough Hall still overrun by houseguests, I really must be there to help her entertain—especially with my brother, the duke, in pursuit of Miss Chilcott."

Katherine tilted her head. "Miss Chilcott? Do I know her?"

"I shouldn't think so. She was not invited to the ball, but she snuck herself in anyway. Well, my brother fell for her and . . . ah well, it has become a very delicate situation, I fear. Her parents are completely opposed to any match between their daughter and the duke."

"That sounds very odd," Lucien said as he pulled out a chair for Louise so she could sit. She thanked him kindly and lowered herself onto it while Katherine and Lucien both reclaimed theirs.

"Yes, I suppose it does. But the duke is determined to make her his bride, so I'm sure he'll get to the bottom of it eventually."

"Well, since you are in town for at least tonight and hopefully tomorrow night as well, we'd like to invite you for dinner—whichever evening suits you best," Katherine said, hoping that her friend wasn't already engaged.

Louise smiled. "That sounds lovely. Huntley suggests we go to the theater this evening—you're welcome to join us."

"Thank you," Katherine said, her eyes meeting Lucien's. She longed to accept the invitation, but she knew she could not. "Unfortunately, the person who attacked me at Cresthaven was hired by someone, and until we find out who, I am still at risk. You know, the shot that was fired at the ball was intended for me."

Louise gasped, her palm pressed against her chest with obvious alarm. "Oh, my dear! No wonder you are staying here." She eyed Lucien. "I didn't want to comment on the impropriety, for in earnest, it is none of my business, and with all the rumors . . . well, I do hope you'll forgive me for imagining that your friendship had risen to a new level."

Katherine swatted her friend on the shoulder. "Lady Huntley, you are just as outrageous as Roxberry's grandmother, except you don't have the excuse of being old and without any obligation to be discreet."

A skinny little maid with a very serious expression entered, carrying a fresh pot of tea and a cup for Louise. Placing the items on the table, she bobbed a curtsy and left. Reaching for the pot, Katherine poured the tea for her friend, refilling Lucien's cup as well as her own in the process.

"My apologies, my lord," Louise said as she slid her fingertips over the ear of her teacup. "Katherine is right. I often say things I shouldn't, and in this instance in particular I do believe I should have refrained from saying anything at all. You are only doing what is right, after all. There is no fault in that, and if Society says otherwise, well, then they can all go hang!"

Katherine couldn't help but laugh. She looked at Lucien, whose lips were puckering with amusement. "Please don't concern yourself on my account, Lady Huntley. I am not so easily offended." His eyes met Katherine's. "On the contrary, it has been an absolute pleasure having Katherine all to myself for a few days. It has given us the opportunity to become properly reacquainted." He stood, while Katherine's cheeks began to burn. "I would be delighted to invite you and Huntley to dine with us tomorrow if you are available then. And if you have some time to spare for Katherine right now, then I daresay she'd appreciate it. I understand she's feeling rather trapped in this house." His eyes darkened. "Word of caution though—nobody must know that she is here. Her life is in danger, Lady Huntley, so I do hope that you will take my warning seriously."

"You have my word on it," Louise replied, her head dipping in acquiescence.

Katherine watched him go, her heart beating a strange tattoo. For the first time in their lifelong relationship, she'd no idea what he was thinking or feeling. It unnerved her tremendously.

"I knew he was planning to ask for your hand," Louise whispered. She was still half turned in her seat, her eyes on the door through which Lucien had just departed.

Katherine sighed. *This again.* "You've no idea of what you speak, Louise."

"Really? From where I'm sitting, the two of you looked very domestic, discussing dinner plans over breakfast." Katherine could feel Louise's eyes on her, but she dared not meet her gaze. Silence spread between them until Louise eventually said, "Tell me, has he kissed you yet?"

Katherine's head snapped up at that question. "Louise!"

Louise merely grinned. "I can see that he has. Now I'll save you the embarrassment of asking if he's done anything more than that."

Good Lord, I'm going to combust!

"Instead, I'm going to ask you why you don't look happier. He is a handsome man, Katherine, and the two of you have always been so close. Surely you can see what a perfect match he would make for you. After all, he obviously cares for you or he wouldn't have risked scandal in order to save you. Besides, I'm sure he could find somewhere else for you to stay if he was determined to do so."

"He wants to keep an eye on me," Katherine said, her voice low with humiliation.

Louise chuckled. "I daresay it's nothing more than an excuse to . . . facilitate certain opportunities—like that of kissing, for instance. He'd never have a chance to do that if you were living with his mama and grandmamma at Roxberry Hall, for instance. Curious that he didn't think to leave you there, don't you think?"

"I . . ." Katherine's throat worked in an attempt to find the right words while she sorted through her muddled thoughts at the same time. "No, Louise. Coming to London with him was my idea. I wanted to be of some assistance, not tucked out of the way somewhere, for if that was the case, I ought to have gone with Sophia." Her voice quivered a little on her daughter's name, for she was terribly worried about her in spite of having recently received a letter from her mother, confirming that Sophia was safe.

"Yes, of course," Louise said. She nodded thoughtfully. The wheels and cranks in her brain were clearly at work. "But the way he looked at you just now . . . Katherine, don't you see that he is desperately in love with you?"

"He is not, or he would have proposed to me properly by now," Katherine blurted. Snapping her mouth shut, she swung her gaze toward the empty plate that sat before her. Only crumbs remained.

"Why would you say that?" Louise asked, her voice a low whisper.

Resting her elbows on the edge of the table, Katherine dropped her face into her hands. In the heat of passion, Lucien had told her he loved her, but how could she believe that he really meant it when he'd failed to ask for her hand the following day? "You know why," she murmured, too embarrassed by half to look her friend in the eye. She shouldn't have said anything, but she'd spent two full days and an entire morning worrying about it.

"Oh!" Katherine heard Louise move from her chair, and a moment later, her arms came about Katherine. "My poor dear."

"So you see, I have acted very foolishly, Louise. I have become a mistress after all, and lost a friend in the process. Heavens! Whatever must he think of me?"

"What must he think of you?" Louise asked with steel in her voice. "Dear Katherine, he is the one who has wronged *you*! You have nothing to be ashamed of. Now, the important thing is to convince him to do the right thing and marry you."

Lowering her hands, Katherine raised her head and looked at her friend. "I don't think he wants to anymore. In fact, he's been very distant with me lately."

"Anymore?" Louise studied her. "You mean to say he has indeed suggested it?"

"He mentioned it a couple of times, but that was before we . . ." She swallowed. "He hasn't said a word about it since, not even in jest."

"And how did you respond when he initially brought it up? Were you open to his suggestion?"

"Not really. When I became a widow, I decided never again to attach myself to any man—that I'd much rather be a companion to my aunt."

"Well, I do hope you've changed your mind about that. Think of Sophia, Katherine, and think of yourself. It would be so much better for you to marry Roxberry."

Katherine attempted a smile, but her mouth wouldn't cooperate. "I know that now, but I fear it is too late. He no longer wants me."

Louise sat back in her chair and crossed her arms over her chest. "Lady Crossby, I do believe you're being an idiot about this."

"I beg your pardon?"

"You heard me." Louise shook her head, her dark ringlets swinging against her cheeks. "To think that a woman like you, who has been married, would know so little about men or people in general. Honestly, you astound me."

Katherine stared at her. "I love him," she said.

Louise nodded. "I know." Her smile was full of satisfaction.

"And I have discouraged his suit with my continuous resistance." She sank back against her chair. "If he asks me now and I refuse him . . . the possibility that I might . . . oh, Louise, what a fool I've been."

"I'm so glad to know that you're finally seeing reason," Louise said, her smile widening until she was practically beaming. "Why, I'm sure the poor man would love to ask for your hand but has quite lost the courage to do so again."

"I think you're probably right," Katherine agreed, yet the doubt that had tugged at her heart for years refused to budge. "But what if you're not? I dare not broach the issue for fear of being spurned."

Louise looked at her with sympathy. "I sense that your marriage to Crossby was not a happy one, though you were always brave in putting on a good appearance for the benefit of others. I'm sorry I didn't realize it sooner, or I would have tried to help."

"There was nothing you could do. He was my husband. Thankfully, we did not see very much of each other."

"Hmm." Louise's eyes met Katherine's knowingly, but she said nothing further about it. "Still, Roxberry is different. You've known him your whole life, Katherine. Surely you can trust him not to hurt you. But if you do wish for him to make the first move, then we shall merely have to nudge him along a little, shan't we?"

"Louise . . . ?"

Louise smiled. "I will arrive for dinner tomorrow evening with Huntley. We'll have a splendid time of it, you'll see."

Katherine groaned. She didn't like the idea of playing games, but she did want Lucien to be hers. If he still wished to marry her, all she wanted from him was a little sign—something that would give her courage.

Chapter 15

Damn! Lucien cursed himself as he entered the park. He had no idea where he was going, only that he needed to walk. Surely there wasn't a man alive in England who was as big a blockhead as he.

A smartly dressed gentleman tipped his hat in his direction, and Lucien almost passed him by without returning the salutation. His mind was in a muddle, his body in constant agony because of her. Having Katherine beneath his roof was torture, especially now that he knew what it was like to have her, to kiss those supple lips, to run his hands over her lithe body as she sighed with pleasure. His touch enflamed her, he could see it in her eyes, and the very thought of it was most provocative.

Lucien's hands clenched and unclenched at his sides. The air was cool today, sharp and crisp. He took a breath and focused on the way it felt as it rushed into his lungs. His sanity was returning, little by little, though he knew it would depart again the instant he returned home and laid eyes on her.

Why couldn't he just ask her the one simple question that was forever churning in his mind? The answer was simple. He'd brought it up before, only to have her toss his offer back at him. After everything they'd recently shared, receiving another "no" from her would likely crush him. He could not risk being denied, not after all the years he'd spent loving her and hoping for her to be his. She'd given herself to him the other night, and while it had been wonderful—better than he ever could have dreamed—she'd done so without any promises being made.

Idiot.

Reaching a cluster of trees, Lucien stopped and scanned the scenery. Nobody else was around, and he plucked his hat from his head and raked his fingers through his hair. He loved her, by God, and because of that, he'd lost his senses and taken her to bed, fully knowing where she stood on the subject of marriage. He'd sworn he wouldn't repeat the mistake—that if they were ever intimate again, it would be because she'd accepted his proposal. Consequently, he hadn't kissed her since their night together either—he simply didn't trust himself to leave it only at that. Not when she stirred such fire in him that all he could think of was how to take her the next time the opportunity to do so arose.

Bloody hell! He had to put the question to her soon, for the sake of his health as much as his peace of mind. He pondered his chance of success. Katherine had seemed a bit tense of late . . . apprehensive perhaps. This morning, she'd been upset, but just before Lady Huntley had arrived, she'd said the most curious thing: *"I suppose that's what I get for wanting the moon, the stars and the sun."* Lucien's heart made a funny thump. If there was any chance at all that she was speaking of him, then he was bloody well going to find out. He hadn't gotten himself this far only to give up now.

With renewed purpose, he put his hat back on his head and marched back the way he'd come. Katherine was his—she'd given herself to him, after all. It was time he stopped being such a dunce about it all and spoke the question that had been on his lips these last few days. The last time he'd asked, she'd been asleep, so that didn't count for much, and before that she'd had her own fears to conquer.

Stopping by the florist on the way, he picked up a bouquet of yellow tulips held together by a lilac ribbon. But when he arrived home, his grand plan of proposing was brought to an immediate halt upon seeing Barrymore and Carlyle alighting from a carriage. He winced. This was not good. If they discovered that Katherine was living with him, the news would hit Mayfair by storm. By God, they'd betted on his success at winning her hand! This could prove disastrous. His grip on the tulips tightened. He hadn't expected them to call on him, and he fleetingly considered backing away and turning the corner. If he could at least enter through the back, then he could get rid of the flowers and warn everyone inside.

Too late, Barrymore spotted him. "Ah! Roxberry, just the man we're looking for." His eyes went directly to the flowers. "I don't suppose those are for Lady Crossby," he said.

"No, they're not," Lucien said, approaching the pair with great reluctance.

Barrymore's eyebrows drew together. "Is there another lady we ought to know about?"

"Just as long as it's not my heiress," Carlyle spoke. He tipped his hat at Lucien. "Roxberry."

"I can assure you that I have no designs on her," Lucien said, "whoever she may be."

"But why are you returning with your flowers? Surely the lady who holds your interest wasn't so cruel as to toss you out without accepting them?" Barrymore asked, his frown deeply serious.

"No, it's nothing like that," Lucien said, not liking what such a confession would do to his pride, even if it wasn't true. "I'm seeing the lady later and thought I'd pick up the flowers early, since I was out for a walk anyway—grab the loveliest bouquet before anyone else has a chance to do so."

"Hmm," Carlyle muttered. "I've always thought you were a sensible fellow, Roxberry. Apparently your practicality extends to every aspect of your life. Will you invite us in? I'd kill for a cup of tea right now."

Pasting a smile on his face, Lucien climbed the steps to his front door and plucked the key from his pocket. He placed it in the lock, took a deep breath and turned it. The door swung open to reveal a very perplexed-looking Parker, his eyes dashing about as he looked from one man to the other. Lucien tried to calm his nerves. He had to protect Katherine from the promise of scandal that presently stood in his foyer. "Parker," he said. "If you'll please take these gentlemen's hats and coats and lead them through to my study, I'll just see if I can find a maid to put these flowers in water." He needed an excuse to go upstairs and tell Katherine to remain in her room until it was safe.

"Surely your butler can do that for you when he's done helping us," Barrymore said. "Here, I'll hold the bouquet for you if you like so you can take off your own coat."

What could he do without raising suspicion? Lucien muttered a silent oath as he gave the flowers to Barrymore and took off his greatcoat. "Thank you," he said. He handed the garment to Parker and addressed his butler. "Please see to the flowers first, and then arrange for some tea to be brought in. I understand Carlyle has a particular craving for it."

"If it's not too much trouble, perhaps we could have some sandwiches too? It's close to luncheon, and I'm not sure I'll make it back home before collapsing from hunger," Barrymore said.

Lucien stared at him. *By all means, invite yourself.* He wanted to toss both men out, but that would be exceptionally bad form. Praying for patience and a heavy dose of divine intervention, Lucien pasted a smile on his face and nodded. "Excellent idea. Parker will see to it right away. This way, gentlemen!"

Standing aside, Lucien waited for his guests to enter his study before closing the door behind them. Suggesting that each man take a seat, Lucien strolled around to the opposite side of his desk and paused, his gaze dropping to the piece of paper lying on the surface before him. It was a letter—a dinner invitation, to be precise—addressed to his sister. The writing curled with elegant swirls, which he instantly recognized as Katherine's. It looked unfinished—halted in midsentence. He frowned. Apparently she'd chosen to oppose his wishes and during his absence had ventured not only downstairs but into his study as well. Once Barrymore and Carlyle departed, he would have to remind her of the danger she faced and how lucky it was that she hadn't been sitting at his desk just now when they'd all walked in.

Moving between his chair and the desk, Lucien sat down across from his guests and smiled. "So tell me, to what do I owe this unexpected pleasure?"

"Well . . . ," Barrymore began, "rumor has it that Lady Crossby is no longer in residence at Cresthaven. People are wondering where she might be. Apparently she's vanished into thin air."

"Surely you must be mistaken," Lucien told him. He leaned back and stretched out his legs but was met with resistance. Soft resistance. Looking down, he spied the obstacle and had to fight for immediate composure. By God if the little minx wasn't staring right back at him from underneath his desk. Had she no consideration for her own safety? Removing his attention from her strained expression, he straightened himself a bit and leaned forward so his elbows rested on the table.

"Whatever the case," Carlyle said, "it's presented the opportunity for a new bet in White's betting book—one with stakes so high that many are likely to fall into debt."

"Are you able to share the specifics?" Lucien asked. He was trying desperately hard not to look down at Katherine for fear that Barrymore and Carlyle might think something amiss.

"Of course," Carlyle murmured. He shifted a bit in his seat, his large frame looking marginally uncomfortable in the much smaller chair. "The bet is in regard to her whereabouts. Everyone wants to know where she is and especially *whom* she's there with. As you already know, most people have you in mind, although there are some who've recently mentioned Starkly. Apparently she was also seen talking to him at the ball, and since both of you are in Town, then surely she must be here too if she's carrying on an affair with either one of you. However, there are those who believe she's left the country, while others think she might still be at Cresthaven after all. You know her better than anyone, Roxberry. If you have any idea as to where she might be and the gentleman whose company she's keeping, then perhaps you'd be kind enough to advise us."

"That doesn't sound very fair," Lucien muttered. "Nevertheless, I will tell you that she did indeed come to Town." He heard a muttered oath from beneath the desk, which he hastily covered with a cough. "However, she quickly left again—alone, I might add. It was my understanding that she would be journeying back to Cresthaven, but if you say she's not in residence, then my guess in regard to her whereabouts is as good as yours, gentlemen."

"Then she has left the country," Barrymore said. "Everyone knows her parents are in Scotland. It's possible she followed them there."

"In this day and age, anything is possible," Lucien said. "Though I personally would not bet on it."

"Then what would you bet on?" Carlyle asked, his eyes widening with expectation.

"Nothing," Lucien replied. "I don't gamble, you see. Especially not when I'm likely to lose."

"Then perhaps you can tell us if there's been some development in the other matter. We've told everyone who mentioned Starkly that they were being absurd and that if she were to attach herself to any gentleman, it would be to you. Be honest with us, Roxberry. Will you be saying your vows soon?" Barrymore asked.

"I don't see how I can," Lucien said. Although he didn't look at her, he could sense Katherine's desire to leap out from under the desk and give them all a piece of her mind. "I mean, if Lady Crossby is not to be found in Society, then surely she must be *out* of Society, in which case there's little chance of a forthcoming marriage between the two of us, when I am here in Town."

"Well, dash it all," Barrymore exclaimed just as the tea and sandwiches arrived. "We were both betting that you would marry her within the next two weeks by special license. Indeed, we stand to lose a great deal if you do not."

"All I can tell you is that no plans have been made." Reaching for a sandwich, Lucien sank his teeth into the soft bread. Barrymore and Carlyle both followed suit. "But I will say this. Each time I've mentioned marriage to the lady, she has denied any wish to venture down that path again."

"You will not ask her again, then?" Carlyle asked, his cheeks filled with food.

With his focus on the bet, the young earl had apparently forgotten his manners—not that Lucien cared. He shrugged, reached for his teacup and took a sip. It was blessedly hot. "I don't know. I believe it will depend on whether or not she can accept that I am by far the better chess player."

Something hard came down over his toes. Her fist, no doubt. Lucien grimaced, and unfortunately the expression did not go unnoticed. "Something the matter?" Barrymore asked.

"The tea was hotter than I expected," Lucien lied. "I believe I've burned myself."

"Well, we shan't take up any more of your time. I think we've learned as much as we're likely to, however little that may be." Barrymore rose, as did Carlyle. "Thank you, Roxberry."

"My pleasure," Lucien said, rising as well. He came around the desk and crossed to the door. "I'll see you out."

As soon as they'd left, Lucien expelled a deep

breath. Disaster had been averted—for now. Turning around, he prepared to return to his study, but he spotted Katherine instead, her slim figure hurrying toward the stairs. "And where, pray tell, do you think you're going?" he asked.

She froze and turned toward him, her eyes refusing to meet his. "To my room."

"If you don't mind, I'd like to have a word with you first." He swept his arm toward the door of his study and waited for her to go toward it. She did not. Lowering his arm, he took a slow breath and fought for patience. "I suspect that you and I are about to have an argument, Kate, and if that is the case, then I'd rather keep it to ourselves than share it with the servants. Now, if you please."

She looked undecided for a moment, but then she turned about and headed back the way she'd come, her posture stiff and decidedly unwelcoming. It didn't have much effect on Lucien. He still wanted to kiss her in spite of his annoyance. "Would you care to explain yourself?" he asked as soon as they were alone.

With raised chin and straight back, she stared back at him. She would not be cowed, for which he could not help but admire her. Instead, she looked quite prepared to defend herself and, if need be, accept the admonishment that she surely expected him to give. "I wished to write an invitation to your sister. I did not think that you would mind if I used your stationery."

"Don't vex me, Kate. You know this has nothing to do with the damn stationery."

Her lips flattened into a thin line. "Very well. I suppose you wish me to apologize to you for thwarting your wishes."

"It would be a start." He hated himself for sounding so strict, but his constant worrying over her had come to a crux when he'd discovered her under his desk. "I do believe I specifically asked you to avoid the downstairs rooms when I am not here in case an unexpected visitor might arrive and see you. The least you could have done was inform Parker of your whereabouts. What if they'd seen you, Kate? The scandal would have been irreparable!"

"I'm sorry, Lucien, but if you recall, it was *your* idea to bring me here. You only have yourself to blame."

He gritted his teeth. In a sense she was right. "All I ask is for you to employ a bit of common sense. Yes, I insisted you stay here so I could protect you, but casting blame will be of little help if you are found out."

She glared at him. "I feel as if I no longer know you. You're harder than you used to be . . . less forgiving and less . . . kind. You unsettle me these days, Lucien, and I find that I do not care for it."

Closing his eyes for a brief second, he shook his head. *She* was the one who drove him to behave the way he did. His constant concern for her well-being weighed heavily upon him, the fear of losing her forever present in his mind. "I am only worried." In fact, he was sick with it.

"I appreciate that." Her tone softened. "And I will do my best not to disappoint you again."

Something about the way she said it, the inflection of her words, gave him pause. He had to kiss her, even if she would break his heart in return. However great the pain he might suffer, he could not allow her to think that she would ever disappoint him. It was his fault that she did though. Due to past experience, she thought herself undeserving of a man's affection. She did not trust that he would accept her the way she was—that he would not care about the discolored marks upon her skin. But rather than lessen the distance between them, he'd broadened it with his own fears of rejection. In short, he'd been careless with her trust.

Looking at her now, her hands clenched at her sides, her posture proud, there was no denying that she was attempting to hide her vulnerability and the pain she surely felt in response to the lack of attention he'd given her recently. If only she understood that he was clinging to sanity by a very thin thread, that if he went to her, he'd want to drown in everything she had to offer. He wanted her as his wife, but she had already told him no twice before. Who was to say that she wouldn't do so again?

On a deep breath, he went to her, his footfalls soft upon the carpet. She didn't move, but she didn't look the least bit welcoming either. Indeed, she appeared wary, which he could understand. "I fear that I am the one who has disappointed you, Kate." He stopped before her, reached for her hand and raised it to his lips so he could kiss her palm.

Her breath caught. "I feel as if my life is spiraling out of control."

"Because of me?" he asked.

"Because of everything." Her fingers quivered. She was not immune.

Lucien gazed back into her eyes and saw the fear-tinged pain that lurched there. "I have made you suffer, though it was not my intention to do so."

"It's all right. I understand."

"So you have said before, but I don't believe that you actually do." Lowering her hand, he placed it over his chest and held it there. "My heart grows frantic whenever you are near."

"So does mine," she whispered.

She pulled at him with her essence, and he was powerless to stop her. He'd decided not to kiss her again unless she was willing to marry him, but it couldn't be helped. She was already in his arms and his lips were soon upon hers, nibbling and kissing until she uttered a sigh that drove him wild.

Without thinking, he backed her up against his desk and lifted her up so she could sit on the edge of it, his hands pulling at her skirts, creating a space for him to stand between her legs. He kissed her harder, pouring into her the passion he'd kept at bay since he'd last held her in his arms. She intoxicated him with her scent—a crisp flavor of lemon, softened with honey. It only made him hungry for more.

"Lucien," she murmured, her fingers digging at his shoulders as he kissed his way along the curve of her neck. "I didn't think you wanted me anymore."

He should have challenged himself to a duel if such a thing had been possible. The pain his stupidity had caused her was unforgivable, but he had every intention of making it up to her now. With a swift tug of her bodice, he bared her breasts, their fullness just as glorious as he remembered. They filled his hands and he kissed his way toward them, his thumb scraping a nipple just before he took the tender flesh in his mouth.

Katherine groaned, her back arching toward him, offering him more. "I want you," he muttered. Reaching between them, he placed his hand against her and slowly circled the area that would give her the greatest pleasure. She shuddered, her breath a little uneven. There was something so exquisitely erotic about touching her like this through the layers of her gown. "I will always want you," he whispered.

Sighing, she tilted her hips. "More," she begged, her words sending waves of hot desire straight to his groin. How he longed to give her more, to take her right there on his desk in broad daylight. He considered it—the urge to do so was powerful indeed—but he had promised himself that he wouldn't. Not until she agreed to marriage.

Regrettably, now was not the time to pose such an important question. Not unless he wished to manipulate her answer, which he did not. *Later,* he promised as he pushed his fingers against her, increasing the friction while his mouth returned to hers. He thrust his tongue inside, speaking without words of his greatest fantasies, of his desire for her and of what was in his heart.

On a jagged groan, she came apart, her hands clutching him close as she shivered with ecstasy. "I love you," she whispered against his shoulder. "God help me, I love you so terribly much."

He should ask her now, and he prepared to do so as he leaned back a little so he could help her adjust the bodice and skirt of her gown. Cupping her face between his hands, he looked at the beautiful features he'd loved for so long. "Kate," he murmured, his heart thrashing about like a caged beast. "I—"

There was a knock at the door. Lucien closed his eyes and willed the unwelcome person away. This could not be happening. He was about to propose to the woman he loved, to assure her of his devotion, and he was being interrupted. The knock came again.

"Will you get that?" Katherine asked.

Lucien gazed past her at the window beyond. "I suppose I must," he said with reluctance. Stepping back so she could slip off the desk, he paused for a moment to appreciate the color he'd brought to her cheeks. "This conversation isn't over," he promised. "We have much to discuss, you and I."

Her lips parted, but she said nothing. Lucien went to the door and opened it to find Parker on the other side of it. "I hope you'll forgive the intrusion," he said, "but it appears you have another caller."

Lucien groaned. His house was suddenly being overrun. "You may tell them that I am not at home."

"I daresay the dowager countess will not take kindly to being lied to," Parker said stiffly. "If I may, I would suggest you go and greet her in the parlor. She is quite eager to see you."

Good God, his grandmother was here? Lucien swallowed. He had to think of some way in which to prevent her from staying at the house. Bloody hell, this was rapidly turning into a very complex nightmare! "I wasn't expecting her to arrive for another two weeks. She's rarely in Town so early in the Season. Is Mama here with her?"

"Apparently—"

"No, she is not," he heard his grandmother say.

Rushing forward, Lucien almost collided with the butler, who was still standing before him. With an apology, Lucien hastily closed the door to his study while Parker stepped nimbly aside, allowing Lucien a clear view of the lady in question. "Grandmamma," he said as he went toward her and reached for her hand. "How wonderful to see you again."

He kissed her knuckles, but she did not smile or say anything amusing at all, the way she usually did. Instead, she was scowling, her hawk-eyes fixed on the door he'd just closed. "What are you hiding?" she asked.

"Nothing," he said, aiming for a nonchalant tone. "Shall we adjourn to the parlor? We'll have some of that peppermint tea you're so fond of."

Her scowl deepened. "Don't try to distract me, Roxberry. It won't work and you know it." She turned toward Parker, assessing the poor man shrewdly. "Tell me, what is my grandson hiding?"

The butler looked perfectly miserable as he glanced from one to the other.

"You are being unreasonable," Lucien told his grandmother. "The study is my own private domain."

"That may well be," she agreed, "unless of course you are up to no good, my dear. Now, if you will please step aside so I can see."

"I will not," he said, panic rising in his chest.

His grandmother looked at him sharply. She then began tugging off her gloves. "Rumors can be devastating to anyone's reputation, you know. From what I hear, Lady Crossby has recently gone missing. Nobody knows where she might have gotten to, though I understand that her location has become the source of a wager over at White's."

"How long have you been in Town?" he asked suspiciously.

"I've only just arrived, but this sort of news has a tendency to travel on the wind. Fortunately for you, however, nobody seems to share my opinion on the matter as of yet."

"And what is your opinion?" Lucien asked, though he had a fairly good idea that he already knew.

"That she is residing in this very house." She smiled at last. "Of course, this has been nothing more than mere speculation until you just greeted me. Now I am convinced, you see, and if I am right in my supposition, then you'd best be straight with me. Lady Crossby doesn't need this sort of scandal, and neither do you."

He felt like the small boy he'd been when he'd found his grandfather's fob watch forgotten in the parlor. He'd picked it up so he could admire it, but he'd been too curious and had somehow managed to break the thing. When his grandmother had entered the room, he'd hastily hidden the watch behind his back, but she'd seen right through him, and although his punishment had been lenient, guilt had shamed him.

Bowing his head, Lucien turned back toward the door, took a breath and opened it. Before him, much like he had left her, stood Katherine, as beautiful as ever. She had not taken refuge under the desk this time.

"Good afternoon," Lady Roxberry said as she strolled into the room behind Lucien. "I see I was correct after all."

"My lady," Katherine said, dipping into an elegant curtsy. She did not meet Lucien's gaze, which was probably just as well right now.

"Please leave us," Lady Roxberry told the butler, whose bland expression appeared to have slipped for the first time Lucien could remember. The door closed with a quiet thud. "Are either of you aware how sticky this situation will likely become if word of your . . . living arrangement gets out?"

"We have considered it," Lucien told her plainly.

"I see," his grandmother remarked. "Then would you please tell me what in blazes you are thinking? Gracious me, Roxberry, I thought you more level-headed than this."

"There is a perfectly good explanation," he said, upon which he told her everything that had happened since the night of the ball—except, of course, the manner in which his relationship with Katherine had progressed. Some things were sacred.

"It does seem rather noble and heroic I suppose," his grandmother said at last, "but that doesn't change the impropriety of it. Thankfully the two of you have always gotten along famously. I'm sure you'll be incredibly happy in your marriage."

"Grandmamma," Lucien gritted. The last thing he needed right now was for his grandmother to involve herself in his proposal.

"Well, you are going to marry her, are you not? After all, it's clear to anyone with a pair of eyes in their head that the two of you have been up to no good lately. Either that, or Lady Crossby has recently grown very fond of rouge."

Lucien groaned. He looked at Katherine, who was indeed a very bright shade of red, her lips still slightly swollen from their kiss. There could be no denying that they'd been doing more than talking moments before his grandmother's arrival had been announced. "I will do the right thing if the lady will allow it," Lucien said. If only he'd asked her sooner, during the two full days of opportunity he'd been given. Now Katherine would likely think he was merely following orders, averting disaster and saving her from the very real possibility of being referred to as his mistress.

"Good." His grandmother's nod was stiff. "You have my blessing, and your mother's, I should think. Your father would be very pleased by this match, Roxberry. He was always quite fond of her ladyship when she was a little girl with braided hair and scruffy shoes. Tell me, my dear, do you still collect flowers for pressing?"

"On occasion," Katherine said, her voice sounding faint. "I'm particularly fond of wildflowers, my lady."

"Yes. I recall that you used to make the most delightful pictures with them." Lady Roxberry turned toward the door. "I'll leave you to it then, shall I? Don't be too long about it though, or I'll have to come back in to ensure that you're behaving properly. A brief kiss is all you're permitted. And just so you know, I do not plan on leaving. If Katherine is to stay in this house, then I shall stay here with her as her chaperone."

"She is a widow, Grandmamma, not a debutante," Lucien said, vexed by the whole situation.

His grandmother stared at him. "And what? You think the gossip will be less harmful to her reputation than if she'd been a naïve young girl?"

"Of course not," he said. "I am well aware that it would be devastating to her and her daughter if anyone should say that she is my mistress."

"Good. Then you will see to your duty. Immediately." She opened the door to leave, then halted, turned back toward them and said, "I'll await you both in the parlor. We can celebrate the news of your upcoming marriage there." The door closed behind her.

"Well, she doesn't mince words, does she?" Katherine said. Lucien turned to look at her. She seemed tense. Who could blame her? "In fact, it is a trait I've always greatly admired."

"Kate . . . ," he began. "I'm so sorry."

Her gaze flickered. "Me too. Had I known it would turn out this way, I never would have come with you, but everything happened so quickly and I didn't think things through. I didn't consider the consequences, and in doing so, I have trapped you."

"I am equally to blame, though I would prefer it if you would use another word than *trapped*. It sounds so calculating and disagreeable."

"Well, I suppose I ought to ease your mind at least. I will marry you, if that is what you wish," she said, her voice so strained it seemed quite ready to snap.

"It is not what you want?" Apprehension flared to life inside him.

"I've told you before that it isn't." She paused, her eyes intense upon his. "However, I must admit that I did consider it after we . . . well, you know. In fact, I rather expected you to ask me again—hoped for it even. But you did not, and I decided that you'd probably changed your mind."

Feeling weak and completely undeserving, Lucien crossed to where she stood. She'd wanted him to ask her again, but he had not—at least not so she'd heard him. "I did ask you, Kate, but you'd fallen asleep by then and you didn't hear me."

"Then why . . . why wouldn't you ask me again the following morning, Lucien? You've had plenty of opportunity." Her eyes brimmed with hope.

"Honestly, upon further reflection, I wasn't sure it was something you wanted, given your previous resistance. I dreaded receiving yet another 'no' from you." Taking her hand in his, he wove his fingers through hers. "Please, Kate . . . I've loved you forever. Save me from this madness, I beg you, and make me the happiest man alive by agreeing to be my wife."

Tears welled in her eyes, and Lucien kissed them away. "Yes," he heard her say, her voice filled with wonder. His heart soared as he swept her into his arms and held her against him, kissing her while she laughed and squealed. The tension that had wound itself around her these past few days had finally come undone. He'd made her happy, not only by proposing but also by assuring her that she was everything he'd ever wanted. Tomorrow they would celebrate with friends.

Chapter 16

"I told you he'd returned for you," Louise said as she seated herself next to Katherine on a pretty ice blue sofa the following evening. They had removed themselves to the parlor after a most delicious meal of roast duck with orange sauce and prunes, while the gentlemen took their drinks in the library. "And people say not to trust rumors."

"Well I, for one, am relieved that he finally plucked up the courage to ask," Patricia said. She was sitting to Katherine's right.

Katherine chuckled. "It was coercion, really." She looked at Lady Roxberry, who was happily sipping her tea.

"Bah!" Lady Roxberry waved her bejeweled hand dismissively. "I've always suspected that boy of having an eye for you, so I'm sure he would have gotten around to it eventually. Still, I can't say I was displeased with the opportunity to nudge things along a little—at the speed he was moving, I would have been long in my grave before anything came of it, and that really would have been a shame. I'm quite enjoying the idea of having *two* great-grandbabies soon."

"Oh!" Louise gasped as she clasped her hands together. "Is there something we ought to know? Come now, Katherine, you can tell us if there is." She and Patricia both nodded with eager encouragement.

Katherine grinned. "Honestly, I can't believe how forward you're both being. Why, I do believe you must have fallen under Lady Roxberry's influence."

"It's about time," Lady Roxberry said. "Naturally, I've been trying to school Patricia since she was a little girl, but she was always a bit too timid. It's a pleasure to see her opening up. But Lady Huntley . . . well, she does show promise, and how surprising that is when your dear mama, the duchess, has always been so very diplomatic."

"I fear I have no patience for diplomacy," Louise said as she picked up her teacup, drummed her fingertips against the rim and finally took a sip. "Or at least not very much. Now tell us honestly, Katherine. Are you increasing?"

"Don't be absurd," Katherine said, her insides quivering with nerves. "How could I be when we're not even married?"

There was a beat, and then a peal of laughter from each of Katherine's guests—including Lady Roxberry herself, who was looking most amused. Katherine stared at them all in shock.

"How, indeed?" Louise said, her voice ringing with mirth. She placed her hand on Katherine's. "My dear, surely you must know that much, having already mothered a child."

The room was getting unbearably hot. Katherine looked longingly at the window. "Yes, of course," she said. "But Roxberry is a gentleman, and while he has certainly kissed me, he has never attempted to do more." Pleased by the steadiness in her voice, she smiled serenely at Lucien's grandmother and prayed she wouldn't call her bluff. Somehow, she had to find a way to change the subject.

"Liar!" Unfortunately, the word came from Lady Roxberry herself.

"I beg your pardon?" Katherine asked, a little affronted by the accusation even though it was entirely true.

"My dear, you needn't keep up appearances for my sake."

"But—"

"Yes, yes, I know what I said." She settled herself against a plump cushion and waved her hand about again. "Surely you understand that I *had* to say that. We all have our duty, after all. But if you think I can't see what's beyond my own nose, then you must be daft. Besides, I didn't insist you switch bedrooms, did I? If that's not a carte blanche, then I really can't imagine what is."

"And why is that?" Patricia asked.

Katherine's shoulders slumped. If only someone would come to her rescue.

Lady Roxberry didn't answer, but she did deliver a very pointed look—one that took precisely two seconds for the other ladies to decipher. "Ohhh . . . ," they breathed, eyes round with interest.

"He wanted to keep me close so he could protect me should the need arise," Katherine said.

"Riiight . . ." Louise dragged out the word. Her reluctance to believe anything Katherine said was plain.

"Oh, you're impossible," Katherine said, knowing full well how unlikely her explanation sounded, given the circumstances. It was especially difficult to convince others of its verity when she didn't believe it herself. It was a half-truth at best. Knowing what she now did, there was no doubt in her mind that Lucien had taken the opportunity to play hero to her damsel in distress with the express purpose of seducing her into his bed and persuading her to marry him.

The door to the parlor opened and Lucien appeared. "Mind if we join you?" he asked, his eyes going straight to Katherine, a smile of appreciation lighting his features as he took her in.

"Not in the least," she replied, trying desperately to avoid the knowing look that Lady Roxberry was giving her. She couldn't see Louise's face or Patricia's, since they were both sitting next to her, but she could sense them smiling with unabashed amusement.

Rotten friends!

"Goodness me, my dear," Huntley said as he followed Lucien into the parlor and looked at his wife, "you look as though you've just been made privy to a state secret. What on earth have you been discussing?" He took a seat in a vacant armchair while Lucien and Gray both went to the sideboard.

"Would anyone care for a drink?" Lucien asked as he reached for a couple of tumblers.

"Sherry, please," Lady Roxberry said. This was seconded by Louise.

Lucien looked at Katherine and raised an eyebrow—a silent question as the mouth of the sherry carafe hovered over another glass.

"Would it shock you if I asked for a brandy instead?" Katherine asked. She needed something stronger than sherry if she was going to recover from her recent interrogation. Her nerves were in a complete tangle.

The corner of Lucien's mouth dimpled. Handing the sherry glasses to Gray so he could distribute them, Lucien took another tumbler and poured a measure. "Not in the least," he murmured.

"Will you answer my question?" Huntley asked. He was watching Louise very closely.

"It was nothing significant. I was just curious . . . or rather, *we* were . . ." Louise looked at the other ladies, while Katherine stiffened.

" . . . about motherhood, my dear," Louise continued. "You see, Lady Gray and I were asking Lady Roxberry and Lady Crossby for advice, since Lady Gray is presently expecting and you and I have been quite—"

"Yes, I think I get the idea," Huntley said. He crossed his arms and leaned back in his chair, looking mildly uncomfortable.

Katherine breathed a sigh of relief, thankful that her friend had refrained from mentioning the real subject of their recent discussion. Gray coughed, apparently to mask what sounded suspiciously like laughter.

Lucien came toward the sofa where Katherine was sitting. He looked terribly handsome in his black evening attire—so similar to the night of the Kingsborough Ball. His hair was calmer than it had been then, however, his jaw smooth due to a late afternoon shave. As he leaned forward to set her brandy in front of her, she caught a faint whiff of his aroma—sandalwood blending with wine and the slightest hint of tobacco. Katherine's insides curled with pleasure, and she suddenly wished she could think of a reason to send Lady Roxberry off to bed and their other guests home.

"I understand from Roxberry that finding the man who hired Lady Trapleigh is proving more difficult than expected," Huntley said. He reached for his brandy and took a sip. "I am sorry to hear it. Nothing is worse than constantly looking over one's shoulder. I've told him that if there's any way in which I can be of assistance, you need only ask. My wife must return to Kingsborough Hall, of course, but there's no reason why I can't remain here if need be."

"Thank you," Katherine said. "I appreciate the kindness."

"The same goes for me," Gray said. "I'm happy to be of service so the two of you can put the unsavory business behind you and start planning your wedding instead."

"Society will turn on its head when it finds out," Patricia said.

Leaning against the mantel of the fireplace, Lucien absently poked at a log, pushing it further into the flames until it snapped and crackled. He grinned. "That's precisely what we're aiming for."

It was another two hours before Patricia announced that while she'd had a lovely evening, she desperately longed for the rest sleep offered. "I'm constantly fatigued these days," she said. "But the worst part of it is that sleep often evades me because I cannot seem to get comfortable with this enormous belly."

"I think you look lovely," Gray told her dutifully.

"And I think I look and feel as if I swallowed a cannonball."

Katherine smiled at her friend. "It will soon be over," she told her reassuringly."

Lucien accompanied them all out while Katherine remained in the parlor with Lady Roxberry, who immediately yawned when Lucien returned. "Well, I'm feeling rather exhausted myself," she said as she rose to her feet.

"You wouldn't care for another sherry?" Lucien asked.

"Oh no. I'll be more content with the tea that I asked one of your maids to send up so I'd have it before bed. You go ahead though, if you like. I'll see you both in the morning." And then she left without saying anything further.

Katherine stared after her, as did Lucien. "No word of warning?" he muttered. "How unlike her." Turning to look at Katherine, his eyes narrowed a little before he finally said, "What were you really talking about earlier, before we gentlemen interrupted? You looked quite flushed, if I recall."

"And so I shall again if we don't change the subject of conversation, but if you must know, they were all quite eager to discover if you and I had . . . well . . . you know."

"Including my grandmamma?" He sounded horrified at the notion, which she supposed was justified, even though he ought to have expected it. He, better than anyone else, knew how surprising the lady could be.

"No, it was mostly Lady Huntley, actually. Your grandmother was apparently quite certain that we'd already been intimate with each other, and she was not opposed to saying so."

"Good God! I'm so sorry, Kate. That must have been terribly embarrassing for you."

She couldn't help but smile. "Yes, I suppose it was, but I survived it." She tilted her head as she regarded him. He still hadn't taken a seat and was instead standing a few paces away, watching her with great intensity. "Aren't you curious to hear her opinion?"

He grunted. "I've little desire to know what she had to say on the matter. In fact, I'm surprised I'm in this room alone with you while she . . ." He frowned, and Katherine waited patiently for him to put it all together. "Are you telling me she approves?"

"She says she cannot because of propriety, and then she reminded me that she didn't insist I switch rooms. She knows we share a door and that we may visit each other whenever we choose, yet she has done nothing to change that. I think we can safely assume that she has turned a blind eye."

"Well, I daresay I ought to advise her on what's required of a chaperone, but that would not be to my advantage," Lucien murmured as he held his hand out toward her.

She accepted it and allowed him to pull her to her feet. "Nor would it be to mine," she whispered. And then she kissed him.

Chapter 17

"**I** have to meet Starkly in an hour," Lucien told Katherine at breakfast the following morning after finishing his paper and setting it aside. It was just the two of them, since his grandmother had recently left to meet with one of her friends. "We'll be heading over to the rendezvous spot together."

"I'm still not comfortable with this plan of yours," Katherine said. "I wish you didn't have to go." Although her apprehension toward Starkly had significantly lessened after Lucien had told her that the earl had once stood up for her against her husband, she was still concerned for Lucien's safety.

As if reading her thoughts, Lucien said, "I have to put an end to this so we can move on, get married and be happy. If I don't confront Donovan, your life remains in danger."

Katherine nodded, acknowledging the truth of his words. How easy it had been to forget the severity of the situation when she'd lain in his arms last night. "Very well, then," she agreed.

Rising from the table, Lucien crossed to where she sat, took her hand in his and kissed it, his eyes locking with hers as he did so. "You must also be careful, Kate. I know this is tedious for you, but please stay upstairs in your room until I return, and keep away from the windows. If anything were to happen to you, I . . ."

His words trailed off, but not before she heard the desperation in his voice. She nodded, hoping to calm his fears. "I promise," she said.

Half an hour later, Katherine was attempting to immerse herself in a book she'd found in the library when Parker knocked on her bedroom door, ashenfaced. "Forgive me for intruding, my lady, but a footman has just arrived from the Gray residency, and his lordship left in such a hurry that he neglected to tell me where he was going. Did he mention his destination to you?"

"Good heavens," Katherine said, coming toward the distressed servant, alarmed by his lack of composure. "Whatever is the matter?"

"Lady Gray is apparently having her baby."

"But it's too early," Katherine said. "She's not due for another month."

"There has also been a complication. I'm not sure what the specifics are, but my understanding is that it's—"

Katherine didn't wait for the man to finish. Dashing past him, she swept out onto the landing and began hurrying down the stairs, tears burning in her eyes as she went.

"Where are you going?" Parker asked with obvious concern.

"To tell the footman where to find Lord Roxberry of course, and then to Lady Gray."

"But you cannot," Parker announced with a bit more authority. "It's too dangerous for you to—"

"If you imagine that you can tell me Lady Gray is suffering through a difficult birth and that I will simply sit here and do nothing, then you are sorely mistaken," she said, spinning about and facing the butler with great annoyance.

"His lordship insists that you remain here, my lady. Besides, I'm sure Lord Gray has the best physician and midwife available to assist."

"That may very well be," Katherine replied, "but ultimately, Lord Roxberry is not my keeper, and in the event that the footman fails to find him and the worst should happen, I believe he'd like to know that I was able to offer his sister some measure of comfort." Not waiting for a reply, she continued on through to where the footman was waiting. "His lordship is visiting Lord Starkly at his residency on Hanover Square, but you'd best make haste, for there's no telling how long he'll be there." Heaven help her, she'd no idea where the footman might find him if he was no longer at Starkly House, since Lucien had failed to give her the location of his meeting.

Thanking her, the footman quickly mounted his horse and took off down the street. Grabbing her pelisse from a hook on the wall and flinging it over her shoulders, Katherine addressed Parker next. "Please send someone to fetch Lady Roxberry."

"Yes, of course," Parker said, following her out into the street. "I don't like you going off on your own, Lady Crossby. If you'll only wait five minutes, I can have one of his lordship's carriages brought round with a maid to escort you."

"There isn't time," Katherine said. "I'm taking a hackney." And before the butler could protest any further, she'd hailed a coach and climbed in, not noticing the other occupants in her haste to get on her way.

A click sounded—the cocking of a pistol—and Katherine's eyes flew instantly to the smartly dressed woman across from her. "Hello, Lady Crossby," Lady Trapleigh said with a smile, "it appears we meet again."

"**A**re you ready to leave?" Lucien asked when he was shown into Starkly's study by the earl's butler.

Rising from his seat, Starkly reached across his desk to shake Lucien's hand. "In a moment," he said. "But before we do, there's something I must tell you." He indicated one of the chairs opposite his own.

Unsure of what to expect, Lucien swept his coat-tails aside and claimed the proffered seat.

Starkly sat as well. As soon as the butler was gone and the door closed, he gave Lucien a serious look. "I didn't want to bring this up until I'd looked into the matter and was absolutely sure," he said, leaning forward so his elbows rested on his desk. "I don't believe Lady Trapleigh's son is in any danger."

Lucien stiffened. "How can you be certain?"

"Because I know where he his." The earl paused momentarily, as if attempting to decide whether or not to continue. Gazing back at Lucien, he eventually said, "Years ago, I created a sanctuary for women who found themselves in a less than favorable situation."

Lucien stared at Starkly in disbelief. "You offered desperate women a place to go for their confinement?"

"They are welcome to stay there until they're ready to return to the life from which they came. The people in my employ help them with that, either by finding them a suitable protector or by ensuring that they can support themselves and their child by some other means."

"But your reputation is in complete conflict with a man who'd be so kind and generous," Lucien blurted. He couldn't believe what he was hearing, though it did align with Starkly's attempt to help Katherine when he'd witnessed Crossby's abuse.

Starkly winced. "Things aren't always as they seem. As you surely must know, there are many upstanding gentlemen who'd like to avoid word getting out about them fathering children on the side. In such instances, I will often take on the responsibility for the sake of the woman in question."

"But why?"

"Let's just say that I harbor a great deal of resentment toward my father and that I would like to make amends on his behalf."

"Am I to understand that Lady Trapleigh was one of the women you helped and that her son is in your care?" Lucien asked carefully.

Starkly nodded. "He is at Guardly, roughly a half hour's ride west of Hereford. After speaking with you the other day, I sent one of my men out to ensure that he was still there and to heighten the security. However, I don't think anyone is planning to harm the child."

Lucien pondered that. "As his mother, Lady Trapleigh would have gone to him first to ensure that he was all right, suggesting that she had no reason to doubt that he wasn't. The threat against her son was a ruse." He felt his heartbeat pick up. "She was merely buying time with the hope of eventually going through with the murder."

"It appears that way. Yes."

Lucien stared back at Starkly. "But Donovan . . .

somehow he must be involved. Unless of course . . ."
Lucien contemplated everything that pointed to Donovan. All they had was Lady Trapleigh's word and a couple of fires to support her claim. "What if Lady Trapleigh arranged for Lady Crossby's investments to be targeted, knowing it would implicate Donovan and remove our suspicions from her in case she got caught?"

"They may have been working together," Starkly pointed out.

"Possibly, though I'm beginning to suspect that the widow has been leading us on a merry chase." At least he hadn't received word from Cresthaven yet, which meant that Lady Trapleigh was still under restraint there.

"We will keep our appointment with Donovan in the event that he is somehow involved. After that, I plan on returning to Cresthaven, and I'll be stopping by the local constable on the way," Lucien said. Clasping his hands together, he leaned forward until his arms rested on his thighs. He looked at Starkly. "I was happy to prevent gossip from spreading when I thought Lady Trapleigh was being blackmailed, but since that no longer seems plausible, I'll have to do what I should have done from the start and have her properly apprehended."

Starkly nodded as he rose to his feet. "We ought to leave now if you wish to keep your appointment with Donovan."

Agreeing, Lucien got up and strode from the room. For now, Lady Trapleigh would have to wait.

Seated at a worm-eaten table at The Fox and Hound tavern, Lucien was stunned when a smartly dressed gentleman approached, offering a small nod by way of greeting. For some peculiar reason, Lucien had been expecting a scruffy ruffian.

"Roxberry?" the man inquired.

"Indeed," Lucien replied, his eyes seeking Starkly, who was lounging lazily at the bar. "And you must be Donovan."

Donovan dipped his head in acquiescence before seating himself opposite Lucien, then he smiled affably. "Let us proceed with business, shall we?"

Lucien leaned forward. "First, I should like to discuss your attempt to harm Lady Crossby."

Donovan's eyes narrowed. "What is this?"

"Nothing whatsoever if you can convince me that there is no connection between yourself and the recent attempts on Lady Crossby's life." Shifting, Donovan moved to get up, but he froze in response to a soft click. The corner of Lucien's mouth drew upward. "I have a pistol trained on you beneath the table, so I suggest you sit back down and tell me everything you know."

"Don't think I came alone, Roxberry," Donovan snarled. "My men will kill you should anything happen to me."

"And I will kill you if they show any sign of trying."

There was a long pause before Donovan, crossing his arms with obvious disapproval, said, "The name of the lady you mentioned is unfamiliar to me."

"Yet word has it that she is a threat to your investments."

"My investments?" Donovan's eyes turned cold. Leaning forward, he rested his elbows on the table. "Now you listen to me, Roxberry. I am not the sort of man who wastes time on long-term ventures. I like fast returns, which is why I've chosen a more unconventional approach to earning a living. Your source is either mistaken or lying to you. Either way, you've wasted my time. Now, if you will excuse me, I have an important race to attend."

"Why should I believe you?" Lucien asked. "For all I know, you may be lying."

"Because I'm not a murderer, you bloody bastard! By God, I've a good mind to call you out for issuing such an insult, but I'd rather avoid the attention."

"What about Mr. Pitkin?" Lucien asked.

Donovan muttered an oath. "I hope you're not insinuating that I'm to blame for that poor devil's taking his own life. Hell, it isn't my fault that some men are fools with their blunt and willing to risk more than they're able to lose. Either way, you and I both know it's only a matter of time before men like him meet a sorry end. But just to be clear, I've never killed anyone." Lucien nodded, and Donovan rose to his feet. "In the future," he said, "have a care with where you lay the blame." Turning away, he strode to the door, passing a flushed-looking man on his way out. Starkly went toward the newly arrived man, exchanged a few words and hurried him toward Lucien's table. Lucien frowned.

"Apparently Lady Gray has taken ill," Starkly said, his features grave with concern. "Her footman here was sent to fetch you . . . something about an ailment pertaining to her delicate condition. From what I—"

"Good God," Lucien exclaimed. He was already on his feet, fear prickling the back of his neck as he thought of his sister. "Thank you for accompanying me, Starkly, but I must be off."

"Yes, yes, of course," Starkly agreed. "Take my carriage—I'll grab a hackney."

"Are you sure?"

"Absolutely. Is there anything else you wish me to do?"

Lucien halted on his way to the door. "I was hoping to return home so I could check on my guest," he said, "but perhaps you can do so for me as I'm sure the Grays will need their footman returned to them."

Starkly nodded.

"And if you don't mind, please inform my butler of my whereabouts."

"I'll see to it at once," Starkly promised.

Parting ways, Lucien hurried over to Starkly's awaiting carriage and flung himself inside, ordering the driver to make haste.

"Are you mad?" Katherine asked as she stared across at Lady Trapleigh. She hadn't changed her clothes since Katherine had last seen her, and she was not alone—a gruff-looking man sat beside her.

"On the contrary, I'm of perfectly sound mind, Lady Crossby. Unfortunately for you, however, your late husband didn't hold you in very high regard."

"I don't understand what my marriage has to do with this," Katherine said, looking to the man sitting next to Lady Trapleigh. "How did you even manage to escape? You were locked in the butler's pantry!"

Lady Trapleigh chuckled. "Remarkable how useful a few hairpins can be, wouldn't you agree?"

Katherine sank back against the squabs of the carriage. How foolish they'd been to untie her, knowing what she'd done. And now Katherine was sitting at the wrong end of Lady Trapleigh's cocked pistol. Sucking in a breath, she silently prayed that they wouldn't hit a bump in the road. "You mentioned Crossby before. Why does my relationship with him signify?"

"My dear, I do believe I ought to allow you the pleasure of figuring that out on your own," Lady Trapleigh purred.

Katherine took a sharp breath. She'd been on her way to the Gray residency to offer her assistance. "My lady, whatever your reason for attempting to kill me, Roxberry's sister needs me. I must get to her as quickly as possible."

"Ah yes, the increasing countess. Tell me, is her life at risk?"

Katherine hesitated, not liking the tone of Lady Trapleigh's voice in the least. "I'm not sure," she said.

"Hmm . . . well, one can always hope, I suppose."

The statement was astounding in its ruthlessness. "How can you say such a thing?"

A measure of sadness lurched within the confines of Lady Trapleigh's eyes. "Don't you find that people will often say and do the most unexpected things for those they love?"

"You . . . you want Lady Gray and me to die because of love?" Katherine could scarcely believe the absurdity of the question, though it did bring another one to mind. "Who on earth are you doing this for?"

"Once again, I've no intention of telling you that," Lady Trapleigh said as the carriage jerked to one side.

"Will you at least tell me where we are going?" Katherine asked, needing to distract herself with conversation.

"To a lovely little apartment where I can keep an eye on you until further notice."

Katherine didn't like the sound of that one bit, but she also knew that the only thing that might save her was the ability to keep calm and rational. She could not allow her fear to take control. Thoughts racing, she grasped hold of one and addressed the widow with purpose. "You lied to us about Donovan, didn't you?"

Lady Trapleigh laughed. "Yes, I thought that a rather clever ploy, really. You and Lord Roxberry are remarkably naïve to even consider that what I told you was true after I deliberately tried to kill you." The weight of her gaze swept over Katherine. "I daresay you would have been very well suited for each other, but unfortunately it's too late for that now."

"What about your son?" Katherine asked. "Does he even exist?"

Lady Trapleigh nodded. "Tobias is just as real as you and I. He's also perfectly safe."

Well, at least that was something, Katherine mused. She wasn't particularly fond of Lady Trapleigh at the moment, but she was happy to hear that her two-year-old son was unharmed. Setting her mind to figuring out Lady Trapleigh's motive, she considered a possible connection between herself and Patricia, for although she didn't think the widow had any plans of killing Lucien's sister, she clearly didn't mind if she happened to die by other means. The more Katherine thought about it, the only link she could think of between herself and Patricia was Lucien, but that was insane. Still, she had to ask. "Does Roxberry have something to do with this?"

"You're obviously very clever," Lady Trapleigh said, the edge of her mouth tilting ever so slightly.

"How is he involved?"

"Now, now . . . let's not get ahead of ourselves. I'd hate to deprive you of the chance to work it all out on your own."

Katherine opened her mouth to argue the point but thought better of it. Lady Trapleigh was determined not to say a word on the matter, and Katherine was swiftly beginning to realize that her best hope of survival would be to start contemplating a means of escape. Hopefully an opportunity to flee would arrive soon enough.

But when they finally reached their destination and Katherine was ushered inside a narrow stairwell, her heart sank. Wherever they were, she very much doubted that any of the people close by would care overly much about her welfare. This was not the sort of neighborhood where gentry ventured, and the scornful look of displeasure that briefly greeted her from a woman carrying a pail of water filled her with despair. She'd get no help from that quarter.

"That's far enough," Lady Trapleigh muttered when they reached the first door on the right. Keeping her pistol on Katherine, she handed a key to her accomplice and asked him to unlock the door.

It squeaked open on rusty hinges to reveal an opulently decorated space in complete contrast to the building's exterior appearance and setting. Oriental rugs dressed the floor of the hallway, leading them toward a spacious room where a comfortable seating arrangement took up one corner, while a generously sized four-poster bed hung with silk veil curtains occupied the other. Katherine took it all in with wide-eyed dismay. "This . . ." Good heavens. She'd heard of such places but had never imagined ever setting foot inside one, for there could be no mistaking what it was—Lady Trapleigh's love nest.

"Do you approve?" the widow asked in a sultry tone.

"It's very . . . err . . . lavish," was all Katherine

could think to say. She'd barely finished her appraisal when she felt her arms being dragged behind her back by rough fingers. In the next instant, a cord of some sort was being bound tightly around her wrists.

Lady Trapleigh chuckled as she gave Katherine a nudge. "Have a seat on that chair over there," she said.

Stepping forward, Katherine contemplated the possibility of making a dash for it. If she leapt to one side, she might be able to catch Lady Trapleigh by surprise. However, Katherine had no weapon with which to defend herself, her wrists were now tied, and with a pistol pressed against her back, she doubted she'd avoid getting shot in the process. And that was without considering that Lady Trapleigh was not acting alone—there would still be a man Katherine would have to somehow overpower. Still, she didn't move forward immediately but glanced around, her eyes settling on a cluster of perfume bottles that stood not too far away on a spindly table.

"I suggest ye do as her ladyship asks," the burly man said as he gave Katherine a hard shove.

The gesture sent Katherine forward with a jolt. Her foot caught against the hem of her gown and she tripped, falling against the table with the perfume bottles on it and sending the entire display crashing to the floor. With a loud thud, Katherine landed on top of the shards of glass and instinctively rolled sideways in an attempt to prevent getting cut, while a pungent smell of roses mingling with jasmine, lavender and an assortment of other scents filled the air.

"Get up," Lady Trapleigh snapped, her pistol trained on Katherine as she spoke.

Katherine made an honest attempt to do so, but it was difficult, restrained as she was and with her long skirts wound about her legs.

With increased exasperation, Lady Trapleigh nodded toward her accomplice. "Hoist her up and help her to the chair."

The man did as he was asked without question, his fingers digging against Katherine's flesh as he yanked her up by her arm and hauled her over to the chair, where he unceremoniously pushed her down onto the seat with a loud grunt.

"Our situations have finally been reversed," Lady Trapleigh said. Handing the pistol to her accomplice, she ordered him to keep it trained on Katherine, then sashayed across to what looked like a jewelry box and flipped open the lid.

Heart pounding in her chest, Katherine watched as Lady Trapleigh removed a folded piece of paper from her reticule and placed it carefully inside the box before closing it again. Whatever was written on the paper, it seemed important—at least to Lady Trapleigh. Katherine closed her eyes, willing her heart rate to drop and for the panic that gripped her body to abate. She had to stay calm for the sake of her daughter. Sophia needed her and could not be left motherless.

And then there was Lucien, the man who'd helped her overcome her fears by making her see in herself the woman that he loved—a woman who was no longer pained by her own reflection. She loved him so terribly much and wanted desperately to share the rest of her life with him.

No, whatever her dismal fate might be, Katherine refused to meet it without a fight. The mere thought of not seeing her daughter or Lucien again was enough to bring tears to her eyes. Stubbornly, she pushed them back.

"I have a few things to see to," Lady Trapleigh said, "but I will return shortly. Keep an eye on her ladyship until then and you will receive the reward we discussed."

The man nodded. "I'll make sure she stays exactly where she is," he promised.

Seating himself opposite Katherine, he stared at her while Lady Trapleigh took her leave, the sound of the front door opening and closing signifying her absence. "If you're good and don't give me any trouble, I'll promise to make it swift when her ladyship gives the order. But if ye try anything funny, I'll shoot ye in the belly and let ye bleed."

Katherine blinked. Her mouth had long since gone dry, and she was finding it difficult to breathe. "Whatever she's offering, I can pay you more," she said as her fingers clasped the large shard of glass she'd managed to grab from the floor when she'd pretended to fall. Turning it carefully around, she wedged it between her wrists and the cord and moved it carefully back and forth in a cutting motion.

The man grinned. "I would never betray Lady Trapleigh," he said. "Least of all when she is acting in his lordship's interest."

Katherine frowned. "Who are you referring to?"

"I don't believe her ladyship would approve of me telling ye that," he said.

Continuing to work at her restraints, Katherine considered every nobleman of her acquaintance. There weren't many she'd had much to do with since her husband's death. But despite her efforts, she couldn't for the life of her think of anyone she'd displeased to such a degree that he would actually want her dead. Perhaps if she could work out *why* someone would want to kill her and whom it might benefit? She still failed to arrive at an answer.

Nodding with understanding, she said, "No, I suppose not." The glass in her hand punctured her skin, and she did her best not to wince in response to the stinging sensation that crept through her palm. With limited movement to avoid attracting attention, she sliced at the cord, praying that it was beginning to fray. "Will you kill me here?" she asked, hoping to distract her assailant. "Or will you be taking me to a different location?"

"Ye sure do ask a lot of questions, don't ye?"

"It just occurred to me that Lady Trapleigh might not enjoy getting her apartment messy, not to mention that it's so much harder to transport a dead body than it is to transport a live one."

"Not if ye keep on yapping it won't," the man grumbled.

Blessedly, Katherine began to feel the cording slip. It was getting looser.

"Stop squirming," the man said a moment later.

Taking a deep breath, Katherine steeled herself. Her eyes shifted toward the jewelry box. If Lady Trapleigh or the man in front of her were of the opinion that she would just sit in this chair and await her execution, then they were entirely mistaken. "I'm sorry, but I'm not very comfortable," she said. "In fact, if you don't mind, I'd be very obliged if I could have some water."

The man scoffed. "You're a long way from Mayfair, and I ain't yer servant."

"I didn't say that you were," Katherine said, scrambling for an idea to get him out of the room. "So I will buy it from you."

He guffawed, showing off a toothless grin. "With what, pray tell? You've nothing on ye that I couldn't just as easily take without offering ye anything in return."

"True, but I *can* sign over to you one of the investments Lady Trapleigh didn't try to burn, thereby providing you with a handsome income of two thousand pounds per year."

The pistol wavered slightly as he gaped at her. "How bloody thirsty are ye?"

Oh dear. Perhaps she'd overdone it a notch? "I'm parched," Katherine said as she met his steely gaze.

Silence settled between them for a lengthy moment while Katherine quietly begged him to take her offer. Thankfully, greed eventually won and the man nodded as he rose to his feet. "I'll be right back," he said.

No sooner was he out of sight than Katherine went back to work on her restraints. With increased vigor, she cut away at them while blood from the cut in her palm started trickling down her fingers. The shard grew slippery, but at least she could feel that the cord binding her wrists was giving way. Knowing that time was of the essence, she gave it a hard tug, successfully snapping it and freeing herself in the process.

Footsteps sounded, and Katherine leapt to her feet. She needed a weapon.

Rushing forward, she grabbed a crystal vase, emptied its contents on the floor and hurried across to the doorway through which her captor would soon be arriving. Clutching the vase by its base, she raised it with both hands, her back pressed flat against the wall. Blood rushed through her veins, but she tried to ignore it and focus on what she had to do. It was either them or her, so the instant she saw the man's profile emerge through the doorway, she tried not to think too much about her actions as she swung the vase directly at his forehead. A groan sounded, followed by the thud that he made as he hit the floor.

Stepping forward on quaking legs, Katherine tried to get a better look. The man was lying facedown and motionless. Close to him, a glass was lying on its side, the water inside it spilling across the carpet. The pistol was there too and Katherine didn't waste a single minute grabbing it, but before she took to her heels, she crossed the floor to the jewelry box. Opening it, she snatched up the piece of paper that Lady Trapleigh had placed there and quickly ran for the door. She was finally free, but in order to remain so, she would have to get out of there before Lady Trapleigh returned.

Chapter 18

Lucien was beside himself with worry as he jumped out of the carriage, which was moving frustratingly slow due to traffic, and continued toward his sister's house on foot. In fact, he ran, ignoring the stares and frowns that attached themselves to him like glue. He was in a hurry, for he knew that Gray would not have sent a footman to fetch him before the baby's arrival unless the situation was critical.

Racing up the front steps of Gray House, Lucien thought of Katherine. Surely she would be all right until he returned, especially with Starkly going to check on her. He winced, knowing how uncomfortable she'd probably be with the earl's company. She would understand Lucien's reasoning though. If Patricia's life was in immediate jeopardy, Katherine would not begrudge his going to her—indeed, she would encourage him to do so.

"How is she faring?" Lucien asked the butler as soon as the door opened in response to his third knock.

"She's very weak, my lord," the butler said, his mouth curved downward and his eyes reflecting a great deal of concern.

"And his lordship?"

"He is beside himself with anxiety. I'd best take you through to him at once—he's in the study."

The moment Lucien caught a glimpse of his brother-in-law, he became painfully aware of just how serious the situation was. "She still lives, doesn't she?" he asked, his voice cracking as he forced out the words. The butler had told him Patricia was weak, but one could never be sure just how much a butler would divulge.

Gray nodded as he took a sip from the glass he held between his hands—brandy, judging from the color. He looked exhausted. "Thank God you came," he said. "I was beginning to think you might not— you're usually home in the mornings, so I couldn't understand what was taking you so long. Even your grandmother arrived before you did."

Lucien looked around, surprised that he'd missed her.

"She's upstairs," Gray explained. "Barged right past Jefferson and myself."

Lucien could well imagine. "Forgive me," he said, "but I went to meet with Donovan, the man I thought to be involved in Lady Crossby's attacks. I'm afraid it took a while for the footman to find me." He took a shaky breath. "Is it possible for me to see her as well?"

An anguished scream filled the air. Gray winced. "She's having the baby—there's also a doctor and a midwife with her."

"But . . . I didn't think she was due for another month." The pitter-patter of feet on the stairs drew Lucien's gaze to the door, beyond which he saw a maid hurrying by.

"Apparently our child has grown impatient," Gray said, smiling bravely as he raised a glass of brandy to his lips and took a sip.

"What does the doctor say?" Lucien asked, fearing the worst. It wasn't uncommon for a woman to die in childbirth, but after suffering the loss of his brother, he wasn't sure if he would survive losing his sister too.

"There's a complication," Gray said, averting his gaze. Crossing to the window, he looked out. "The baby's turned the wrong way."

"But Patricia will survive?"

There was another heart-wrenching scream, and Gray's body tensed. "I don't know," he said as he dropped his head into his hands, taking on a defeated look that Lucien didn't care for in the least. "I just wish there was something I could do for her. I feel so helpless."

Failing to find the right words, Lucien decided to toss propriety and do the unthinkable. Crossing the floor, he embraced his brother-in-law. "She's a strong woman, Gray, and she's been through this before. I'm sure she'll pull through along with the baby," he said as Gray hugged him back, clearly needing whatever strength and compassion Lucien could offer.

Half an hour passed—the longest of Lucien's life—before the doctor finally arrived in the study, announcing that although Lady Gray had lost a great deal of blood and was still at risk, she and the baby had both survived the ordeal. "You may go up and greet your new son," the doctor said. "Just be aware that your wife is very weak. She requires a great deal of rest, so you mustn't stay too long."

"Come along, Roxberry," Gray said as he set his glass on his desk. "You should accompany me, as I'm sure she's eager to see you."

Lucien nodded, accepting the invitation, but when he saw his sister and how pale she looked, he had to struggle to fight back the tears. Nestled in the crook of her arm, peacefully asleep, lay a tiny being with a wrinkled brow. Patricia's eyes opened at the sound of their arrival, and when she saw them both, she offered them a weak smile that almost broke Lucien's heart. "How are you feeling?" Gray asked as he seated himself by her bedside and reached for her hand, his face filled with paternal pride.

"Not at my best, but I daresay it was worth every effort," Patricia said.

Eyeing his grandmother, who stood silently to one side, Lucien was struck by how shaken she looked. There was no denying that the birth had almost ended in disaster.

"Isn't he handsome?" Patricia asked, drawing Lucien's attention back to her.

"He certainly is," Lucien whispered.

"I'm thinking we should name him after Gavin," Patrica said, her eyes meeting Lucien's for the briefest of moments before she looked at her husband. "If you agree."

"I can't think of a better namesake," Gray said.

Lucien felt his heart squeeze with a rough onslaught of emotion. "Our brother would have been honored by the gesture."

Patricia nodded. "I didn't have the opportunity to tell you last night, Lucien, but I'm so pleased that you're marrying Kate. It's important to make the most of the time we've been graced with. I'm glad to know that you are making the most of yours." Her words grew heavier as she spoke, and she eventually closed her eyes. "Now, if you'll both forgive me, I'm extremely tired and would like to get some rest."

Wishing his sister a speedy recovery, Lucien went to the door while Gray kissed his wife and whispered a few endearments to her. "Lady Roxberry?" he asked when the dowager countess made no move to leave along with him and Lucien.

"If you don't mind, I should like to remain here so I can watch over her." Her voice was full of emotion. "I can sit just over there without disturbing anyone."

Nodding, Gray allowed the request, taking his leave of the two women as he exited his wife's bedchamber. "Will you join me for luncheon, Roxberry? It's almost time, and I'd appreciate the company," Gray said as they headed back downstairs.

Torn between Gray's request and the desire to return home so he could check on Katherine, Lucien paused with indecision. "Thank you," he finally said, "but I—" *Knock, knock!*

"I wonder who that can be," Gray murmured as they arrived at the bottom of the stairs. They paused there while the butler went to open the door.

A muffled exchange could be heard in the entryway beyond, then the butler returned. "Lord Starkly has arrived, my lord. May I show him in?"

A pained expression settled upon Gray's face. He was clearly in no mood to entertain Starkly and was probably considering denying him entry. "I believe he's here to see me," Lucien said. "When I hurried over here, he promised he'd check on Lady Crossby. I'm sure he only means to assure me that all is well."

Gray sighed. "Very well then, show him in—we'll be in the library," he said, addressing the butler. Turning away, he started toward the room in question. "Come along, Roxberry."

Seating himself in a deep leather armchair, Lucien watched as Gray poured himself another brandy.

He'd offered Lucien one as well, but Lucien had declined, considering it too early in the day for that sort of thing. He wasn't about to stop Gray though—Lord knew the man probably needed to dull his senses. The bottle was readily available.

"Roxberry isn't in much of a drinking mood this morning, but perhaps I can convince you, Lord Starkly?" Gray announced the moment Starkly was shown into the room.

Coming to a halt, Starkly looked at Gray, frowned and finally said, "I appreciate the offer, but I'd rather not." Accepting that he must drink alone, Gray replaced the stopper on the brandy carafe and swept his arm toward the area where Lucien was sitting. "Then by all means, have a seat."

"Thank you, but I prefer to stand, since I doubt I'll be staying long." Starkly looked directly at Lucien, who'd leaned forward in his seat, not liking the earl's tone one bit. "I'm sorry it took so long for me to arrive, but finding an available hackney took longer than I'd expected. I regret to tell you that when I finally did arrive at your home, Lady Crossby was not there."

"*What*?" Lucien was on his feet in a heartbeat. "Are you quite sure?"

"Your butler says he saw her step out into the street and climb into a hackney, so yes, I'm quite sure."

"Did he tell you where the blazes she was going?" What the devil was she thinking? She wasn't a simpleton, for Christ's sake, and ought to know better—especially after everything that had happened. Clearly she'd taken leave of her senses.

"I was hoping you would be able to tell me that, Roxberry, since your butler informed me that she'd decided to come here after receiving the same news you did about your sister." Raking his fingers through his hair, Starkly muttered an oath. He turned to Gray. "Forgive me for barging in like this. I hope things are not as bad as I feared. Your wife . . . is she—"

"She is presently resting with my son," Gray said as he took a large gulp of his drink.

"Then I must congratulate you, Lord Gray," Starkly said.

Gray nodded his thanks and said, "But what of Lady Crossby? She's not here, and I daresay she would have arrived by now if she was the first to be informed of Lady Gray's condition."

"I'm going to file a missing person report right away," Lucien said, already heading toward the door. "And then I'm going to insist that every available runner in London starts searching for her."

Gray looked a little stunned. "I'm sure she'll show up soon enough. I mean, even with the threat against her taken into account, I doubt she's in any real danger at present. After all, if you were meeting with Donovan before coming here, then he's unlikely to have gone after Lady Crossby, and since Lady Trapleigh has been detained at Cresthaven, she can hardly be much of a threat."

"You're probably right," Lucien said, "yet I can't help feeling as though something is horribly wrong. As you say, she should have been here by now if this was her destination." His stomach twisted and his heart thumped. He should have taken Katherine with him when he went to meet with Starkly. What had he been thinking, letting her out of his sight for even a second?

A loud banging sound came from the hallway, accompanied by the clicking of heels upon the polished parquet. "Sounds like you're being invaded," Starkly said.

Voices sounded, followed by a quick succession

of footsteps, as if someone was running while another person was hurrying after them. The three men stood, frozen, as a flurry of billowing fabric appeared in the doorway. Lucien stared as a woman burst into the room without as much as a by-your-leave.

Before him stood Katherine, and as relief weakened his limbs, he was spellbound by the wild beauty that graced her as she stood there gasping for breath, her hair tumbling over her shoulders and her crumpled gown in slight disarray. In her right hand, she held a pistol. "How is she?" she asked, eyes wide as she looked at Gray. "I'm so sorry I couldn't get here sooner, but I—"

"Forgive me, my lord," Gray's butler announced as he came up behind her, "but I tried to tell her to wait. She wouldn't hear of it, however, and pushed straight past me. I must say it was rather unexpected—took me completely by surprise."

"It's quite all right," Gray said. "We were actually hoping that Lady Crossby would arrive. Weren't we, gentlemen?"

"Oh, absolutely," Lucien said, exceedingly happy that Katherine was standing there before him in the flesh, yet anxious to discover what had happened. And where on earth had she gotten the pistol from? Stepping forward, he took her hand in his own and led her over to one of the chairs, where he encouraged her to sit. Once she had done so, he carefully pried the pistol out of her grasp and handed it to Gray. "Tell me everything," he whispered as he crouched before her.

"It was dreadful, Lucien. I should have listened to you, but I was a fool and so terribly worried when the footman came looking for you with news about your sister." Reaching out, she caught hold of Lucien's arm and pierced him with her eyes. "Please tell me she's all right."

"She has given birth to a son," Lucien said, unwilling to delve into the details at the moment, since Gray seemed blissfully distracted by Katherine's arrival. "She's resting right now, but I'm sure she'd love to see you later. Until then, why don't you tell me what happened? Why did it take you so long to get here?"

Katherine took a deep, shuddering breath. "I hailed a hackney in front of your house and climbed in to find Lady Trapleigh waiting for me."

Lucien stilled. "Lady Trapleigh? You mean she's here? In London?" Anger rose inside him. He clenched his fists. By God he would have to have a word with Katherine's butler for failing to inform him of this.

Katherine nodded. "There was a man with her—an accomplice of sorts."

"Did they hurt you?" Lucien asked as he squeezed her hand. When she flinched, he looked down to find the wound on her palm. Wild fury rushed through him, hot and fierce.

"No," she said, her eyes holding his. "I cut myself on a piece of glass when I tried to escape."

"They held you captive?" Lucien felt his throat tighten at the very thought of it.

Katherine nodded. "They took me to Lady Trapleigh's . . ." She stopped herself, straightened her back and tilted her chin a notch before saying, " . . . trysting place."

"Good Lord!" all three men exclaimed in unison as they stared back at her, wide-eyed.

Katherine couldn't decide whether they looked utterly uncomfortable with her mention of such a thing or if they might be intrigued. Whatever the case, their interest only grew as she related the rest of her story.

"Bravo!" Lord Gray exclaimed as soon as she mentioned hitting her captor with the vase.

Katherine looked to Lucien, who was watching her with something that could only be defined as deep admiration. "Yes," he said. "Bravo indeed."

"I know where this place is," Starkly said.

"Of course you do," Gray muttered.

"Perhaps we should go and see if Lady Trapleigh's accomplice is still there. If we're lucky, we might find Lady Trapleigh as well," Starkly continued, ignoring Gray's comment completely.

"Lady Crossby comes with us," Lucien announced. "I'm not leaving her behind this time."

"Splendid," Starkly said, "then I suggest—"

"One moment, gentlemen," Katherine said. "While I understand the need for haste, there is something I would like to look at first. You see, I have brought with me a letter belonging to Lady Trapleigh—a letter she seemed to be quite protective of. I realize it may be nothing, perhaps merely a note from an admirer . . . but what if it's not? What if it gives us some answers?" She looked to each of the men in turn. "I think we ought to read it before we do anything further."

"Then open it," Lucien urged her, encouraging her with a smile.

"Yes, do hurry," Starkly added. "I'm quite eager for the opportunity to chase after those villains."

"Trying to atone for all your sins?" Gray asked.

Starkly nodded. "Something like that."

Acquiescing, Katherine plucked the folded piece of paper from the pocket of her pelisse and handed it to Lucien, who immediately unfolded it and started to read. Was it just her imagination, or was he growing paler by the second? He flipped the page over to see if there was anything on the back, clearly unsatisfied with what the letter contained.

"Well?" Gray asked. "What does it say?"

Lucien opened his mouth to speak, then closed it again. Eventually he handed the letter to Starkly. Katherine rolled her eyes and groaned. This was growing tedious. She ought to have read it herself.

"By Lucifer's . . . ahem . . . forgive me, my lady." Starkly looked mildly embarrassed. "What I meant to say was, this is extremely unexpected."

"Would one of you please tell me what that letter says? I'm about to expire from the suspense of it all, and if you'll only look at poor Lord Gray, it seems he's faring no better," Katherine exclaimed.

"You hit it on the nail, my dear," Lord Gray said, saluting her with his half-empty glass of brandy.

"I think you ought to sit down for this, Katherine," Lucien said.

She lost her patience with him then. "I *am* sitting down!"

"Right. Sorry. I think perhaps this letter has addled my brain." He handed it to her. "Here, perhaps you ought to read it yourself, because if this is to be believed, it appears as though the man who's to blame for Lady Trapleigh's attempts on your life is already dead and buried."

"He's *what*?" Katherine asked, her gaze dropping to the signature at the bottom of the page. Her heart practically stopped. There, accompanied by his seal, was Charles's name, scrawled in his own hand. It took a moment for her brain to accept, and then, desperate to understand the meaning of it all, she started to read.

My dearest lady,

As I lie here, consumed by sickness and awaiting nothing but death, my only thoughts are of you and our son. It is my hope that you will one day find it in your heart to forgive me for the choices I have made, but you know as well as I that I had to marry her. Revenge, however, is not as sweet as I had hoped, but rather bitter, as it turns out. If only I had been capable of letting go of my anger, my resentment and my hate, then perhaps we could have been happy together. As it is, my efforts have been in vain—sooner or later, my wife's lapdog will return to England, and I will have no say in what happens next. If there is one thing I cannot bear, it is the thought of him winning her, but you know this well enough already, for I have spoken to you about it on numerous occasions. Unfortunately, it is too late for regrets. Stay strong, my love, and look after our boy.

Yours always,
Charles Langdon

Katherine read the letter again. She looked up at Lucien. "If I understand this correctly, my late husband had an ulterior motive for marrying me—one that was so important to him that he sacrificed his own happiness."

"That seems to be the gist of it," Lucien agreed.

"But that's ludicrous!"

"I'm assuming you're the lapdog in all of this," Starkly said, addressing Lucien.

"I suppose I must be, though I don't understand

where all of this animosity is coming from. We grew up not far from each other, you see, attended Eton together and were later enlisted in the same regiment. I confess I never cared much for the man, not even when we were children. He had a competitive streak that bordered on the obsessive, not to mention an arrogant attitude that always raked my nerves, but it never occurred to me that he harbored such resentment toward me." Lucien frowned. "Perhaps Lady Trapleigh can enlighten us further if we manage to catch her. Thank you for your hospitality, Gray, but we really must be on our way now. If there's anything you need—anything at all—please don't hesitate to ask."

"Give her ladyship my love," Katherine added, looking at Gray, "and tell her that I will call on her as soon as possible."

Lucien, Starkly and Katherine exchanged a few more words with Gray, then headed back out into the street, where they hailed a hackney, directing it toward the same area from which Katherine had fled only one hour earlier.

"**W**ell blast it all, he's gone!" Lucien said as he stared at the vacant spot on the floor where Lady Trapleigh's accomplice was supposed to have been. "And there's no sign of Lady Trapleigh either, is there?"

"I'm afraid not," Katherine said.

"Surely there must be a way in which to correct this disaster." Raking his hand through his hair, Lucien turned to Starkly. "If I were Lady Trapleigh, I think I'd make a run for it. She knows Lady Crossby will have told us what happened and what the consequences will be once we catch her. It's likely that she will attempt to flee the country. Can you head over to the Home Office? Once you explain what's transpired, I'm sure that someone will arrange for the roads leaving London to be watched, though I do suggest that you ask them specifically to do so—the ports too for that matter. I doubt she'll return to her estate, but you never know—perhaps you should tell them to check there as well."

"I'll see to it right away," Starkly said. He eyed Katherine. "I hope you can someday forgive me for not doing more in order to help you."

"As I've recently discovered, you did more for me than I ever would have expected. It is I who should ask your forgiveness for thinking the worst of you all this time."

Starkly grinned. "I daresay it was an unavoidable mistake, given my reputation."

With a bow, he took his leave.

"We ought to get going as well," Lucien said as he took Katherine by the hand. "You've had quite the ordeal today—I'd like to take you home so you can rest."

Rest. Yes, that was precisely what she needed on top of that morning's activities. And perhaps something to eat as well. It was past noon, and she was beginning to feel rather peckish. After all, she hadn't even had the glass of water she'd requested earlier. Passing it on the way out of the apartment, she said, "Sounds like a splendid idea."

Returning home, they found a letter from Katherine's butler waiting for them. "It's from Carter," Katherine said as she read the missive. "He says that we ought to be aware that Lady Trapleigh escaped last night."

Lucien grunted. "I daresay we could have used that information earlier. Perhaps then you wouldn't have acted so recklessly." His eyes met hers, and she saw in them the fear he'd had of losing her.

Katherine wouldn't argue that she had taken a risk by leaving the safety of Roxberry House, or that it had almost cost her her life, but she wasn't sure she wouldn't have done so even if she'd known about Lady Trapleigh. "My only thought was of Patricia, and that I had to try and be there for her—to help her in whatever way I could and to offer her comfort."

"I know," he said, "and your selflessness is one of your finest qualities, but even you must admit that you should have allowed Parker the time to ready a private carriage."

"Fear for your sister's life made it impossible for me to sit and wait for him to do so. My judgment was clouded by circumstance," she said. "I'm sorry."

"All that matters is that you're safe now," he said as he pulled her into his arms and kissed the top of her head. "If all goes well, Lady Trapleigh and her accomplice will soon be apprehended by the authorities."

Katherine dearly hoped so. She longed for it all to be over so they could bring Sophia home and move on with their lives.

"I still can't believe you rendered a man unconscious with a vase," Lucien said a while later as they sat across from each other in the upstairs salon with a few plates of food between them.

"Neither can I. Slammed it right into his skull,"

she confided. "Impressive what a life-threatening situation can do to a person. All I knew was that I had to escape."

"And you did brilliantly, my dear. I couldn't be prouder of you, though I do believe I will have to ask Parker to lock away the crystal."

Katherine chuckled as she bit into a chunk of cheese. "Do you fear for your life, my lord?"

"I fear for my sanity," he whispered as his eyes met hers. "You've no idea how terrified I was when Starkly arrived to inform me you'd gone missing. It felt as if my heart was being ripped from my chest."

Looking at Lucien, she knew that it was true. "I love you too," she said as she reached out her hand, wrapping it around his larger one. "It will be a relief to put all of this behind us."

"I couldn't agree more," Lucien said, "but until word arrives that Lady Trapleigh has been caught, we must still be careful."

"I suppose this means that I must continue my confinement," she said, disliking the notion.

Lucien nodded. "It's for the best, Kate. We have to do what we can to keep you safe until she's apprehended." Picking up a grape, he offered it to Katherine.

"What if she's never found?" The thought of looking over her shoulder forever was unbearable.

"I don't know what we'll do then, but let's not worry about that until we have good reason to. She's only just gone missing, and if Starkly can rally the Home Office, then I've every confidence she'll turn up soon enough."

Katherine sincerely hoped so, not only because she wanted to move on with her life but also because she wanted answers—answers that only Lady Trapleigh could give her.

"Begging your pardon," Parker announced, appearing in the doorway, "but her ladyship's bath is now ready."

"Thank you," Lucien said.

"Speaking of Bath, will you accompany me when I fetch Sophia home?" Katherine asked.

"Of course." He smiled as he rose and held his hand toward her. "But first I will escort you to your room."

Heat prickled Katherine's skin and her pulse began to dance in response to the dark gaze he was offering her. She chastised herself for her silliness, for it was hardly as if he was going to toss out the maids and make love to her in a small tub. Yet there was something devilish about him right now—something that stirred her blood and excited her senses, even though she couldn't quite define what it was.

"Here we are," Lucien said as they entered her chamber, where two maids stood ready to assist, one busily heating more water in a pot that hung over the fire. Lowering his lips to Katherine's ear, he whispered, "Feel free to request some privacy once they've helped you disrobe."

A hot flush rose to Katherine's cheeks and she felt her stomach tighten, but before she had a chance to gather her wits and respond, Lucien had left the room, closing the door behind him.

"If you'll please step this way, my lady," one of the maids said, "we'll help you out of your gown and into the bath."

In a daze, Katherine complied, allowing the two maids to bustle about. The pampering felt good after the day's hectic events. "Would you like us to wash your hair as well?" the maids inquired as soon as Katherine had lowered herself into the water.

"No, thank you," Katherine murmured. "In fact, I can wash myself if you'd be so kind as to hand me the soap."

They looked a bit hesitant about that, as if worried that they might be chastised for not doing what would ordinarily have been expected of them.

"It's quite all right," Katherine assured them. "It's just that I'd like to be alone with my thoughts."

"Very well then," the maids said, bobbing curtsies as they took their leave.

Once they were gone, Katherine sighed heavily, closed her eyes and leaned back against the edge of the tub, luxuriating in the feel of the warm water against her skin. It was most soothing.

A soft click sounded, followed by the hushed tread of footsteps upon the plush carpet. Opening her eyes, Katherine found Lucien gazing down at her with smoldering eyes. He was dressed in a moss green velvet robe. A smile tugged at Katherine's lips. There could be no doubt about his intentions, and the knowledge made her brazen.

Picking up the soap that was sitting on a small dish beside the tub, she rubbed it between her hands to produce a thick lather. Raising one arm, she then swept the lather slowly along the length of it. "As you can see, I followed your advice—not a maid in sight."

"Thank God for that," Lucien murmured, his eyes fixed on the motion of her hand as she slowly soaped herself.

Finished with one arm, she directed her attention to the other, attempting the most sensual movements she could manage. Lucien's lips parted and his breathing grew increasingly labored, judging from the heavy rise and fall of his chest. Katherine's heart soared, happy with the effect she was having on him.

How invigorating it was to be looked upon with the deep longing that glowed in his eyes.

Sitting up, Katherine brought her breasts out from beneath the surface of the water and ran her fingertips across them. Lucien groaned, the sound a gentle plea of encouragement that brought out the wanton within her. Arching her back, she applied the soap, then set it aside and began to massage each breast, reveling in how full and heavy they grew beneath her touch. When she carefully squeezed one of her pebbling nipples in the same way Lucien had done before, a surge of energy rushed between her thighs, where it swirled about until it began to ache.

"Do you like touching yourself like that?" Lucien asked. His voice sounded raspy.

"I like that you're watching me do it," she murmured, for it was the truth.

"Tell me how it feels," he urged as he untied the sash of his robe and allowed the garment to slip from his shoulders. He was naked beneath, and heavily aroused. Katherine couldn't help but stare, her movements stilling as she did so. "Don't stop," he muttered. "A woman ought to know how to take her own pleasure. I want to watch you take yours."

A gasp escaped Katherine's lips at the wickedness of his suggestion. Surely she couldn't be *that* bold.

As if reading her mind, Lucien placed his own hand upon his erect member and said, "Please, Kate—do it for me."

His words broke her and she quietly nodded, increasingly impassioned by the indecency of it all and loving the groans that came from Lucien each time she tugged at her nipples.

"Lean back," he told her, his voice hoarse and insistent. She did as he asked, lowering her body farther into the water. "Now raise one leg. Hitch it over the edge of the tub and lift your hips." Again she complied, producing a position so scandalous it would have made a harlot blush. "Now show me . . . show me where you want me the most."

Katherine looked at him and at the figure he portrayed as he stood there before her completely nude, his eyes blazing with intense need. He was at his most vulnerable right now, and the knowledge—the trust he was placing in her—dissolved all of her own apprehensions.

Slipping her fingers along her leg, she carefully touched the juncture between her thighs.

"Yes," Lucien muttered, "like that."

Stunned by how good it felt, Katherine did it again. She'd never thought to give herself pleasure before and had certainly never imagined doing so with someone watching. Now, as tingles started up her legs and waves of heat spiraled outward along her limbs, she found it difficult to understand why. Her fingers found the spot that Lucien had stroked the day before, and sparks took flight, urging her to accelerate her movements, to tense her muscles and tilt her hips until finally, she shattered before him.

"My God," Lucien gasped, and before Katherine could return to solid ground, he'd scooped her up in his arms and marched across to the bed, clearly not caring how wet the bedclothes would become.

Setting her down against the pillows, he climbed up between her thighs and lowered his head to her most intimate part. Katherine squealed from the shock of it, but with one flick of his tongue, he swiftly made her writhe beneath him as she gasped for air.

Heavens, this feels good!

He spread her wider with his hands and thrust one

finger inside her while his tongue continued to work its magic. It wasn't long before Katherine felt the stirrings of another climax coming on fast, so when he added a second finger, she promptly flew apart on a scream of ecstasy.

"I have to have you now," he told her earnestly as he leaned over her, his hand caressing her waistline.

Katherine blinked. "I didn't think I'd be able to do that so soon after . . . you know."

Lucien grinned. "My dear, as long as you're in the mood, I don't see why you shouldn't come for me as often as you choose."

"Good heavens, Lucien. Does your mother know that you talk like that?" His wicked words had made her all hot and desperate again.

"Heaven forbid," he said as he lowered his lips to hers, kissing her thoroughly and with so much passion that Katherine had to wonder how she'd never noticed his desire for her until now. "I suggest we keep it that way," he added.

His hand slipped between them, teasing her gently. "Don't stop," she whispered as she tilted her hips in invitation.

Lucien chuckled. "Why, Kate, I do believe you've lost your inhibitions."

"I daresay you may be right."

"Hmm . . . I like it." He nibbled her shoulder. "You're ready for me now, and I've no desire to wait another second to claim you."

And as he slid inside her, filling her, Katherine knew she'd rather die than be separated from this man. "I love you," she whispered as he kissed his way along her neck.

"I love you too," he muttered, his hands shifting to her hips as he thrust himself in and out of her. "I always have."

Once again, as if by magic, the tingles started. They rose up her legs to pool between her thighs, where the intensity of them grew gradually stronger until she felt herself burst with blinding light. A deep, guttural groan escaped Lucien a second later, and she felt him spilling himself inside her. The thought would have terrified her last week, for she'd vowed never to remarry, unwilling to suffer the torture that Charles had subjected her to. Now, however, she thrilled at the possibility of carrying Lucien's child, so when he quietly settled himself beside her, cradling her close, she felt nothing but happy contentment.

Chapter 19

Seated in a secluded corner of the dining room at The Fox and Hound, Laura Islington, Countess of Trapleigh, stabbed at the chicken she'd ordered from one of the waitresses. She was furious. If she ever got her hands on Mr. Hendricks again, she would wring the imbecile's neck—finish him off before the authorities got to him. She never should have trusted him to watch over Lady Crossby while she made arrangements for the lady's disappearance.

Leaning back in her seat, Laura drummed her fingers against the tabletop and took a healthy sip of her wine. What a mess this had turned out to be. If only she hadn't botched up that shot at the ball, but when she'd seen Lady Rebecca approach the spot where Lady Crossby had stood, she'd taken a risk, hoping to kill Lady Crossby before Lady Rebecca had gotten any closer. Instead, she'd managed to shoot the one person she'd actually come to like. It was a veritable catastrophe!

Picking up her knife, she diced the potatoes and forked a few pieces of them into her mouth. What the hell was she going to do? Even the treasured letter that Charles had sent her had disappeared. She took another sip of her wine, hoping to drown the pain that caused. She'd been desperately in love with him, poor devil that he'd been. It was tragic really, the way in which a life could be shaped by the evil deeds of others.

It had broken her heart when he'd told her that he was getting married, but she'd understood his reasoning—had known that she and Charles could have no future together as long as his past haunted him. Now, as he lay cold and alone in the ground while his widow seemed increasingly ready to do the one thing he had hoped to prevent, Laura thought of everything Charles had given up—years of his life wasted in an unhappy marriage, the chance to share his future with the woman he loved . . . his health.

There was no doubt in Laura's mind that it was his marriage to Lady Crossby that had killed him by prompting the deep depression that had eventually led to his addiction. His only satisfaction throughout it all had come from knowing that he'd finally bested Roxberry, but if Roxberry were to marry Lady Crossby anyway, then all of Charles's sacrifices, including her own, would have been for nothing. Laura couldn't allow that to happen. Her love for Charles and her devotion to his cause left her with little choice but to stop Lady Crossby by any means necessary. This would be her final tribute to Charles—to take Lady Crossby away from Lord Roxberry forever.

A thought struck her, and she smiled. There was time yet if she hurried. Finishing her meal and downing the remainder of her wine, Laura paid the waitress and started for the door. She was about to be bold and reckless, no doubt, but that didn't frighten her. Presently, the only thing she feared was failure, because when it came to the man she loved, she would do anything for him, even if it meant sacrificing her own life by risking capture.

It was late by the time she arrived at the back entrance to Roxberry House, but Laura had intended it that way. Standing in the shadows, she watched from a distance as a groom flirted with a scullery maid. The door to the mews stood open, forgotten by the couple, allowing Laura a view of the space beyond.

"I think I'm going to turn in," the groom said, pulling the scullery maid toward him. "Care to join me?"

"You know as well as I that Parker will sack us on the spot if he finds out," the scullery maid said.

"Oh, come now—everyone's gone to bed. It's unfair that you should work as hard as you do without any amusement. At least let me ease your burden a bit." He tugged her closer. "How about giving me a kiss?"

She did, her free hand going about the groom's neck while water sloshed from her bucket. Laura took the opportunity to sneak past them and enter the house. "Did you hear something?" she heard the scullery maid ask as the door squeaked shut.

"Not a thing," the groom assured her.

Expelling a breath, Laura headed down a hallway, past the kitchen and toward the servants' stairs. She paused to listen. Everything was perfectly still. With quiet footsteps, she started up the steps, jumping at the sound of a grandfather clock chiming midnight as she entered the downstairs hallway. Composing herself, she went toward the next flight of stairs and began her upward journey. Her eyes had grown accustomed to the darkness, which was occasionally interrupted by the glow of streetlights through some of the uncurtained windows. Even so, she'd no idea where Lady Crossby might be sleeping and would have to make a guess. Hopefully, she would pick the correct bedroom and avoid an altercation with Roxberry.

Arriving on the landing, she paused for a moment as she looked about. To her left was a room with the doors flung open. Squinting through the darkness, she determined that it had to be a salon of some sort. She swiveled her head to the right and started down the corridor. There were four doors, two on each side of her. On a deep, steadying breath, she reached out and tried one of the door handles. It was unlocked, and the door opened easily enough. Laura entered the room as silently as a burglar and glanced about, studying the space. It looked like a comfortable bedroom, though the bed was empty. Grabbing one of the pillows, she moved on, entering another room, wherein she found Lady Roxberry fast asleep, the occasional snore reverberating through the air. Backing out of the room, Laura went to the other side of the corridor and tried a different door. It swung open effortlessly and she stepped quietly inside, the heavy breathing of deep slumber flowing toward her.

Crossing the floor, Laura hovered at the edge of the bed and looked down at the sleeping form of Lady Crossby. Laura had never taken a life before, and she was well aware that doing so would not be easy. But she'd loved Charles—she still did—and she wanted to do this for him.

Clutching the pillow between her fingers, she took a deep breath and fought for resolve. She then raised the pillow over Lady Crossby's head and carefully brought it down over her nose and mouth. There was a beat, then Lady Crossby's hands flew up in an attempt to push the pillow away. Leaning forward, Laura pushed down harder while Lady Crossby's body began to writhe back and forth, her legs kicking out in an attempt to push away her assailant. She caught hold of Laura's wrist and pushed at it with such force that Laura momentarily lost her footing, loosening her hold on the pillow just enough for Lady Crossby's scream to be heard.

Fear hugged Laura and she quickly pushed down on the pillow again, muffling Lady Crossby's sounds of distress. If only she could hold the pillow in place a few seconds longer, Laura was sure she'd succeed in her task, but in the next instant, strong hands grabbed her arms and pulled her backward, and then she heard the deep rumble of Lord Roxberry's voice saying, "What the hell do you think you're doing?" He turned her around and began shaking her, dark fury lighting his eyes. His gaze shifted toward the bed. "Kate? Are you all right?"

"Y-yes," Lady Crossby gasped. Sitting up, she stared accusingly at her attacker.

"I'm happy to hear it," Lord Roxberry said. He then shoved Laura aside and crossed the floor to the door. Shutting it, he turned the lock and pocketed the key. He glared at Laura. A cold shiver slithered along her spine. "You have a great deal of explaining to do," he said as he addressed her. Crossing his arms, he jerked his chin toward a chair. "I suggest you sit down this instant."

Lucien had been to war. He had fought against the French and watched his countrymen drop like flies, fully aware that he might be next. Hell, he'd sat at his brother's bedside, holding his hand as he'd drawn his last breath. Even so, nothing had ever terrified him as much as the thought of losing Katherine, so when he'd heard her scream as he'd made his way back upstairs from his study, he'd feared the worst.

His fear, however, had since turned to fury. By God, he'd never been as angry with anyone as he now was with Lady Trapleigh. He had a good mind to wring her neck for what she'd just done. Thankfully, he'd arrived on the scene just in time to prevent the worst possible outcome. He shuddered as he picked up the tinderbox on the mantelpiece and lit an oil lamp. "Are you sure you're all right?" he asked Katherine. She didn't look at all well as she sat there on her bed with the coverlet pulled up around her. Grabbing the jug of water that stood on the dresser, he poured a glass and handed it to her. He noted that her hand trembled as she took it, her lips quivering ever so slightly as she placed the glass to her mouth and drank. The incident had clearly shaken her, and with good reason. Muttering an oath, Lucien turned toward Lady Trapleigh. "You'd better start talking," he growled.

"I think the letter speaks for itself," she said, raising her chin with defiance, "and since I know you must have read it by—"

"The hell it does," Lucien bellowed. He would not allow such arrogance to pass. Not when the woman before him had just made a third attempt on Katherine's life.

Lady Trapleigh drew back, visibly stunned by his outburst. "Then by all means, tell me what you wish to know," she said, sounding annoyingly put out.

The nerve!

He ought to fetch the constable this instant and be done with it. In fact, it was what he should have done in the first place, back at Cresthaven. Devil take it though, he was curious. He wanted her to explain the letter, and he sensed that so did Katherine.

"What I wish to know," Lucien bit out, "is why you're so eager for Lady Crossby to die, and what Lord Crossby's role has been in all of this."

Lady Trapleigh straightened her shoulders, her pride testing Lucien's patience to the fullest. Lacing her fingers together in her lap, she looked first at Katherine and then at Lucien. "Lady Crossby's late husband didn't marry for love, for if he would have done, he would have married me." She turned her head toward Katherine. "Indeed, the poor man could barely stomach his wife."

"I am well aware of it, though I fail to comprehend his reason for deceiving me," Katherine said. "Once we were married, I saw very little of my husband, and in those rare instances when we did meet, he was always angry with me. All charm and kindness toward me vanished on our wedding night. After that, he chose only to see me in the dark, for brief encounters necessitated by his duty toward the Crossby lineage."

"I know," Lady Trapleigh murmured.

Lucien felt ill just thinking about it.

"The truth of your failed marriage is simple enough," Lady Trapleigh said, "for you see, you were just a means to an end—a woman unfortunate enough to be loved by the wrong man."

Katherine frowned, and Lucien straightened himself. "What do you mean?" he asked.

Lady Trapleigh offered a smile. "The real target in all of this, Lord Roxberry, has always been you."

This got Lucien's full attention. "Lady Trapleigh," he said, his patience wearing thin. "I would appreciate it if you would explain the entire mess to us, as opposed to speaking in riddles. What the devil do you mean?"

"To be blunt, Lord Crossby despised you—always has," Lady Trapleigh told him.

"But he and I never socialized with each other, even though we were neighbors. I just can't think of a single thing I could have done to deserve such wrath."

"You might not think so, and yet you did, always managing to be one step ahead of him in everything. His father whipped him for it, you know—for not doing as well as you at Eton, for never winning any of the races in which you also competed. You've beaten him at everything his entire life—even in the army, where you were promoted to captain, forcing him to endure the greatest humiliation of all by making him follow your command.

"Eventually, his failure as a man, not only in the eyes of his father but in his own, began to consume him. Achieving that honorable discharge from the army served a very important purpose though. It allowed him to return home before you so he could take from you the one person he knew you cared about more than life itself—Lady Crossby. He charmed her in every conceivable way until she finally agreed to marry him— pressured no doubt by her parents, who longed for their daughter to marry a *titled* gentleman. Once the vows had been spoken, he deliberately set out to destroy her."

Bloody hell! This was madness if it was true.

Lucien glanced across at Katherine, who looked just as stunned as he felt. "I had no idea," he said.

"I doubt anyone else knew how deep his resentment toward you ran. Even with his dying breath, Charles's father accused him of being less of a man than you and a great disappointment to the Crossby name. I imagine it must have been very difficult for Charles. He felt like a failure, and he blamed you for that."

"Tell me, how long were you his mistress?" Katherine asked.

Lady Trapleigh attempted a smile, but it was a sad one. "Lord Crossby and I became lovers a few years before you married him, and we remained so throughout your marriage. We loved each other, and I accepted the choice he made to marry you, even though I wished he would have married me instead—especially when I discovered that I was carrying his child." She laughed bitterly. "It's a pity things turned out the way they did, for I do believe we could have been a happy family if it hadn't been for Crossby's deep-rooted need for revenge."

"What I don't understand is why you would try to kill Lady Crossby now. With Crossby dead, there's no need for . . ." He stopped himself and considered everything he knew. His mouth dropped. "You still want to fulfill his wish by preventing me from marrying her. But that's . . . that's . . ."

"Love," Lady Trapleigh said.

Lucien shook his head in disbelief. "No. It's insane! Have you no consideration for your son?"

Lady Trapleigh shrugged. "He's being raised at an estate close to the Welsh border by people who can offer him a proper future. His father was married and his mother is famous for having bedded half the men in England. The last thing that child needs is to be associated with me." She shook her head, looking weary. "All I wanted was to grant Charles his final wish."

"Well, I can't tell you how pleased I am by your lack of success," Lucien stated as he took Lady Trapleigh roughly by the arm, pulled her to her feet and steered her straight toward the door. "You can look forward to a lengthy sojourn at Newgate now."

"**I**s it finally over?" Katherine asked Lucien when he returned to the bedroom after ensuring that Lady Trapleigh had been escorted off the premises by two Bow Street Runners.

"I believe so," he said, "for us at least." Sinking down next to her, he pulled her against him and she instinctively breathed him in, that familiar scent of sandalwood filling her senses.

It felt wonderful to be held in his strong embrace . . . safe. "It was lucky that you arrived when you did." Turning in Lucien's arms, Katherine gazed into his eyes. "I could have died."

"I know, my sweet," he whispered gently as he placed a tender kiss upon her forehead. "I'm sorry I wasn't here with you when she arrived."

"You couldn't fall asleep?"

"No." Twining his fingers with hers, he raised her hand to his lips and placed a soft kiss upon her knuckles. "So much has happened lately, I fear my mind was incapable of rest. Will you please forgive me?"

"Always," she murmured.

His lips brushed hers, and in the next instant, she felt his hand caressing her thigh. After being shot at and kidnapped, she could finally enjoy being loved without fearing for her life, and as she sank further into Lucien's embrace, Katherine understood what it meant to be truly happy.

Epilogue

Two weeks later, after fetching Sophia home from Bath, Lucien swept Katherine across the ballroom floor of Darwich House, her skirts twirling about her legs as they moved in time to the waltz being played. They were not the only popular couple that evening, and there could be no denying that Lady Darwich had been crowned the luckiest hostess in Town. Only a week had passed since Lucien had married the love of his life by special license, so he was amused to discover that marrying a widow who'd almost been murdered by her late husband's mistress was no longer the topic du jour—not when the Duke of Kingsborough had just announced his betrothal to a woman who'd been nobody of consequence until it had been discovered that she was the Marquess of Deerhurst's granddaughter. Lucien smiled at the thought and decided that he would have to get Kingsborough to tell him the details of that story later.

And then of course there was Mr. Neville to consider. The fact that Lucien had only just heard of *that* scandal this very evening was a testament to how absorbed he'd been by his own troubles these past few weeks.

Leading Katherine in a wide circle that took them past the orchestra, Lucien met her eyes. They were alight with wonder. "You seemed preoccupied just now," she said, her cheeks dimpling as she spoke. "Any thoughts you'd care to share?"

"I was just appreciating my own good fortune," he confided. "I still fear that this is but a dream from which I'll soon awaken."

"I hope not, for I would miss you terribly if that were the case." She smiled, and his heart gave a little shudder.

God, how he loved this woman.

"Then perhaps I'd best keep dreaming," he whispered as the dance drew to a close. Taking Katherine by the arm, he led her over to the refreshment table, where he offered her a glass of lemonade.

"Congratulations on your wedding," Mr. Goodard said as he approached. "I can't say that it came as a surprise, but I am very happy for you both."

"So are Carlyle and Barrymore, I assure you," Lucien said with a chuckle. "They both wagered on her ladyship and I tying the knot before the end of the Season—placed their bets at White's, you know."

"I say, I wish I would have been that predictive," Mr. Goodard said.

"You could always bet on yourself," Katherine suggested with a hint of mischief. "How are things progressing with Lady Julie?"

An expression of deep melancholia descended upon Mr. Goodard's handsome face. "Alas, I cannot tell the lady's mind. She has me quite perplexed, though I was relieved to discover that her interest in you, Roxberry, was a ruse. Still, I find it impossible to discern whether or not she looks favorably upon my attempts at flattery or if she'd rather be rid of me altogether."

"Mr. Goodard," Katherine began sympathetically, "I believe—"

"Surely her intentions will become known with time," Lucien said, deliberately cutting off his wife. He tried not to look at her just then, for he was well aware that she was probably scowling.

"I'm sure you're quite right," Mr. Goodard said. "In the meantime, I shall see if she'd like to dance."

"Care to explain yourself?" Katherine asked as soon as Mr. Goodard was out of earshot.

Lucien took a sip of his drink as he stared out over the ballroom. "Winning your hand wasn't easy, my dear, but it was worth every effort. I daresay I'm doing Mr. Goodard a favor by *not* divulging the true nature of Lady Julie's heart."

"And just when I thought you were being perfectly beastly," Katherine murmured. "Your intentions prove you to be a veritable romantic."

He had no chance to respond when Lord and Lady Huntley walked up to them. "I must say that after everything, I had rather expected to attend a grand Society wedding. Imagine my disappointment when I heard you'd married in secret," Lady Huntley said. She smiled adoringly at her husband as she added, "Would you be kind enough to pour me a glass of lemonade?"

"Certainly," Huntley said. He picked up an empty glass from a tray on the table and proceeded to do as his wife had asked, saying, "Please forgive her ladyship. What she *meant* to say was congratulations.

Isn't that right, my dear?" He handed Lady Huntley her glass.

"My friend is well aware that I am thrilled on her behalf, isn't that so, Lady Roxberry?" Lady Huntley smiled as her gaze shifted to Lucien. "I do believe she's made an excellent match for herself. Truly, I couldn't be happier."

"It's kind of you to say so, my lady," Lucien said, offering the countess a slight bow.

Her smile never faltered as she added, "That said, I will personally have you skewered if you ever do anything to upset her."

A sound not entirely dissimilar to that of a strangled giggle escaped Katherine, while Huntley snorted in response. "At last her true nature is revealed," he muttered.

"Understood," Lucien said, addressing Lady Huntley. To Lord Huntley he quietly murmured, "You wife has quite a vicious bite."

Huntley nodded. "And I hear that yours can take out a man with a vase."

Lucien bit back a smile, his forehead creasing as his brows drew together. "Should we live in fear?"

"Just treat her like a princess and you'll be fine," Huntley said.

"You do realize that we're standing right here, don't you?" Lady Huntley asked, her arms crossed as she eyed both gentlemen.

"Heaven forbid we dare to forget it," Huntley said, but when his wife opened her mouth, undoubtedly intending to make another rejoinder, her husband smoothly stopped her by asking if she'd do him the honor of partnering with him for the next set.

"Would you care to follow suit?" Lucien asked Katherine when they were once again alone.

She nodded her consent. "Just as long as you're not issuing your invitation out of concern for your own head."

"Not at all," Lucien said. "I am merely trying to protect Lady Darwich's crystal."

Katherine laughed, her dark curls swaying as she shook her head with merriment. "You really are incorrigible, you know."

Taking her hand in his, Lucien led Katherine into a country dance. "I'm beginning to realize as much," he said with a wink.

"Roxberry," a female voice called once the dance had ended and Lucien was leading Katherine away from the dance floor. He recognized it immediately and was therefore not the least bit surprised to find his grandmother coming toward them.

She was looking quite elegant in a plum-colored evening gown, her hair wrapped neatly in a turban to match. "May I suggest that you keep your passion for your wife in check or you'll have no choice but to run outside and cool off?" There was an edge of mischief to her tone.

Lucien heard Katherine wince beside him, or was that him who'd made that sound? Certainly his grandmother was known for being bold, so he really ought not be surprised by such a statement. And yet he was. They were out in public, for heaven's sake! He coughed to conceal his slight embarrassment. "We were merely dancing," he stated. "Nothing wrong with that."

Hester Marvaine, Dowager Countess of Roxberry, gazed back at him unblinkingly. "You were looking at her as if you were quite prepared to gobble her up right there on the dance floor."

"I most certainly was not," Lucien protested.

"You most certainly *were*," his dear grandmother insisted.

Katherine tugged at Lucien's arm as if hoping to extricate herself so she could escape. He wouldn't allow that. If he was to suffer his grandmother's candor, then by God, so would she—for good and for worse and all that. He grinned.

"What's so funny?" his grandmother asked.

"You are, of course." The matriarch frowned. Clearly she did not approve of that notion. "After all, considering all the stories you've told me of your younger years, I cannot help but wonder if you're not being a tiny bit hypocritical."

Katherine gasped. "Roxberry," she hissed. "Apologize to your grandmamma." She turned toward the lady in question. "Please, my lady, I'm so terribly sorry."

"Thank you, my dear," the dowager said, her spine straightening a fraction, "but Roxberry does make a fine point, though I would like to remind you that things were different back then."

"How so?" Lucien asked, unable to hide his mirth. He was having a wonderful time needling her, and the fact that she allowed it was what had always made him love her as dearly as he did. His mother would never have been so tolerant.

"Well, for one thing, there was a revolution going on," his grandmother said.

Lucien quirked a brow. "I hardly see how French politics would have had any bearing on your discretion in regard to flirtation."

His grandmother sighed as if he'd been the most

obtuse person on the planet, and then to confirm the notion, she said, "No, I don't suppose you would."

Katherine groaned.

Deciding to salvage what little affection his grand-mother held for him after such a discussion, Lucien reached for her hand and raised it to his lips. "Will you dance with me later?" he asked. "Perhaps a qua-drille?"

His grandmother chuckled. "Only if you promise to remain on your best behavior. I won't allow you to look at *me* like that. As a matter of fact, I'll stomp on your feet if you do."

Lucien smiled. "I promise to restrain myself." He looked around. "Has Mama arrived, by any chance? I haven't seen her yet."

"She decided to stay home in the end," his grand-mother said. "Another megrim, I believe."

Again? This was becoming a bad habit of hers—no doubt a result of the melancholy she'd been suffering since her husband's death. Silently, Lucien made a note to address the issue soon.

"Oh, if you'll excuse me, my dears, I'm just going to have a word with the Dowager Duchess of Kings-borough," Lucien's grandmother said. "Fetch me when it's time for us to dance, will you? A quadrille sounds lovely indeed."

At Lucien's side, Katherine shook her head. "I don't believe I'll ever grow accustomed to the way in which you talk to each other," she said as they watched the dowager countess walk away.

Lucien considered that. "No, I don't believe I would ever have dared say such things to *your* grand-mamma."

"Good Lord, no! She would have eaten you alive!"

"I'm well aware of it," Lucien grinned as he guided

her toward the French doors leading outside into the garden. "In fact, there's nobody else I can be so forward with—except you, of course."

Turning her head at a slight angle, Katherine looked up at him, her eyes locking with his as they stepped out onto the terrace. The air was cool, the cloudless sky strewn with stars. "I do hope you're ready for me to respond in kind."

"I say, is that a challenge?" he asked as he guided her down some steps and onto a graveled path.

She shrugged. "If you like."

"Hmm . . . I do believe I like it a great deal."

"Well, then perhaps I ought to tell you my reason for bringing you out here."

Lucien frowned. "I think you must be confused, since *I* was clearly the one who brought *you* out here, my dear. You accepted my arm and I guided you out onto the terrace, down the steps and to this very point on the path."

"That's just something you think, Lucien, when the truth of it is that I felt an uncanny urge to fling myself at you in there. I thought the cover of darkness would serve us better."

Her impish tone made him laugh. "It certainly seems as if you've gotten the better of me."

"Not yet, but I'm about to." Giggling, she pulled away from him and raced around the corner of a neatly trimmed hedge.

Intrigued, Lucien hurried after her, his eyes squinting through the murky darkness until he caught sight of some fluttering silk. "Got you," he said as he snatched hold of her wrist and pulled her toward him.

"Shh . . . ," she whispered. "I would hate for us to be discovered."

"And why is that?"

"Because then it will be at least another hour before I'll be able to do this." And twining her arms around his neck, she rose up onto her tiptoes, pressed her lips against his and kissed him with so much love and tenderness that he would forever look back upon this wondrous moment as one of many, in their happily ever after.

Don't miss how the Kingsborough Ball began!

Keep reading for excerpts from
THE TROUBLE WITH BEING A DUKE
and
THE SCANDAL IN KISSING AN HEIR

Available now from Avon Books

The Trouble With Being a Duke

"**I** really must commend you on the pie, Mrs. Chilcott," Mr. Roberts said as he picked up his napkin, folded it until it formed a perfect square and dabbed it across his lips with the utmost care and precision. "It is undoubtedly the best one yet—just the right amount of tart and sweet." The slightest tug of his lips suggested a smile, but since he wasn't a man prone to exaggeration, it never quite turned into one.

Isabella stared. Was she really doomed to live out the remainder of her days with such a dandy? Mr. Roberts was unquestionably the most meticulous gentleman she'd ever encountered, not to mention the most polite and the most eloquent. In addition, he never, ever, did anything that might have been considered rash or unexpected, and while there were probably many who would think these attributes highly commendable, Isabella couldn't help but consider him the most mundane person of her acquaintance. She sighed. Was it really too much to ask that the gentleman who planned to make her his wife might look at her with just a hint of interest? Yet the only thing that Mr. Roberts had ever looked at with even the remotest bit of interest was the slice of apple pie upon his plate.

Isabella wasn't sure which was more frustrating—that he lacked any sense of humor or that he valued pie more than he did her. The sense of humor was something she'd only just noticed recently. Unable to imagine that anyone might be lacking in such regard and taking his inscrutable demeanor into account, she had always assumed that he favored sarcasm. This, it turned out, was not the case. Mr. Roberts simply didn't find anything funny, nor did he see a point in trying to make other people laugh. This was definitely something that Isabella found herself worrying about.

"You are too kind, Mr. Roberts," her mother replied in response to his praise. "Perhaps you would care for another piece?"

Mr. Roberts's eyes widened, but rather than accept the offer as he clearly wished to do, he said instead, "Thank you for your generosity, but one must never overindulge in such things, Mrs. Chilcott, especially not if one desires to keep a lean figure."

Isabella squeaked.

"Are you quite all right, Miss Chilcott?" Mr. Roberts asked.

"Forgive me," Isabella said. "It was the tea—I fear it didn't agree with me."

Mr. Roberts frowned. "Do be careful, Miss Chilcott—it could have resulted in a most indelicate cough, not to mention a rather unpleasant experience for the rest of us."

Isabella allowed herself an inward groan. The truth of the matter was that she'd been forcing back a laugh. Really, what sort of man would admit to declining a piece of pie because he feared ruining his figure? It was absurd, and yet her mother had nodded as if nothing had ever made more sense to her. As for the threat of a cough . . . Isabella couldn't help but wonder how Mr. Roberts would fare in regard to their future children. He'd likely barricade himself in his study for the duration of their illnesses—all that sneezing and casting up of accounts would probably give him hives otherwise.

Her father suddenly said, "Have you heard the news?"

"That would certainly depend on which news you're referring to," Mr. Roberts remarked as he raised his teacup, stared into it for a moment and then returned it to its saucer.

"More tea, Mr. Roberts?" Isabella's mother asked, her hand already reaching for the teapot.

"Thank you—that would be most welcome."

Isabella waited patiently while Mr. Roberts told her mother that he would be very much obliged if she would ensure that this time, the cup be filled precisely halfway up in order to allow for the exact amount of milk that he required. She allowed herself another inward groan. He'd just begun explaining why two teaspoons of sugar constituted just the right quantity when Isabella decided that she'd had enough. "What news, Papa?" she blurted out, earning a smile from her father, a look of horror from her mother and a frown of disapproval from Mr. Roberts. A transformation Isabella found strangely welcome.

"Apparently," her father began, taking a careful sip of his tea while his wife served him another generous slice of apple pie, "the Duke of Kingsborough has decided to host the annual ball again."

"Good heavens," Isabella's mother breathed as she

sank back against her chair. "It's been forever since they kept that tradition."

"Five years, to be exact," Isabella muttered. Everyone turned to stare at her with puzzled expressions. She decided not to explain but shrugged instead, then spooned a piece of pie into her mouth in order to avoid having to say anything further.

The truth of it was that the annual ball at Kingsborough Hall had always been an event she'd hoped one day to attend—ever since she was a little girl and had caught her first glimpse of the fireworks from her bedroom window. She hazarded a glance in Mr. Roberts's direction, knowing full well that a life with him would include nothing as spectacular as the Kingsborough Ball. In fact, she'd be lucky if it would even include a dance at the local assembly room from time to time. Probably not, for although the life she would share with Mr. Roberts promised to be one of comfort, he had made it abundantly clear that he did not enjoy social functions or dancing in the least.

Perhaps this was one of the reasons why he'd decided to attach himself to *her*—an act that she'd always found most curious. Surely he must have realized by now that they had very little in common, and given his current station in life, he could have formed a favorable connection to a far more prosperous family. Of course he would probably have had to attend a Season in London in order to make the acquaintance of such families, and his reluctance to do so certainly explained why he was presently sitting down to tea in her parlor instead of sending flowers to a proper lady of breeding.

Isabella had on more than one occasion brought the issue regarding Mr. Roberts's displeasure for socializing to her mother's attention, complaining that her future would consist of few diversions if she were to marry him, but her mother had simply pointed out that the only reason young ladies attended such events was with the direct purpose of drawing the attention of the gentlemen present. Once married, there would be little reason for Isabella to do so and consequently no point in engaging in anything other than the occasional tea party. And as if this had not been enough, her mother had added a long list of reasons why Isabella should be thankful that a man as respectable and affluent as Mr. Roberts had bothered to show her any consideration at all. It had been rather demeaning.

"Well, it's nice to see that they seem to be recovering from the death of the duke's father," Isabella heard her mother say.

"I couldn't agree more," Isabella's father said. "It must have been very difficult for them, given the long duration of his illness and all."

"Indeed," Mr. Roberts muttered without the slightest alteration of his facial expression.

A moment of silence followed until Isabella's mother finally broke it by saying, "Now then, Mr. Roberts, tell us about that horse you were planning to buy the last time we saw you."

And that was the end of the conversation regarding the Kingsborough Ball—but it was far from the end of Isabella's dreams of attending. In fact, she didn't spare a single thought for anything else during the remainder of her tea, though she must have managed to nod and shake her head at all the right times, for nobody appeared to have noticed that her mind had exited the room.

"Was afternoon tea as delightful as always?" Jamie, Isabella's younger sister, asked when they settled into bed that evening. At thirteen years of age, she was a complete hoyden and just as mischievous as any boy her age might have been, getting into every scrape imaginable. After deliberately sneaking a frog into Mr. Roberts's jacket pocket three months earlier, she'd been barred from attending Sunday tea. Her punishment for the offense had included two weeks of confinement to her bedroom, as well as some choice words from Mr. Roberts himself. Needless to say, Jamie's approval of the man had long since dwindled.

"It was better, considering I was hardly aware of Mr. Roberts's presence at all."

Jamie scrunched her nose. "Honestly, Izzie, I don't know why you suffer the fellow. He has no sense of humor to speak of, is much too reserved to suit your vibrant character, not to mention that there's something really queer about him in general. I don't think you should marry him if he offers."

Isabella attempted a smile as she settled herself into bed, scooting down beneath the covers until she was lying on her side, facing her sister. They each had their own bedroom, but with the nights still cold, Jamie often snuck into Isabella's room so they could snuggle up together, talking about this and that until sleep eventually claimed them. "I have to think rationally about this, Jamie. Mama and Papa are struggling to keep food on the table, and there's also you to consider. I want a better life for you than this, with more choices than I've been afforded."

Jamie shook her head as well as she could, considering she was lying down. "I don't want you to sacrifice yourself for me. I'll never be able to forgive myself for being the cause of your unhappiness."

There were tears in her young eyes now that

made Isabella's heart ache. Isabella loved her sister so dearly and knew that her sister loved her equally. "It's not just you, Jamie, but Mama and Papa as well. Mr. Roberts will ensure that they want for nothing."

"And in return, you will probably have to kiss him." Jamie made a face.

Isabella's hand flew up to whack her naughty sister playfully across the head. "What on earth do you know of such things?" Was there anything more appalling than talking with one's kid sister about kissing?

"Enough to assure you that you might want to think twice before giving that particular right to a man like him."

With a sigh, Isabella rolled back against her pillow and stared up at the ceiling. Jamie was right, of course, but what was Isabella to do? Her family's future depended on her seeing this through to the end. Really, what choice did she have?

"So, what did you daydream about this time?" Jamie asked, changing the subject entirely.

"What do you mean?"

"You said before that you barely noticed Mr. Roberts's presence during tea. I assume your thoughts must have been elsewhere."

"Oh!" Isabella sat up, turning herself so she could meet her sister's eyes. "The Kingsborough Ball. Papa says they're hosting a new one. Oh, Jamie, isn't it exciting!"

Jamie jumped up. "You have to attend."

"What?" It was preposterous—absurd—the most wonderful idea ever. Isabella shook her head. She would not allow herself to entertain the notion. It would only lead to disappointment. "That's impossible," she said.

"Why?" The firm look in her sister's eyes dared her to list her reasons.

"Very well," Isabella said, humoring her. "I have not been invited, nor will I be."

"We'll sneak you in through the servant's entrance. Cousin Simon can help with that, since he works there."

Isabella rolled her eyes. Trust Jamie to have that problem already worked out. "I'm not an aristocrat—they will notice I don't belong," she countered.

Jamie shrugged. "From what you've told me, the Kingsborough Ball is always masked, is it not?"

"Well, yes, I suppose—"

"Then no one will notice." Jamie waved her hand and smiled smugly. "Do go on."

"I . . . I have no gown that I could possibly wear to such a function, and that is the deciding factor. No gown, no ball."

"Ah, but you are wrong about that," her sister said, meeting her gaze with such cheeky resolve that Isabella couldn't help but feel a growing sense of apprehension. "There's always the one in the attic to consider, and I'll wager—"

"Absolutely not," Isabella said. She knew exactly which gown her sister was referring to, for it was quite possibly the most exquisite thing Isabella had ever seen. It had also given rise to a string of questions that would probably never be answered, like how such a gown had found its way into the Chilcott home in the first place. Fearful of the answer and of the punishment they'd likely have received if their parents had discovered they'd been playing in a part of the house that had been off limits, they'd made a pact to keep their knowledge of the gown a secret.

"But Izzie—"

"Jamie, I know that you mean well, but it's time I faced my responsibilities as an adult. The Kingsborough Ball is but a dream that will never amount to anything more."

"A lifelong dream, Izzie," her sister protested. Jamie took Isabella's hand and held it in her own. "Wouldn't you like to see what it's like living it?"

It was tempting of course, but still, wearing a gown that had in all likelihood been acquired under dubious circumstances, as it was one her parents couldn't possibly afford, would be harebrained. Wouldn't it? After all, it had probably been hidden away for a reason. Her mother had never mentioned that it existed, which was also strange considering it would make an excellent wedding gown for Isabella when she married Mr. Roberts. No, there was something about that gown and its history. Isabella was certain of it, for the more she considered it, the more wary she grew of what she might discover if her questions were one day answered.

In any event, she couldn't possibly wear it to the Kingsborough Ball. Could she? She would be betraying her parents' trust by doing so. It would certainly be the most daring thing she'd ever done. And yet . . . this would be her last chance for a fairy-tale experience. Closing her eyes, she made her decision. She would do it. Isabella would seize a moment for herself—one night of adventure that would have to last a lifetime. She only hoped that she wouldn't one day look back on it with longing and regret.

The Scandal
in Kissing an Heir

Kingsborough Hall, Moxley, England
1817

Daniel Neville, heir to the Marquisate of Wolvington, removed himself to a corner of the Kingsborough ballroom—as good a place as any for a man who'd been labeled an outcast by Society.

Overhead, candles held by three large chandeliers spread their glow across the room, the jewels worn by countless women winking in response to the light. This was true opulence, and nobody did it better than the Kingsboroughs. Why, there was even a glass slipper sculpted from ice and a pumpkin carriage sitting outside on the lawn—a touch of fairy-tale splendor indicative of the theme that the dowager duchess had selected for her masquerade.

And what a masquerade. Never in his life had Daniel borne witness to so many feathers. They were everywhere—attached to gowns, on the edges of masks, and sprouting from women's hair.

The ball gowns were marvelous too. These were not the boring dresses generally on display at Almack's. Certainly, one could still tell the debutantes apart, due to their tepid choice of color, but they all had a bit of something extra, like crystal beads that sparkled when they moved.

It was refreshing to see, and yet as he stood there, watching the spectacle unfold, Daniel felt nothing but bland disinterest. It was only one hour since he'd arrived, but it felt more like four. God help him, but he'd never been so bored in his life. Perhaps he should have remained in London after all. At least there he had his friends to keep him company and could avoid the constant reminder of how unwelcome he was among the finer set. His aunt and uncle were in attendance of course, but as soon as they'd entered the ballroom, they'd been approached by Lady Deerford. Daniel had hastily slipped away in order to avoid the countess, who had a renowned tendency to talk the ear off anyone willing to listen. In hindsight, he was beginning to think that nodding his head in response to whatever she had to say would have been preferable to this self-imposed solitude. Recalling the glass of champagne in his hand, he took another sip of his drink and decided to request a brandy from one of the footmen at the first available opportunity. Stronger stuff would be required if he was to get through the rest of this evening. He watched as a group of ladies approached on their tour of the periphery. There were three of them, one being the Countess of Frompton. If Daniel wasn't mistaken, the two young ladies in her company were her granddaughters—typical debutantes dressed in gowns so pale it was hard to discern where the fabric ended and their skin began. It would do them both a great deal of good to get married, if for no other reason than to be able to add a touch of color to their attire.

As they came nearer, Lady Frompton glanced in Daniel's direction. Their eyes met briefly, then her ladyship quickly drew her granddaughters closer to her, circumventing Daniel in a wide arc that would have been insulting had it not been so expected. They weren't the first to avoid him that evening. Indeed, the three youngest Rockly sisters had beaten a hasty retreat a short while earlier when they'd realized who they'd been heading toward on their own tour of the ballroom. Daniel hadn't been surprised, for his reputation was so tarnished that he could probably ruin a lady by merely glancing in her direction. Why he'd bothered to attend the ball at all, when the chance of enjoying himself had been as distant a prospect as traipsing through the African jungle, was beyond him.

Well, not entirely.

He needed to find himself a wife, or so his uncle had informed him last week when he'd discovered that Daniel had hosted a most outrageous party at his bachelor lodgings—an event that had been sponsored indirectly by his uncle via Daniel's monthly allowance, where vingt-et-un had been played until most of the courtesans and gentlemen present had been divested of their clothing. What made the incident worse was the fact that Daniel had been so deep in his cups that night that he'd offered his mistress the diamond earrings his father had once bestowed upon his mother. They had been a treasured family heirloom but would now grace the lobes of Solange.

"You're a bloody curse on this family!" Daniel's uncle, the Marquess of Wolvington, had said as soon as Daniel had entered his study the following day. The marquess had then delivered a long list of reasons as to why he'd thought this to be the case. "It's time you grew up and learned a thing or two about responsibility, or you'll end up running your inheritance into the ground after I'm gone. Heaven help me, I'd love nothing better than to disinherit you and allow Ralph to take up the reins, but—"

"My nephew?" Daniel had said, unable to help himself in light of the fact that his uncle would rather entrust his entire fortune to an infant.

"I doubt he'll do any worse than you." Daniel had winced in response to this retort, but he'd done his best to hide all signs of emotion as his uncle continued, "Your sister's a levelheaded woman, her husband too. I'm sure the two of them would be prepared to act wisely on Ralph's behalf, but since the law prevents such an outcome, I rather think it's beside the point.

"That said, your aunt and I have come to a mutual agreement—one which we hope will encourage you to get that head of yours on straight. You will cease your gaming immediately, or we will cut you off financially, which, to clarify, will mean that you will have to work for a living unless you wish to starve. Additionally, you will stop associating with loose women, engaging in haphazard carriage chases, or anything else that's likely to embarrass the name your father left you. And finally, you will get yourself engaged within a month and married by the end of the Season."

Daniel had stared back at his uncle in horror. The older gentleman, however, had looked alarmingly smug and satisfied with his new plan. Daniel had turned to his aunt, whose presence had only served to increase Daniel's humiliation tenfold. Although she was not his blood relative, she had always been kind toward Daniel, had treated him like the son she'd never been blessed with, and had often stood up for him against his uncle, who'd been more stern and restrictive. "He cannot be serious," he'd said, hoping to incur a bit of sympathy from her.

She'd glanced up at him, eyes crinkling at the corners as she'd offered him a sad little smile. "I'm afraid so, love, and I have to say that I am in full agreement. You cannot continue down this path, Daniel—it will be detrimental if you do. Please try to understand that we're only looking out for your best interests, as well as those of the family at large." Her eyes had been filled with disappointment.

Of course he'd understood, but he'd still been furious with both of them.

A wife—ha! Raising his glass to his lips, Daniel took another sip. As if finding one here was likely to happen when no self-respecting parents or guardians would allow their daughters and wards within a ten-foot radius of him.

No, Daniel was there because it had been Kingsborough who'd issued the invitation. They'd moved in the same circles once, and Daniel had always enjoyed the duke's company immensely. Things were different now though. The duke had reformed, abandoning his rakehell ways in favor of supporting his family. There was much to be admired in the strength of character Kingsborough had shown, and Daniel had wanted to offer his friend some respect for everything he'd been through—the difficulty he must have endured in dealing with his father's demise. But with so many people in attendance, Kingsborough had only been able to speak with Daniel briefly, as there were many others who craved his attention.

Daniel fleetingly considered asking one of the widows to dance, but he decided against it. No sense in wasting time on fruitless pursuits, since none of them had any inclination to remarry. They'd gained their independence and had every intention of holding on to it. The only thing he could hope for was to enjoy the comfort of their beds later, but that would hardly hasten his progress to the altar, nor would it improve his aunt and uncle's opinion of him if they happened to find out. Knowing them, they'd probably decide he'd gone too far in thwarting their wishes and cut him off before the month was up—an unwelcome prospect, to say the least.

Across the floor, he finally spotted someone who would appreciate his presence. He and Casper Goodard often gambled together, and Daniel decided to go and greet him. With wife hunting being a futile endeavor here, sharing a bit of friendly banter over a game of cards would be a welcome distraction.

Squaring his shoulders, Daniel started to head in Goodard's direction when a flutter of red met the corner of his eye. Glancing toward it, he took a sharp breath . . . and froze.

Who on earth is that?

Next to the terrace doors, partially concealed by a pillar and an oversized arrangement of daffodils, stood a woman unlike any other he'd ever seen before. Her hair was black, and from the looks of it, exceptionally long, for it wasn't cut in the style that was fashionable but piled high on her head in an intricate coif. And her skin . . . it was not the milky white tone that made most English women appear a touch too pale for his liking. On the contrary, it looked bronzed— as if she'd been basking in the afternoon sun. It took a moment for Daniel to come to his senses and realize that he was not only staring openly at her but gaping as well. Quickly snapping his mouth shut, he cursed himself for being such a fool—it was just hair, after all.

And yet he suddenly had the most bizarre and uncontrollable urge to unpin it and run his fingers through it. Of course, it didn't hurt that the woman promised to be a tantalizing beauty if the fullness of her lips was anything to go by. Unfortunately, the upper half of her face was concealed by a mask, but if he could only get close enough, he ought to at least be able to see the color of her eyes.

He began going over all the ladies he'd ever been introduced to, attempting to recall someone who shared her attributes, but it was to no avail. Clearly, he'd never encountered this woman before, and he found the mystery most intriguing.

Moving closer, he watched as she tilted her chin in profile, her jawline fine and delicate beneath her high cheekbones. A lock of hair falling softly against the sweep of her neckline had come to rest against the bare skin of her right shoulder, and the unexpected urge he felt to brush it aside and place a kiss there in its stead was startling. Daniel hesitated briefly. Women didn't affect him, and whatever was said to the contrary was untrue, for the charm and soulful eyes he chose to display were no more than tools he applied in his endless pursuit of pleasure. He was methodical in his seduction. If he placed a kiss against a lady's shoulder, it would be for a reason, not because he couldn't stop himself. The fact that he'd felt a helpless need to do so now, however brief it had been, disturbed him.

Whoever she was, she couldn't possibly be an innocent, dressed as she was in scarlet silk. He wondered if she might be somebody's mistress, or if not, then perhaps a widow he hadn't yet met—one who might be willing to remarry? As unlikely as that was, he could always hope.

Knowing that the only way to find out would be to talk to her, he decided to do the unthinkable—ignore etiquette and address her without being formally introduced. After all, it wasn't as if his reputation was likely to suffer further damage at this point, and considering her gown, he thought it unlikely that hers would either. Dressed in such a bold color, the lady could hardly be a saint.

One thing was for certain, however—he needed a wife, and he needed one fast. If her reputation did suffer a little from his talking to her, then so be it. Perhaps he'd marry her and tell all the gossipmongers to go hang. The corner of his mouth lifted at the very idea of it. What a satisfying outcome that would be. Hands clasped behind his back, he stepped up beside her and quietly whispered, "Would you care to dance?"

Rebecca flinched, startled out of her reverie by a deep, masculine voice brushing across her skin. Turning her head, she caught her breath, her body responding instinctively as it flooded with heat from the top of her head all the way down to the tips of her toes. The man who stood beside her was nothing short of magnificent—imposing even, with his black satin mask that matched his all-black evening attire.

His jawline was square and angular, his nose perfectly straight, and the brown eyes that stared down at her from behind the slits of his mask sent a shiver racing down her spine—there was more intensity and determination there than Rebecca had ever seen before in her life. He wanted something from her, no doubt about that, and as nervous as that made her, it also spoke to her adventurous streak and filled her with excitement. "Good evening," she said quietly, returning his salutation with a smile.

He studied her for a moment, and then he smiled as well, the corners of his mouth dimpling as he did so. Oh, he was a charmer, this one. "I hope you will forgive me, considering we haven't been formally introduced, but I saw you standing here from across the way and found myself quite unable to place you. Naturally, I had no choice but to make your acquaintance. I am Mr. Neville at your service, and you are . . . ?"

Rebecca knew her mouth was scrunching together in an attempt to keep a straight face. Oh, how she'd love to tell him exactly who she was. The knowledge would undoubtedly shock him, but unfortunately the risk of discovery was far too great for her to divulge her true identity.

Rebecca gazed up at the gentleman before her. "This is a masquerade, Mr. Neville, is it not?" she asked, deciding to keep his company a little while longer. How pleasant it was to be in the presence of a young and handsome gentleman for a change, rather than suffer the attentions of men who coughed, croaked and hobbled their way through what remained of their lives, as was the case with the suitors her aunt and uncle kept pressing upon her.

"It is," Mr. Neville said, dragging out the last word with a touch of wariness.

"Then part of the amusement comes from the mystery of not always knowing the identity of the person with whom you're speaking. Wouldn't you agree?"

She watched as Mr. Neville's eyes brightened and his smile turned to one of mischief. "Tell me honestly," he said, ignoring her question, "are you married?"

"Certainly not," she said, attempting to sound as affronted as possible, which in turn made him laugh. Surrendering, she allowed the smile that threatened to take control of her lips. "If I were, I would have ignored you completely and rudely walked away."

"Is that so?"

"Quite."

"Well, then I suppose I should inquire if you have any brothers that I ought to live in fear of."

She grinned this time and shook her head with amusement. "You are incorrigible."

"I've been called much worse, I assure you."

"I do not doubt it for a second." And it was the truth, though she had no intention of sharing any of the adjectives that were presently coursing through her own mind, like *magnificent* and *delicious*. Her cheeks grew instantly hot and she cringed inwardly, praying he wouldn't notice her blush. Heaven forbid if either word ever crossed her lips—the embarrassment of it would likely be impossible to survive, particularly since her mind had now decided to turn those two words into one singular descriptive, namely *magnificently delicious*. Her cheeks grew hotter still, though she hadn't thought such a thing possible.

"Would you care for some air? You're looking a bit flushed."

Oh dear.

She'd rather hoped he wouldn't have been able to tell. Looking over her shoulder, she considered the escape the French doors offered. She wouldn't mind the cooler outdoors right now, not only to cure her overheated reaction to Mr. Neville but also to avoid for just a little while longer the task she'd set herself. Looking the way she did, how on earth was she to make a good impression on any of the young gentlemen present? She wasn't sure, though she knew she'd have to figure it out before the evening ended and she lost her chance altogether.

Her eyes met Mr. Neville's, and the promisè of trouble in them only compounded her instinct to dismiss him as a possible candidate. But instinct could be wrong, couldn't it? So far, he was the only person she'd spoken to, the only man who'd asked her to dance. Granted, hiding behind a pillar probably hadn't helped her much in that regard. Still, despite her better judgment, she couldn't help but acknowledge that when Mr. Neville looked at her in that particular way, she lost all interest in the other gentlemen present. Perhaps she ought to consider him after all.

"It's very kind of you to offer," she said as she looked him squarely in the eye, "but I must consider my reputation. Why, you look precisely like the sort of man who'd happily kiss me in some secluded corner without a second thought for the consequences."

Mr. Neville's mouth quite literally dropped open. She knew her words were bold and inappropriate and that she probably ought to have been mortified by what she'd just said. But she wasn't. Mr. Neville's reaction was entirely too satisfying to allow for any measure of regret. Folding her hands neatly in front of her, she stared back at him instead, challenging him to respond while doing her best to maintain a serious demeanor.

"I . . . er . . . assure you that I would do no such thing," he blustered, glancing sideways as if to assure himself that nobody else had heard what she'd just said.

It was all too much, and Rebecca quickly covered her mouth with one hand in a hopeless attempt to contain the laughter that bubbled forth. "My apologies, but I was merely having a bit of sport at your expense. I hope you'll forgive me—and my rather peculiar sense of humor."

He leaned closer to her then—so close in fact that she could smell him, the rich scent of sandalwood enveloping her senses until she found herself leaning toward him. She stopped herself and pulled back.

"Of course . . . *Nuit*." His eyes twinkled. "I must call you something, and considering the color of your hair, I cannot help but be reminded of the night sky. I hope you don't mind."

"Not at all," she said, attempting a nonchalant sound to her voice, though her heart had picked up its pace as he'd said it, the endearment feeling like a gentle caress of her soul.

Who was this man? Could she really have been so fortunate to have stumbled upon the man of her dreams? A man who might potentially agree to marry her once she confessed to him the true nature of her situation? She dismissed the hope, for it was far too naïve and unrealistic. Besides, Mr. Neville's suave demeanor screamed rake and scoundrel rather than incurable romantic, which was what she would need. In fact, he was probably precisely the sort of man she should try to avoid, although . . . she made an attempt to look beyond the debonair smile and the lure of his eyes. Could he be genuine? Surely, if he really was a rake, he wouldn't have been so shocked by her suggestion that he might try to compromise her. Would he? She wasn't sure and decided to give him the benefit of the doubt instead.

The edge of her lips curled upward into a smile. "How about a refreshment," she suggested. "A glass of champagne, perhaps? And then I believe I'd like to take you up on that offer to dance."

"Yes, of course," Mr. Neville said as he glanced sideways, undoubtedly trying to locate the nearest footman. There was none close by at present. "If you will please wait here, I'll be right back."

Rebecca followed him with her eyes as he walked away, his confident stride reflecting his purpose. She was not unaware of the looks of reproach he received from those he passed, and she couldn't help but wonder if her instincts about him had been correct after all. Was she wasting her time on a scoundrel? She hoped not, for she'd quite enjoyed their conversation. It had been comfortable and unpretentious, spiced with a sense of humor.

As he vanished from sight, she gave her attention to the rest of the guests. One gentleman, she noticed, was making his way toward a cluster of young ladies with quick determination. She watched him, wondering which of the women had caught his interest. But right before he reached them, another gentleman cut in front of him and offered his hand to one of them—a lovely brunette dressed in a dusty pink gown. Placing her hand upon his arm, the pair walked off without as much as acknowledging the presence of the first gentleman. Rebecca wondered if they'd even seen him. Perhaps not, she decided, except that the second gentleman suddenly looked back, grinning with victory at the first gentleman.

What cheek!

She was just about to turn her attention elsewhere when a man's voice said, "I don't believe I've ever had the pleasure of making your acquaintance."

Turning her head, she was forced to look up until her eyes settled upon a handsome face, but where there was something playful about Mr. Neville's features, this man looked almost menacing—as though he was not the sort who was used to having his wishes denied. "I really wouldn't know," Rebecca told him, feigning boredom as she did her best to still her quaking nerves. Whoever he was, he was huge—the sort of man who could easily fling her over his shoulder and carry her off without anyone being able to stop him. "Perhaps if you told me your name . . ."

He smirked. "Lord Starkly at your service. And you are?"

She offered him a tight smile in return. She was not about to play the same coy game with this man as she'd done with Mr. Neville. That would only lead to trouble. But she could hardly give her real name either, so she said, "Lady Nuit."

Lord Starkly frowned. "I don't believe I—"

"This is a masquerade, my lord, is it not?" She heard the impatience in her voice but didn't bother to change it. "Let's just say that I'd rather not give away my real name for personal reasons."

"Yes, of course," Lord Starkly said, his features relaxing a little. The predatory glimmer returned to his eyes. "I understand completely why a woman such as yourself would prefer to remain incognito, though I—"

"A woman such as myself?" Rebecca asked, unable

to keep the blunt tone of indignation from seeping into her voice. She shouldn't have been shocked, considering her gown, but she didn't seem to be able to stop herself.

"Come now, *Lady Nuit*. There's no need for you to keep up your charade for my benefit. I mean, what other reason would a woman possibly have for engaging in conversation with Mr. Neville unless she was already a fallen angel? Not to mention that your attire is rather indicative of your . . . ah . . . experience in certain areas." He paused, leaned closer and lowered his voice to a whisper. "I trust that you are his mistress or perhaps hoping to become so, which is why I decided to hurry over here and proposition you myself."

Rebecca could only stare at him, agog. Who was he to so blatantly insult a woman as if she was nothing more than bothersome dirt tainting his boots? She so desperately wanted to hit him that she could barely contain her enthusiasm to do so, her fingers already curling into a tight fist at her side. And what was it he'd said about Mr. Neville? That keeping his company was what had led him to believe that she was a doxy in the first place? Disappointment washed over her. She should have known. Mr. Neville had only his own interests in mind as far as she went, and they would not include marriage. He might have more charm than Lord Starkly, but when it came to it, they were cut from the same cloth—libertines through and through. Neither man would do. Rebecca needed the permanence and security of marriage, not to a relic but to a man of her own choosing, if she was to escape the future her aunt and uncle had in mind for her, and for that, she would have to look elsewhere. Deciding she'd had enough of Lord

Starkly's presence and hoping to be gone before Mr. Neville returned, she resolved to walk away and find someone else entirely.

With a swift "If you'll please excuse me," she spun on her heel, only to barrel straight into Mr. Neville, who'd just come up behind her with two champagne flutes in hand, the bubbly liquid spilling onto both of them in the process.

TEN THINGS I LOVE ABOUT YOU
978-0-06-149189-4

If the elderly Earl of Newbury dies without an heir, his detested nephew Sebastian inherits everything. Newbury decides that Annabel Winslow is the answer to his problems. But the thought of marrying the earl makes Annabel's skin crawl, even though the union would save her family from ruin. Perhaps the earl's machinations will leave him out in the cold and spur a love match instead?

JUST LIKE HEAVEN
978-0-06-149190-0

Marcus Holroyd has promised his best friend, David Smythe-Smith, that he'll look out for David's sister, Honoria. Not an easy task when Honoria sets off for Cambridge determined to marry by the end of the season. When her advances are spurned can Marcus swoop in and steal her heart?

A NIGHT LIKE THIS
978-0-06-207290-0

Daniel Smythe-Smith vows to pursue the mysterious young governess Anne Wynter, even if that means spending his days with a ten-year-old who thinks she's a unicorn. And after years of dodging unwanted advances, the oh-so-dashing Earl of Winstead is the first man to truly tempt Anne.

The Casebook of Barnaby Adair novels from
#1 *New York Times* bestselling author

Stephanie LAURENS

WHERE THE HEART LEADS
978-0-06-124338-7

Handsome, enigmatic, and deliciously dangerous, Barnaby Adair has made his name by solving crimes within the *ton*. When Penelope Ashford appeals for his aid in solving the mystery of the disappearing orphans in her care, he is moved by her plight—and captivated by her beauty.

THE MASTERFUL MR. MONTAGUE
978-0-06-206866-8

When Lady Halstead is murdered, Barnaby Adair helps her devoted lady-companion, Miss Violet Matcham, and her financial adviser, Montague, expose a cunning killer. But will Montague and Violet learn the shocking truth too late to seize their chance at enduring love?

LOVING ROSE
978-0-06-206867-5

Rose has a plausible explanation for why she and her children are residing in Thomas Glendower's secluded manor. Revealing the truth would be impossibly dangerous, yet day by day he wins her trust, and then her heart. But when her enemy closes in, Rose must turn to Thomas to protect her and her children.

LAU6 0814

At Avon Books, we know your passion for romance—once you finish one of our novels, you find yourself wanting more.

May we tempt you with . . .

- **Excerpts** from our upcoming releases.

- Entertaining **extras**, including authors' personal photo albums and book lists.

- Behind-the-scenes **scoop** on your favorite characters and series.

- **Sweepstakes** for the chance to win free books, romantic getaways, and other fun prizes.

- Writing **tips** from our authors and editors.

- **Blog** with our authors and find out why they love to write romance.

- **Exclusive content** that's not contained within the pages of our novels.

Join us at
www.avonbooks.com

LYS3 0310

Give in to your Impulses!

These unforgettable stories only take a second to buy and give you hours of reading pleasure!

Go to *www.AvonImpulse.com* and see what we have to offer.

Available wherever e-books are sold.

AVONIMPULSE